FINALE

ACADEMY OF STARDOM - BOOK FOUR

BEA PAIGE

To Pen, Xeno, Dax, York and Zayn.
Thank you for dancing your way into my head.
Thank you for changing my life.

Bea Paige xoxo

And now the end is near, and so I face the final curtain ~
Frank Sinatra, I Did It My Way.

PLAYLIST

Dear Reader,

As you know, music plays an integral part in Pen and the Breakers' story. Throughout the series there have been specific songs to go with each important dance scene. I've loved hunting through music to find the perfect song and have had lots of help over the course of writing the series, notably from Erica aka my *Music Pimp*, and the members of my Facebook group ~ Queen Bea's Hive.

All the songs listed below can be found on Finale's <u>Spotify</u> <u>playlist</u>.

PROLOGUE

Dax

MOTHERFUCKING CUNT.

I'm going to kill the bastard. I'll wrap my hand around his throat and squeeze. I'll do it with a smile on my face and peace in my heart. I'll watch with glee as the blood vessels pop in his eyes, as they bulge out of his motherfucking head. I'll absorb his oxygen like some soul-sucking monster and enjoy every last fucking breath.

He dares to come after my brothers?

He dares to threaten the girl I love?

He dares to taunt her with messages that have twisted her up inside?

He doesn't get to fuck with her, with us.

He *will* die.

Snapping my head up, my fingers curl into my palm. My

muscles tense with adrenaline. My heart fucking kickstarts into a higher gear as I will myself to get to my feet.

Xeno was right when he said that violence was brewing inside of me.

I feel it now. It's an inferno, burning me up from the inside out. I've felt it smouldering inside my chest ever since Frederico had a knife pressed against Kid's throat. Wait, who am I trying to fucking kid? It was ignited ever since the moment I allowed the only girl I've ever loved back into my heart. It's grown in size since I held her in my arms and fucking loved her with every part of my tainted, broken soul. Loving us has put Kid in danger and that knowledge has fuelled the fire inside. My need to protect her spreads like liquid heat inside my veins with every passing day. I made a promise to her as a kid, and I will not break it. Not now, not ever.

We sealed that promise with a kiss, her first kiss, one that scorched away all kisses that came before that point until they were nothing but dust. I had known in that moment, when she'd looked up at me with flushed cheeks and love in her eyes, and asked me if I'd always protect her, that I would. That I would *die* to protect her. She was always my hope, my *home*, and I was always her dark angel.

So, you see, it doesn't matter that I'm bleeding out.

It doesn't matter that my skin is pale, and my heart is fighting to keep me alive.

It doesn't matter that Xeno is roaring at me to stay the fuck down, or York is beating a man to a pulp to get to me. It doesn't matter that Zayn is cutting through more men to do the same, his knife glinting in the light, blood dripping from the blade.

All that matters right now in this fucking moment is Kid. If it's the last thing I ever do, I will kill that cunt David. I will set her free of the cage he's inflicted on her soul.

That's my final vow as I push myself up off the floor and stagger towards him.

"No fucking more!" I roar.

1

Pen

"HOW IS SHE?" Dax asks quietly, leaning against the doorway of the bedroom in this unfamiliar house, his huge frame taking up the space.

"Asleep, finally," I reply, my fingers lingering on Lena's hair as I gaze down at her. My heart is heavy, my throat constricted as I try to prevent the sadness from pouring out of me. I need to be strong. I *have* to be strong for her.

"I'm glad she's resting now."

"She's exhausted," I say quietly, stroking her cheek. Her face is still blotchy from all the crying she's done over the past few hours since finding Mum dead. "When she climbed into bed, she barely registered me in the room with her, Dax. She's been so lost in her own pain, so exhausted from the grief..."

My voice trails off as I lean over and press a delicate kiss against her temple. Right now she's curled up into a tight ball beneath the duvet cover. She's made herself as small as possible in self-comfort just like she used to do when she was younger, when she would wake up from a nightmare.

"I'm sorry, Kid," Dax says, his voice cracking in sympathy. I blink back my tears, refusing to let them fall. I will not break in front of Lena. Not today, not ever.

"She's heartbroken. Confused. She can't understand why mum *killed herself*," I continue, the words bitter and sarcastic on my tongue. I hate lying to Lena, but what's the alternative? Telling her the truth? How can I tell her that our psycho brother is back and he killed our mum with his bare hands? That he strangled her, robbing her of breath. How can I tell Lena that he left a note reminding me that we'll never be free of him, that he will follow through on his threats just like he promised he would? How can I tell her that she could be next? That her own brother would snuff out her young life just to spite me.

My hand falls away from the soft strands of her hair and my shoulders drop. As much as I want to curl up on the bed next to Lena and forget the past few hours. I can't. I'm not sure that I'll ever sleep again knowing I'm to blame for my sister's grief, knowing he's out there just waiting to strike.

"Kid—" Dax begins, reading my body language and the defeat I feel.

"This is my fault," I say, each word cutting me open a little bit more. I grit my teeth, willing myself not to cry.

Sighing heavily, Dax doesn't respond with words, he simply steps into the room and takes my hand pulling me up into his arms. I press my cheek against his broad chest and breathe him in, my fingers curling into the material of his top as I try my hardest to hold in all these emotions threatening to spill out of me.

"No. Don't do that. Don't you even think about taking the blame for this. This is *not* on you. It's always been *him*," he whispers vehemently into my ear, his arms tightening around me.

I don't answer. I can't. The tears I've held inside all day begin to fall and I can't stop them or the muffled sobs that follow. Dax's kindness, his love and concern, unravel me.

"L—ena," I sob, shoving my hand over my mouth, not wanting to break here, not wanting to wake her.

"I've got you," Dax says as he wraps his arm around my shoulder, and guides me from the room and further along the hallway in this house I've never stepped inside before tonight. I turn into his side, burying my tear-streaked face into his chest as I attempt to swallow down the sobs, concerned that she'll hear and wake up.

"Take the room furthest on the right. I've got it ready for you all," a kind, female voice says as Dax hesitates in the hallway unsure where to take me.

I blink back my tears, swiping at my cheeks, trying to focus on the pretty blonde woman before me. I remember her from the photos in Hudson's other house. She's just as beautiful in the flesh. For a moment I wonder what she makes of all of this. This is her home, and we've brought trouble and heartache right to her front door.

"I appreciate it, Louisa," Dax rumbles, hugging me to his side tighter and pressing a kiss against the top of my head. "We're sorry to intrude like this."

Louisa nods, her eyes kind, if a little wary. "You're not

intruding when you've been invited. Besides, the kids are with their Grandad this weekend." She hesitates, her eyebrows pulling together in a frown as she looks at me. I can tell there's more she wants to say but must think better of it. "The others are downstairs in Hudson's office if you need them."

"Will you tell them I'm staying put with Pen, that they should come up as soon as they're done?"

"Of course, I will." Louisa flicks her eyes to me and gives me a gentle smile. "I'm sorry for your loss."

Swallowing hard, I nod, not able to even thank her because how can I explain that I'm not crying for my mum, but for my sister's pain. Stepping around us, Louisa heads towards the stairs at the end of the hallway that lead downstairs to the main portion of the house. This is the guest wing; it alone has five bedrooms, or at least that's what Hudson explained when we arrived an hour ago. I guess I was paying more attention than I thought at the time. The fact we're in the Freed's home and not at the Breakers' flat is telling. When Beast suggested he bring us here instead of back to their flat, not one of the Breakers questioned it. Were they expecting more from David? Isn't killing my mum enough for one day? That thought makes me tremble and Dax looks down at me with worry.

"It's going to be okay, Kid," he says, pushing open the bedroom door.

"You can't promise me that," I reply as we step inside the room. He kicks the door shut behind him and guides me towards the large king-sized bed. Sitting on the mattress, he pulls me down onto his lap.

"It *will* be okay."

"How? How can you promise me that now after what's happened today?"

"We'll find him. I swear on my life, we'll make David pay."

"He killed our mum, Dax. He murdered her to hurt Lena, knowing that her pain would tear me apart. This is because I stood up for myself, because I danced the way I did, because I fought back."

"No—"

"Yes, it is," I retort, cutting him off. "It's just like Frederico said, I provoked the monster. David won't rest until you're all dead, until Lena is dead, until there's just me left. I've got this sick feeling in my stomach. I know he won't stop until I'm *his*." And I mean that in the worst possible way. He's already proven that he has no problem selling women into sexual servitude. David has always wanted me in a way a brother should never want a sister, so what's to stop him from owning me in the same way. That night back at Rocks when I was a kid, I'd seen the truth of his depravity right there in his eyes, and I know, without a shadow of a doubt, that's what he has planned for me.

"That *isn't* going to happen," Dax exclaims, but there's no denying the fear that flashes in his gaze before he blinks it away. He's thinking the same thing too. That David wants me as his sex slave. My stomach curdles and I swallow down bile as I push those thoughts away.

"You don't know that."

Dax wraps his arms tighter around me as if his presence alone is enough to ward off the evil just waiting to snatch me away from him. "I do. I *do* know that."

"He managed to get to Mum, Dax!" I cry. My chest rattles

with more emotion that I don't want to set free, afraid that if I do, I might never find the strength to recover.

"I would *die* before I let him hurt you or Lena! We all would," Dax replies, squeezing me tighter against his chest. I believe him, I do, and that only makes me more fearful, not less. I can't lose him, any of them. I won't survive it.

"No! Don't talk like that. I wouldn't be able to bear it!" Twisting in his lap and straddling his thighs with mine, I claw at his shoulders, my fingernails digging into the back of his neck as I press my forehead against his. For a moment, all I can do is hold on tight and stare into the eyes of the man I love. Dax is so fucking strong, so powerful, it would be easy to hide behind him just like I did as a kid. But I can't. Not anymore. Today I may be torn apart by my sister's grief, but tomorrow I *have* to be stronger. Stronger than ever before. I need to be able to defend myself, to protect Lena. I'm done feeling helpless when it comes to David.

"We're not going anywhere, Kid. You have us for life, nothing and no one will take you from us, or us from you. I fucking swear it."

Pulling back, I drop my arms from his shoulders and curl my fingers into fists in my lap as rage and violence bubbles just beneath the surface of my fear. I feel it clawing at my limbs, reminding me that I have a choice. I can choose to run, to hide behind the Breakers, behind Grim and Beast, or I can fight back. There really is no choice.

As Dax whispers words of love and comfort in my ear, I allow the rage and the violence to take hold. I let it become more than just a feeling. I allow it to spread like vines around my internal organs, squeezing tight, robbing my lungs of breath and my heart of human kindness. I started this by drawing my brother out. This time, I'm going to be the one to end it. "It's not enough," I mumble, trying and failing to articulate how I feel.

Lifting my chin so that I look at him, Dax's eyes flare with concern. He rests his large hands over my fisted ones, their warmth a stark contrast to my coldness. "Tell me what you're thinking, Kid," he urges, watching me closely.

"I want you to teach me. I want the Breakers to teach me how to be strong."

"This is just a blip—" he responds.

"A *blip*?" I spit the word out, regretting my reaction immediately.

"That's not what I..." He heaves a sigh, then tries again. "I just meant that you *can* be vulnerable, you can lean on us. Do that now, let us be strong for you." I shake my head, panic rising in my chest because he's not getting it. "You're already so strong," he pushes on. "So fucking strong. I'm just saying that every once in a while you *can* break—"

"No," I reply, cutting him off and hating the way my voice sounds so harsh. "I don't mean it like that."

"Then what do you mean? What are you saying exactly?"

Swallowing hard, I push away the girl who thought prison was the answer for David and replace her with someone far more ruthless, someone cutthroat, someone with claws and teeth not movement and passion. "I'm done being a victim. The second he left that note I knew."

"Knew what?"

"That when he comes, and he *will* come, that I have to be ready for him..."

"Kid, listen—" Dax begins, his eyes flaring with understanding. He knows what I mean. He gets it now. Understanding leaches into his eyes, the grey-green swirling with worry.

"I want you to teach me how to fight back. I want you to teach me how to be like you all. I want you to teach me how to *kill* David."

2

Pen

DAX STIFFENS, his hands tightening over my own. "He'll never get close enough to you, Kid. You won't need to fight back. We'll protect you. This time we'll do it right."

I frown, my body vibrating with frustration, with anger, regret and fear. "Don't you understand? I can't be vulnerable anymore, Dax. I *need* to know how to defend Lena, to kill David if it gets to that point. *When* it gets to that point."

"You don't know what you're asking of me," he replies, his gaze flicking behind me.

I turn to find Xeno, York and Zayn entering the room. All three look as haggard as I feel, the beauty of our coming together as a group tainted once again by my brother. If nothing else, his timing is on point. He ruined that special moment in the basement three years ago when I first laid eyes on the mural, and he's tainted our love once again today.

"Titch?" York asks, immediately reading the situation and not liking it one bit. "No!"

He begins to shake his head, already responding to my unspoken words. He sees it in my eyes. He sees the change in me, my intention, my rage, my determination to end this once and for all.

Climbing off Dax's lap, I stand my ground and fix my gaze on Xeno. Of the four, I know he'll understand how I'm feeling. It wasn't so long ago that he wanted to kill my brother himself, that he was willing to sacrifice his own life to protect me despite my protests.

"Tiny?" he questions, flicking his gaze between Dax and me.

"I was *wrong* before. This has changed everything. David's too dangerous. When he comes for me I want to be prepared. He doesn't get to live. Dax is going to help me make sure of that."

"The fuck, Dax?!" York exclaims, scowling.

"I haven't agreed to anything," he replies, but when I cut a look at him over my shoulder he sighs heavily and I know he'd do anything I ask, even teaching me how to kill my brother.

"Pen, this is grief talking," Zayn says, stepping towards me. The look he gives me is one of regret and sorrow, as though what happened today is as much his fault as it is mine. "Tomorrow you'll see clearer."

"No!" I snap, shaking my head. "It isn't grief. This is *self-preservation*. This is *realisation*. This is me growing the fuck up. Even if David was thrown behind bars he'd find a way to get to

Lena, to you all, to me. This *only* ends when he's dead. I'm just sorry I was too stubborn, too fucking self-righteous to see that before now."

York shakes his head, stepping towards me. "It's *vengeance*. You're too good for that. Too fucking pure, Titch. Don't sully your soul, don't darken it for that monster. Trust me when I say there's no coming back once you head down that road."

"I disagree. This is Tiny being *smart*," Xeno says, earning him glares from York and Zayn, and a sigh of resignation from Dax.

"You can't be fucking serious! What happened to your mantra '*I kill so you don't have to*'? Has that suddenly changed?" Zayn snaps, his shoulders tensing as he glares at Xeno. "You were willing to fly to Mexico, into certain death, to try and kill that fucker, and now you're okay with Pen seeking him out and doing the same? Do you want that on your conscience, Pen's light snuffed out because she killed her brother when it should've been one of us?"

"I didn't say that. Fuck, you know that I don't want Tiny to step into the darkness," Xeno replies, glancing from Zayn to me despairingly. "I don't want you with blood on your hands even if it belongs to that cunt. Of course I fucking don't!"

My heart constricts at his words, at his dedication to us all, at the love I see blazing in his eyes as he stares at me. It hurts him to love so completely, to fear for us, to feel our pain, but he does it anyway. "Xeno, *I* know that, but you understand why I need this. Don't you?"

He nods. "Yes, I do. I understand only too well." Stepping towards me, Xeno scrapes a hand through his hair. He stops before reaching me, the shaking in his hands telling me that he's close to losing control. Swallowing hard I meet his gaze and grit my jaw, drawing on the last reserves of strength inside of me. I need to be strong, not just for Lena, but for him, for all of them.

"I need to do this."

"I will always step in, Tiny. I will kill for you. I will take David's life and bear the burden of it. I will always be that man because I fucking love you, just like I love you all," he says, looking between us.

"Good. Then we protect Lena and Titch. We keep them *safe* until David's dead," Yorks adds, focusing on me. "You don't have to get involved. You don't have to blacken your soul."

Xeno shakes his head, turning his attention to York. "You're missing the point, York. Tiny *needs* to be able to defend herself. She needs to be able to do that. She feels powerless. We can help her to find strength."

"You're implying we'll let David get close enough to hurt her!" York roars back, frustration and fear winning out in the moment. "That ain't gonna happen!"

Xeno strides over to York and grabs hold of his upper arms. "For better or worse, Tiny walks in our world now, and we *all* know how fucking dangerous it is. David isn't the only one she needs to worry about. You know that."

"But—"

"I know you'll walk into the fires of Hell to protect her, York. We all would, but sometimes that's not enough. She needs to be able to protect herself."

York throws his hands up in the air, dislodging Xeno's hold, and glances at Zayn who blows out a frustrated breath. The look that passes between them is a mixture of frustration, understanding and defeat.

"Xeno's right," Dax says, finding his words as he stands behind me.

"Not you too?" Zayn questions.

Dax reaches for my hip, and when I don't pull away, wraps his arm around my waist and hauls me back against his chest. "At the very least, we teach Pen how to protect herself. If that means knowing how to kill a man should she ever find herself in a position when that's the only choice she can make, then that's what we *have* to do."

"But we can and *will* protect Pen and Lena," Zayn insists, scraping a hand over his face as though trying to rub away what he's seeing, hearing.

"It isn't enough," I say, repeating my words to Dax earlier. Zayn flinches, my honesty cutting him deep, cutting them all. I see the invisible lashes and the pain my words cause. The truth hurts. It really fucking hurts.

"Pen—" he begins, but I cut him off.

"I have to claw some power back. I have to. This will help. Will you help me do that?" My eyes fill with tears, but I blink them back as I look between Zayn and York. I have to have their agreement too. It's important to me that they're behind me on this. "Please?" For a moment neither answer, then altogether they nod. "Thank you," I whisper out, my body sagging with relief as a wave of exhaustion washes over me, the last reserves of energy that was keeping me upright leaving my body in a rush.

"You need to sleep," Dax whispers against my ear, guiding me the couple steps back to the bed on heavy limbs. Sitting down on the side of the bed, Dax helps me take off the hoodie I'm wearing, leaving me in York's shirt that I'd borrowed earlier today and my own loose fitting trousers. He strips down to his t-shirt and boxers, York, Xeno and Zayn following suit, an unspoken agreement that we'll be spending the night together. All of us.

"What if Lena wakes up?" I mutter.

"Gray has the room next to Lena. He'll come and get one of us should she wake up," Zayn says, closing the distance between us.

"He's still here too?" I ask as he drops to his knees and removes my trainers and socks.

"Yes," Zayn confirms, looking back up at me. His fingers slide upwards from my ankles, over my calf muscles, and across my thighs as he reaches for the waistband of my trousers. Lifting my arse slightly, Zayn pulls down my trousers, discarding them before placing his hands back on my bare thighs. He sighs, his head dropping for a moment as his tan hands, dark against the lighter shade of my skin, begin to massage the tension from my muscles. I watch, transfixed. His hands are a contradiction, capable of such tender kindness and such bloody violence.

"Where's Beast?" I ask, realising that I haven't thanked him for tonight.

"He wanted to report back to Grim," Xeno explains, climbing onto the bed behind me, the warmth of his bare chest heating my back. "He doesn't like leaving her alone even though we all know that she can handle herself. Gray offered to stay in his place," He begins to massage my shoulders as Dax and York climb beneath the covers. I feel the heat of their gazes burning my skin as they watch us.

"Are there any leads?" I ask.

"Apart from the note left for you, nothing of consequence.

The cameras dotted around the housing estate haven't worked for years. It looks as though the local council's money only stretches to prettying up the estate on the surface with the regeneration of the area, and not ensuring the residents safety. There are no prints at the flat. No eye witnesses as far as Beast's men have been able to find out so far. Nothing," York explains heavily. He shifts on the mattress, frustration clear on his face.

"Fuck," Dax murmurs next to him.

"Someone must've seen something. They couldn't have interviewed everyone on the estate already. It's only been a few hours," I say, turning to face them both. My gaze latches onto Dax's. "What about those kids who were hanging about the estate when we visited Lena a few weeks back? They're the type to see all kinds of shit, right?"

Dax nods. "It's a good place to start. I'll go back to the estate tomorrow. See if I can speak to them."

"You do realise that even if they did see David, they ain't gonna tell you jackshit, right? No one saw anything because everyone turns a blind eye. David has a reputation. You're not the only one scared of him, Pen," Zayn points out, his fingers stilling on my thighs as he looks from Dax to me. "Aside from the fear your brother instils in people, there's a code on the street. You know that."

Dax scowls, his face darkening. "I don't give a fuck about the code. If those kids know something, I'll find it out."

"Dax, they're just kids..." I say, swallowing down the nausea I feel at the look on his face. If I can barely tolerate their violence against men, then how the hell will I deal with violence against kids. The answer is I won't. I can't. No matter how I feel about my brother and what I want to do to him, I draw the line at hurting kids. "No."

His gaze meets mine and I see that muscle flexing in his jaw as he grits his teeth, then he nods his head, a flutter of shame shadowing his features. "There are other ways to be persuasive."

"I agree, there is," Xeno says. "Dax, you'll head back to the estate first thing. See what you can dig up."

"I'll go with him," Zayn adds. "We can swing by our flat and make sure it hasn't been turned over or bugged or some shit."

"Is that why we came here tonight?" I ask, stiffening beneath their warm hands.

"Yes. We couldn't risk taking you both back to our flat just in case David knows where we live. There are plenty of people who would back your brother. We've got to be smart," Xeno explains, confirming what Dax had said earlier.

"Beast made the right move bringing us here. It gives us a little bit of time to get our heads straight, sort out a plan and make sure the flat's clear," Zayn says.

"And what is the plan?"

"Hudson's brothers, Max and Bryce, left an hour ago to head back into the city. Tomorrow they're meeting with some contacts of theirs who run the larger shipping ports along the south coast to see if they can put some feelers out. It's likely David arrived in the country by boat in one of the smaller ports, otherwise Interpol would've picked him up if he'd come in via the airports or Channel Tunnel."

"I see." My head drops back against Xeno's chest as he works his fingers across my shoulders, they curl over, reaching my clavicle as his thumbs dig into the tight knots. I let out a moan of appreciation.

"How long will we stay here for?"

"Long enough to make sure the flat's secure, put out some feelers and move your things from the Academy to our place. A couple days, max," Dax says, casting a look over my head to Xeno.

"Wait. You want me to move in?"

"There's no way you're staying at the Academy after this. Of course you're living with us, *permanently*," Xeno says, his voice brooking no arguments. He presses a soft kiss against my temple to temper the abruptness of his response.

"But Lena..." I begin, wanting so much to move in with them, even if the circumstances overshadow the warm feeling in my stomach. It's all I've ever wanted, to live with them, to never be parted again.

Zayn squeezes my thighs gently in reassurance. "...Will move in too."

My eyes fill with tears as I look down at him. "She's not your responsibility," I whisper, my voice catching as reality settles in.

"She's your family and that makes Lena our family too," he counters.

"Zayn's right," York adds, drawing my brimming eyes to him.

"You don't have to do this. You don't owe me anything."

York makes an annoyed sound. "You're so used to handling everything yourself, but that stops today. Let us help you. We want to do that. Fuck, Titch, haven't we made it clear enough? We. Love. You."

"I know, but—"

"No buts! When people love and care for each other they step the fuck up. Lena needs you, but she also needs a roof over her head. Right now that's going to be too difficult for you to do on your own. We'll help you to give her that, okay?" he continues.

"Okay," I croak, so choked up with gratitude that I can barely speak. Even with Grim's generous wage, there's no way I could cover the cost of rent, bills, and food, not to mention all the things a teenage girl needs. "Thank you. I don't know what to say..."

"You don't have to say a damn word, Kid. We're a family. Understand?"

"Yes," I reply, letting out a long, steadying breath.

"Good. Now let us soothe you, Pen. We got you, okay?" Zayn murmurs, his hands firm but gentle, matching the pressure of Xeno's fingers. I nod, and for long minutes the pair massage my aching muscles, easing some of the tension I feel. When my eyelids begin to droop, Xeno presses a gentle kiss against the top of my head.

"Get under the covers, Tiny."

Zayn's hands fall away, and he grips the mattress either side of my hips before standing. Leaning over, he presses a delicate kiss against my lips. "I love you, Pen," he whispers.

"I love you too."

Pulling back, he cups my cheek, pouring all the love he has for me into that one look. I wish I could fall into his night-time eyes forever, wrapped up in the weightlessness of his love.

"Sleep," he urges.

With the little energy I have left, I crawl towards Dax and York and settle between them both. Instinctively, I press my cheek against York's chest, wrap my arm around his waist and snuggle into his side breathing in the lingering scent of his after-shave. Heady notes of pineapple and jasmine waft over me and I relax into the richness of his scent.

"We'll keep you safe. I *promise*," he says passionately, brushing away the hair from my face and pressing a kiss against my forehead. We both know it's his last attempt at convincing me that I don't need to learn how to kill David.

"I know you will, and I love you all for it," I mumble, trailing my fingers over the oak tree tattoo on his chest. "But please understand, I need to learn how to protect Lena, to kill David if that's what it comes down to."

"I do understand. Fuck, I do," he replies, drawing me closer, hugging tight. Behind me, Dax spoons my body. His thick arm folding over both me and York, holding us both in that protective, loving way of his, knowing that it isn't just me who needs his affection.

"Cute," Zayn remarks from the side of the bed, as he looks down at the three of us. "Looks like I've lucked out on being the big spoon once again." A smile plays about his eyes, a soft chuckle releasing from his lips to let us all know he's just kidding.

"If you're that bothered, you can spoon me. There's plenty of room. This bed is huge," Dax replies with a smile in his voice that draws the tiniest bit of laughter from me. Their brotherhood, their love for one another, warms my heart like nothing else. They don't even realise it, but they're *my* light in all this pain and darkness. They always were. Always will be.

Zayn sighs and slips under the covers behind Dax. "I draw the line at spooning you, *big boy*."

"Afraid you might like it?" Dax asks, snickering as he nuzzles my neck. His cock hardens at our closeness, but he doesn't act on it, knowing that what I need most in this moment is his unwavering comfort, and their warmth and affection.

"I love you, mate, but not that much," Zayn retorts with a huff.

"Stop talking, Tiny needs to sleep. She needs *rest*," Xeno admonishes, a clear instruction as to how he believes the rest of this night should go. In all fairness, as much as I love and adore them all, my mind isn't on sex right now. I want safety, friendship, closeness. I want to fall asleep in their arms, in their warmth, so that tomorrow I can face the day and all the shit that's bound to come with it. Xeno pulls back the covers and climbs in behind York. He tucks the pillow beneath his arm, propping his head up a little as York trails his fingers up and down my bare arm, pressing gentle kisses against the top of my head. I can feel his heart thumping beneath his rib cage. It thunders in love, compassion and solidarity.

"Close your eyes, Tiny. Sleep," Xeno gently commands, watching me. My heart lurches, squeezing at the love he shows me, *us*. I know how hard it is for him to live with that love, and the pain it causes keeping it under control, but he's stronger than he gives himself credit for. "We'll all be here when you wake up and every day that follows for the rest of our lives."

And without a shadow of doubt, I know that they will, but only if David isn't alive to ruin it.

3

Dax

"FUCK. Not one arsehole is willing to talk," I say, swiping a hand over my face as we stand by the Bentley parked at the housing estate. "Too shit scared."

"Yeah, we all know that wanker has a reputation around these parts." Zayn replies, pushing off the car. He nods towards a kid sitting on top of a garage. He's smoking a blunt and eying us both from beneath his beanie hat. "What about him? Was he one of the kids Pen mentioned you wanting to speak to?"

"No! Fuck, that's Justin!"

Zayn frowns. "Justin?"

"Yeah, I teach him dance at the Academy for Madame Tuillard. He's a good dancer but he's also a little shit. Way too fucking cocky, and an arsehole to Sydney."

"Who the fuck's Sydney?"

"His best friend's little brother. Cute kid. Talented. But the butt of Justin's jokes."

"Well, maybe we should have a little chat with Justin. See if he saw anything or knows someone that might."

"Yeah. It can't hurt."

As we approach, Justin stands up and takes one last drag of his joint then chucks it over the side of the garage. The smell is pungent and reminds me of those nights in the basement of Jackson Street when we'd all get high and laugh until we cried. "Alright, Dax?"

"Been better. What're you doing around here?" I ask him.

"Just hanging out. What're *you* doing here?" He pins me with his gaze and smirks.

"You're right, he is a little shit," Zayn says, laughter in his voice.

"You should try teaching him. Thinks he knows every damn thing there is to know about dance. He reminds me of someone actually."

Zayn laughs. "I do know everything about dance. Just because you've got this new teaching gig on the side, doesn't make you an expert all of a sudden. I was always the choreo genius. You know that."

I shake my head and return my attention to my most frustrating student. He could actually be an exceptional dancer if he didn't let his ego get in the way. That's why Sydney is better, because he has no ego, just pure love for dance. "Hanging out on your own? Where's the rest of your crew?"

"Chilling at a friend's place. Needed some fresh air."

"You call that joint fresh air?" I ask, raising my brow.

"What are you, *my dad*?" Justin responds, pressing the flat of his hand against the edge of the garage roof and flipping over the side in a forward roll. He lands on his feet before me, kicking up dirt and grit from the pavement.

"Woah, you really are a cocky little shit!" Zayn says, shaking his head.

Justin rolls his eyes "Not cocky. Just certain of my skills, that's all." He looks between us both then up at the block of flats we've just come out of. "So, I'm guessing you're here because of what happened to that hag, yeah?" He lowers his voice and looks at me with excitement in his eyes. "Rumour around here is that her daughter finally had enough, and *murdered* her."

"Watch your mouth!" I admonish, clipping him around the back of the head. "That hag happens to be the mother to two people we care about. So hold your fucking tongue!"

"Shiiiiittt! Fuck, man. I didn't know that. I was just kidding, that's all. I thought she might owe you a debt or something and you were coming to collect, being as you're gangsters."

"I'm not a gangster. I'm your dance teacher, *that's all.*"

"Yeah, and I'm a fucking virgin."

Zayn barks out another laugh and wraps his arm around Justin's shoulder, pulling him into a headlock. "I fucking like you, you little twat," he says, before shoving him away again.

"Thanks... I think," Justin replies, his cheeks blushing a little. I don't know much about the kid, but I do know that he doesn't have a father figure and his mum works all hours of the day to provide for him. Pretty much the same story for most of the kids who live around here. It's rarer to find a kid who doesn't come from a broken home than kids that do. Sad as fuck if you ask me.

"I'm guessing you wanna speak to someone who might've

seen something, yeah?" Justin asks, side-eying us both, before casting his gaze further afield, as though he's expecting someone to step out of the shadows and tell him to shut the fuck up.

"You know something?" Zayn asks, beating me to it.

"I don't, but I know someone who might. Follow me." Justin strides off towards the block of flats opposite to the one Lena and Pen had lived in with their mum. There are four, twenty-story flats on the estate. Fucking ugly monstrosities that until recently blighted the landscape. I'm talking graffiti covering the walls, both inside and outside of the buildings. Broken down lifts, smashed windows, fucking piss in the hallways. It was a dive; add in litter covering every inch of the place, including used needles and condoms, and it wasn't exactly prime real estate.

"So who's your friend that lives here?" I ask.

"Rafe."

"Rafe? I didn't know he lived on this estate," I say as we cross the newly revitalised green space that sits right in the centre of the four high-rises. The local playground where Kid first met Zayn has now been updated with wooden play equipment and one of those outdoor gyms that have popped up in local areas all over London.

"He doesn't, but his older brother Jefferson has a place here," Justin replies, jumping up onto a wooden picnic table. He grins then does a backflip, landing on light feet. Zayn glances at me and I can see that he's mildly impressed by the kid's tricks.

"Jefferson? That name sounds familiar." I remark. "You say he's Rafe's older brother?"

"Yeah, Jefferson Sloane. He's part of the Callous Crew."

"Ah fuck, yeah, I know him. He was the guy who got beaten

to a pulp by Beast in the cage at Tales a little while back," I say. "Talented fighter, if a little hot-headed."

"See, I fucking knew it! Only *gangsters* get into Tales. One day I plan on getting into that club. Is Grim really as shit hot to look at as Jefferson says? I swear he's got a permanent hard-on for her. Then again, maybe it's that other mysterious chick he's been pining over for a while now..."

"Yeah, Grim is hot. She's also way off limits. That's a tree I'd advise him never to bark up, not unless he wants to become a eunuch," Zayn comments with a grin.

"What the fuck's a eunuch?" Justin asks, popping a piece of chewing gum into his mouth.

Zayn and I burst out laughing, and I give the lad a gentle shove. "Look it up on Google, but be prepared to see some fucked-up shit, and *do not* let Sydney or Olivia see. That shit ain't for their eyes!" I warn him.

"Yeah, sure. Whatever," Justin replies, stopping dead in his tracks when someone wolf-whistles from one of the balconies on the block of flats we're walking towards. He points. "There's MDMA."

"MDMA?" Zayn asks, looking up and shading his eyes from the mid-morning sun that's peeking out from behind the tower block and doing its best to fucking blind us. "That's a fucking drug."

"No, it's Jefferson... *Mad Dick Magenta*. MDMA is his tag. Get it?"

Zayn pulls a face. "Mad Dick Magenta? Are you for real? Why has he called himself that?"

"Because he's a *mad dick* of course, and he happens to like the colour. His tag is all over London, The dude is fucking epic at parkour and graffiti. Last week he climbed up the civic centre in broad daylight and spray painted his tag on the wall right outside the mayor's office. The police were called but no one could catch him. He just did his Spiderman shit and escaped across the rooftop."

"Spiderman shit? Escaped across a rooftop? I think you're high, Justin," I point out.

Justin shakes his head, looking at me with a wide grin, the whites of his eyes pink from the joint. *Yeah, fucking high.*

"Nope. See for yourself," he replies, pointing towards the tower block whilst shoving another piece of chewing gum into his mouth.

"What the ever loving fuck?" Zayn exclaims, his mouth dropping open in surprise.

I follow his gaze, and for a moment I can't see jackshit with the sun blinding me, then a cloud blocks out the sunlight and about six stories up, Jefferson Sloane is hanging from the bottom of what I assume is his balcony about to drop to his death. Rafe is peering over the side of the balcony, a mixture of awe and horror on his face.

"Hey, get the fuck down from there!" I shout.

Beside us, Justin doubles over and laughs. "That's like telling Fuck Boy Blue to not, well... *Fuck.*" Then he cracks up again as though he's just said the funniest thing in the world.

"Fuck's sake," I mutter under my breath, side-eying him.

The kid needs to stop smoking Mary-J, that's what he needs to do. I make a mental note to call his mum and let her know what her son's up to. I'm no snitch, but someone needs to look out for the kid. He might hate me for it in the short term, but I know his type. The kids got an addictive slash destructive personality. I've met loads like him over the years. By the time he's twenty he'll be doing crack and on the short road to death. Well, not on my watch. He might be a cocky little shit, but he's a good kid underneath it all, and talented. He just needs a little help to get things right, and clearly hanging about with Jefferson Sloane ain't doing much for him.

"Did you know that Danny has slept with over a hundred women. He's like, fucking epic, man. The guy's a babe magnet."

"Danny? Who the fuck is Danny?" Zayn asks, one eye on Jefferson as he dangles one handed from the balcony.

"Fuck Boy Blue, of course!" Justin says, rolling his eyes like Zayn's some old shit with memory problems. "Well, Fuck Boy for short or otherwise known as Danny Bleu. Then there's Jade Robertson."

"Let me guess, Jacked up Jade?" Zayn retorts, scoffing.

"No, *Sick Prick Jade*, actually. You wanna fuck with someone's head, hire out Jade. He really does have a cruel streak. It's just as well Rafe is Jefferson's little brother and I'm his best mate, otherwise he would've practised being an arsehole on us way before now."

I frown at that. Not liking the sound of that cocksucker. "Hmm."

"Anyway, that pretty much makes up Callous Crew. I've been practising my parkour skills to see if they'll take me on. Rafe said I should steer clear, but he's just a chicken-shit..." Justin's voice trails off, his thoughts lost beneath awe and wonderment as he stares up at Jefferson who swings his legs and lets go of the balcony only to land lightly on the one below without falling to his death.

"Fuck me!" I exclaim, my eyes widening at the insanity of

what I've just witnessed. "I'll tell you something, kid. You need to listen to Rafe. He's got his head screwed on. You, on the other hand, *do not* need your head splattered all over the concrete."

"Ah, whatever. Jefferson might be insane, but he's fucking cool as shit... Watch," Justin insists.

It takes Jefferson or should I say, *Mad Dick,* all of three minutes to make his way down to the ground. He drops from one balcony to the other like he really is fucking Spiderman. There's no safety harness, no ropes, just his skill. If I thought Justin was cocky, then I guess he's got nothing on this prick.

"Yo, T-Bone, what's up?" Jefferson shouts from the other side of the green, his attention on Justin as he approaches us.

"*T-Bone?* What's with all the goddamn nicknames?" Zayn grumbles under his breath.

"It's a graffiti writer thing," I reply with a shrug. "Asia's real name is Alicia and Camden was once known as Bling. How do you not know that?"

Zayn rolls his eyes, turning his attention back to Jefferson. "So here he is, *MDMA,*" Zayn mocks. It takes Jefferson a second to realise who Justin's with and once he does, his cocky demeanour changes to one of respect, even if there's still a lot of bravado on display.

"Dax. What're you doing here?" the motherfucker has the audacity to ask like this is his territory and we're encroaching. "You good?"

"I'm here to ask a few questions, and I'll be better once I know you're never gonna let Justin join your crew. Like your little bro, he's a good dancer and I need all his limbs in working order, not to mention his brain kept intact. That little show you just put on can plant ideas into young, impressionable heads and that, my friend, I ain't cool with. Understand?" I finish with a smile, but we all know it's a warning veiled in good natured banter. Jefferson nods, hearing me loud and clear.

"We ain't looking to take anyone on. Besides, doing back-flips off of a couple benches isn't exactly impressive. It takes a lot more than that to get into the Callous Crew." He glances over at Justin, who frowns, the cuss slowly filtering through his high. The poor kid is downright dejected. Looks like joining Callous Crew is higher up on his wish list than becoming a professional dancer. I'm going to have to do something about that, but first...

"So, what can I do for you?" Jefferson asks, before I can question him.

He folds his arms across his chest, and I notice the way he winces slightly at the movement. I'm betting he's got a couple of cracked ribs from the recent fight with Beast. Which makes the stunt he's just pulled doubly stupid. There's a yellowing bruise under his eye and one on his jaw too. Though, despite his cocky attitude, I've got to give him props, he's got balls stepping into the ring with the best fighter in London. Especially since I'm betting he's barely eighteen. I'd even hazard a guess that he might even be under age, and if that's the case, it ain't us he needs to worry about but Grim. She's a lot of things, but the rules of her fight club are simple ones. No weapons, no mercy and no minors. Unlike some other underground fight clubs dotted about the UK, Grim is very strict when it comes to chil-dren fighting in the ring. Ever since her half-brother, Ford, threw a fight against Beast to save his life, it's a no-go for her.

"Justin here said you might have seen something the other night?" Zayn asks, cutting to the chase.

"The other night?" Jefferson tips his head to the side as though trying to recall, but I notice how he glances over at Justin, clearly pissed off that the kid's opened his mouth.

"Yeah, you know when that drunk-arse bitch was found dead. You said that you saw..." Justin's voice trails off as soon as he realises his mistakes. One, he's just cussed out Pen and Lena's mum *again*, and two it's suddenly dawned on him that Jefferson isn't too pleased to be drawn into this. Justin pulls an '*oh fuck*' face.

"... Oh, *that* night. Yeah, I saw you guys coming out of the flat with Pen and Lena before the cops came. Beast was there and some other bloke I didn't recognise."

"You know Pen and Lena?" Zayn asks.

"I live on the estate, don't I?" he retorts with a shrug. "What happened to their mum, did she overdose? Everyone knew she liked to drink and do drugs. Wasn't a secret."

Stepping closer to Jefferson, I glare at him. He's actually not much shorter than me, but where I'm built, he's wily. All muscle, sure, but built like an athlete, not a boxer. He's light-weight to my heavyweight, but if he fucks me off then I've got no issue teaching him a lesson. The guy's fair game. If he can step into a ring with Beast then he can take a pummelling for trying to act like he doesn't know shit.

"Listen, we need to know what *else* you saw. People around here ain't talking and that leads me to believe they're very aware of who killed our girl's mum. The fact that Justin here is about to drop a bollock tells me you saw more than just us leaving the flat, am I right?"

"Fuck me. You're with *Lena*? Ain't that what they call jail-bait? For you, I mean. For me, she's fair game. I love an older woman, even if it is only by a few months," Justin says, grinning stupidly.

"No, idiot, they're talking about Pen. Lena's *older* sister," Jefferson says, clipping him around the back of the head before I can.

"Ow, fuck!" he exclaims, rubbing the spot and looking between us both. Suddenly the penny drops. "Wait, *Pen* as in that dancer who came to our lesson that time?" He starts gesticulating with his hands, mimicking the curves of a woman. "She had such a sexy fucking arse—"

"Continue along those lines, *T-Bone*," Zayn snaps, referring to his nickname with as much contempt as he can muster, "and I don't give a fuck if Dax is your teacher, I'll give you a hiding for disrespecting our woman like that!" Zayn snaps, turning from *laid-back-and-friendly* Zayn to *I'm-gonna-pull-a-knife-and-cut-you* Zayn in less than a second.

"Wait, shiiiiitttt, *our woman?*" Justin blurts out, not in the least bit scared by Zayn's threat and unable to control the verbal diarrhoea due to all the Mary-J. Reason number two for calling his mum: the kid has zero filter when he's high, all the street smarts he's acquired over the years disappearing under the influence of a Class B drug. We'd get high as kids, sure, but we never lost the smarts.

Zayn steps closer to him, a warning look on his face and I throw my arm out. "He's just a kid. Leave it be." We both know he wouldn't hit a child, but there's nothing wrong with Justin thinking he might, it might make him think twice about getting so high that he doesn't realise until it's too late that he's pissing off some very dangerous people.

Jefferson grabs Justin by the arm and points to the block of flats he just scaled down. "Rafe is waiting on you. Get inside!" he says, pushing him away with a shove.

"But...!"

"Inside now or I'll call your mum and tell her you've been smoking weed again."

"Fuck's sake. Fine!" Justin turns to me and gives me a sheepish smile. "Sorry, man. I didn't mean to offend you."

I jerk my chin. "Get going."

"Sorry about Justin," Jefferson says as soon as he's out of earshot. "He's a royal pain in my arse, but like a little brother to me. Him and Rafe have been tight since they were in nappies. His mouth runs away from him sometimes."

"That'll be the joint we caught him smoking a second ago. You give him that?" I ask.

"The little fucker!" Jefferson exclaims, running a tattooed through his hair. "No, I didn't. He must've nicked it from my stash. He said he was going to the shop. I should've known. He's a liability, but Rafe loves him, and I happen to give a shit about my brother's happiness and his. So I let them hang out at my place. Better than hanging out on the streets."

"Or from balconies..."

Jefferson meets my gaze, and I can tell he wants to respond with a cutting remark, but wisely thinks better of it. Instead, he blows out a breath. "I wouldn't put them in danger. I'm always telling Justin to concentrate on dance."

"Yeah, yeah. We get it, you're a nice guy." Zayn responds, his voice loaded with sarcasm. "Let's cut to the fucking chase, shall we? What did you see?"

"A pizza delivery driver. That's what I saw."

Zayn scowls. "The fuck? You better not be feeding us bullshit. I might not hit kids, but then again you're almost a man, and I prefer using a knife."

"Yeah, I heard." Jefferson doesn't even flinch at the threat or the fact that we're assuming he's under eighteen. He's gutsy. There aren't many people who'd hold their nerve when the Breakers threaten them with violence. Either we're getting soft, or Jefferson Sloane, aka Mad Dick Magenta, is a lot tougher than we give him credit for.

"Well?" I prompt.

"That's honestly what I saw," he says, perching on the picnic bench beside us and propping his feet up on the seat.

"But there's more to it than that, am I right?" I say.

He nods tightly. "I was smoking a joint on my balcony, just chilling, when I saw the delivery driver pull up. Honestly, the only reason he caught my attention was because Mrs Ray, a sweet old lady who's lived on the estate since it was built back in the fifties, stopped dead in her tracks the second she laid eyes on the bloke. She dropped her pint of milk, and it smashed all over the concrete. Then she just turned on her heel and went inside her flat. For an eighty year old, she sure as fuck moved fast."

"Then what?" I ask, urging him to continue.

"Then I did a really fucking stupid thing..."

Zayn cocks his head. "And what was that?"

"I decided to go check this dude out. I was high, bored, feeling restless over a bit of pussy..." I raise my brows and he just shakes his head as though to dislodge the thought of that *bit of pussy* from his head. "By the time I reached the block, the delivery driver was coming down the stairs, a flight above me. I got that feeling in my stomach, you know what I mean, when you know you need to make yourself scarce," he says, looking at me for agreement.

"Yeah, I know what you're saying. That feeling has saved all of us countless times in our line of business," I agree. Call it street smarts, self-preservation, whatever. Most people who've grown up in this kind of environment learn pretty quickly to trust their instincts. That's why Mrs Ray turned on her heel and returned to her flat when she saw the delivery driver. Self-preservation had kicked in, and that *only* happens when there's a threat to your safety.

"What happened next?" Zayn asks, resting his foot on the bench and giving a mother and her child a brief smile as they walk by. Jefferson doesn't answer until they've left.

"The delivery driver passed by me, pulling off a pair of black gloves and shoving them in his pizza bag. There was something sticking out of the corner of the bag. I don't know what it was, maybe the handle of a knife or something? But it wasn't even that that made me glad I'd stayed hidden. It was the fact that the guy was smiling."

"Smiling?" I ask, my blood running cold.

"Yeah, *smiling*, in a sick, twisted way, like he'd just fucked someone up and was getting a kick out of it."

Zayn looks at me and I nod. "And this guy, describe him to me."

"Maybe mid-twenties? He was wearing a cap, light brown hair. Straight nose. Stubble. About your height and physique. Good looking, I guess, with a side of fucking psycho," he says, nodding at Zayn. "That's all I got."

"And the license plate of the moped. You didn't happen to notice that?"

"No. Sorry. I didn't."

I nod my head, and hold my hand out to Jefferson. He takes it in a firm grip. "Thank you. We appreciate you telling us this."

"It's the least I can do. What you're doing for my brother and Justin, well... it means something to them even if neither will admit it." He hesitates for a moment then stands. "Look, admittedly, I should've come forward earlier, but you know how it is. Especially lately. I heard about what happened at Rocks. Frederico was batshit crazy thinking he could take on the Skins. I'm sorry about your uncle."

"I'm not," Zayn replies, grabbing his mobile from his back pocket and reading a message on the screen. He wanders off, leaving me alone with Jefferson.

"Right. Well, see you around then." He drops my hand and moves to walk away.

"Wait..." I say, glancing over at Zayn who has his phone pressed to his ear. Catching my eye, he shakes his head at my concerned expression, telling me without words that it's nothing to worry about.

"Yeah?" Jefferson stalls, waiting for me to speak.

"I need to ask you a favour," I say, locking eyes with him.

"Okay..." He's cautious. Frankly, he's right to be. Favours come hand-in-hand with danger in the kind of circles we move in.

"As you might've gathered, we're looking for that guy you saw here. It's really fucking important that we find him. I'm asking you and your crew to keep your ears to the ground and your eyes peeled. If you see him again, you give me a call immediately. Rafe has my number. If you can't get hold of me, call

Grim or Beast, I'm assuming you have a contact number for them given you've fought at Tales."

"Yeah, I do, and Dax...."

"What?"

"I know how this shit works," he says, meeting my gaze with a steady one of his own. I already know where this is going, but I'm not going to give him a helping hand. I'm asking him for a favour and therefore he's going to want one in return. It's only fair. If he didn't ask for one, I would've been more wary of him, not less. I wait. "I want a favour in return."

"Done."

"Aren't you going to ask what it is?"

I shake my head. "Nope. Though, if I were betting a man, I'd figure it has something to do with that *piece of pussy* you mentioned earlier."

Jefferson's mouth drops open. "How the fuck...?"

I laugh, pointing my finger at his face. "Let's just say I recognise the look of a man who's got his head in a spin over a woman. Whatever you need, whenever you need it, just let me know."

With that I turn on my heel and catch up with Zayn who's still talking on his phone. When he eventually finishes the call I give him a look.

"Just Beast checking in," he explains. "I filled him in on what we found out from Jefferson. He's going to call Hudson and see if Interpol can find out if there were any reports of stolen mopeds from the local pizza deliveries in the area. Failing that, they might be able to pick up CCTV footage in the surrounding area. It's a good lead."

"Let's hope so. Have Beast and Grim had any luck with their contacts?"

"Not so far, and he's mad about it. Grim too. They've got everyone working on finding David, but he's like Jack the fucking Ripper. A fucking psychopath that no one could catch."

I shake my head. "Not this time. We'll find David, and when we do, he's going to understand what it feels like to be on the receiving end of violence. I fucking guarantee it."

4

Pen

"THANKS FOR LETTING US STAY," I say to Hudson and Louisa two days later at breakfast. "I appreciate it."

"Yeah, ditto," Xeno adds, wrapping his arm around my waist and pressing a kiss to the top of my head.

"Did you sleep better last night?" Louisa asks, looking between us both. We're standing at the far end of the dining room, away from the others. Xeno holds a mug with his free hand and the smell of expensive, freshly roasted coffee wraps around us. It's weirdly comforting.

"We did, thank you." My cheeks heat, but there's absolutely no judgement in Louisa's eyes, just warmth and understanding.

"I'm glad." She smiles gently then flicks her gaze to Xeno. "That look tells me that perhaps you didn't?"

He shakes his head. "Dax and Zayn not being here might've

freed up the bed, but I woke up with York practically crushing me. The bastard used me as his personal cuddle toy. I think he thought I was Tiny. The arsehole got a bit of a shock when he woke up to find a fist in his gut."

Hudson's lip twitches in amusement and Louisa grins.

"Funny, Bryce has a habit of doing the same in his sleep. Normally it's Hud who bears the brunt of his *affection.*" She wiggles her eyebrows then smothers a laugh at the look Hudson gives her. "You know it's true, Hud."

"Luckily for everyone I'm very tolerant," he replies, his cheeks tinge pink a little at Louisa's insinuation. We all know she's talking about *morning wood.* I don't think there is a guy on this planet who doesn't wake up with a boner. "You get used to it after a while. Comes with the territory."

"Yeah, I guess it does," Xeno replies with a smirk.

A smile pulls up my lips, but it falls quickly. How can I feel joy, however small or fleeting, when Lena is hurting so much? I glance over at her. She's sitting at the dining table with York by her side. All morning he's been trying to distract her with conversation, talking about everything and nothing despite her lack of interest. He's taken it upon himself to help her deal with her grief and I couldn't love him any more for it. If anyone can break through her cloud of grief, York can.

"She's so withdrawn. She's barely talked these past couple days and hasn't even questioned why we're here. It's not like her," I say, watching Lena as she pushes her food around her plate distractedly, only to drop the fork a moment later, giving up entirely on eating. I frown.

"It's going to take time," Louisa says, squeezing my arm gently.

"She's not eating either," I reply, stating the obvious.

"She will. You'll make sure of it."

I nod, heaving out a sigh as I meet Louisa's gaze. "I'm sorry I didn't get a chance to meet Max and Bryce. I wanted to thank them before we left today. It can't be easy opening up your house to a bunch of strangers. I'm sorry we brought trouble to your door."

"You're not strangers. I feel like I know you all already. Eastern has told me a lot about you, and Hudson thinks very highly of you all. Besides, this isn't going to be the last time we see each other now, is it? We have plenty of time to get to know each other."

"Wait, you think highly of *me*?" Xeno questions Hudson with a smirk, trying to come off unbothered by the compliment.

"Is that really such a surprise?" Hudson responds.

"Yeah, actually it is..." Xeno shifts on his feet, cutting Hudson a guarded look before breaking out into a smile. "Well, you aren't the arsehole I originally thought you were either."

Hudson laughs, shaking his head. "Thanks, I think... So, what are your plans? You're welcome to stay longer if that's what you need. The kids' grandfather is happy to have them for a few days more."

"Thanks for the offer, but we'll be heading off today. Dax and Zayn have had our flat thoroughly checked over and it's clear," Xeno explains.

"Good to know. I've got my contacts at Interpol checking on the lead the guys informed us about yesterday. We owe that kid Jefferson," Hudson says, lowering his voice. "As soon as I hear anything, I'll be sure to let you know."

Louisa frowns, shaking her head. "Not here," she says,

flicking her eyes to Lena before looking at me and changing the subject. "Are you certain you don't want to stay longer? I know Grim would be upset if we let you leave before you were ready to, and right now it's best not to anger Grim given her current condition," Louisa says with a wry grin.

Hudson smirks, humour in his eyes. "Oh, I dunno, watching Beast piss Grim off is probably the funniest thing I've seen in a while. I'm not sure he'll survive the pregnancy. Bryce reckons he won't make the third trimester. Max thinks she'll shoot him before the fourth month is over and I reckon she'll string him up by the balls the week before the baby's due. "

Xeno smirks and Louisa gives Hudson a shove. "Hey, don't be such an arse. Making bets about a pregnant woman! You wait until I speak with Max and Bryce." She clicks her tongue in annoyance and female solidarity.

"I might be interested in wagering a bet myself. What are the odds?" Xeno asks casually, adding fuel to Louisa's ire. She raises a brow at him, unimpressed, and I swallow a laugh. I like this woman.

"Seriously, these men!" she says, reaching for me once more. Her warm fingers wrapping gently around my arm. She's very touchy feely, and for a brief moment I imagine the kind of mum she is to her kids. A good mum, *kind*. I bite on the inside of my cheek feeling all kinds of ways that I don't want to pick apart right now. "Anyway, getting back to the point in hand, I just wanted you to know that we're genuinely happy for you to stay here longer if you think a change of scenery would help Lena to heal. It's not going to be easy for her to go back home given what happened there."

I swallow hard, tears pricking my eyes at her kindness whilst the violence I feel brewing inside gains traction. The concoction of such conflicting emotions is a heady one, poisonous in its intent. I feel myself unravelling, their kindness my undoing.

"Pen...?" she questions gently.

Forcing the feelings aside, I plaster on a smile. "That's really kind of you, but Lena and I are moving in with the guys for the time being."

"*Forever*," Xeno corrects me.

Hudson nods in approval. "That's probably wise. Grim's men will continue to guard your sister when she's at school, and now that Gray has been introduced properly he will become her personal bodyguard."

"What will I tell her? Right now she's distracted by her grief, but eventually she's going to question what's going on," I say, chewing on my lip.

"You might not agree with me, but I think you should tell her the truth. It may be a shock to hear, but in the long run it will be better for her. Secrets have a habit of getting all twisted up if they're not shared. She might accept Gray better and understand the gravity of the situation more," Hudson suggests.

"I don't know if I can," I reply, following Hudson's gaze, my stomach churning with anxiety at the thought of breaking the news to her.

Gray is currently sitting opposite Lena, his dark blonde six o'clock shadow covering his cheeks and chin. With a shaved head on one side, and a curtain of blonde hair on the other, he's attractive in a silent, thoughtful way. I can't get a good read on him. Right now, he's nursing a black coffee, his unreadable gaze focused on Lena who's staring off into the distance, the fluffy scrambled eggs and bacon left untouched before her. My heart squeezes in pain. Seeing her like this *hurts*.

"I'm considering taking Lena out of school for the time being. She'll have questions then, I'm sure..." My voice trails off as I sigh heavily. The pressure of keeping her safe weighing heavily on my shoulders. "The guys have offered to pay for a tutor until this whole situation has been dealt with."

Xeno squeezes me tighter, understanding how hard it is for me to let them help financially. He made the suggestion as we were getting dressed earlier, and whilst I hate taking Lena out of school and away from her friends, it would be for the best until we can guarantee her safety.

"Given the circumstances, I think that's a good idea. I have a friend who could help in that department. She's a retired teacher. I'll give her a call if you want?"

"I'd appreciate that..." My voice cracks, overwhelmed with everyone's kindness. It's not something I'm used to. How fucked up is that? I'm tearing up because of kindness, something that I've been woefully lacking my whole life.

"Hey, it's okay, Pen," Xeno murmurs.

"I'm fine," I say tightly, brushing off his concern with a forced smile, whilst inside I battle with a sudden, fierce anger. Anger at my mum for never loving me. Why did she hate me so much? Why didn't she save me from David's wrath? Why did she drink to escape?

Those questions have always burned in my mind, and now I'll never have the opportunity to find out. I'm not foolish enough to think Mum and I would ever have fixed what was broken, but eventually I would've confronted her. Xeno, sensing my imminent breakdown, hauls me closer to his side.

"Come on, you should eat too. You can't take care of Lena if you barely have the energy to stand upright," he reminds me.

Louisa nods, her eyes cast with worry. "Yes, *please*, eat. There's plenty to go around. I hope you like—"

"Pen?! PEN!" Lena stands suddenly, her chair toppling over from the force. My skin prickles at the sound of her misery and heartbreak. It scratches down my spine, piercing my gut and fanning my rage, the violence and my need to lash out at the man who did this to her, to us.

"Lena!" I call back, shrugging out of Xeno's hold and rushing forward.

Her head whips around, her eyes frantic until she focuses on me. They're filled with a never ending sadness so deep that I fear we both might drown.

"Hey, Lena..." York says softly, reaching for her hand with gentle fingers and empathy, but she shakes him away, focusing only on me.

On the other side of the table Gray stands, concern etching his features with shadows and lines. I've only spoken a handful of words to him, but the way he looks at Lena tells me he's a good man, that her sorrow affects him too, just like it does all of us.

"Pen!" Lena cries as I pull her into my arms and hold her close. Her wails of grief fill the air and make the hair on the back of my neck stand. I break with her, for her, but there are no outward signs, just unending sympathy and a hate that expands and billows until I feel sick with it. I've always hated David, I've wished him dead countless times, but I've never wanted to make that happen with my own bare hands until now.

"Hush, I'm here. I'm here."

"She's dead, Pen. She's gone!" she wails, her tears wet and warm against my cheek. Her body doubles over in agony as grief tries to drag her to the floor.

"I know, Lena. I know," I murmur, supporting her weight as I ease her back into the chair York has picked up off the floor and placed behind her.

"She's never coming back, is she?" she asks me as she cries for a mother who loved her fiercely but never extended that same kind of love, *any* kind of love, to me. "Pen, tell me this is all a dream. Tell me Mum's okay. *Please.*"

I shake my head, blinking back my own tears, refusing to let them fall, determined to remain strong, unbreakable. I dig deep, knowing that all I can do right now is tell her the truth.

"Mum's never coming back, Lena. I'm sorry. I'm so, so sorry."

5

Pen

WE ARRIVE at the flat later that evening. Dax and Zayn have already brought over mine and Lena's belongings and put them in Dax's room. Four boxes each, that's all we have to our name. Not that it matters. Possessions mean nothing so long as we have each other.

"I thought you'd want to share. For now at least," Dax says when I enter the room and notice that all of his stuff is gone, replaced with our things instead.

"But where will you sleep?" I ask, chewing on my lower lip as I survey the room.

"With Xeno. York and Zayn fucking snore. I won't get a wink of sleep with those two bastards."

"I don't fucking snore, prick," Zayn says, bringing in one last bag filled with Lena's toiletries and makeup. He strides into the bathroom and leaves them on the vanity. "I'd offer to help unpack, but I know girls can be particular about their stuff and where it should go. Besides, I need to shift my shit over to York's room given Gray has taken mine."

"He's staying too?"

"Just temporarily. We've asked him to watch over Lena whilst we're at the Academy all day. It makes sense that he stays here rather than travelling back and forth from his place. The guy's a closed book for the most part, barely talks, but he's respectful, courteous, and is a skilled bodyguard according to Beast," Zayn explains.

"Can we trust him?" I ask, lowering my voice even though the door to the bedroom is shut. "I know he's been watching over Lena for a while now, but being with her constantly.... I just feel like that's my responsibility. He's a stranger to her."

"Both Beast and Grim vouch for him. Beast has known him for eight years, since he was a kid of twelve. Grim officially hired him two years ago. Neither will go into details about his history but they're one hundred percent behind him. I trust their word. They've proved themselves loyal allies."

"He's only our age? He seems older somehow," I remark.

"Yeah. It can get like that when you've grown up in this life," Dax mutters.

"Hud's arranging for the tutor to come over once the funeral is out of the way. So Lena won't be alone with Gray anyway."

Frowning, I chew on my lip some more, a nasty habit of mine when I'm uncomfortable about something. I know what I'm about to say isn't going to go down well, but I've been going over and over it in my mind and there's no alternative.

"There's something I wanted to say," I begin, but right at

that moment my phone pings with an incoming message. Pulling it free from my back pocket, I quickly glance at the screen. It's another message from Clancy. She's been desperate to talk with me after Zayn told her what went down when the guys were collecting my stuff from the Academy yesterday, but I've been too distracted with Lena to call back and have only managed a couple of quick texts.

"What did you want to say?" Zayn asks as I drop my phone on the bed. I'll reply to Clancy later.

Dax narrows his eyes at me. "I might not be York, but I know that look, Kid. What is it?"

"*I* want to be here for Lena, not some stranger she barely knows."

"You are, Pen, but you're one person and you can't do it all," Zayn points out.

"That's my point. I'm going to call Madame Tuillard tomorrow. I'm giving up my spot at the Academy—"

For a beat silence descends, then Dax narrows his eyes at me. "The *fuck* you are!" he exclaims, the sudden fury in his voice making me jump. He strides over to me and grips my shoulders, ducking his head to look me in the eye. "You are *not* giving up on your dream. No fucking way."

"It doesn't seem so important anymore," I counter, telling him a half-truth in the hope he'll leave it at that. I shrug my shoulders as though it really doesn't mean anything to me to leave my dream behind when, truthfully, it absolutely does. It fucking kills me, but it's *nothing* compared to this feeling I'm carrying with me now. York was right, I *do* need vengeance. I may not have loved my mother, but Lena did. David's broken her. Day by day I've watched her withdraw into herself, and I want payback.

I want him dead for what he's done to her.

Stepping out of Dax's hold, I start hanging up Lena's clothes in the wardrobe.

"Fuck that, Pen! Dax is right," Zayn says fiercely. "You do not let that cunt win. This is what he wants, what he's always wanted. You do not fucking give up your dream. Hear me?"

Gritting my jaw, I turn to face them both. "What's the point wasting my time there waiting on David to make his next move when that time could be better spent hunting him down and helping Hudson draw out Santiago. You know I'm right."

"We can still do all of that, Kid, but you give up dance, the very essence of who you are, and David's already won. You may as well just offer yourself up to him now and be fucking done with it!" Dax shouts, his eyes blazing with anger. He's never, not once, shouted at me like this.

"Tell me, after everything that's happened, what else am I supposed to do, Dax?" I ask beseechingly, needing him to understand.

"You keep fighting, that's what you do. You keep dancing. You embrace the warrior within you, the one that danced on the table in Tales and brought the four of us to our goddamn knees. You funnel that girl still within you who took the punches and the kicks from that motherfucker and survived them."

"It's not as simple as that," I say, balling my fists.

"It *is* that simple. You dance. You fight. You win. End of."

"But how can I dance knowing what he's done, what he wants to do? How can I carry on like nothing's happened? Tell me, how?" I ask Dax, begging him to provide me with all the answers he's so certain of. Dance is a joyful experience for me, even when I use it to work out all of my emotions. I don't want to feel fucking joyful right now. I want the rage, the anger, the violence.

"You're *still* that girl who never lost faith in her dream even when everyone else lost faith in her. You are Pen-motherfuck-ing-Scott. Understand me?"

My shoulders drop. "I don't know if I am anymore. I'm so full of fucking fear and rage and this feeling of... of *violence*. I've never felt this way before, not even in all the years he beat me," I hiss, pulling at my clothes, feeling uncomfortable in my own skin. "I've always turned to dance to keep me sane, to purge my feelings, but I don't want to purge this violence. I don't. If I do, if I let it go then I've got nothing left to hold onto and I won't be able to fight him. I need to fight him," I retort, anger making my words sharp, deadly.

"You're wrong. You have *us* to lean on!" Zayn counters, frustrated at me, at the situation. I don't blame him, but I can't help the way I feel. "Let us help you."

"You are. You're going to teach me how to fight. To *kill*," I spit, hating myself for sounding the way I do. I don't recognise my own voice and the monstrous violence fuelling it. "What good is dance when all is said and done? It won't protect me from David. It's only ever acted as a beacon for his hatred. It brought him here after all."

Zayn flinches, his nostrils flaring. One minute he's glaring at me, the next he's striding across the room and grabbing my hand. "Come with me, right the fuck now." He doesn't give me a chance to protest, he simply pulls me from the room, throwing a look over his shoulder at Dax. "Get the guys. They're needed in the studio. Tell Gray to order pizza, put a movie on or something. Have him keep Lena company, keep her occupied whilst we deal with this *situation*."

"I am *not* a situation," I protest, indignation riling me up further.

"Don't fucking fight me on this, Pen, or so help me God, I'll do something we'll both regret!"

"Zayn, I know what you're trying to do," I begin, trying to pry my fingers free of his hold, but he shakes his head and squeezes tighter, refusing to let me go. "I'm not going to change my mind. I'm leaving the Academy."

"That's bullshit, Pen!" he seethes, kicking open the studio door so hard it crashes against the wall. I half expect Lena to come running, but I guess she's still too lost in her own pain to notice what's going on between us right now and, honestly, that's a relief. I don't want to add to her burden.

"Zayn, would you stop!" I trip over my feet in my haste to keep up with him as he maintains a crushing grip on my fingers. Once we're in the centre of the room, Zayn lets my hand go and with a heaving chest, rounds on me.

"We promised we would help you to learn how to fight, to kill. We're doing that not because we want to, but because we know you need to feel in control again. I get it, even if I don't like it, but I'll be damned if you turn your back on dance because the guilt over what's happened has messed with your head and twisted you up inside. You are *not* leaving the Academy."

"The fuck?!" Xeno exclaims, stepping into the studio at that exact moment. York and Dax follow behind, both staring at me.

Dax in anger and York with shock. Xeno glares at me, a mixture of confusion and fury showing on his face.

"I *am* leaving the Academy," I repeat, jerking my chin and levelling my gaze at them all. I'm panting now. My chest heaving. I'm so overwhelmed with intense emotion I can barely temper my feelings as I glare at the men I love, all the while hating myself for feeling so screwed up inside. I hate that I'm ruining their dreams as much as my own, but the second I saw those purple fingerprints wrapped around my mum's throat and her lifeless eyes staring up at me, something fundamental changed within me.

Something *snapped.*

I broke.

I'm not that girl they loved. Not anymore.

And I'm so fucking mad about it.

I want to tear at the air, at the spectre of David that has always haunted my every waking moment and inhabited my nightmares. He's always been there in the background, but up until now dance has always kept me steady, countering his presence. Over the years, dance has allowed me to temper the hurt and the pain, the anger and the bitterness. It has kept my soul intact even when my body's been bruised and beaten, and my heart broken from abuse. It's kept the spark in me alive.

But that spark is no longer a bright light in a sea of darkness, warming me, soothing me. That spark has turned into a roaring inferno full of rage and violence. By killing my Mum, by fulfilling his promise, David's taken my coping mechanism, my escape, and twisted it into something unrecognisable.

I don't want to dance.

I want to *kill.*

"Pen, you have to listen to us," Zayn pleads, taking my hands in his. The warmth of his palms seeps into my skin, pulling me out of my thoughts momentarily. I lock gazes with him and shake my head. I'm not stupid, Zayn has brought me into the studio for an intervention. He thinks he can goad me into dancing, that once I succumb to the power of movement that I'll be okay again, that I'll change my mind and let them save me. That I'll go back to the girl he loves. That they all love.

But I *can't*.

My need to dance has been replaced with my need for violence. I want him dead. God help me. I want him dead.

Fisting my fingers, I wrench my hands free from Zayn's hold and swing at the air, throwing a punch at David's ghost. Zayn steps back, absolute desolation casting a shroud over his features.

"Pen—"

Zayn's voice is drowned out by the ghost of David's. I can hear him now. I can hear his voice goading me, taunting me.

"Mark my words, Penelope, you're going to regret ever fucking me over."

I claw my fingers, racking them over the apparition before me, wishing for blood and getting nothing but thin air.

"Just know this, Penelope. I'm gonna kill your precious Breakers, then I'm going to kill Lena and then when you've lost everyone you love, I'm coming for you. When that day comes, there will be no one left to protect you."

"NO!" I shout, frantic as I punch and kick. Oblivious to anyone but the phantom taunting me.

Whore. Bitch. Slut. Slapper. Scum.

Worthless.

Little.

Cunt.

All the horrible things he's ever said to me over the years bombard me now as I punch and kick. Rage and scream. Fury wraps around me and where once dance would have soothed my soul, all I feel is rage. All I long for is his death. And right there in the dance studio surrounded by the men I love, I lose myself to the broiling violence.

6

Zayn

POWERLESS. Helpless. Fucking useless.

That's how I feel watching Pen lose herself to the agony her cunt brother has caused.

Tears stream down her face but there's no relief from them, only pain. Hardship.

She's hurting and there's not a damn thing any of us can do for her but let her ride this out. Pen needs to purge herself of everything she feels. Then and only then can she begin to rebuild, to fight back. A pain-filled cry tries to escape from her lips, but she stuffs her fist into her mouth to muffle the sound and collapses to the floor instead, still conscious of Lena even as she suffers her own pain.

"Titch..." York says, his voice cracking with emotion. He moves towards her, but Dax holds out his arm and shakes his head, knowing she needs to do this. She needs to let it go. He keeps his gaze fixed on her, and I see the fierceness of his love and compassion flare in his eyes.

Watching her like this, breaking apart, is gutting. It slices through the toughened outer shell we all wear and spreads us wide open. Her vulnerability is humbling. It takes courage to bear herself like this even if she doesn't realise it in the moment.

For long minutes, we watch as she slams her fists against the floorboards repeatedly, echoing the dance she performed only a few weeks ago in the theatre at the Academy. Truth be known, Pen has never danced with as much emotion, or as much power as she had in that moment. Not even that night at Tales when she slapped us all in the face with the force of her talent, anger and passion. We'd all watched her from our seats at the back of the theatre and held our motherfucking breath as Pen had looked directly into the camera, into the eyes of her demon, and sent him a message that could only be interpreted one way.

It was a clear *fuck you* to David, and was the most powerful thing I've ever witnessed.

Right now we see that dance in its rawest form, stripped back to its very essence. This is pure emotion, not movement. This is all the broken, ugly darkness, all the debilitating fear, bone-crushing anger and muscle-trembling violence she's held inside for so long. It pours out of her now, a river of emotion staining the floor with her tears.

Yet, despite the pain she's exorcising and the loudness of her grief and fury, she barely makes a sound. Amidst it all, there's still a part of her aware that Lena sits in the other room and that's how I know that whilst Pen might be breaking apart, she *isn't* broken.

She's so fucking strong.

"She's going to hurt herself," Xeno mutters, his face contorting with sympathy, empathy and excruciating pain. It hurts him to see her like this. Now it's his turn to step forward, wanting to break her out of this storm of emotion that's shredding her so completely.

"No, Xeno. Don't," I warn, shaking my head. "She needs to ride this out. We have to let her. She's strong enough."

He glares at me, and I see his need to disagree. Instead, he grits his jaw, nodding sharply. He knows I'm right. Pen is strong enough. She has always maintained an inner core of steel, a thread of strength that has gotten her through every hardship she's ever suffered. She might be rejecting dance right now, but it's who she is, and I know she won't turn her back on it because we won't fucking let her.

So we watch and we wait.

This haemorrhaging of everything inside of her isn't just about her brother's heinous act or her sister's pain. This is about her mum too. This is about a woman who never loved her, who was cruel and abusive, who allowed her son to beat her. It's about the unimaginable pain of not feeling loved, of surviving abuse through sheer force of will. This is grief and guilt, abandonment and disappointment, *fury*. It's empathy for a woman who doesn't fucking deserve it. This is all of those emotions rolled up into an inevitable tsunami of pain that only now finds its release. It breaks out of her like the fucking dead clawing out of mud and soil. It shreds her apart and we're with her, feeling every crack and every tear. We absorb it, take it on. We watch as she battles thin air, as she rages, her teeth bared, her eyes wild until she flips onto her back, crushes her hands over her face, and sobs.

After a while the muffled sobs become silent whimpers and when, eventually, she curls onto her side, I go to her. My gaze flickers to Xeno as I kneel on the floor behind her. He rips his glassy eyes away from Pen and turns to York who's swiping at his tear-stained face. Lowering his voice, Xeno whispers something under his breath. York nods, flicking his gaze to me before leaving the room. He comes back half a minute later.

"Gray's got it covered. They're watching a movie. Lena's finally eating."

Xeno nods, closes the door then jerks his chin. York and Dax move towards us whilst Xeno strides over to the surround sound system and places his mobile into the dock. Scrolling through his music, he finds the track he's looking for and presses play. My throat closes the second *Look After You* by Aron Wright begins to filter through the speakers.

"Fuck," Dax says, blowing out a long breath and swiping a hand over his face as he stares at our girl. I know he wants to haul her into his arms just like I do, but he holds back from the urge, understanding like the rest of us that this is a delicate moment.

Turning my attention back to Pen, I rest my hand on her arm as one by one the guys sit down on the floor around her. Xeno places his hand on her hip whilst Dax reaches for her leg, his large hand squeezing gently. York strokes her hair, his fingers sliding over the silky strands. We all need to touch her. We need to connect, need to show her that we're here, that we always will be.

She lies still, her eyes pressed shut, her face covered in tears as we comfort her with gentle touches, silent but for the music playing.

Around us, the words of the song cloak us with meaning. They're poignant, they speak for Xeno, for all of us as her men, her Breakers. Music, as much as dance, has always been a form of language between the five of us. As kids we used music to express how we felt when we didn't know how to do that with words. We would play songs that would reflect our feelings and emotions, listening together, silently understanding what we were incapable of saying. Then we would dance to that music, adding in another layer of communication between us, strengthening our bond. This song choice is Xeno opening the door on that old form of communication, because right now, none of us can bring ourselves to say the words without fucking crumbling. We want Pen to know that she isn't alone. That she will never, ever, be alone again.

That we will look after her.

We will help her to heal, to grow. Our home is hers now, as it is Lena's, and we will *never* abandon them, just like we won't let her abandon dance. It's who she is. It's the very core of Pen. It's what drives her. It's what brought her to us, bound us together, what ripped us apart and what, ultimately, brought us back together again. We won't allow her to turn her back on it through misplaced guilt, crushing grief and an overwhelming need for vengeance.

Right now she's cast adrift, but we *will* anchor her. We will guide her, show her the way back to who she is because we know what it's like to lose ourselves, to lose our passion for dance. We lost it when Pen walked away, and we got it back again because of her. She reignited our love for dance and we'll be damned if we allow her to turn her back on it.

As the music plays, we continue to soothe her, pressing our fingers over her body. We're four pairs of hands, four beating hearts with one simple goal: to love her.

To motherfucking *love* her.

Slowly, she rouses. Her eyelids flicker open as she pushes upwards, our hands falling away as she shifts into a seated position. Pen's the quiet calm after the storm when there's nothing left but a desolate landscape, littered with the debris of shattered dreams and broken fucking hearts. She's at a turning point. I see it, understand it. Either she embraces the devastation and chooses to rebuild back stronger, or she lets it damage her beyond repair.

"Titch?" York says gently, reaching for her, but his hand falls away when he reads her body language.

Pulling her legs up, she rests her chin on top of them, wrapping her arms around herself in comfort. Dax's nostrils flare as he sucks in a breath at the rejection and York shifts uncomfortably, swiping a shaking hand through his hair. It may seem like nothing to a stranger, but the Pen we know would have reached for one of us instead. She's cutting herself off, and I realise then what path she's choosing.

That hurts. It motherfucking hurts.

Xeno, sensing what I do, meets my gaze. His green eyes flash with determination as he hardens his features. I've seen that look before. I understand its meaning well enough. This is Xeno ready to fight until he gets what he wants. It's a look the three of us have experienced at least once before when we've fallen into a dark place, only to be pulled back out by Xeno, kicking and screaming, but *fighting*. He's saved us from ourselves before, and now he's going to do the same for Pen.

Dax and York notice. The tension rises.

"We're here, *always*," Xeno says, resting his hands on her feet and ducking his head to meet her gaze. "The four of us are *here for you*. We will teach you to fight. We will teach you to embrace the darkness..."

She lifts her head from her knees and locks gazes with him. "He has to die." Her voice is cold, deadly, like the jagged edge of my knife, but there's fight in it. That gives me hope, because where there is fight, there is passion, and where there is passion, there is *always* dance.

Xeno grits his teeth. "Yes. He does."

Pen breathes in deeply, her lungs filling with air. She holds her breath for long moments before letting it out slowly and as she does, the music changes from heartfelt promises to something equally as powerful, invigorating in its meaning. *Don't Cry* by Bugzy Malone and Dermot Kennedy plays and, once again, I lock eyes with Xeno over Pen's shoulder, instantly understanding the message within the song.

"We will be your light when the world gets too dark," he continues. "We will be the lyrics in every song and the step in every dance. We'll remind you every fucking day who you are. But know this, Tiny, if you want to learn how to kill a man, then it comes with one condition. You don't turn your back on dance. *Understand?*"

She doesn't respond, stubborn to the end, but here's the thing, so are we. Pen *will* keep dancing.

We'll make sure of it.

7

Pen

"GET UP, PEN," Xeno demands, his voice low, determined. He stands, Dax, York and Zayn following suit.

I remain on the floor, my arms wrapped around my legs as I drag my gaze away from Xeno and stare at my reflection in the mirror. I'm tired, my face is pale, drawn, tear-stained, but despite the weakness I see before me, there's also something else...

Inevitability.

My Breakers will fight me every step of the way. I know that, I love them for caring enough to try. But here's the thing, we all know that dance isn't going to save Lena. It's not going to save the boys I love and it sure as fuck won't save me.

Dax widens his stance, folding his arms across his chest as he glares at me. "You heard him. Get up, Kid." Turning my head slowly, I look up at Dax, my dark angel, and see the challenge in his gaze. "Get. Up," he repeats.

I say nothing, allowing his demand to wash over me and the words of the song to register in my muddled head. The beat vibrates up through the floor, my teeth rattling with it. Gone is the soothing words of love and support and in its place is something angrier, harsher. It's like a slap in the face because I thought they got it. When they'd supported me with their presence a moment ago, I thought that they understood where I was coming from. I see now that isn't the case.

"Enough is enough, Titch." York this time.

Fuck this. I won't be coerced.

With my anger, other feelings return, and even though my body feels heavy, exhausted from my breakdown, my mind starts to latch onto the one thing that's going to keep me going. The need to kill. Pain begins to radiate from my hands, and I turn them over, looking at my palms and the redness of my skin. Some of my nails are broken, some bleeding where I raked them over the floorboards imagining David's face. I'm going to kill that bastard with or without their help.

"Titch. Stand. Now!"

Pressing my eyes shut, I try to block out their voices and the music, concentrating instead on the end goal, on David's lifeless eyes, so similar to my Mum's, wide and vacant. Dead. Only then will I find peace.

"You do not belong on the floor. Titch. Get the hell up."

Jerking my head up to the left, I lock eyes with York's icy gaze and flinch at the fire I see in them. He reads me expertly. He knows my mind, he sees my truth and his nostrils flare, his arms falling to his side as he begins to tap. It's sudden, angry.

His steps pound the floor barely inches from my crossed legs. It's a challenge. He's pushing me to react.

"Get the fuck up, Titch!" York roars.

He stamps his feet in harsh beats all the while staring at me. Ball. Shuffle. Change.

Stomp. Slide. Stamp. Stomp. Slide. Stamp.

STAMP.

York gets too close, and I'm forced to shuffle away from his pounding, angry feet, only to find Dax's legs pressing into my side. I jerk away, but he crouches down, grabs my upper arm and yanks me to my feet. I try to pull free from his hold, but his fingers just curl tighter. He snarls, then lowers his mouth to my ear.

"You don't get to turn your back on dance, not because of that cunt," he seethes, his anger as broiling as my own. Letting me go, Dax doesn't give me a chance to respond, instead he spins on his right foot and kicks out in a pirouette. His body is light, but filled with incredible power as he moves. The music feeds his anger and his steps as he dances. I swallow hard, refusing to look at him. Dropping my head, I twist on my feet and walk towards the door.

"No! You're staying."

"Get out of my way, Zayn," I say, trying to step around him. He simply blocks my path, planting a firm hand on my shoulder. "I can't do this."

"You face this. Right the fuck now," he replies, twisting me around. He wraps one arm around my waist and lifts my chin firmly, his fingers digging into my skin, forcing me to look. "Do you see that? Do you see how you brought them back to life? You did that with dance, Pen. *Dance* brought us back together," he repeats, hammering his point home. "It *healed* us. You stop dancing, then what we have together, it will fucking die. It might not happen right away, but it will happen. This is who we are underneath all the fucking bullshit. Do you really want that?"

"Please, don't do this. I *can't*..."

The words of the song seep into my thoughts, coating me in guilt. They goad me as much as his words flay me open. This is a song about fighting. About darkness, about refusing to give up, refusing to give in. But it's Zayn's words that hit me harder, like a punch to the stomach.

I'm winded from them.

"We need each other, Pen."

He's right, I need them so much. I need *us*, but I need Lena safe more. They said they would teach me to defend myself against David, to kill him should it get to that point, but what they don't understand is that I *have* to be the one to end his life and I can't do that if this violence and rage I feel right now is tempered by dance.

"He's ruined everything," I croak, and for the briefest of moments, Zayn loosens his hold on my face. Everything was ruined because of my brother. Everything that happened to us was because he forced me to walk away from them. I wasn't strong enough then to fight back, but I have to be now. I have to be. "I can't do this if you force me to dance..."

Zayn growls, moving forward so that I'm forced to move with him. He's too big, too strong for me to fight off. "You can. You will," he insists.

When I try to plant my feet on the floor, Zayn lifts me off the ground and strides with me towards Xeno. He hasn't taken his eyes off of me this whole damn time and I see how his body vibrates with energy, with tension that's only heightened by York's angry tap and Dax's enraged steps as they both continue to dance behind him. Two very different dances. Two completely different men, both connected by history, by brotherhood, by *dance*.

Swallowing hard, I drag my gaze away from them and back to Xeno. His fingers curl around my wrist and he pulls me out of Zayn's hold. I slam into his chest, the air forced out of my lungs. Grasping my face in his curled fingers, Xeno slams his lips against mine. I gasp, shocked by the sudden kiss as he slides his angry tongue into my mouth, bruising my lips and my heart. Gone is the man who stroked my hip with gentle fingers and in his place is the Xeno who can't keep a lid on his emotions.

Volatile. Dangerous. Unhinged.

"You can only push so far until we're forced to push back," he says, the words a dark threat against my lips.

Panting, I try to shake out of his hold, but he grins, then twists me around and yanks me back against his chest, holding me firm just like Zayn had a moment ago.

"Zayn, get your knife. Now!" he orders, his voice low, menacing with intent.

"Why?" I ask, hating that my voice wobbles.

Zayn's gaze flickers with something that I can't interpret in the moment, then he nods curtly before turning on his heel and striding from the room. Whilst he's gone, Xeno forces me to watch Dax and York dance once more.

"Don't you feel that?"

"Don't," I bite out, twisting my head away, only for his fingers to tighten around my jaw as he jerks my head back around. Every dance step, every movement, is a hammer smashing through my determination.

They're warriors. Brothers. Fighters.

Monsters.

They're my lovers. My best friends. My heart.

They're the other pieces of my soul.

My chest heaves. My skin itches with the need to shred myself from this feeling. David has well and truly messed with my head. He's done the one thing I vowed to never let him do. He's taken my love for dancing and twisted it into something painful, something I want to push away, not embrace.

Xeno's soft breath tickles my cheek as he leans over me, tightening his hold. "I don't fucking believe in God, Tiny, but I do believe in angels. Dax was always your dark angel, but you, you were always mine. You brought me back to life. Fuck, don't you understand that?"

"Xeno..." My voice breaks, and I will myself to gather the pieces of myself and hold them together. *Strong. I have to remain strong.*

"Look at them!" he demands as Dax flips forward then slides into the splits at the same time as York leaps over his head, dropping to the other side. His feet move so fast I can barely follow the tap steps. My eyes drag up his body, then meet his gaze. For a moment I think he's going to say something to Xeno, but he grits his jaw, twists around and holds his hand out to Dax. Their eyes meet and they both nod, a silent agreement made between them as York pulls Dax to his feet. Then with their hands still joined, they press their foreheads together, their free hands reaching up and grasping each other's shoulder. York grits his teeth, and as the next beat of the song drops, he taps in a way that reminds me of how a boxer would move his feet in a fight. Dax's top lip curls up in a menacing glare that completely contradicts the love in his eyes.

This is two powerful men facing off. Two best friends fighting for each other. For us. For me.

My heart fucking swells in shame, in love, in fear and frustration.

"See how they fight, Tiny. See how they *fight*."

I swallow hard, choking back the tears. Dax pushes against York, forcing him backwards, their foreheads still pressed together.

Dax, the bare knuckle fighter. York, the boxer.

York taps, Dax counters with steps of his own. York grins wickedly then shoves Dax backwards. They part, bouncing on their feet. Sparring, dancing, fighting. I watch, entranced, as they merge the disciplines into a mashup of movement that takes my argument and strangles the life out of it.

York throws the first punch. Dax ducks, his right leg sliding out as he spins away before rising up on his toes and jabbing his fist in an uppercut. York jumps back, his feet move quickly as he bounces on his toes, waiting, intermittently cutting into a tap sequence then back to bouncing as though he can't contain either side of his personality. Dax launches forward, throwing a punch that clips York's jaw. The force of the punch throws York's head to the side and I suck in a breath at the blood that splits his lip, but York won't be deterred. Grinning with bloodied teeth, he pulls back his fist throwing all his weight behind it as his whole body moves with the punch, but Dax spins away in a barrel jump before he can even reach him. York doesn't give up. He comes for Dax, chasing with fast feet, tapping and sliding, throwing punch after punch whilst Dax dodges and weaves until, eventually, they're no longer fighting but dancing once more.

It's breathtaking.

"Don't you *see*, Tiny?" Xeno asks, drawing my attention back to him and the way his thumb slowly circles my jaw, easing over the tenderness from Zayn and his bruising grip.

"I know I've seen enough..." I bite out, battling the overwhelming desire to join them.

Lost within their movements, sweat beads on Dax and York's skin, and I feel the heat from their bodies as they move around us. It blankets us, and is comforting in a way that I wish it wasn't right now.

"No you haven't. You've not seen nearly enough," Xeno counters, pressing his nose into my hair and breathing in deeply before continuing. "You're not the only one battling the violence inside. We do it every second of every day, and the *only* thing keeping us from fucking tearing everyone and everything apart is *you*. You gave us back our souls through *dance*. Don't you get it? We'd become senseless, soulless creatures without you, without movement. *Together*."

"Please, Xeno, you have to stop..." I'm begging now, and I don't care how that sounds. I don't want to be forced into seeing this, into feeling this way, into wanting to dance.

"No, Tiny. I won't. You've seen the monsters we hide. They scared you." I whimper at his words, at the truth I can't deny. "Didn't they, Tiny?"

"Yes."

"And yet you're so willing for us to become those monsters again."

"No." I shake my head fiercely. "This isn't about you. It's about me, about what *I'm* capable of."

"That's where you're wrong. This is about all of *us!*"

"Stop it," I whimper, crying now. I hate myself for it. For the tears that continue to fucking pour and not give me any relief. I feel weakened by them and it angers me.

Soft Pen. Kind Titch. Loving Tiny. Sweet Kid.

Flipping me around in his arms, Xeno narrows his eyes at me. "I won't stop until you listen."

"I have to let dance go."

"No."

"Yes," I argue.

"Tiny, when you walked away before we didn't just lose you, we lost the ability to dance, to find our home within the steps. A part of us *died*, Tiny."

"This is different! I'm not leaving you. I'm just not dancing. That's all."

"Bullshit. You're turning your back on who you are, on us as a family, a fucking crew. Fuck, I ripped myself open for you, Tiny, and for what? For you to abandon us like this?" His words hurt, scoring more pain on top of pain. When will it end?

"I didn't know how hard loving me would be, and I'm sorry, okay? I'm sorry it hurts you so much. I'm sorry I can't be who you need me to be."

"Don't you remember what you said to me?" he asks, his voice lowering. There's a tremor to it that guts me.

"No, I don't," I respond, swallowing hard, remembering only too well. I remember how he danced that day in the Freed's home gym. I remember how raw, how passionate, how utterly breathtaking he'd been. How *real*. I saw who he truly was that day and loved him for it. I still love him for it.

"You said that you didn't want to punish me. I believed you."

"I don't want to punish you," I whisper, feeling my resolve splinter and crack at his vulnerability.

"You said that we'd all suffered enough."

"Please, don't do this. I'm not strong enough. I *need* to be strong enough."

"We're asking you, Tiny," Xeno continues. "No, we're fucking begging you. Don't turn your back on dance. We need it as much as we need you, and we *can't* dance without you. It would destroy us."

"I *can't* be her, Xeno. I can't be that girl if I want to beat David. If I want to *kill* David." I drag in a fortifying breath and continue on. "If I want to survive in your world, I have to let that side of me go. Dance softens me. It makes me weak."

"No it doesn't!" His fingers curl into my upper arms, and behind him Dax and York stop dancing, their attention focused on us now. Their chests heave with breathlessness, their muscles ripple with exertion and their skin shimmers with sweat. I swallow hard, dragging my gaze away from them and forcing myself to speak my truth.

"Softness gets your heart broken. Kindness makes you weak. Love makes you a burden and sweetness makes you a target. I understand that now."

"You're so fucking wrong, Tiny. Dance has always been the key. Always. It gave you *strength* when you felt weak. It gave you a *voice* when you didn't have the words to speak. It's what bound five broken souls *together* and made them one unit.

Dance is your greatest weapon, *our* greatest weapon. It always has been. We were never weaker than when we were apart, absent of dance."

"No," I reply stubbornly, all the while knowing that there's a whole lot of truth in his statement that I don't want to acknowledge. His words have impact, his fierceness is like a pair of scissors snipping at my resolve.

"No? Then let us remind you what we look like without dance," he says, letting me go with a shove. I fall back against a firm chest. Zayn's chest. A moment later, a blade is pressed against my throat.

"Zayn, what are you doing?" I stiffen, fear cutting off my tears as I'm reminded of that night when Frederico threatened my life and died for it.

"Showing you the monster buried inside," he replies, his voice dark, unrecognisable.

Xeno, Dax and York step forward. Something about them shifts. Something that scares me. Gone is the compassion, the protectiveness, the fierce, undeniable love, and before me stands men void of humanity.

"Please..."

Dax locks his gaze with mine. "Do you *see* the monsters?" he asks, stepping forward.

"Yes," I pant.

Xeno cants his head, his thick curls falling sideways.. "Can you *hear* them?"

"Yes," I whisper, shivering at his guttural, monstrous voice.

Zayn runs the flat edge of the knife against my neck. I feel the cool metal against my hot skin and a shiver of fear runs down my spine. "Can you *feel* them?" he asks me.

"Y—yes."

"Now tell me again why you think turning your back on dance is the right decision," Xeno presses, steeping closer. He takes the knife from Zayn, grabs the handle and turns the knife on himself. I let out a screech as he presses the tip against his chest, right over his heart. "Because the way I see it, dance is the *only* thing stopping us from losing our souls and letting out these monsters once and for all. The four of us have been walking a tightrope for years. Balancing on a thin length of rope, holding onto the last shred of our humanity. Since returning, since being with you again, *dancing* with you again, that tightrope has turned into a wooden plank. Something safer, stronger. But if you give up dance then so do we, and our safety net is gone. We'll fall into the pits of Hell with no way of clawing ourselves back up. I'd rather die than let that happen."

"No," I whimper.

"Yes," he hisses, digging the knife deeper. A fleck of blood blooms against his white t-shirt, growing as he cuts his skin.

"If you want to be a monster, a *real* monster like your brother, then turn your back on dance. Take away our safety net. Fuck, you may as well take this knife and stab me in the motherfucking heart and kill me. Kill Dax, York, Zayn. Do it!" he seethes, all the while digging the knife in further, the tip slicing through his t-shirt and skin.

"STOP!" I yell, pushing out of Zayn's hold and grabbing Xeno's hand, pulling it and the knife away from his chest. We stand glaring at one another; my rib cage expands and contracts like a bellow fanning the flames of a fire. Dax and York step on either side of Xeno, their nostrils flaring and chests heaving. "I can't lose you. I can't lose any of you," I whisper.

Zayn steps forward and gently takes the knife from Xeno. He slides it back into its sheath then hands it to me with shaking fingers. "Do you understand now, Pen?" he asks me, his voice breaking, pleading.

I nod, swiping at my face.

"Then tell us, Titch, *why* do you need to keep dancing?" York asks, swallowing hard. He swipes at his split lip with the back of his hand, smearing the blood across his pale skin.

"To stop me from turning into a monster," I whisper.

"No," Xeno replies, shaking his head. "You have to keep dancing to make sure that *we* don't."

8

Pen

A KNOCK on the studio door has the desired effect of an ice cold bucket of water thrown over us. Gray's entrance, and the familiar rumble of Beast's voice on loudspeaker, cutting short the much needed conversation between the five of us.

"What is it?" Xeno snaps.

"Beast's on the line. He needs to speak with you. All of you. Now."

"We've just got back from Hudson's place, what the fuck could be so urgent that it can't wait until tomorrow?" York asks in irritation.

"Is Rocks on fire urgent enough for you?" Beast growls through the loudspeaker.

"What the fuck?!" Zayn exclaims, striding over to Gray and snatching the phone from him. "Say that again, Beast."

"Rocks is up in flames. I called the second I found out. You need to get your arses over there ASAP! Grim and I are on our way there now," he says, before ending the call.

For a moment Zayn just stares at the phone in his hand, in shock like the rest of us. Gray is the one who forces us into action. "I'll stay with Lena and Pen. You go," he says.

Zayn's head snaps up and he looks over at the others before shaking his head. "I want the other ghosts who've been watching over Lena stationed outside the flat and the entrance to this building. We're not leaving until they get here."

Gray takes the phone back from Zayn and punches out a text message. "Done. They'll be here in ten." Focusing his attention on Xeno, Gray's eyes flick between the sheathed knife in my hands and the bloodstain on Xeno's t-shirt. He frowns.

"I think you're needed in the lounge," Xeno says, effectively dismissing him.

"Pen?" Gray asks, focusing on me now.

"Don't overstep," Zayn warns, his voice tight.

"I'm just doing my job."

"Your job is to guard Lena. *That's* your job," Dax reminds him.

Gray nods. "No disrespect intended," he says, but he doesn't leave. Instead, he looks at me, a question in his eyes.

"I'm good. We're good. Please just go be with Lena. I need a moment with them," I say quietly.

He hesitates for a moment then nods. "Lena's calmer," he says a little awkwardly. "I thought you should know."

"Thank you, Gray."

With one last terse nod of his head he turns on his feet, leaving us alone once more.

"I haven't got a problem with Gray watching over Lena, but Pen is our responsibility, not his," Dax grinds out the moment the door shuts, a streak of possessiveness showing.

"I agree, but now isn't the time to lay down ground rules," Xeno says, snapping his head around to look at Zayn. "Get your shit. We leave as soon as the ghosts arrive.

"And us?" York asks, folding his arms across his chest.

"I need you both here, just in case."

"In case of what?" I ask, not liking the sound of this.

"I'm covering all bases, Tiny."

"You think David's behind this?"

"I don't believe in coincidences."

"You think he'll come for me... *Right now?*"

"We have to assume the worst. At the very least, this is him trying to fuck with us. Fuck with you," Xeno says, resting his hands on my shoulders and squeezing lightly.

"Well, it's working..." I reply, hating that it's the truth.

"He knows your weaknesses and your strengths, Tiny. Physical violence never broke you as a kid, so he's trying to grind you down with emotional warfare and mind games. Don't let him get inside your head like that. Nothing's changed. We stay strong. We dance. We fight. Right?"

Chewing on my lip, I drop my gaze to the blood stain on his t-shirt. Reaching for the hem, I lift it up and inspect the wound. It's a small cut that sits in the centre of his chest, right over his heart. The blood has already started to congeal. "You should see to that before you go," I say, gently feathering my fingers around the edge of the wound and avoiding his question altogether. It really isn't more than a scratch but that means nothing. This wound is as significant as all the other invisible scars Xeno wears on the inside. That thought pulls me up sharp. Do I really want to be that person who scars him some more? The truth is, I don't. I don't want to hurt any of them, and turning my back on dance will hurt them more than I ever imagined it could. Lifting my eyes up I look between the men I love.

"Fuck, I'm *sorry...*"

"No need for apologies, Tiny," Xeno responds, grabbing the back of my neck and pressing a hard kiss against my lips before pulling back. "This is what we do, right? We're there for each other, no matter how fucking ugly it gets."

"Yes," I agree.

"Good." Xeno nods, then jerks his chin at Zayn before striding out of the studio.

"We'll be back as soon as we can," Zayn says, taking my hand and squeezing it firmly. He drops a gentle kiss to my lips. "We'll talk when we get back, okay?"

"Okay," I agree watching him leave.

"Fuck!" Dax curses, expressing my thoughts exactly.

It's been one thing after the other but, really, what did we expect? David is a bastard. "This has him written all over it," I remark coldly. "Hit hard, then hit even harder. He wants us on our knees and he's doing a good fucking job at getting us there."

"He's *trying* to get us on our knees. He won't succeed. This bond we have, it's unbreakable," Dax counters.

"So what now?" I ask, feeling at a loss. This last hour, let alone the past few days, has been a fucking rollercoaster. I've felt every emotion in the book and then a few more. I've got emotional whiplash and all I really want to do is sleep and forget for a few precious hours, but I refuse to do any sleeping until Xeno, and Zayn have returned home. I won't rest until they're back.

"How about a dance...?" York asks after a beat, a smile in his eyes and that cheeky laughter back. God, I love him. He's nothing if not persistent, and there's a familiarity about that which makes me smile despite everything that's gone on between us.

"You just had to go there, didn't you?" Dax says, shaking his head, the tiniest hint of a smile pulling up his lips.

"Of course I fucking did. Mate, Xeno practically stabbed himself in the heart to show Titch how much dancing with her means to us. I figured she's got the message by now..." He turns to look at me, a hint of hesitation in his eyes as he searches my face. "You *have* got the message, right? Because you never actually agreed to anything," he asks.

"Yes. I got the message. We dance. We fight."

"We, as in *us*?" York presses, pointing between us. "Not as in we, the Breakers. I gotta be sure, Titch. This time I need you to spell it the fuck out for me, because I feel like I'm losing my touch when it comes to reading you."

"We, as in the Breakers... as in, I'm a Breaker too now, right?"

"Well, thank fuck for that!" Dax exclaims, beating York to it. In two strides I'm in his arms and being lifted up off of my feet as he hauls me close. "For a moment back there I thought we'd lost you for good."

"You'll never lose me. *Never*," I say passionately, meaning every word. "I'm just sorry I got lost for a bit." Shame fills me and I drop my head, averting my eyes. I pushed them to their limits. It was a fucked up thing to do even if it was unintentional.

"Kid, you're human. Flawed, just like we are," Dax murmurs, folding me against his chest in a hug, and almost squeezing the breath out of me. "We love you, regardless. We will fight for you, alongside you, against you if we need to, but we will never, *ever*, stop loving you."

"Erm, what the fuck, *big boy*. Me and Titch were having a moment just then and you just had to sweep right in and wrap her up in your big tree-trunk arms so I can't get a look in!" York complains, but the lightness in his voice and the rumble of laughter in Dax's chest as he eases me from his arms, tells me it's all in jest.

"Sorry, man. I was feeling a bit selfish just now," Dax replies, shrugging his shoulders as he opens up his arms and gestures for York to join us. I twist around to face York, my arm wrapping around Dax's waist and wait.

He rolls his eyes. "Really? I can't hug our girl without you getting all up close and personal as well?"

"Not tonight, no."

"Anyone would think you actually want my dick," York says, raising an eyebrow.

Dax shakes his head. "York, shut the fuck up and get in here before I change my damn mind."

"Fine!" York strides over, kisses Dax on the cheek in an affectionate—if not slightly domineering way—then drops a kiss to my forehead, sandwiching me between them both.

$\text{\textit{\textbf{Ł}}}$

"WHAT'S GOING ON, PEN?" Lena asks me as I sit on the edge of the bed in my pyjamas a few hours later. She's sleepy, and even though it's almost two in the morning, she's refusing to sleep. "Where did Xeno and Zayn go?"

"Something happened at Rocks. Nothing for you to worry about, Lena."

"I'm not a child, you know..."

"Seriously, you just need to sleep. It's been a rough few days. We'll talk in the morning, okay?"

She yawns, burrowing beneath the blanket until only her head is peeking out from the top of the covers. Her pretty blue eyes regard me. "I miss her so much. Is that wrong, Pen? I mean, to miss Mum when she was so horrible to you."

Her voice cracks and my heart squeezes at the guilt she feels. I never really thought about what it would be like for her, knowing she was loved when I wasn't. I was only ever happy for Lena that she *was* loved because at least she didn't have to feel as worthless as I did. Resting my hand on her leg, I squeeze gently. "Of course it isn't wrong. You loved her, she loved you. Our relationship bears no reflection on yours. You feel any way you want," I say.

"Do *you* miss her, Pen?" she asks quietly, a wariness in her eyes that makes my stomach turn over.

"She was getting sober. She was finally turning her life around. I'm sad that she didn't get to show us how she would've been without the addiction," I reply. It's the only kind thing I can say in the moment. I don't want to hurt Lena with my fucked up relationship with Mum. That's between us. *Was* between us.

Lena sighs, swiping at another rogue tear. I know there's

more she wants to ask, but I guess hearing the truth would be too much at this moment, and she doesn't pursue it. Instead, she changes the subject. I'm more than a little relieved. There are a lot of things we need to discuss eventually, but right now I don't have it in me to have *that* conversation.

"How long are we staying here, Pen?"

"For as long as we need... *Forever*, if that's okay with you?"

"We're not going back to the flat?"

I shake my head. "Do you want to live in the flat after..."

"After what happened there?" she finishes for me. I nod and she shakes her head. "This place, it's lovely..."

"But?"

"But it's not ours. I mean, it's more yours than mine. I'm just your little sister. I'll get in the way."

"The hell you will!" I reply.

"You're not my mum..." It's an argument she's thrown at me dozens of times in the past when I've acted like her mum, because ours was too out of it to do the same. This time it means something different. She feels like a burden, that she's not my responsibility.

Climbing on the bed beside her. I pull back the cover from beneath her chin so I can get a better look at her. "No, I'm not your mum. I'm your big sister and you have never been, nor will you ever be a burden. People you love aren't burdens, Lena."

"What about the guys?"

"They want to help. They want you here. Besides, we come as a package, you and me. I wouldn't have it any other way."

She gives me a small smile. "They love you a lot, don't they?"

"Yes, they do."

"I'm glad, Pen. I'm glad you have people who love you."

"Me too, Lena. Me too."

Resting my head on the pillow, I lay down and smooth her hair back off her face. After a minute or so Lena's eyes drift shut. "What about Gray?" she asks sleepily.

"What about him?"

"Does he love you too? Is that why he's here?"

A smile pulls up my lips. "No, Lena. He doesn't love me. Gray's here to watch over you..."

Her eyebrows pull together in a frown and I instantly regret my words. If she asks why then I'll have no choice but to tell her the truth. Fortunately, she loses her battle against exhaustion and finally drifts off to sleep, leaving me wondering how the hell I'm going to tell her the hardest truth of all, that David killed our mother.

Zayn

BY THE TIME we reach Rocks, the club is being eaten alive by flames. Thick, black smoke billows up into the sky, smothering the surrounding buildings in a noxious blanket and blocking the light from the street lamps that line the road. The smoke is so thick that the second Xeno and I step out of the car my lungs fill with the acrid smell and I'm choking on the stench.

"Jesus, fuck," I mutter, my eyes watering as I pull my scarf up over my nose and mouth.

A few locals are gathered nearby filming the fire with their phones, no doubt uploading it onto fucking social media to get more views or whatever the fuck these vacuous pricks need these days to get their kicks. I can't help but snarl at the twats, my bad mood worsening with every passing second.

"Come on. I think I see Grim and Beast," Xeno says, indicating for me to follow him.

Yellow police tape is pulled right across the street, from one lamp post to another, and a cop car is parked just beyond it, the engine off with its blue light still flashing. Further along the street, parked closer to Rocks, are two fire engines and their crew who are battling the fire that's doing its best to spread to the neighbouring buildings. To the left, a good distance from the fire and the apparent stream of smoke that is blowing our way and not theirs, is Grim and Beast.

"That heat is intense," Xeno remarks, ducking beneath the yellow tape and walking straight past the cop car, giving nothing but a cursory glance at the police officer who looks like he's just stepped fresh out of the police academy.

"Stop! You can't go down there. Can't you see there's a fire? This street has been cordoned off for a reason. I have orders to keep everyone back until it's safe," the cop blurts out as we stride past him.

"That's *my* club," I respond, cutting him a look that tells him I'm in no fucking mood as I continue walking. "And I don't give a shit about your orders."

Xeno gives me a look and I shrug. Whilst Jeb never made a will, as his only next of kin I get it all. The club, his house and all his possessions will pass to me once everything's gone through probate and his estate is settled. The fact I killed the bastard has no bearings on the outcome, given Interpol covered it up and I literally got away with murder. Truth be known I don't fucking want any of his shit, least of all this club. All of it was bought with blood money, a lot of it mine.

"Stop!" the young copper orders, but it's half-hearted. I'm pretty sure, given Beast and Grim are already standing way past the barrier in the shadow of a darkened alley, that this young cop is either affiliated with them or his partner is. When we reach the pair it's obvious the latter is true.

"Cheers, we appreciate the info," Beast says to another police officer as we approach. This cop is a lot older, and given the relaxed way he is with Beast and Grim, well acquainted with the pair.

"You're welcome. I'll get back to the kid. He's new, wet round the ears and eager to impress. You know what I mean?" the copper replies, giving Xeno and me a curt nod. We may not have met before, but he certainly knows who we are.

"Yeah, I hear you. Is he *good* though, right Benny?" Beast asks, flipping his gaze to the kid who's currently watching us all and looking nervous as shit. I hold in a laugh, pretty fucking apt name for a bent copper.

"I wouldn't have partnered with him if I didn't think he was."

"I'm glad to hear it, but I need you to make sure he's on our side before we reel him in, yeah?"

"Of course, Beast." Benny nods, turning his attention to Grim. "It's good to see you, Grim."

"You too, Benny. Next time you're at Tales the drinks are on me, okay?"

"That's very generous of you. Thank you." He casts a look over his shoulder, jerking his thumb. "I'd better get back to the lad."

"I didn't know you had bent coppers on your payroll," Xeno

scoffs . "Do the punters of Tales know you entertain the enemy as well?"

"Good evening to you too, arsewipe," Beast replies, folding his arms across his chest and scowling. "How Grim chooses to run her business is none of *your* damn business."

"Well, actually, when her name's still on the deed to our clubs, it fucking is," Xeno snaps back, clearly still fucked up over our interaction with Pen earlier and taking it out on Beast and Grim. Not the wisest move of the century, though I don't blame him. I'm still feeling out of sorts too.

It ain't every day the girl you love almost turns her back on dance and the brother you love holds your knife to his chest, ready to die if she didn't change her mind.

Beast snarls, but Grim just rolls her eyes, swatting at Beast's chest. "Just cool it lads. It's hot enough here as it is, we don't need you two causing a scene to add to this shitstain of a night." She turns to face the burning building, her skin cast in an orange glow making her look as fierce as her reputation, like some sexy arse fire demon from the pits of Hell. Beast throws his arm over her shoulder and glances over me at the top of his head, eyebrows raised. I look away, not in the least bit interested in getting into a brawl with the man. Grim might be hot, but Pen is the only woman who lights my fire.

"What's the deal then?" I ask, wanting nothing more than to wrap this up and get back to Pen. We've still got shit to iron out and I've got a motherfucking headache.

"The place is a write-off," Beast remarks. "Ain't no saving it now."

The firefighters are working hard to put out the fire, but just like Beast said, they're losing the battle. Pretty soon the place will be gutted. Not that I give two shits. I never wanted it anyway. The only happy memories I had of that place were the ones with Pen in them, but they've long since been overshadowed by everything else that's gone on. Besides, after the carnage of a few weeks back, the place is bound to be haunted by all the men we killed from Dante's Crew. I deal with the ghosts of the men I've killed on the daily, I don't need to own a place that reminds me of that fact.

"What do you know?"

Grim lets out a heavy sigh, and it's only then I notice the shadows around her eyes and the tightness around her lips. Being the owner of Tales and having a reputation like she does must be pretty fucking difficult to manage at the best of times, without adding pregnancy to the mix.

"Benny's one of my men on the inside," Grim explains. "The reason we found out about the fire tonight even before the fire brigade did was because Benny happened to be first on the scene. He's aware that you and I have an affiliation. He thought I'd want to know, and he was right."

"Well then, we owe Benny a few drinks too. Give him the details to Jewels nightclub. He can bring his other half and the evening will be on us," I say, before Xeno can jump in and stop me.

"Fuck sake, why not invite the whole police force and be done with it," he mutters under his breath instead.

"And speaking of your nightclubs," Grim says, ignoring Xeno's outburst. "I've got my lawyer to draw up some papers transferring Jewels and Chastity back into your names. As soon as this shit is over it'll be done. I did have a question though, should I be adding Pen's name onto the deeds?"

"Yes," both Xeno and I respond simultaneously. We haven't discussed it directly with Pen, but it was a unanimous vote between the four of us. We want her as our partner in life, and in business. What's ours is hers. That goes without saying.

Grim smiles. "I thought as much. I'll be sure to get Pen's details added."

"So what are we looking at here?" Xeno asks, folding his arms across his chest as we watch Rocks turn to ash before our eyes.

"Well, this fire wasn't an accident," Beast remarks more than a little sarcastically.

"David or Santiago?" I ask.

"Maybe some other fucking crew looking to stir up shit?" Xeno offers, clearly hoping that's the case. It's much easier to deal with a threat that we can see than one we can't. We're all fucking pissed off that David has managed to enter the country and murder his own mum without being caught. None of us have any fucking clue where the cunt is right now. The fact we haven't heard shit at all from Santiago is fucking with our heads too.

"Honestly, given what happened recently, I didn't think David would have the balls to act again so soon. I figured this would be Santiago sending a message via another crew. I was wrong." Grim pulls out a padded envelope from her handbag, handing it to me.

"What's this?" I ask, taking it from her, frowning at the name penned in black ink on the front of the envelope. "It's addressed to you."

"Fucking genius right here," Beast jokes, winking at me. I ignore the fucker.

"This was delivered to Tales just before we left to come here. I opened it up in the car on the way over after we called you. There's a note inside and something else too. You might want to be careful pulling it out."

"Grim, I don't like surprises. Want to give me a heads up?" I say.

"It's a note and a... severed toe."

My hand hovers inside the envelope, my fingers brushing against a piece of paper. "You're shitting me, right?"

"She's deadly fucking serious. Made Grim chuck up her guts when she opened it. David's a sick bastard."

Pot, kettle, black, I think, wisely keeping that thought to myself.

"I'm not normally so squeamish..." Grim's voice trails off as she lifts the back of her knuckles to her lips, then swallows. We all know she's seen worse than a severed toe before. Pregnancy really is throwing her out of whack.

"Fucking lovely," Xeno exclaims, watching me carefully as I pull the note free and hand him the envelope with the fucking toe inside.

I hold the folded note in my hand. Even in the fiery orange glow from the fire, there's no mistaking the blood stain on the paper. "I don't suppose we know who the toe belongs to, do we?"

"We do as a matter of fact. Read the note first," Beast insists.

I read the note.

"How the *fuck*...?" I question, snapping my head up as I

hand the note to Xeno who takes it from me, swearing under his breath as he reads. "Do we know if it's true?"

"I called Hudson who rang his contact at Interpol. He texted me just before you arrived. The coroner confirmed that Pen's mum is indeed missing a toe."

"That sick bastard" I exclaim, getting that twisted up feeling in my stomach. I'm not an anxious man. That's not what this feeling is. This is me needing to vent. Usually the monster inside of me wins out on nights like this and I end up in a knife fight. That's not an option right now.

"Jefferson mentioned to you and Dax that he thought he saw the handle of a weapon sticking out of the bag David was carrying, right?" Grim asks.

"Right," I agree.

"The fucker went prepared," Xeno mumbles. "But why wasn't there any blood?"

"Once the heart has stopped beating the blood doesn't pump out from a wound the same way as it does if the person is still alive. There would've been some blood, sure, but the living room has parquet flooring, and it wouldn't have taken much to clean up," Beast says, matter-of-factly.

"Did the coroner tell you this?" Xeno asks, sliding the note back into the padded envelope, and handing it back to me. I try not to think about the toe inside and how badly it's going to affect Pen.

"No. Comes with the territory." Beast responds with a shrug.

"But why didn't we know about all of this sooner? She's been at the mortuary for a couple of days," I ask.

"For exactly that reason. She's been on ice since they picked her up," Beast explains. "The report was only concluded an hour ago. David strangled his mum and severed her toe for the soul purpose of sending another message. Then he put back on her sock and shoe, and cleaned up the fucking mess." Beast shakes his head like he isn't a man who's severed body parts before. The only difference between Beast and David is that Beast does what he does because he's protecting the woman he loves, and David does it to hurt the woman he's obsessed with.

"He went with a formed plan in mind," I growl, my hand instantly going to the knife tucked into the sheath strapped to my waist. Feeling the worn leather of the handle calms me a little. "This isn't just him acting out like some spoilt fucking kid. He's messing with Pen's head. He wants to break her."

"No shit," Beast mutters.

"Why send the note to you though, given it's clearly addressed to Pen?" Xeno asks.

"Pen works for Grim at Tales. It's common knowledge," I suggest. It's the most logical answer.

"I don't think so," Xeno disagrees. "Why fuck off Grim, one of the most powerful gangsters in London. It doesn't make any sense. Yes, Grim might've hired Pen but that means shit. As far as everyone is concerned, it was a good business decision. Pen brings in the punters. She makes Grim a lot of money. David might be a possessive twat, but he was fine with Pen working for Jeb the past three years. This is no different," Xeno counters, giving me that fucking look again. The one where he knows shit and I don't. Then the ball finally drops.

"Except—" I say.

"Except David wants to make it perfectly clear to all of us

that he knows a lot more than we originally thought and that, my friend, is a motherfucking problem," Beast finishes for me.

"You're damn right it is," Xeno agrees, locking eyes with Beast.

"Fuck!" I exclaim.

Grim folds her arms across her chest and sighs. "Looks like we've got a snake in the grass."

10

Pen

AN HOUR after Lena finally falls asleep, I hear a light tap at the door. Sliding off the bed as quietly as possible, I tiptoe over and open it. Zayn's leaning against the doorframe, his forehead pressed against his arm, a bleak look in his eyes.

"You're back," I whisper, reaching for him. My hand cups his cheek, and for a brief moment he presses his eyes shut, leaning into the warmth of my palm. "Are you okay?" It's a stupid question because, clearly, he isn't.

"You'd better come," he says, pushing off the door and taking my hand in his. He smells of smoke and ash, of fire and destruction.

"How bad is it?" I ask as we walk towards the living area. He doesn't answer, instead he suddenly pulls me against his chest and hugs me fiercely, his arms folding around me as he buries his face into my hair. "Zayn. Just tell me. I can handle it. What happened tonight, it was just a... *blip*," I say, reusing Dax's description from a couple days ago. I know it sounds lame, it wasn't a blip, more of a mountain.

"Does that mean you're staying at the Academy, that you'll still dance?"

"Yes."

"Thank fuck," he replies, cupping my face in his hands and kissing me roughly. He tastes of whisky as my tongue curls around his, and we try to reassure each other with love. With his thumbs stroking my cheeks, Zayn pulls back, sighing heavily. "This is going to get worse before it gets better. We're gonna need to dance more than ever, Pen. *All* of us."

Before I can even respond to that statement, he takes my hand and pushes open the door to the living area. I'm surprised to see Grim and Beast standing by the kitchen island with Xeno and Dax. The fact they're both here doesn't bode well. York is talking quietly with Gray by the front door, and beyond I can see another two men I don't recognise. I'm assuming they're the ghosts Zayn demanded were sent to watch over us before he left earlier this evening with Xeno.

"Pen. I'm just gonna say this now," Grim says the second she notices us. "If I get my hands on your brother before you do, I'm gonna string him up and gut the bastard for what he's done. I'm sorry, he doesn't deserve to live it up in prison with fucking digital tv and goddamn all-inclusive meals at the mercy of the bloody Queen of England."

"Please, don't call him my brother. He's never been family," I respond, not bothering to argue because I agree wholeheartedly. It's time to take a leaf out of Grim's book.

"I'll take that as an approval," she replies, a dark smile pulling up her lips as she strides across the room and pulls me into a hug. "How's Lena doing?"

"Not great. She's sleeping right now," I reply. We move to the sofa and I sit between her and Zayn.

"That's good at least," Xeno says, taking a seat opposite us whilst Beast sits to Grim's left.

"You know, I wasn't sure I believed all the talk about David until now. I just thought he was your average two-bit sociopath with a superiority complex, but I agree with Grim, the guy's fucked in the head. The sooner he's put down the better," Beast says to me before lifting his feet up onto the coffee table, dirty boots and all.

Xeno cuts him a look, but doesn't say anything. It's only when Grim taps his leg that Beast removes his feet. I would've smiled had I not felt like throwing up. Once the rest of the guys have joined us on the sofa, including Gray, Xeno clears his throat.

"Rocks has burned to the ground. As you've probably gathered, it was an arson attack."

"Shit," I exclaim, glancing at Zayn who blows out a steadying breath. "Was nothing salvageable?"

Xeno shakes his head. "Not a thing, the place is gutted. I'm betting accelerants were used to ensure the most amount of damage in the quickest amount of time. The arsonist knew what they were doing."

"It was like staring into the pits of Hell. Nothing but charred remains," Zayn adds, heavily, his tone serious and full of weight.

Reaching over, I squeeze Zayn's hand. "I'm sorry. I know

you had mixed feelings about the club. But it's still a blow."

He shakes his head, letting my hand go and reaching for the bottle of whiskey on the table. He pours himself a generous shot, knocking it back. "It's nothing but bricks and mortar, and honestly, I don't give a shit that it's gone... There were more bad memories attached to that place than good."

Zayn chews on his lip, glancing over at Xeno. Something passes between them. "What am I missing here?" I ask. I know these men better than anyone and this low mood isn't just about the club burning down or our confrontation earlier.

"There's more, Pen..." Zayn says, confirming my worst fears. He turns to face me, his knees brushing against mine.

"What?" I whisper.

"Fuck man, don't beat about the bush. Just tell her," Beast says, earning him a dig in the rib from Grim.

"Tell me what exactly...?" My voice trails off when a terrible thought occurs to me. I swallow hard, hoping to God that I'm wrong. "The club has been closed since that night everything went down, so no one was hurt, *right*?"

Grim rests her hand over mine and squeezes it gently before Zayn pulls out a folded note from his pocket. I see a dark stain of red on one corner of the lined paper and swallow hard. It doesn't take a genius to work out what that stain is or who the note is from. With trembling fingers, I take the note from Zayn, and avoiding the blood, I unfold the note and read it out loud.

Eenie, meenie, miney, mo.... Catch a piggie by its toe... Mum was just the starter, Penelope. Didn't she have pretty toes?

"Fuck!" I exclaim, dropping the note. It flutters to the floor as bile rises up my throat at the words and the insinuation. "Please tell me he isn't saying what I think he's saying?"

Xeno locks eyes with me and nods. "We'll make him pay, Tiny."

"I—" My hand clamps over my mouth, the taste of bile burning the back of my throat. I gag.

"How?" Dax snaps. I've never seen him look more murderous than in this moment. He's practically vibrating with rage, and those thick veins on his forearms that I love to drag my tongue over when we make love, bulge beneath his skin as his fingers curl into fists on his lap.

"With a handheld saw I imagine. Fucking awkward to do," Beast replies, earning him another dig in the ribs from Grim and a grunt of annoyance from Xeno.

"Beast, now's not the time," she snaps.

"He wanted to know how..." Beast shrugs, then clamps his mouth shut and holds his hands up when Grim gives him a death glare.

Dax stands abruptly. "That's not what I fucking meant."

"My bad. Apologies, Pen," Beast says, grimacing as he realises his mistake. The fact that he can talk about chopping off limbs without even flinching reminds me just what he's capable of. "Sincerely, I'm sorry. I forget not everyone has the stomach for this shit."

I just nod, not having the words to respond. Isn't it enough that David took her life, but removing a toe so he could send another sick message? That's beyond fucked-up. My hands begin to tremble as I look at the note on the floor and try not to picture the fear in my Mum's eyes as her own son held her down and strangled her to death. I don't even want to know where the toe is. I only hope it's not in this flat.

"How did *you* get it?" Dax asks, pointing at the note on the floor.

"David sent the toe with this note by courier to Tales for the attention of *Grim*," Zayn explains, picking up the note and placing it on the coffee table in front of us.

Dax frowns "*Grim?*"

"What the fuck? Why?" York asks, sitting forward in his seat. "I mean, no offence, Grim, I'm kinda glad you received it and not Pen—because a fucking toe—but why you?"

Up until now he's been silent, watching me closely as though he's half expecting me to grab the nearest weapon I can lay my hands on and go on a rampage. Truthfully, whilst I might feel like doing exactly that, my body has other ideas. I can feel the beginnings of shock setting in as my teeth start to chatter and my skin covers in goosebumps.

"That was exactly our reaction too," Zayn says.

"It's because I work for you, isn't it?" I say quietly, feeling like the room is closing in. How many more people that I care about will have a target on their backs because of me?

Grim shakes her head, and squeezes my hand gently. "Not to toot my own horn or anything, but no one would come after me blatantly like that just because I happened to hire you. This is much, much more than that. David is playing with us. This is a game to him. It's just one big mindfuck."

"What are you saying exactly?" I ask Grim, shifting uncomfortably in my seat, trying not to pass out.

"We believe David's got someone on the inside, a mother-fucking traitor," Beast growls.

All eyes turn to Gray who raises his eyebrows in surprise. He's been sitting quietly all this time, just observing in that thoughtful, unobtrusive way of his. "Me?" he questions, pointing at his chest. He's calm, not in the least bit perturbed by the sudden rising tension in the room.

Grim lets go of my hand and leans forward, resting her elbows on her knees as she perches her chin on her steepled fingers. "You know me better than that Gray. If I thought it was you, then your pretty face and the contents of your skull would be splattered across the wall by now."

Gray grins, and it's the first time I've seen him look anything other than moody and thoughtful. "Which is exactly why I'd never betray you."

"I hope the threat of death ain't the only reason, son," Beast adds, a smile in his eyes.

"That and the fact that you're the only family I've ever had," Gray replies sincerely. "You never need to worry about my loyalty. Not now. Not ever."

Xeno nods. "Good to fucking know, because if I find out you're a fucking traitor it won't be Beast and Grim you'll need to worry about. It will be *us*." Xeno lets that threat hang in the air, and the guys glare at him too just in case he didn't get the message.

Gray nods, his top lip twitching with mirth that he shuts down when Dax snarls at him. "I wouldn't expect anything less, but just so you know, I've been looking out for Lena for weeks now and there ain't nothing I'd do to hurt her. She's just a kid."

"Do you have any idea who it might be?" I ask Grim, forcing myself to breathe and ignoring the dark spots in my vision.

She presses her lips together in a hard line. "Not right now, but when I find out who the snake is they're going to regret ever fucking with us."

"When will this end?" I mutter, those dancing black spots growing in size. I blink them away, forcing myself to remain strong, to not fucking crumble again even though the walls feel like they're closing in. Everywhere we turn there's another enemy, more snakes waiting to strike, to strangle, to poison, to *kill*. Grim grasps my hands in hers and ducks her head to look me in the eye.

"Do *not* let him get in your head. You hear me, Pen. Do not let that bastard rule you. Trust us to take care of this."

"I trust that you'll do everything you can," I reply, grateful for her friendship, her support. "But I want you to promise me something, Grim."

"Anything, Pen."

"That when the time comes, I'm the one who kills him."

Beast whistles under his breath. "Fuck me!" he exclaims, but I refuse to look at anyone but Grim. I know she understands. I know she gets it. My Breakers love me. They love me enough to want my soul to remain pure, and I know, I *know* that given the chance they'll kill David for me. I can't have that. I won't. This isn't about me keeping *my* soul intact. They've dirtied theirs up, darkened their souls with their actions over the years we've been apart, and I refuse to allow them to blacken them further. It's time I taint my own a little bit. Besides, David's my responsibility.

"I have to be the one to do it, Grim. I *have* to be."

She nods, a mixture of both respect and sadness in her gaze. "You have my word, Pen," she promises, before drawing me into her arms and hugging me tightly.

11

Pen

"DO you think Mum was in pain when she died?" Lena asks me the following evening whilst we're lying in bed.

My chest tightens at her question, my stomach flipping over. Right now, I have a choice, I can lie and protect her from the evil in the world or tell her the truth and hope to God she forgives me for my part in Mum's death.

"Pen?"

Turning sideways, I reach for her, tucking a stray strand of hair behind her ear. There's so much left unsaid. Not just between me and Lena, but me and the guys. We still need to talk through what happened yesterday, but right now Lena needs to hear the truth no matter how hard it will be to comprehend. "Lena, there's something you should know..."

"What is it?" she whispers, stiffening beside me as her eyes rake over my face. She knows me well enough to know that what I'm about to say isn't going to be good.

"Mum didn't overdose."

For a moment she just stares at me blankly, allowing my words to sink in. Then she sits up abruptly. I rise with her. "Was it *cancer*...?" she asks accusingly, her voice wobbling around the words. It's every worst nightmare, isn't it? Cancer, the secret killer, the taker of life, the ruiner of families. Except this time, David's the cancer. I want to cut him out of our lives for good. I want to rid us of him by any means possible.

"No, Lena." I shake my head, but she doesn't seem to hear me. Her thoughts jumping to conclusions and her words running away with them.

"Is that where she was going twice a week? Was she sneaking off to get radiotherapy or chemo or something? Why didn't you tell me, Pen? I could've said goodbye!"

Reaching for her hand, I hold it, squeezing tightly. "It *wasn't* cancer. She was seeing a therapist."

"What do you mean?" she asks, her face a mask of confusion. "Then what was it? A heart attack? A stroke? What?" She gulps, her eyes brimming with tears.

"The world is full of evil people..." I begin, hating the look in her eyes.

"What are you getting at?" she whispers out.

I take a deep, steadying breath and squeeze her hand tighter. "Mum didn't die of natural causes, Lena. She was murdered." Shock pales her skin, the colour draining as the seconds tick by. "If I could protect you from this, I would, but I can't, Lena. The truth would've come out sooner or later. It's better that you hear it from me. I'm so sorry."

"Who?" she whispers eventually. The tremble in her voice makes me want to take back my words, stuff them deep inside and never, ever, let them out again. I squeeze her fingers tighter, trying to anchor her so she's strong enough to hear the truth.

"It was David."

She shakes her head. "No..." The tears that were wobbling on her eyelashes fall, and with them so does my heart. It drops into my stomach, a flailing, bleeding mess.

"Yes. David killed Mum. He did it to leave me a message, Lena."

"No..." She shakes her head, disbelief in her gaze.

"You have to know the truth no matter how painful," I plow on, needing to get it all out before I lose my nerve. I can't take the truth back now. All I can do is leave it between us like a rotting piece of flesh, filled with maggots, the stench overwhelming.

"I'm so sorry."

"No!" Lena shakes her head, anger blazing in her eyes. "NO!" she shouts, ripping her hand out of my hold and scrambling off the bed. She stands in the middle of the room, shaking with shock. Her teeth chatter, her hands tremble as she glares at me as though I'd wrapped my fingers around Mum's throat and squeezed the life from her myself.

"What did you do?" she asks, her question framed as an accusation that pierces my heart, that *guts* me. "Pen, what did you do?"

My mouth dries, my tongue heavy with guilt, but I force myself off the bed and face her. "I finally stood up to him. This was his response."

"*You* did this!" she screams, spittle flying from her mouth, tears pouring down her cheeks. I flinch, her words a stinging slap across my face.

"No," I counter, hating that she's right, because I did do this. I provoked the monster.

Behind her the bedroom door slams open. York and Dax enter first, followed by Gray who hovers in the doorway, looking between us both. Behind him I see Zayn and Xeno, standing in the hallway. Xeno moves forward, but Zayn holds him back, I snatch my head away, concentrating on Lena.

"What's going on?" York asks. Neither of us answer him.

"Lena, please... You don't understand," I say, choking back my guilt, hating the way she's looking at me now. I step forward, holding my arms out, wanting nothing more than to pull her against my chest. I want to comfort her, to tell her she's safe, that we'll protect her, that I never meant for this to happen. "He's the cancer, Lena. He's evil. David killed our mum. I didn't mean for it to happen."

"Fuck," York mutters.

She swipes at her face, then points a shaking finger at me. "You *had* to do it, didn't you?"

"Had to do what?"

"You couldn't just leave them in the past," she accuses, glaring at the guys over her shoulder before turning her wrath back on me. "All those times you snuck off in the middle of the night to go be with them. To *fuck* them."

"It wasn't like that..."

"Bullshit." She laughs, and the sound is so like my mum's laughter that a shiver runs down my spine. I wrap my arms around myself, gritting my jaw as I take all her bitter, hateful words. "It's all your fault. You knew how he was about you, but you had to keep pushing it."

"They were my friends. He is my *brother*," I remind her, hating the fact that she understands more about David's twisted feelings towards me than I'd thought.

"But you're not just friends with them now, are you? Did he kill Mum because he was so fucked off that she could never stop you from being with them? Not back then and not now!"

"Don't do this, Lena. You don't know what you're saying. David is *sick*. I was just trying to live a life free of his abuse. I needed love too. I *need* love too."

"You need to be *fucked*, you mean!"

"That's enough!" Dax snaps, stepping towards Lena. He grasps her arm, but she snatches it away, bitter tears running down her cheeks.

York opens his mouth to speak but I shake my head at him. "Don't. She needs to get it out. I'm okay," I whisper, swallowing down the lump in my throat. This isn't Lena talking. This is grief and confusion. It's easier to blame someone who'll love you unconditionally than a man she's not strong enough to fight against.

"Did you know he used to beat on her too, Pen? He'd hurt *her*. All those times you snuck out to be with them, he would turn his anger on Mum. She took your beatings when you were out fucking around with them! Mum would lock me in my room, and I would lie in bed listening to him smack her about. I would hear her begging him to stop, and I couldn't do *anything*. I was too young, and you weren't there!"

I clutch at my stomach, winded by her words. "Lena, I didn't know... Why did you never say anything? I'm so sorry."

"Don't you dare!" she cries, stepping away from me as I try to reach for her.

"Lena. I didn't know," I repeat, but she shakes her head fiercely.

"No, you're not sorry. You *made* this happen. You *willed* it to happen. You never loved Mum. You always *hated* her!" she accuses, and I can't even deny it because every word is true.

"I never meant for this to happen..."

"Yes you did! You think I didn't hear all the times you wished her dead when you thought I was sleeping. How you begged for God to take her, so you didn't have to live with her anymore. I. Heard. You!"

I stumble backwards, my legs hitting the bed. "Oh God, Lena. You were never meant... I didn't mean for you to hear that..."

"You. Made. This. Happen!" she screams, coming for me like a wild cat.

"Fuck this!" Dax snaps, stepping between us. She pulls up sharp, looking up at him with rage in her eyes.

"Get out of my way!"

"The fuck I will! You calm your arse down."

"She did this!"

Dax shakes his head. I can't see his face, but I recognise the fury in his voice all too well. "Now you listen to me very carefully, Lena. I don't give a fuck how much you're hurting or what you need to tell yourself to make you feel better. Pen is *not* at fault here. Your fucked up brother is. *He* killed your mum. *He* put his hands around her motherfucking throat and strangled her until she couldn't breathe anymore. Not Pen."

"Dax, don't..." I beg, reaching forward and pressing my

fingers against his back. Lena's bottom lip begins to quiver, her face crumpling. Seeing her like this, so full of hate and loathing, pain and anguish, it's almost too much to bear. I know this isn't what she really thinks, I *know* that, but it doesn't hurt any less.

"No, Kid. She doesn't get to shit on you like this, not after everything you've done to protect her over the years," he says to me, before turning back to face her.

"I'm—"

"Did you know that the first night I met Pen she was black and blue from the *beating* David gave her," Dax says, cutting her off. "She was a year younger than you, Lena, and that beating she took, it was for *you*. She stepped in to protect you. It took her over a week to recover physically, and even then she still bore the marks of his violence. She still fucking does. But you've never seen that because Pen has kept it all hidden on the inside. She protected you from it. She's still protecting you."

"Dax, she doesn't need to hear this," I whisper.

"Bullshit. This is *exactly* what she needs to hear," he retorts.

"I—I'm..." Lena looks at me, the hardness in her eyes softening to guilt and even more pain. There's so much fucking hurt, all because of David, but Dax doesn't let up.

"That night and all the occasions before it, Pen took David's beatings whilst your mum chose to save you and not her. You had your mum's protection, Lena. Who did Pen have, huh? Tell me that. Who the fuck did she have?"

"I'm sorry!" She's sobbing now, her hands covering her mouth as she shakes her head, but he refuses to stop.

"I'll tell you who she had. Fucking no one, not until that night when she came into our lives. So don't you dare make her feel guilty about wanting affection, *friendship*. As far as I'm concerned, your mum was as bad as David. She may not have hit Pen, but she hurt her all the same by doing nothing, by treating her like a piece of shit, by never being the mother she needed."

Lena looks at me, her head shaking. Tears falling down her cheeks, snot bubbling out of her nose. "I'm sorry," she croaks, stumbling towards me.

Dax grips her arms, and she drops her head between her shoulders, sobbing quietly, all her fight gone as quickly as it came. I watch as he tips her chin up gently so she looks at him. "Lena, Pen loves you," he says, softer now. "She has loved you both like a mother and a sister since before she ever became friends with us. She has kept you out of harm's way your whole life. Don't take out your pain on her, she doesn't deserve it."

"I know. I'm s—sorry."

Dax nods tightly, then lets her pass. She stares at me, uncertain for a moment. "I didn't mean it. I didn't mean what I said."

Reaching for her, I fold her into my arms. "It's okay. I know you didn't. I know that, Lena."

She buries her head in my shoulder and sobs, and all I can do is hold her. Forgive her. Love her.

"Titch?" York steps closer.

"I've got this," I reply, shaking my head. "Just give us a moment, okay? I need to talk to Lena alone."

He nods. "Let's go, Dax," York says, guiding him out of the room and past Xeno and Zayn, both of whom are watching me with guarded expressions. Xeno steps forward again, but I shake my head.

"Please, don't. Not right now."

He nods, and motions for Zayn to follow him, leaving Gray standing in the doorway.

"Is there anything I can do?" he asks after a beat.

"No, there isn't."

"I was planning on getting an early night, but I'll be in my room if either of you need me," he says, and with one last flick of his eyes towards Lena, he's gone.

As soon as the door clicks shut, I guide Lena back to bed. She climbs under the covers, allowing me to tuck her in. I give her a sad smile, using the sleeve of my top to wipe away her tears. "If I'd known what he would do, I would've protected Mum, just like I protected you."

"He would've killed you, Pen. Dax was right. You were just a kid yourself. Fuck. I can't believe I said all that shit to you. I'm a horrible, horrible person." Another sob breaks free, and she chokes it back, stuffing her fist into her mouth.

"Lena, you're hurting. You're angry. You have every right to be, but you were right, I did hate Mum. I hated her because she didn't love me, because she let David hurt me. She wasn't a mother to me. That hurt. It still hurts. But here's the thing, I'm so, so glad she was a mother to you."

"Oh, Pen," she wails, gripping hold of the edge of the duvet.

"Hush, it's okay, I know. I know. I love you so much, and that's why I asked Grim and Beast to protect you. David threatened your life, Lena. He said he would hurt you if I didn't do what he wanted."

"Hurt me?" she whispers. I nod. "What did he want you to do?"

"He found out that the Breakers were at the Academy. He wanted to know *why*."

"To dance... Right?" I shake my head and her voice trails off. She's so young, naive in a lot of ways, but she's not stupid.

"They've been away for three years, Lena, doing bad things for bad people. We didn't part well. When they joined the Academy at the beginning of term, we weren't friends. Far from it. Our path back to where we are now, it hasn't been easy. There's still so much to work through."

"They love you though, and you love them. Everyone can see that..."

"They do, and that as much as anything else is why David's doing what he's doing."

"I'm scared," she admits, burrowing beneath the duvet.

"I didn't want to tell you. I wanted to protect you from the truth, but I knew, eventually, you'd ask questions and the longer I left the truth buried the harder it would be for you to process. There's so much more to what's going on. I just can't fully explain it all right now. You have to believe me, Lena, despite my feelings towards Mum, if I'd had any idea about David's plans I would've made sure that one of Grim's men was watching over her too."

"Grim? Who's Grim?"

"She's my boss, my *friend*. She owns a nightclub called Tales. That's where I dance on the weekends. Gray works for Grim, it's why he's here, to help keep you safe. I asked her for help, and she gave it to me."

"But *why* does David want to kill me?" she croaks, fear fluttering across her tear-stained face.

"Because he knows how much I love you. Because he will hurt everyone I love just to make me suffer. Because he's fucked up, Lena. It's why Gray's here, why you're not going back to school for a while. We need to keep you safe."

"Oh, God, I think I'm going to be sick."

Flinging back the covers, Lena runs into the en-suite bathroom. By the time I reach her she's emptying the contents of her stomach down the toilet. All I can do is rub her back as she heaves and heaves, her last meal splattering the porcelain bowl. When she's finished I pass her a damp washcloth and a glass of water, then help her back to bed. Climbing beneath the covers, I pull her against my chest, stroking her hair as she shivers against me, her teeth clacking.

"I will never, *ever*, let him hurt you. Between us all, we'll keep you safe... I swear it."

Lena nods, her arms tightening around my waist, her tears falling silently as I hold her. My promise is all I can give her in the moment, but deep down I know it's not enough. David will find a way to get to her, but only if I don't get to him first.

12

Pen

"KNIVES ARE ONLY EVER useful in hand-to-hand combat. If you find yourself in a situation where it's you or them and you have a gun, you use that. *Every* time, okay?" Zayn says as he circles me, a no-nonsense look on his face.

"Okay, understood." I nod my head tersely, holding tightly onto the fake knife he's given me to train with. It has a leather handle like an ordinary knife might, but a wooden blade. I feel like a kid playing 'goodies' and 'baddies'. Right now, I'm the baddie.

"Zayn's right. We all carry a knife with us, but a gun will take down your attacker, or at least injure them enough so that you'll have a chance to escape. Next resort is a knife, and failing that, your fists," York says from the corner of the dance studio.

He's already taken me through some basic boxing punches, and the three of us are covered in a sheen of sweat from the exertion.

"Gun first. Got it." I roll my shoulders, feeling the ache in muscles I didn't know I had. I thought as a dancer I'd used them all, clearly I was wrong.

"It's not likely that you'll ever be in a position to have to defend yourself like this, because between us, we're going to make sure that no fucker gets close enough to hurt you," Zayn says. "Nethertheless, Xeno was right. You're moving in our world now and aside from David, there are plenty of people who might try to take a shot at you to get back at us."

"Fantastic," I mutter. "Maybe Lena should have some training too?"

"It's not a bad idea," York agrees. "Gray could train her. I'll speak with him about it later. Right now they're chilling in the lounge watching Pretty Woman. I'm pretty sure Gray would rather remove his eyeballs with a wooden spoon than watch that shit, but he's a good guy and is taking it like a man."

"Says the guy who loves black and white musicals," Zayn retorts with a roll of his eyes.

"Hey, don't mock me. Those films are classics."

"And Pretty Woman isn't?" I ask, smothering a laugh. It's moments like these, amidst all the shit, that give me hope, purpose. I want this to last forever. I want us to be free from the threat of our enemies once and for all.

"You'll have to ask Dax. Wait, maybe it's Xeno... One of them has the hots for Julia Roberts." York grins, winking at me.

"I'll be sure to ask when they get back," I say, tucking that little titbit away for later. Dax and Xeno headed over to Jewels and Chastity Nightclub respectively to catch up on business, leaving Zayn and York to start my training. Not that I'm complaining. They've both been incredibly patient with me as I've fumbled through the past few hours of training.

"Hey, don't listen to York, Pen. Julia Roberts has nothing on you," Zayn says, flashing me his chipped-tooth smile.

"It's cool. I don't blame them for fancying Julia Roberts, she's totally hot and worthy of their adoration. Just so long as it's me they think about when they're jacking off, I'm alright with it," I blurt out, my cheeks flushing at the sudden rush of words.

Zayn's black eyes scan my heated skin before he smirks and says, "Believe me, Pen, we've all been jacking off to thoughts of you. We've been doing it for years now."

"Well, shit. Is that why you've been taking extra long in the shower these past couple days?" York asks, laughter in his voice.

"Well I ain't gonna rub one off in bed with you sleeping next to me, now am I?" Zayn remarks.

"Hey, you can whack off all you like. It's not as if I haven't seen you come before. As a matter of fact, your orgasm face is highly entertaining," York jokes before proceeding to mimic Zayn in post-coital bliss.

We all burst out laughing, and it's the best feeling. The rush of joy almost better than sex. Almost.

"Okay, let's get back to it," Zayn says, calming down first. "Anything you want to add, York, before we move on?"

York straightens his face and nods, serious once more. "Like I explained earlier, Titch, you want to attack first. Don't hesitate. Your height and weight put you at a disadvantage, so you need the element of surprise. Your attacker will underestimate you based purely on what you look like. If you're backed into a corner and you've lost your weapons then I want you to use light, fast jabs to keep your attacker at bay. It will keep them on the defence, and you might be able to get a heavy cross punch in. Hit them as hard as you can at this point, then once they're down, that's when you run."

"I'll try." I give him a wry smile feeling every inch the tiny woman that I am. Being petite and a dancer is a plus, but as a boxer, not so much.

"You just need to build up your strength, Titch," he says, trying to reassure me. "Besides, Zayn's going to teach you how to correctly handle and use a knife in combat. Not to mention the fact that Xeno is planning on making you a gun toting badass bitch, so it's unlikely anyone will get close enough for you to need to use your fists."

"Regardless, Pen needs to be prepared for all eventualities, and it's up to us to make sure she gets it right."

"I appreciate it," I say, looking between them and I do, so fucking much. Having them to train with, to spar with, is giving me something to focus on. It's allowing me to funnel all my pent up anxiety and the simmering rage within me into something useful. I don't feel so helpless, and that's a good thing.

"Let's move on then," Zayn says, manoeuvring the fighting dummy torso so that it's positioned directly in front of me. "This dummy is usually used to teach boxing jabs and to get a feel at what it might be like to hit a human, but it's also useful for me to show you the most lethal places to strike your attacker with a knife."

"Okay."

"The biggest area of the body to hit is clearly the torso, but the heart and lungs are protected by the ribcage and it's not easy to get a precise hit to the heart when your opponent is physically moving and you only have a small blade," Zayn explains, sliding his fingers lower. He points to the stomach area. "You can stab anywhere here, and whilst it will cause damage, it isn't lethal, but it will hurt like a bitch. I've fought men who've been stabbed in the stomach and kept going for a long time after. In a life or death situation you need to go for the places with the least resistance but the most impact. We want these fuckers bleeding out on the first jab with a knife."

I swallow hard. "So where then?"

"There are three places that would be more effective for you given your size and weight. I might be able to stab a person in the heart, lungs or liver because I know which ribs to slide the blade through and have the strength behind the stab in order to hit those targets, but you need to be smart, not strong."

"What about *my* favourite place?" York asks, pointing to the back of the dummy's head.

"You have a favourite place to stab someone?" I ask, pulling a face.

"Well, yeah. We all do..." His voice trails off when he hears how that sounds. "Okay, that's pretty fucked up. Forget I said anything."

Zayn flicks open his blade and presses it against the back of the dummies head at the base of the spine. "York's preference is to stab here. Doing so will cause instant death so long as you sever the spinal cord, but it isn't very easy to do. The spinal cord is encased in vertebrae, and discs that, whilst spongy, are tough."

"So don't stab there then?"

"I wouldn't recommend it for you unless your attacker is face down on the floor and already injured enough not to be able to fight back."

"Okay so what are the three best places for me to stab?"

Zayn motions for York to step closer. He lifts up York's arm and points to his armpit with the tip of his knife. "Inside the armpit is a large artery called the Axillary artery. It supplies blood to the arm and fingers and because it's so close to the heart, if severed, blood will spew out like a fucking geyser. Much like York when he's coming."

"Thanks for that, bro," York grins.

"But only go for this area if your attacker isn't wearing thick heavy clothing. It'll be too hard to slice through the material."

"Got it," I nod, taking it all in. Half of me is disgusted by the thought of sliding a knife into another person, the other half is impressed by Zayn's knowledge.

"The second place is the groin area, in the crook of the leg," Zayn indicates, again using his knife to press against that area on York's body. He's wearing jogging shorts, and Zayn's hand slides up the material so that he can show me exactly where he means.

"Oy, watch the motherfucking crown jewels, will you?" York protests, his hand reaching down to cup his junk.

Zayn grins mercilessly. "Is that *fear* I see in your eyes, York?"

"You bet your arse it is. I've seen you use a knife and I'm not happy that thing is so close to my dick and bollocks. I happen to want to keep them intact, and I'm pretty fucking sure Titch wants that too. Am I right?" he asks me.

"Yes, you're right," I agree with a grin.

"Thought as much."

York lets go of his junk as Zayn removes the knife, though he remains on one knee in front of him and I find myself having to force myself not to think dirty thoughts with him crouched before York like that. Even so my cheeks heat and I really, really hope York's not able to read my mind right now. Refusing to look at him, I concentrate on Zayn instead. "And the third spot?" I ask, swallowing hard.

"Back of the knee. You'll find the popliteal artery which is basically an extension of the femoral artery. It's close to the surface of the skin, and if you slice through that there will be rapid blood loss."

Zayn gets to his feet and motions me over. "I want you to have a go at stabbing those areas. Not too hard. You might be holding a fake knife but jabbing hard is gonna hurt."

"Why not the throat? Isn't that a good place to stab?" I ask, looking away when a flash of guilt crosses Zayn's face. It was only the other day he had a knife pressed against my throat, and whilst he had no intention of hurting me, it still gives me shivers.

"Only if you have an extremely sharp blade. There is tough cartilage in the neck area that you need to slice through before reaching the Carotid artery. My recommendation would be to stab straight into the neck beside the Adam's apple, then pull the knife sideways. Again, this is harder than you think, so stick with the places I've shown you."

"I will."

"Good. Now let's make this a little more realistic. York I want you to go for Pen as if you're about to attack her. Let's see if she's remembered her training."

York doesn't hesitate, he comes for me and my first instinct is to just lash out with my blade, forgetting everything they've both taught me.

"You're going to have to do better than that, Titch," York says, disarming me within moments.

"Fuck!" I grind out, instantly feeling like a fool.

"Remember what I said, Pen. If your attacker is throwing his weight at you in a punch then you want to use that opportunity to duck down and stab him in the armpit. Let's practise that now."

I nod, taking back the wooden knife from York and trying again. For the next ten minutes York keeps attacking whilst Zayn calls out instructions and corrects my mistakes, and with every minute that passes, I feel my anxiety lessen and my strength return.

Eventually Zayn calls time out and I'm so exhausted from all the training that my arse drops to the floor. I lay flat out, breathing heavily. York and Zayn both lay down next to me, one on either side.

"That was intense," I manage to say after a couple of minutes, my heart rate finally getting back to normal.

"You were amazing," York says, turning to his side, pushing up on his elbow so that he can peer down at me. He grins and I see the way his eyes light up with lust.

"What?"

"That was really fucking hot," he says.

"I have to agree with York there," Zayn murmurs, pushing up onto his elbow too.

I look between them, a sudden rush of heat warming my belly as they stare down at me. York rests his hand on my stomach, sending goosebumps scattering across my skin at his touch. Zayn, on the other hand, dives in for the kill and presses a hot kiss against my mouth that has my lips parting and a moan releasing. I'm vaguely aware of York cursing Zayn for being a sneaky son-of-a-bitch and getting in there before him, but that doesn't stop him from sliding his lips along my collarbone, or grazing my skin with his teeth.

Our moment of bliss doesn't last long, however, when the sound of the door opening, and a deep cough interrupts us. They both pull away and I sit up, looking over my shoulder at Gray.

"I'm sorry to interrupt, but Lena needs you... She's crying and I can't console her." He gives me an apologetic look, but I shake my head.

"That's okay. We're finished here anyway," I say, trying hard to hide my disappointment. We've had little precious time alone together, and I'm acutely aware of their needs as much as my own. Regardless, Lena has to come first, so with one last lingering look at my guys, I sigh, then head out of the studio and back to my sister, her heart-wrenching sobs forcing me back to reality.

13

York

TITCH SITS BESIDE ME, stoic, whilst Lena falls apart in her arms. The officiant ends the service with kind words that makes Lena sob louder and Titch stiffen in her seat. Placing my hand on her thigh in solidarity, I squeeze gently, letting her know that I'm here for her, that however she chooses to express her sorrow is fine by me. That not feeling sad about her mum's death is okay too. That I understand.

"I'm alright," she says, folding her arms around Lena and glancing up at me, a determined look on her face. I nod, knowing she believes that to be true.

"I know."

Her gaze cuts across to the wooden casket and the simple spray of white Calla Lilies sitting on top of it. "I will pay you back every last penny," she murmurs.

"No, you won't."

"I *will*."

I don't argue with her. Now isn't the right time. Despite appearances, her head is all over the place. For the past few days, since Rocks was burnt to the ground, the only thing keeping her sane has been learning to fight. Everything else has come second to her single-minded goal to be strong enough to face David. Dax and I have been teaching her self-defence. Zayn has been showing her how to handle a knife, and Xeno will be teaching her how to shoot a gun. Slowly, the girl who loved to dance, who used the movements of her body as a weapon, is turning into a different kind of warrior. The softest parts of her, hardening with her need to protect Lena, to face her brother when the time comes.

"I guess that's it then," she says, as we stand outside the crematorium in the remembrance garden staring at her mother's flowers that will be gathered up later and incinerated with the body. I wrap my arm around her shoulder and pull her into my side, silently comforting her whilst she gathers her thoughts.

"Is there something wrong with me, York?" she asks quietly.

"Wrong with you?"

Heaving out a sigh, Titch looks over at Lena on the other side of the remembrance garden. She's quietly sobbing, and Dax is talking with her softly, his hand resting on her shoulder. Despite what he said to her that night she ripped into Titch, there are no hard feelings. Dax cares for Lena in a brotherly, protective way, the same as we all do.

"I don't feel anything for Mum. All the sadness I hold inside is for Lena and what she's lost. When I think of Mum and who she was to me, I just feel anger, resentment. Hate. What kind of person does that make me?"

"There's *nothing* wrong with you, Titch. Get that thought out of your head," I reassure her.

"She was *murdered*, and all I can think of right now is that I'll never have to feel worthless around her again. I'm broken inside."

"Titch. You're no more broken than the rest of us are."

"I'm not sure that makes me feel any better," she replies quietly, watching Xeno and Zayn make small talk with the officiant.

"Perhaps that wasn't the best comparison to make. All I'm saying is, you can't force yourself to feel sad if you don't. That doesn't make you a bad person, Titch. No one expects you to cry for the woman who mistreated you."

"You heard what Lena said, she took the beatings for me..."

"No," I reply, cutting her off. "She took the beatings for *Lena*. If you'd been there at the time, then it would've been you. Don't make her out to be someone she wasn't."

"If you're right, York, and feeling this way doesn't make me a bad person, then *why* do I feel so fucking twisted up about it? Why do I feel like the *worst* person in the world?"

"Because you have a conscience, my love, and a big, beautiful heart," I tell her, pressing a kiss to the top of her head.

"*My love...?*" she whispers, the tiniest hint of a smile in her voice. "I'm your love?"

"Well it certainly ain't *big boy* over there. Though I appreciate the attraction. Dax is all man, isn't he?" I remark, wanting to get her to smile again. I miss that, her joy. It's fucking gutting to see her struggle so much with all her emotions. That bastard, David, has so much to answer for.

She cocks her head, staring at Dax. "He *is* good looking, isn't he?" she muses, a playful tone in her voice. "I've seen the looks you give him."

I chuckle at that. "Flirty banter, Titch. I'm not into men that way."

"Hmm," she hums, her cheeks flushing a little pinker. I get the impression that it's not an '*I don't believe you,*' kind of hmm, but a '*I'd like to test that theory.*' Interestingly, I'm not averse to the idea of testing any theory that gets her rocks off, but right now isn't the appropriate time to discuss our sexual desires. I've never sought out a man for sex, ever, and Titch is literally my heart and soul, but the way she responded to me sliding my fingers into Dax's mouth that night we had a threesome, well... I wouldn't mind turning her on like that again. Fuck, if it didn't make me hard as rock. I'm pretty sure Dax felt the power of that moment too.

"I ain't afraid to admit that I love Dax, like I love Xeno and Zayn. I appreciate their appeal. I'm not being funny, Titch, but have you seen what we look like in these suits... We give The Rat Pack a run for their money."

Titch laughs, and this time it's a *real* laugh, not a half-hearted one, and even though she smothers the sound with her hand, it does stupid fucking things to me... And my cock, well, let's just say I'm mentally telling it to calm the fuck down. Now is neither the time nor the place for my cock to act pre-pubes-cent, for fuck's sake. I spent way too many times rearranging my junk as a teenager after Titch would laugh in that carefree way of hers. Now, I can't even do that without giving the officiant another reason to pray for me tonight.

"I might have to agree with you there," she replies, her cheeks flushing a little. She glances at me, a spark in her gaze that I haven't seen since we had sex in the basement of Jackson Street.

I'm not sure if it's there because I've finally made her laugh, or if it's because she fancies the fuck out of us in these suits. Honestly, I don't care either way, I'm just relieved to know that the Titch we all know and love is still there buried beneath this woman trying to hold herself together under the weight of this shitstorm we're wrapped up in.

"Pretty sure I'm Frank Sinatra reincarnated," I say, hoping for another smile at least.

"Wait, I thought it was Fred Astaire...?" Titch asks, biting her lip, that spark igniting between us. I can almost feel it sizzle over my skin, and this time I have to discreetly adjust myself. Lena really doesn't need to see me turned on at her mum's funeral.

"Hey, I'll be whoever you want me to be, do whatever the fuck you want me to do, so long as you keep looking at me the way you are right now," I reply hoarsely.

She drops her gaze, her cheeks flaring. "York, I—"

"Maybe we should continue this conversation later?" I mutter, framing my request as a question.

"Later," she agrees, turning her attention back to the flowers before us. There's a large display of yellow, pink and white flowers shaped into the word Mum. "Thank you for these. For everything today. It means a lot to Lena, and that means every-thing to me."

It might be traditional to have flowers at a funeral, but I know for a fact that the only reason we paid for them was because, like Titch said, it was important to Lena. If it was down to the rest of us the bitch would've been chucked on a fucking pyre like the evil witch she was.

"You're welcome," I say, wisely keeping those thoughts to myself.

"Wait, who are those from?" Titch asks, pointing at a large wreath of blood-red roses resting against the letter M.

"Grim and Beast, most likely. They said they would be sending some."

She shakes her head. "No, those are from Beast and Grim," she replies, pointy at a small posy of pink tulips.

"Clancy and River?" I suggest.

Titch shakes her head. "I asked them not to."

"A friend, maybe?"

"Mum didn't really have friends. Acquaintances from the pub, maybe."

"A well-meaning neighbour?"

"Mum *hated* red roses, said they reminded her of my father. Besides, none of Mum's neighbours would have that kind of money to spend..." Titch's voice trails off as she looks up at me, her face paling. That one look has my stomach turning over.

"Let me," I say quickly, but she shrugs out of my hold and reaches for a small white envelope placed between two large roses. She plucks it free, holding the envelope in her hand. For a moment she just stares at it, and I find myself praying that her mum wasn't the sad, lonely woman Pen described but had loads of friends who clubbed together to buy her this wreath.

Ripping it open, Titch reads the card, a strangled cry bursting free from her mouth a moment later.

"He's here," she whispers, her head snapping up.

"Let me see," I exclaim, taking the card from Titch and reading it.

> **You look beautiful in that dress, Penelope.**
> **Hasn't Lena grown up?**
> **Eenie, meenie, miney, mo...**
> **Who's toe should I take next?**

"He's here!" she repeats, looking frantically about her with wide, startled eyes. "We need to get Lena out of here, right the fuck now!" Her voice rises with every word, catching Xeno and Zayn's attention who are standing the closest to us. They break away from the officiant who looks a little stunned by her outburst, and stride over to us.

"Titch," I say, grabbing her shoulders and forcing her to look at me. "We've got ghosts dotted around the crematorium. If he was here, we'd know about it."

"Then how does he know I'm wearing a dress?" she accuses.

"Just a lucky guess, nothing more."

"What's going on?" Xeno asks, looking between the two of us, alarmed by Pen's sudden change of mood.

"This came with those flowers," I explain, passing him the card.

"Motherfucker!" Xeno exclaims, his hand immediately reaching for the gun that I know he's got strapped to a holster beneath his suit jacket.

"Xeno," I warn, shaking my head as the officiant approaches, Dax and Lena following behind.

"Everything okay?" the officiant asks.

"Everything's fine," Xeno replies curtly. "But we need to get going."

"Pen?" Lena questions, clearly not buying it.

"I'm not feeling all that great. That's all. It's been a long day," she says, taking Lena's hand in hers. "I'd like to go home now."

Zayn nods, pulling out his phone. "I'll get Gray to bring the car up."

"That's understandable. I'm very sorry for your loss," the officiant says in that serene way all people of the cloth seem to be perfect.

Lena gives him a tremulous smile. "Thank you for the beautiful service."

"You're very welcome. If there's anything else I can do...?"

"We're good," I reply, placing my hand on the small of Titch's back as I guide her towards the car that Gray has driven up from the carpark. I might be ninety-five percent certain that David isn't here, but that doesn't mean to say I want to take a chance on the five percent possibility that the fucker has somehow managed to bypass the ghosts and has his sights set on our girl and Lena right at this fucking moment.

"Wait," Titch exclaims, stopping suddenly. She drops Lena's hand and turns to face the officiant. "That wreath, did you happen to see who delivered it?"

He frowns "It was delivered by the florist about an hour before the ceremony started. We thought perhaps there was a mix up and that's why it wasn't added to the flowers in the hearse. We asked the driver to leave the flowers here so that the others could be added to it when the hearse arrived."

"Do you remember the name of the florist?" Xeno asks.

"Why? Is there a problem with the wreath?"

"No, not at all," Titch reassures him. "We'd just like to thank the person who sent the flowers. There isn't a name on the card."

"Ah, I see. Well, let me think..." He cocks his head to the side, trying to remember. "Eva's Florists. Yes, that's it. I'm sure it was Eva's Florists."

"The one in the high street?" Titch asks.

"Yes, that's the one."

"Thank you," she replies, casting Xeno a look before grabbing Lena's hand and climbing into the SUV, closing the door behind her. The officiant nods then walks back to the building, no doubt needing to get ready for the next service. How fucking depressing.

Dax loosens his tie, and pops the top button of his shirt waiting until we're alone before speaking. "Looks like we've got a lead."

"Or a wild goose chase," I remark.

Zayn scoffs. "Yeah. I happen to agree with you, York. David isn't stupid enough to leave a trail." "Regardless, I need you two to check it out," Xeno says, looking between Dax and Zayn. "See what you can find out. York, you go with Gray, take the girls home. Keep them distracted until we get back."

"Where are you going?" I ask.

"Tales. Hudson's meeting Grim and Beast tonight. I want to fill them in. Perhaps Hudson can get Interpol to pull their fingers out of their arses and help us out."

Dax grunts. "Yeah, and pigs might fly. They've done jack-shit for us so far."

We all laugh at that, because so far they've been less than fucking useless and we're quickly running out of options. Sooner or later David's going to make his next move, and with the way things are going, we won't see him coming until it's too fucking late.

14

Pen

BY THE TIME Lena falls asleep, it's almost midnight, but I'm too wired to sleep. Instead, I head towards the living area and the low rumble of voices coming from beyond the closed door.

Pushing it open, I step into the room and am relieved to find that it's just the four of them. I might've gotten used to having Gray around, but that doesn't mean to say I *want* him around. Though to be fair to the guy, he's pretty good at knowing when to disappear so that we can have some privacy and Lena seems comfortable around him, so that's a plus in my book.

Xeno sits forward in his seat, his slim black tie dangling between his parted legs as he looks at something on his phone. He's still wearing his suit from the funeral but has removed his jacket. In fact, they're all still wearing their suits, minus the jackets, except for York, who changed the minute we arrived home earlier. He's in a pair of joggers and tight muscle shirt that shows off his defined abs and pecs.

"Titch, everything okay?" he asks, catching me staring.

"I can't sleep."

"It's the stress," he replies, getting up and leaping over the back of the sofa in one effortless move that probably would've made my heart flutter if I didn't feel so on edge. Picking up on my low mood, he frowns, offering me his hand. "It's been a long day. You've barely eaten. Let me make you something to eat, yeah?"

"No, thank you. I'm not hungry."

"A drink then?" He guides me to the sofa, and I perch on the edge of the cushion, hating how tense and wound up I feel.

"Water is fine."

"Coming right up," he says, casting a look at Zayn who shifts closer and wraps an arm around my shoulder.

"So, did you find out anything?" I ask, some of the tension leaving me as I relax into Zayn's hold, my hand resting on his thigh.

"We spoke with the manager of the florist. She was the one who delivered the flowers today. It was a last minute rush order yesterday afternoon, apparently," Dax explains, rolling up the sleeves of his shirt. My gaze falls to his tattooed arms and fingers, a sudden flush of heat reminding me that despite this fucked up day, I'm still capable of feeling *something* other than the urge to bludgeon David to death for what he's done.

"Did you get any details?"

Dax pulls a face. "The poor woman was fucking terrified of us. She looked like she was about to have a heart attack when I asked for the details of the booking."

"I'm not surprised, have you seen the way you look?" York jokes.

Dax rolls his eyes. "Anyway, I managed to convince her to give me all the information she had."

"Which was...?" I prompt.

"A landline number," Dax says, but he doesn't look too pleased about it.

"That's good though right? Can't that be traced to an address?"

"It can. It has. But it's another dead end," Xeno explains.

My heart sinks. "How come?"

"It's a phone booth located in Hammersmith. I'm sorry, Pen."

"Fuck!" I exclaim, the growing anxiety making me feel sick.

"It's not a complete loss. Interpol has added the area to their search. They've got an approximate time of the phone call when they pull up CCTV footage of the area," Dax continues.

"What about the night David murdered mum...?"

"Working on it," Zayn pitches in.

"They *still* haven't found anything yet?" I rub my fingers over my forehead, feeling a headache coming on.

"Apparently there's a lot of CCTV footage to go through. It's going to take a bit of time," Xeno explains, pressing his lips into a hard line, as frustrated as I am by the wait.

I nod, feeling dejected. "So what now?"

Zayn puffs out his cheeks, letting out a slow breath. "Now we wait."

"I hate this," I say, standing suddenly, feeling the need to move, to do something to stop this ball of anxiety from growing inside. "I hate feeling like this."

York places the glass of water on the coffee table with a slice of cake that I hadn't asked for. "Why don't you sit down? We can watch a movie or something. It might take your mind off things?"

"I don't want to sit. I don't want to watch a movie..." I exclaim, my fingers stretching out then balling into fists. "I want to..."

"Want to, what?" Zayn prompts gently, urging me to open up.

"I don't know. I just don't feel right," I say, trying to explain this twisted up feeling inside. "Everything's wrong. I feel on edge."

"I know what will help," Xeno says, glancing between the guys, a silent conversation going on between them all.

"I'll let Grey know where we are should he need us," Dax says. Understanding what that one look means.

"Where are we going?"

Zayn gives me a warm smile, even if it is blighted by his concern for me. "Don't worry, not far."

"I'll be right behind you." Dax says, briefly squeezing my arm as he passes by. I jolt at his touch, my nerves firing at his proximity and the weird tension filling the air.

"Follow me," Xeno says, eying both Zayn and York before striding over to a door on the far left of the kitchen. I'd always assumed it was some kind of storage cupboard. Obviously assuming wrong when Xeno pushes the door open and steps inside the darkened space beyond, Zayn following behind. They disappear, swallowed up right before my eyes.

"This flat isn't the only part of the building we own," York explains as we follow them.

I hesitate, peering into the darkness. "Are we going to pass through a load of smelly old fur coats and into a magical world with animals that can talk and a witch who wants to kill me?" I ask, trying to temper the anxiety in my chest as I blindly step inside. "Because, honestly, I could do without the shock."

Behind me, York laughs. "No, Titch. This ain't Narnia. Let me turn on the light." He reaches around me, his chest brushing gently against my back as he turns on the light switch.

"Stairs to heaven then?" I ask, as my eyes adjust to the light and I take in the staircase leading upwards to a small landing above.

"Depends on what your idea of heaven is, I guess?"

"That sounds ominous."

York chuckles. "I'm just kidding. Come on."

We climb the stairs, and I come to a standstill when I open the door at the top. "What the hell?" I screech, speechless for a moment as I take in the large, secluded balcony that's covered with glass on all sides, including the ceiling, and opens out into a large room that's set back into the building. It's almost the same size as their living room downstairs. "How did I not know about this?"

"Too much going on, I guess," York shrugs, guiding me into the room, his hand gently resting on my lower back. I shiver involuntarily from his touch, and he eyes me carefully. I read the hesitation on his face, but he doesn't remove his hand. "We come up here when we want to get away from shit. The view's pretty fucking spectacular. Especially at night."

Sliding his hand around my waist, he hugs me to his side, drawing me fully into the room. Ambient music is playing gently, and the space is lit up with soft lighting. In one corner of the room, set back off from the balcony, sits a sunken hot tub. On the other is a large exercise mat that you might find in a gym, a row of dumb bells lined up against a mirrored wall, and a running machine.

"Do you like it?" Zayn asks, sitting on a l-shaped sofa that's positioned within the glassed-in balcony. Behind him, Xeno is reaching into a mini fridge, and pulls out five bottles of beer.

"It's beautiful..."

My voice trails off as York steps in front of me, enclosing me in his arms. "Is this okay?" he asks softly, wanting my reassurance as he holds me against him, searching my face. He knows I'm feeling raw, sensitive to everything, including his affection, and he's cautious with me.

I nod. "Yes."

"You don't seem certain?" he pushes, concern furrowing his brow. "Titch?"

"I'm certain that I love you all. I'm certain that I'm afraid, that I'm angry, that I wish this was all over. I'm certain that I *want* to kill David, that I want to see the life drain from his eyes. I'm certain that I need to be stronger. I'm certain that I need to be able to dance for you all..." I take in a shuddering breath, my stupid eyes brimming with tears that I blink back furiously. "I'm certain that I want to dance for *me* but I'm not sure if I can."

"And what aren't you certain of?" Zayn asks, watching us both closely.

"I'm not certain we'll survive this. I'm not certain that you won't get hurt. I'm not certain that Lena won't be damaged beyond repair because of my brother. I'm not certain that when it comes down to it, that I'll be able to kill David..." I hush out, that truth, painful.

"You don't have—" Xeno reminds me, but I shake my head.

"I do. I'm certain of *that* at least," I finish, all of my jumbled up thoughts tumbling out of me. It feels good to let them go, to let them out.

"Titch," York says, drawing his attention back to him. "Do you know what I'm certain of?"

"What?"

"I'm certain that you're the strongest woman I know. I'm certain that we'll come out of this, *all* of us. I'm certain we'll live until we're old and wrinkled, and that Dax will turn into an ugly, fat bastard, *eventually*." He laughs at that, mirth twinkling in his eyes. "I'm certain that one day your belly will be filled with my son."

"Fuck you, York," Xeno mutters, but there's a smile in his voice that warms my heart.

"And finally, I'm certain that I fucking love you," he says, reaching up to cup my face, the pads of his thumbs rubbing over my cheekbones as he bends over to kiss me. My fingers curl into his top as I kiss him back, our tongues dancing, our lips caressing. We part only when our kiss shifts from loving to passionate.

"I love you too," I whisper against his lips, before stepping out of his hold and wandering over to the window to take in the spectacular view of our hometown lit up beneath us.

Pressing my fingers against the cool glass, I allow myself a moment to settle the thrumming beat of my heart and the rush of heat beneath my skin as I stare at the twinkling lights of Islington below. My eyes are drawn to the spot where I assume the approximate location of Rocks, based on the landmarks I recognise. Letting my mind wander back to the nights we spent there as teenagers, I remember all those incredible times when we danced there together. Despite all the shit that happened at Rocks since those days, I still hold onto those memories. Treasure them.

"Will you rebuild?" I ask, knowing they'll understand what I'm talking about.

Behind me, Zayn approaches with a bottle of beer. "Here," he says, dropping it over my shoulder.

"Thanks." I lift the bottle to my lips and take a sip.

"I haven't really thought about it, honestly," he replies, wrapping an arm around my waist from behind as he perches his chin on the top of my head. "When this is all over, we'll make a decision together."

"Together?"

"Yeah. We always make important decisions together, the four of us... *Five* of us now," he corrects himself. "You've always been a part of us, even when we weren't together. Your opinion is important. It matters."

"Thank you," I reply, resting my hand over his, feeling both loved and respected.

Zayn tightens his arm around my waist, and we stand together, silently drinking our beers. A minute or so later, the door to the room opens and Dax enters.

"Everything good?" Xeno asks him.

"Yeah, Gray's chilling in the lounge, Lena's sleeping, and the ghosts are still watching the place. We're good for a bit," he says.

I watch his reflection in the glass as he grabs a beer from Xeno and sits on the couch next to York. He's still dressed in his suit, the material of his trousers and shirt tight over his bulging muscles.

"Thank you, Dax," I say.

"You got it, Kid."

Focussing my attention back on the view, I find myself relaxing in Zayn's arms. The combination of being held by the man I love and the alcohol flooding my bloodstream is just the tonic I need. It's a moment of reprieve that we all need badly.

"Can anyone see in here from the outside?" I ask.

"They can if we choose," Xeno explains, stepping up beside us. "Right now the privacy glass is on. One flick of a button and anyone looking our way can see right in." He points to the opposite building, an office block by the looks of it, and grins. "Pretty sure some of the people who work there have gotten a good view of each of our arses at least once over the last year when we've forgotten to switch the glass to private."

"It's never switched to privacy glass when I'm up here. I have a fine arse and don't see why others shouldn't enjoy the view," York says.

"You're such a dick," Zayn mutters, chuckling.

"Yeah, pretty sure those lucky office workers have seen that too," he replies, and we all laugh with him.

"We actually picked this flat because of this very room," Xeno continues once we've calmed down. "None of the other properties have this feature. In a weird kind of way it reminded us of Jackson Street. A room to hang out together in. No TV, just a music system and each other for company."

"And a hot tub," I add, a smile in my voice.

"And a hot tub," he agrees.

Xeno stares out of the window, drinking his beer as we stand in companionable silence whilst Zayn slowly rubs his thumb up and down the skin on my bare arm. Goosebumps litter my skin, not because I'm cold, but because something shifts in the air around us. A familiar warmth pools in my lower belly at their presence.

Beside me Xeno sighs and I turn to look at him, my gaze roving over his features. There's a sudden tenseness in his jaw, and a tightness around his mouth that I desperately want to soothe. When I left Lena sleeping, I thought, perhaps, I wanted to do more training, needing physical exercise that wasn't dance to help tire me out. I realise now that what I want most of all is *them*. I need intimacy. I want conversation, laughter, their touch, their kisses, their hands and tongues, their cocks. *Them.* We've been so at odds, thrown from one crisis to another over the last week or so that I just need to reconnect, and I think they need that too.

A frown pulls together Xeno's eyebrows, pulling me out of my thoughts and very much in the present. "What is it?" I ask gently, wanting to pull him into my arms, but not wanting to step out of Zayn's. He turns to face me, uncertainty in his gaze.

"It's okay to feel fucked up inside, Tiny. You don't need to hide anything from us. We love you regardless. *I* love you, no matter what. Understand?"

"I do, and I'm so grateful for you all. For everything. I love you all so much..."

"But," Xeno prompts, eying me carefully.

"But I'm terrified that he'll take you all away before we've really had a chance to just be together. Sometimes I find myself wishing I was fourteen again just so that I can be with you all as we were before everything went wrong. I'd take all those beatings over and over again to just be that kid, and *happy* with you all."

"Fuck, Tiny, you're breaking my heart here, and you know I don't have one of those," he mutters, a half-smile pulling up his lips, making this serious moment lighter somehow. I'm glad of it.

"Jesus fuck, me too," York agrees from his spot on the sofa.

Reaching for a strand of hair that's fallen free from my hair tie, Xeno tucks it back behind my ear. His fingers linger on my skin, trailing heat as he slides them along my jaw. Behind me, Zayn presses a kiss against the curve of my neck. I swallow, my heart pounding to a different rhythm.

"Xeno," I whisper, and the sound of his name on my tongue is needy and full of want.

"This room up here, it's just for us. Whenever we need to get away, we come here and we forget the shit going on around us, even if it's just for a little while," he says, taking the empty beer bottles from Zayn and me, and placing them on the floor by his feet. "I know you've been through hell, and we don't expect a damn thing from you, but I can't deny that I fucking want you, Tiny. I need you so—"

Pressing my finger against his mouth, I shake my head. "I need you too. I need *all* of you more than I can explain," I say, cupping his cheek with my hand. "But I'm so fucking scared I'm going to lose you... that I feel myself drawing away to save myself from the pain. Does that make sense?"

Xeno grips my wrist in his hand. "It makes perfect sense, but you don't need to do that. You won't lose us, any of us. I fucking swear it."

"Feeling like this, looking over my shoulder, waiting for him to strike again, it's making me crazy. Every hour, I swing wildly between fear and rage until I don't know what side is up and what side is down."

"Then we'll make sure that we're here to keep you steady, grounded," Zayn says, dropping a tender kiss to my temple in reassurance.

"We'll be here to love you until all you can think of is us," Xeno adds as Zayn pulls my hair back from my shoulder and kisses a trail of heat up my neck, his teeth scraping over the sensitive flesh.

Pressing my eyes shut, I let out a low moan of pleasure as I reach up and cup the back of his head. I angle my neck so that Zayn can run his lips across the tender flesh beneath my ear.

"Please, just make it all go away. Make me forget, if only for a little while."

"Oh, Tiny, we're going to do more than make you forget. We're going to fuck you until your body and your thoughts are filled with nothing but us," Xeno promises before pressing a kiss against my palm, his lips trailing over my skin to the pulse point on my wrist. He licks me there, his teeth grazing over the sensitive flesh as his eyes flash with hunger and promises of pleasure. "Take off your clothes," he orders.

15

Xeno

TINY LOOKS at me with wide eyes. Her cheeks are flushed, and her pupils are blown. There's a hint of apprehension in her gaze but a hell of a lot more lust as Zayn leads her to the mat on the other side of the room. Dax meets York's gaze as they stand, a small smile appears. Something passes between them, a silent agreement that intrigues me. Whatever they're thinking, I trust that it'll be for Tiny's benefit.

Grabbing my mobile phone, I scroll through my playlist and select a song, blue-toothing it to the sound system before chucking my phone on the sofa. *Let It All Go* by Birdy and Rhodes begins to play. Their haunting voices saying everything I can't.

Tiny needs to let go of all the fear, all the pain, the guilt, and this feeling of uncertainty.

She needs to rid herself of it all, and we're going to help her to do that. We're going to take control of the situation. We're going to pleasure her until all she thinks of is us, until she's in fucking paradise and not trapped in her head.

Fuck David.

Fuck Santiago.

Fuck every last thing trying to break us apart.

Together we're stronger. We always were. We always will be.

Tiny bites on her lip, her cheeks flushing pink as she looks between us all. Her trust in us, her love for us makes me want to be a better man, for her, for my brothers, for the life we'll have together.

"Let us see you," Zayn says, his voice hoarse as he reaches for the hem of her t-shirt and lifts it slowly upwards, revealing her perfect skin, inch by inch.

Goosebumps bloom across her skin, her dusky pink nipples hardening beneath the thin lace of her bra as Zayn drops her top to the floor. She swallows hard, her gaze fixed on Zayn as he brushes his fingers down the middle of her flushed chest. When he cups her tit, rubbing the pad of his thumb over her nipple through the material, my fucking cock hardens, straining against my clothes.

"You're so fucking beautiful," he murmurs, his voice reverent, worshipful.

"A-to-the-fucking-men to that," York agrees, his gaze fixed firmly on Tiny as she arches her back and presses her tits into Zayn's hands. He massages them gently, and she lets out a low moan as he pulls down the material of her bra, freeing her creamy mounds, and sucks one peaked nipple into his mouth. I watch intently as his plush lips, framed with stubble, grazes her skin. It turns me the fuck on, watching my best friend pleasure her, watching her skin pink up from the friction.

"Fuck," Dax groans, cupping his junk, and rubbing himself through the material of his trousers. Next to him York grins, swiping a hand through his hair, those strange-as-fuck eyes of his roving over every inch of her skin. The three of us are greedy, drinking in the sight. We palm our cocks, watching intently as Zayn pleasures our girl. The way he holds her, moves with her, is a slow dance. If she realises what he's doing, she doesn't push him away. Instead she reacts instinctively, moving with him. Her thigh lifts up over Zayn's hip as he supports her back, dipping her backwards so he can better access her beautiful tits. It's the first time she's danced since before her mum was found dead, and fuck if it doesn't ease the ache inside a little.

"Zayn," she whimpers.

The neediness in her voice has my cock leaking pre-cum, and by the look on Dax and York's face they're struggling too. I've slept with a lot of women over the years, but no one has ever affected me the way Tiny does. I know it's the same for them.

Everything about her is a fucking turn-on. Her beauty, her voice, her body, the way she moves, the way she dances, the way she moans and laughs. Her strength, tenacity and courage. I love her like I've never loved anyone.

"Suck her tits until she comes," I demand, unable to hold back my needs, wanting to take control of her pleasure, theirs, mine. It's who I am. A bossy fucker for the most part, but being able to control this aspect of our lovemaking helps me to manage the uncontrollable emotions within me. My best friends understand that.

Zayn grunts in acquiesce, drawing her back up slowly so that he can grasp either side of her ribcage with his hands, alternating between flicking her nipples with his tongue and drawing them into his mouth. She unhooks her leg from his thigh in one smooth motion, her toes pointed before she rests it back on the mat, and naturally places her feet in second position.

"I can't get enough," Zayn says, making a low, rumbling noise in his throat as he sucks on her nipple greedily. He continues to kiss and lick until her knees are buckling and breathy pants release from her parted lips.

"Don't stop," Tiny cries out, her fingers sliding into Zayn's hair as she tugs on the strands, her mouth dropping open in bliss.

"I don't intend to." Zayn smiles, flattening his tongue against her nipple, leaving a trail of saliva across her skin before he bites down with just enough pressure to skirt the edges of pain and pleasure.

"Oh, God, I-I need…" she moans, one hand releasing from Zayn's hair as she slides it down her body, reaching for her clit.

"York," I snap, jerking my chin.

"I thought you'd never ask." Grinning, he steps up behind Tiny and wraps his arm around her waist. "No, my love. Allow me," he admonishes, his voice dark, rasping, as he replaces her hand with his and slides his fingers beneath the waistband of her sleep shorts. She jerks, York's fingers finding her clit beneath the material. My gaze flicks between his hand hidden beneath her shorts and Zayn gently teasing one pretty, erect nub with his tongue.

Fuck, I bet she's dripping wet.

Pressing the heel of my palm against my chest, I rub at the love and the pain that always comes hand in hand when it comes to Pen and my brothers. Dax notices, giving me a look of concern, but I just grin, no longer afraid of what hurts me. I let the love I feel for Tiny, for my brothers, in. I embrace it whole-heartedly, and as I do, I let go of the fucking pain. I let it go.

Dax nods, smiling, his attention turning back to Tiny as he strips off. First he removes his shirt, then his suit trousers, shoes, socks and finally his boxers until he's standing naked, cock in hand. York's eyebrows raise, his gaze dropping to Dax's dick briefly before concentrating on our girl once more. "Titch, tell us what you need," he asks her.

She groans, leaning her head back against his chest, and looking up at him with heavy-lidded eyes. "You're mouth on me, *everywhere,*" she replies, reaching up and grasping the back of his neck as she pulls him down for a kiss.

"Fuck, yes," York groans into her mouth, their lips colliding, teeth clashing, tongues fucking as they kiss.

"Take off her shorts," I order, stripping off my clothes until I'm naked, my cock painfully hard, my balls fucking tingling. Jesus, I need her lips wrapped around my dick. I want to sink my cock into her mouth and fuck her.

Zayn reaches down and pulls off Tiny's shorts leaving her bare. He shifts to the side, angling his body so I can see York sliding his thick fingers between her pretty, pink folds. His hands are fucking glistening. She's so damn wet. Hips gyrating, Tiny seeks out more pleasure as York and Zayn bring our girl to climax. Her moans get louder, her grip on Zayn's head tighter as she presses her tits into his mouth, and gyrates her hips, desperate to come.

Briefly, Zayn pulls back and motions for Dax to join them. "Get the fuck over here, now," he demands, dropping on his knees before Tiny.

York grins, removing his hands so Zayn can cup her arse and lift her off her feet. With York supporting her back, Tiny jumps, and in one graceful motion, has her legs wrapped around Zayn's shoulders as he buries his face between her legs. She cries out in ecstasy, as he fucks her pussy with his tongue, the slippery, wet sounds making my cock weep and my balls tighten. Dax joins the trio, his large, tattooed hands grasping her tit as he bends over and sucks her nipple and the surrounding flesh into his mouth. She gasps at the assault, her eyes rolling back in her head as York grasps Tiny's chin with his glistening fingers.

"You really are fucking perfect," he grinds out before kissing her, swallowing her moans into his mouth.

"That's it, make our girl come." I groan, sliding my fist up and down my cock. My fucking balls tightening as I feast on what I'm seeing like a starving man. I can't get enough. I'm fucking greedy as my gaze flicks between the four of them, dancing over soft curves held in a tattooed hand, creamy thighs wrapped around broad shoulders, and hungry lips devouring breathy moans.

My brothers *love* Tiny whilst I watch. They make her come whilst I jerk myself off and when she screams out her orgasm, her back arching, her legs shaking, they continue to pleasure her until she's spent. Squeezing my dick to stop myself from coming, I step towards the group and cup Tiny's face in my hands. Her head lolls on York' shoulder as she blinks up at me, dazed and glowing in the aftermath of her orgasm.

"You're ours. Forever, Tiny. *Ours*. Now, I want you to get on your knees."

"W—what?" Her pupils constrict and dilate. Lust and alarm fighting for dominance.

"On your knees, beautiful," I repeat, wrapping my demand up in affection and love.

Zayn slides her legs off his shoulders and steadies her hips as she stands on wobbly legs. Behind her York cuts me a look, his eyebrow raising. Resting her hands on Zayn's shoulders, she lowers to her knees, her eyes fixed on me the whole damn time and fuck if I don't want to drown in the warmth of them.

"Pen," Zayn says gently, drawing her attention away from me and back to him.

His mouth and chin are still covered in her cum, and she smiles, almost shyly, as he wipes a hand over his face, swiping away the evidence of her orgasm before planting a passionate kiss on her bruised lips. "Your taste makes me fucking high. I could eat your pussy morning, noon and night for the rest of my godforsaken life, and never need a proper meal again."

York barks out a laugh. "Greedy motherfucker. There's this thing called sharing."

"I *can* share, but fuck you lot, tonight *I'm* the big spoon!"

Tiny's cheeks flush pink, a laugh bubbling up her throat at their banter. It's a beautiful sound.

"We can discuss whose bed Tiny's sleeping in tonight, later. Strip!" I command.

"What's wrong Xeno, your balls turning blue," York jokes,

drawing a chuckle from both Dax and Zayn. "Sucks, doesn't it...? Oh, wait, *that's* what you're angling for."

"Shut the fuck up, York."

"Fine," he replies, rolling his eyes but stripping nevertheless. Zayn follows suit until the four of us are butt naked and standing in a circle around our girl.

Tiny's hot stare roves over each of us in turn, a smile lighting her eyes as she drops her gaze from my heaving chest to my hand wrapped around my cock. Truth be known, I'm so close to coming, that I'm fucking terrified I'll loosen my grip and come like some horny teenage boy without an ounce of fucking control. I've got a motherfucking reputation to keep up here, so I tell my cock to fucking behave as I step closer to Tiny.

"Is this what you want?" she asks, a slow sexy smile spreading across her face as she reaches for my cock, her warm fingers sliding over the head. Her dark eyes burn into my soul like a heat-seeking missile as she looks up at me, licking along the slit.

"Fuuuuccck!" I exclaim. Dax, Zayn and York echo my words as they watch Tiny give me the best motherfucking blowjob of my life. Honestly, we are all so turned on that it's like a motherfucking Russian roulette, except our dicks are the guns and spunk the fucking bullets. No one wants to be the one to come first. Each one of us has our pride at stake.

"You want me to make you come, is that it, Xeno?" she asks, pulling back and licking the tip of my cock like we've been doing this our whole lives. Fuck, we will be. That I do know for sure.

"Yes," I grind out, my fingers sliding into her hair, my arm muscles flexing as I push my dick against her lips, urging her to take me deep into her mouth once more, but clearly tonight she's trying to kill me.

"Yes, what, Xeno?" she asks, stroking her hand up and down my shaft, her saliva making it slick.

"Yes, *please*, suck my cock and make me come, Tiny." I'm not a man who usually begs, but fuck she's well and truly got me by the balls, literally.

"You only had to ask," she mutters, her small, delicate hand stroking my shaft as she cups my balls and gently squeezes. My hips jolt as her lips wrap around the head of my cock once more, and it takes everything in me not to come like a fucking geyser.

"Jesus, fuck. I'm gonna blow my load just watching this," York says, stroking his cock as his eyes fixate on Tiny's mouth around my dick.

Tiny moans, sucking me deep into her throat, her lips wrapping tightly around the shaft of my cock. I feel an impending orgasm building in my balls, gathering fucking speed and there's nothing I can do to stop it, but Tiny draws back, releasing me with a pop. I groan in protest, my fingers curling into her hair, but she grins evilly, shaking her head.

"Tiny..."

"Not yet," she replies.

"I think I like this game," York says, chuckling. If I didn't think it would spoil the moment, I'd fucking throat punch him right now. My balls haven't been as high in my body since I was a pre-pubescent kid.

"Come closer. All of you," Tiny urges, looking up at us with heavy-lidded eyes, and even though she's the one on her knees, the power is all hers. Dax, York and Zayn step closer, the heat in the room growing dense.

"Look, it's a cock circle," York comments, always trying to crack a joke at the most inappropriate moments. He's such a fucking jackass.

"Hmm," Tiny agrees, reaching for his cock, whilst still sliding her fist up and down mine. She wraps her hand around his dick and slides him into her mouth. His eyes roll back in his head and his hips jerk.

"Motherfucker!" he exclaims as she sucks him off for a moment before moving onto Dax, releasing my cock to wrap her fingers around Dax's. She bites her lip, staring at his huge dick before her pink tongue peeks out from between her bruised lips and slides along the thick vein pulsing along the shaft. If I was a lesser man, I might be intimidated, but I'm not. It's not as if the rest of us have small dicks, he just happens to have a giant one.

"Kid, you're killing me here," he grinds out, his hands cupping her face as he guides her up and down his cock. He's careful not to go too deep, always the one to stay restrained for Tiny. I'm not surprised she nicknamed him her dark angel.

York groans as she curls her fingers around his dick whilst sucking off Dax. When he's close to coming so she lets his cock go and switches hands, reaching for Zayn this time. Just like the rest of us, he can't contain his reaction and swears like a sailor as she jacks him off whilst sucking Dax's dick like a motherfucking lollipop.

Another rush of blood fills my cock, and the familiar sensation of an oncoming orgasm rolls through me just by watching her suck Dax's cock and stroke Zayn's. She alternates between the two of them. Sucking Zayn next, whilst stroking Dax's dick. Both York and me are watching intently, jerking ourselves off. Then she shifts again, twisting around and takes my dick in her mouth, her tight lips and warm wetness setting me off like a fucking firecracker.

I come long and hard, my fingers wrapped in her hair as she swallows my cum down. As soon as I'm spent, she reaches for York and half a minute later he's coming. Moving around our *cock circle*—fucking York, I'm going to kill him for putting that phrase in my head—she sucks off Dax next. He comes with a roar that I swear to fuck shakes the windows, and then, finally, finishes off Zayn.

"Holy. Fucking. Shit," York exclaims, saying what we're all thinking as he passes a shaking hand through his hair.

"I couldn't agree more," I say, positive that if I don't sit down soon, I might just fall the fuck down. Tiny stands, her cheeks flushing furiously as if she's surprised at her own actions. Giving us all a gentle kiss against our cheeks, she smiles almost shyly but there's a hint of a confident woman just beneath the surface, and boy, do I fucking like it.

"Was that okay?"

"Okay? Pen, if we weren't already committed to you one thousand percent, you can bet your arse we are now. That was the sexiest fucking thing I've ever experienced in my entire life. *Ever*," Zayn says with a light laugh.

"Good," she murmurs, her hands feathering over his scarred chest. She glances over at the jacuzzi, eyeing the water. "I've never been in a jacuzzi before—"

"Then that will have to be rectified, right the fuck now," Dax says, swooping down and picking her up in his arms. She giggles as he strides across the room, steps into the warm water, and drops beneath the surface with Tiny still in his arms.

"Let's get wet!" York says, punching the air and practically dive bombing into the water. He slips under the surface, rising up as droplets slide down his body, then slams his fist against the button on the rim of the jacuzzi.

"Sit the fuck down, you idiot," Dax grumbles, wiping water droplets off his face.

"You know you fucking love me," York retorts, settling down beside Dax, his arm draping across the ledge behind his back.

Tiny laughs again at York's antics. "Oh my God, this feels so good," she says, wriggling in Dax's lap as the bubbles churn the water, making it frothy.

"A man could get a complex over here," Zayn says, climbing in and taking a seat opposite the trio.

"I meant the bubbles," she replies, giggling again in that carefree way I haven't heard in years, let alone since we've been reunited.

"Thanks," Dax grumbles with a smile in his eyes.

Tiny bites her lip, her hand snaking up from under the surface of the water as she grasps his cheek. "I didn't mean it like that," she says after thoroughly kissing him. "You make me feel good. You all make me feel good."

"You can mean it any which way you like so long as you kiss me like that again," he replies.

"Beer anyone?" I ask, striding over to the fridge, not bothering to wait for their reply. Grabbing five bottles, I remove the caps, observing them for a moment. My heart fucking swells with my love for them all, and for the first time ever it feels *good*.

"Are you just going to stand there, with your one-eyed snake giving us all the stink eye, or are you getting in?" York asks, smirking.

"Ha-fucking-ha." I give York the finger as I saunter over, not giving two fucks that I'm sporting a semi, and step into the jacuzzi, handing them all a beer before sinking beneath the surface of the water next to Zayn.

"Cheers," Dax says, and we all raise our bottles, chinking them against each other.

For the next few minutes, we drink our beers, and sit in companionable silence, enjoying this moment of peace, satiated and at ease with one another. That is, until Tiny adjusts her position in Dax's lap and smiles provocatively. "So, what now?" she asks.

16

Pen

"HOW ABOUT A GAME of truth or dare?" York suggests, swiping his hand through his hair, slicking it back off his forehead.

Xeno rolls his eyes. "What are we, fucking teenagers? I've got better, more adult ideas on my mind," he says, taking a swig of his beer as he looks at me.

"Yeah, we all know what those *ideas* are because we're all thinking them ourselves," Dax chuckles, his fingers sliding along my thighs beneath the water. He teases me, gently cupping my pussy and allowing me to rock into his hand before removing it and placing it on my thigh once more. Every now and then he circles his hips, and I feel his cock sliding across the skin of my lower back, and my core clenches, desperate for more.

"What's wrong with a game of truth or dare?" I say, biting

on my lip as another familiar hand slides up my thigh reaching for my pussy. I glance at York, holding in a moan as he looks at Xeno and Zayn as if he isn't circling my clit with his finger right now.

"Yeah, why not? We never did play the game when we were kids. Come on, Xeno, you might enjoy it," York teases, his fingers doing the same to my pussy.

A dark glint shines in Xeno's eyes. "Fine, but lets up the ante a little, shall we?"

York grins. "Oh, I like it. How's this going to play out?"

"Ah, fuck, no," Dax grumbles. "You two are a fucking night-mare when you get like this."

"Like what?" I ask, coughing on a moan and trying not to fidget too much in Dax's lap because his boner is growing by the minute and I'm getting off on York's fingers.

"York goads Xeno into doing things he's not interested in and Xeno gets his own back by shifting the goalposts. I'm pretty fucking certain they both get off on the high stakes. Ain't that right, Zayn?"

"Yeah, that's exactly right," he replies, shaking his head and taking a deep pull from his bottle of beer.

"So what are the stakes then?" I ask, stiffening when Dax reaches between my thighs and finds York's hand there. York chokes back a laugh, and Dax presses an open-mouthed kiss on my shoulder to stifle his own reaction. I'm not sure if it's a laugh he's trying to hide or a grumble of annoyance, but when neither move their hand, and they begin to pleasure me in tandem, I'm guessing it's the former.

"Yes, what are the stakes?" York asks nonchalantly, hiding

the fact that his fingers are currently intertwining with Dax's whilst they rub me off.

It takes all my willpower not to moan and give us away. Thank God I can use the recent lovin' and the heat from the water as an excuse for my flushed skin. I don't think either Zayn or Xeno would be pissed off if they knew what was happening under the water, given what's just taken place between us all, but there's something thrilling about the secrecy of what we're doing that turns me on and takes my mind off of everything else going on.

"Okay, so these are the rules. This is a *hard* truth and *no holds barred* dare. If you choose truth, then the questioner doesn't hold back on what truth they want to hear. I'm talking deep. No pussyfooting around. Go for the jugular. Got it?"

We all nod. Well, to be fair, I kind of groan my agreement seeing as York's finger is slowly circling my clit and Dax's finger is dipping into my pussy.

"If you choose dare, and then refuse the dare because you're too chicken-shit, then you pay a fine of five thousand pounds. It goes into a savings account for Lena's university fees, or whatever she wants to put it towards for when she's older."

"What? No," I protest.

"Those are the rules, Tiny," he replies, challenging me with his stare.

"That puts me at a disadvantage, because I don't have any money, let alone five thousand pounds to throw about like that."

Xeno shrugs. "Then do the dare," he says, shrugging.

"Fine," I say, deciding then and there, I'm going to choose a truth. It's not like they don't know everything there is to know about me already.

"We'll take it in turns to ask the question or provide the dare. So, either make your dare really fucking good or make your truth really hard to answer."

"Fuck sake," Zayn mutters, glaring at York.

"You're fucking on!" York laughs, removing his hand and squeezing my thigh. He leans over and presses his lips against my ear. "Hold onto that thought." Half a beat later, Dax has gently removed his finger, leaving me wanting and totally wound up.

"So who's going first?" Xeno asks, sliding a little lower beneath the water. He keeps his gaze on me, his eyes sparking when our feet touch. He slides his foot up my inner calf, then higher still, grinning mercilessly at me as it reaches my inner thigh. When he presses the ball of his foot gently against my pussy, I bite on my lip. My clit is already throbbing from York and Dax's treatment, and now Xeno is teasing me with his foot. Who knew *that* could feel so good?

I bite on my lip to stifle the moan and Xeno grins sexily before sitting back up. It's all I can do not to slap the water in frustration. These guys are determined to torture me. I guess this is payback for me mercilessly sucking their cocks and teasing them in turn.

Despite being on my knees surrounded by four alpha men, in that moment I had felt powerful. It was the most erotic, thrilling thing I've ever done, and I plan on doing it over and over again.

"I'll go first. Let's get this over with," Zayn says, rolling his eyes whilst the three of them laugh.

"Okay then, mate. Truth or dare?" York jumps in and asks before the rest of us can.

"Truth, you cocksucker," Zayn snaps, narrowing his eyes at York. "There's no way I'm taking a dare. I know what you're like. You'll probably ask me to climb this building butt naked."

"Actually, that's not a bad idea," York muses. "I mean, I'd give you time to train, maybe you could get Jefferson from Callous Crew to give you some advice, huh? I bet he wouldn't hesitate to scale this building, the fucking daredevil."

Zayn raises a brow, unimpressed. "Just ask the fucking question, York."

For a minute, York contemplates his question then clears his throat. His demeanour changes from joyful to serious as he examines Zayn. "How many times over the years did Jeb cut you?"

Blanching, Zayn's skin pales. It's clear from his reaction that he's never had this discussion with the guys and he's certainly not happy talking about it. I understand his reluctance to open up about something he feels ashamed of. When you suffer physical abuse like we have, you either try to hide it from everyone or pretend it doesn't affect you in any way. To make matters worse, Jeb abused Zayn as an adult, and that can't be something that's easy to bear. It's obvious he doesn't want to revisit it. "Fuck you, York. I'll pay the damn fine," he snaps, looking away from us all.

"The fine is only applicable if you don't take the dare," Xeno says, his voice even.

Zayn snaps his head around to look at Xeno. "Fuck this shit." He moves to stand, and I reach for him, grasping his fingers.

"I'm sorry, this was a bad idea. You don't have to say a thing if it's too painful," I say.

"The fuck he doesn't," York counters. "Sit down, Zayn, and let it out. You don't have to hold onto that shit anymore. Why the fuck did you think I asked the question? Titch isn't the only one who needs to let stuff go."

Zayn's nostrils flare, but he sits back down. "You've seen the state of my chest. Let's just say it was a lot and leave it at that."

"How many times," York insists.

Zayn's nostrils flare. "Forty-six. He took a knife to my chest and cut me on forty-six different occasions. Are you happy now?"

"The *fuck?*" Dax grinds out, his fingers tightening on my hips.

"Of course I'm not fucking happy. I love you man..." York says earnestly.

"What's done is done. I got my own back. The fucker's dead."

"You said you took the punishment for our wrongdoings. Is that right?" York persists, not letting Zayn close down the conversation.

"Yeah, I was cut whenever one of you talked out of turn towards him or simply pissed him off for some stupid reason only he could come up with. Some cuts were more painful than others, but I'd bare every single one of those cuts again if it meant making sure one of you wasn't punished instead," Zayn says, lifting the bottle of beer to his lips and knocking back the remaining liquid.

"Zayn," I whisper, sliding off of Dax's lap and into his arms.

"It's alright, Pen. I'm good." He folds his arms around me, and I press a kiss against his cheek, my fingers running over his scars beneath the water.

"You're a good man," I say, pressing a kiss against his lips.

"One of the best," York says in earnest. "We owe you one."

Dax and Xeno nod in agreement, their silence a sign that they're just as cut up about his confession as York and I are.

"Actually, you owe me forty-six *ones*," Zayn replies with a grin, and even though it isn't funny, we all laugh, feeling lighter for it.

"Okay, Xeno, your turn. Truth or Dare?" Dax asks him.

"I'm pretty fucking sure you know everything there is to know about me. I'll take a dare."

Dax grins wickedly. "No sex with Tiny for the next two months, including foreplay," he says without preamble.

"What? That's not a dare, that's a fucking punishment!" Xeno exclaims.

"Mate, suck it the fuck up. Dare's a dare. The question is, are you man enough?"

"You fucking arsehole! I always knew you were jealous of my dick. Afraid of a little competition, are we?"

"Me, jealous of *your* dick?" Dax scoffs, rolling his eyes. "I'm not being funny, but have you seen the size of my cock?"

"We all know that it's not the size that matters, but what you can do with it that counts," Xeno counters with a smirk.

Dax grins. "Isn't that what every small-dicked man says?"

York barks out a laugh, throwing his head back. "Where's the fucking popcorn? This is *gold*! I knew playing this game was genius."

"I know, let's ask Tiny, shall we?" Xeno says, turning to me.

"Wait, what? Are you actually *admitting* you've got a small dick?" Zayn asks, his face deadpan as he joins in on the banter.

"Fuck off. No, I'm not... Tiny?"

I blow out a breath looking between Dax and Xeno. "You seriously expect me to answer that?"

"This can be your truth," Xeno suggests. "Come on, Dax won't be offended when you put him in his place. He's still your dark angel after all. Can't give him all the kudos for every damn thing. He's *got* to be shit at something."

"What is this, some kind of cock-off?" I retort, rolling my eyes.

For a beat there's stunned silence until all four of them burst out laughing. I join them, my heart expanding with all the camaraderie and banter. It reminds me of how we used to be, and what we can have in the future if we get through everything stacked against us.

"Seriously though... Give me your truth," Xeno persists, wiping at his eyes. I don't think I've ever seen him laugh so much he's cried. Normally that's York or Zayn, and even then they've been high.

"Well, that's easy. I don't even think about it. I love you all equally, your *cocks* included. Also, I'd just like to point out that *I* get to decide who I have sex with and when. Just saying..."

Dax flicks some water at Xeno, smirking, and for a moment I think Xeno is going to punch him. Instead he just smiles. "I'll take the goddamn fine, you cock, because there is no way in Hell that I'm abstaining from loving our girl for two fucking months."

Dax laughs. "Thought you might." A look passes between them, and I realise then that Dax dared Xeno the impossible so that he would have no option except to pay the fine and Lena would have a nest egg for her future. God, I love these guys.

"Who's next?" York muses, pointing between himself and

Dax. He captures my gaze, and something flares within them. A challenge maybe? I remember our conversation from earlier, and the way the two of them seem so at ease with each other, both as people and sexually, and an idea forms in my head. "Remember, Titch, if you're gonna go for a dare, go big or go home, right?" York reminds me.

Dax looks between us, his eyes narrowing, but there's a hint of something playful too, and that gives me the courage to go with the flow. Biting my lip, my cheeks heating and my clit throbbing at the thought of what I'm about to do, I open my mouth and let the words tumble out. "This is a joint dare, for you both," I say.

"Hmm, a joint dare? Interesting," Xeno interrupts, looking between the three of us. "Before you make the request, Tiny, I'm going to make a suggestion."

"What's that?" Zayn asks, shifting me so that I'm sitting across his lap, bridal style.

"I think we should up the ante even more."

"*More?* Why the fuck would we agree to that, Xeno?" Dax asks, shaking his head.

"Done!" York exclaims with a grin, steamrolling into the agreement without so much as considering what it is Xeno might suggest.

Dax groans "Thanks, man, now I can't say no without looking like a pussy."

"But you'd be a pussy with a really *big,* monster dick..."

Dax leans over and whacks York around the back of the head. "I could fucking murder you sometimes. It's just as well that I love your crazy, annoying arse."

"There is always an out," Xeno interjects.

"Yeah, yeah, five thousand pounds. I know."

"Not this time. I'm upping the ante, remember? You can refuse Tiny's dare but then you'll have to pay twice the fine. That's ten grand into Lena's pot *each*."

"Fucking perfect. Cheers, York. Talk about getting stitched up," Dax grumbles, but honestly he doesn't look too pissed off about it. I'm betting ten grand is pocket change to them both, and for the first time I wonder just how much they're worth. "Fine. Let's do this." Dax looks at me, his elbows resting on the side of the jacuzzi, his thick, tattooed fingers swirling in the water. "What's the dare, Kid?"

"Yeah, what's the dare, Titch?" York teases, he's eyes glinting.

Biting on my lip, I debate whether I should go ahead with it. What if I'm reading things wrong and they're not as open sexually as I think? "Maybe this isn't such a great idea," I murmur, dropping my gaze away. Fantasies are just that for a reason. Just because the thought of them kissing and jacking each other off is a turn-on for me, doesn't mean to say it will be for them. I don't want to make them do something they don't want to do.

"Fuck that! Say it, Titch. Whatever it is, we can always say no. We have that choice," York reminds me.

"Go on, Kid. Be brave. *Dare* us," Dax orders, his voice lowering in a way that makes my toes curl.

"Okay, I dare you to kiss each other. Full tongues, and...." Xeno stiffens beside me and Zayn's eyes widen as he takes a sip of his beer. Cleary, neither of them were expecting this turn of events.

"And?" York asks, focussing on me intently.

"And jerk each other off," I blurt out, my cheeks blushing furiously.

"Atta girl," York smiles as though he knew exactly what I was going to dare them to do.

Zayn chokes on his beer and Xeno's eyes pop open in shock. I don't think I've ever seen either of them as stunned or as speechless as they are right now.

"Fuuuucccckkkk," Zayn says, recovering from his shock. "Smart move, Pen. Smart move. Good way to rinse the guys of their cash."

"I wasn't trying to rinse them of anything," I whisper, my cheeks burning now with embarrassment. Neither Dax or York have said a word, or even moved an inch, and it's starting to feel really awkward. What the hell was I thinking?

"You weren't? Woah... Does this turn you on, wanting to see them kiss and touch each other?" Zayn asks gently. The amusement in his voice is gone. He's not judging, just curious. I'm so grateful for that because right now Xeno is burning a hole in the side of my head. I'm not sure if he's on board with my desires or disgusted by them.

"Yes. It turns me on," I say, feeling brave as I glance at Xeno. "I mean. You all turn me on and well, I just... It's just something that..."

"No need to explain, Titch," York shrugs like it's no big deal. "I ain't afraid of my sexuality. I love women, specifically you, and if it turns you on wanting me to kiss and touch *big boy* over here, then I'm game."

"You are?" Xeno asks, shaking his head, clearly still shocked, but there's a hint of amusement in his eyes that relaxes me a little.

"Why the fuck not? Dax?" York asks, turning to Dax.

Dax shifts forward, his hands dropping beneath the water. "Well, it's not as if I haven't touched York's cock before today..."

"Fucking hell," Zayn says. "Why am I the last to know anything?"

"It was by accident," I explain. "When we were together before, Dax was half asleep and—"

"And he grabbed my dick," York finishes for me.

Zayn laughs and shakes his head. "Well, shit."

"I do have one request though," Dax says, flicking his gaze to Xeno for approval.

"And what's that?" Xeno asks.

"If I'm gonna jerk off York for our girl's pleasure then I'm gonna need my own visuals, because as much as I love York, and admit he's a good-looking fucker, I might need a little help in making sure I don't let anyone down. Catch my meaning?"

"Yeah, I get you. Zayn, are you in?" Xeno asks.

"If by in, you mean inside of Pen, then of course the fuck I am."

"Oh, God," I mutter, thinking maybe I've bitten off more than I can chew here.

"And we kiss first," Dax adds. "Because when I'm giving York a hand job I'm going to need to be focussed on you. Okay, Kid?"

"I'm good with that," York agrees, winking at Dax who just rolls his eyes.

"Deal," I find myself saying, or rather, panting. "Shit, is it getting hot in here?"

York smirks. "It's about to, Titch. It's about to."

Before I'm even able to prepare myself, York shifts his body towards Dax, grabs his face in his hands and slams his lips against him. For a minute I think Dax is going to pull away, but when he grips York's hair tightly and slides his tongue between York's parted lips I know he's all in.

"Fuck," I exclaim, my body reacting instantly. I press my thighs together to ease the throbbing I feel between my legs, but Zayn tuts in my ear.

"Relax your legs, Pen. You watch and I'll play," he urges, running his hand up my shin and over my knee, his hand disappearing beneath the water as he reaches for my pussy. When his finger slides between my pussy lips, I let out a moan, momentarily closing my eyes as he gently teases my clit. Behind me, Xeno shifts closer and reaches around to cup my breast, his thumb and forefinger twisting my nipple.

"Don't take your eyes off Dax and York. Enjoy the show, Tiny, and we'll enjoy you."

My eyes snap open, then fixate on Dax and York kissing. It's almost violent the way they grip at each other, and nothing like the way both of them have kissed me before. We've been passionate, sure, but this is something altogether different. When York pulls back suddenly, I see that his bottom lip is bleeding a little and it should make me feel guilty, but when York swipes his finger over his bottom lip and smiles, that guilt disappears and is replaced instead with lust that billows and expands inside of me.

"Bring it on," York challenges, and this time it's Dax who slams his mouth roughly against York.

They kiss like they fight, with passion and mutual respect, and when they begin to moan, enjoying the kiss beyond the fact that it turns me on, my toes curl and my clit spasms. It's about the most erotic thing I've ever witnessed, and it does crazy things to my body.

"Oh God. I'm going to come," I pant, as Zayn fingers me expertly and Xeno licks and bites my neck and shoulder, his hand cupping and squeezing my breasts. When Dax grips York's jaw in his fingers and tongue fucks his mouth, my orgasm barrels out of nowhere and I'm crying out as it rushes up and out from my clit in one spine-tingling shockwave. When I come down from my orgasm high, York and Dax are sitting on the ledge of the jacuzzi staring at the three of us, droplets of water rolling over their skin, their cocks standing at attention.

"Now the fun really begins," York says, smirking. He reaches for Dax's cock, his fingers wrapping around the base and starts to gently stroke him. Dax jerks in his hold, his expression neutral until I stand, then his gaze darkens with lust as water runs in rivulets down my body. My eyes flick downwards to his cock and the lazy way York jerks him off.

"Fuck," Dax mutters, looking from me to York's hand gripping his cock and up to York who smiles. "That feels good, mate," Dax admits, before turning back to me.

"I—" But I can't find the words to express how turned on I am. All I can do is watch transfixed, my mouth parting as Dax's tattooed fingers reach for York and begin stroking up and down his cock.

"Fucking hell," Zayn exclaims. "You really are taking this dare seriously."

"We're taking Titch's needs seriously. What turns her on, turns me on," York says.

"Ditto," Dax agrees.

My nipples peak into hard points as I watch them, and I

slide my hands up to cup my breasts, wanting to give them something back in return. Their attention makes me feel powerful. Brazen. Swallowing hard, I find my voice. "What do you want me to do?"

"Climb out of the jacuzzi and grab the ledge, Kid," Dax instructs roughly.

"Okay," I reply, stepping between Xeno and Zayn and out of the jacuzzi, dropping to the other side. Turning to face them, I press my stomach against the lip of the jacuzzi and wait.

"Zayn, I want you to fuck our girl for us. Take her from behind and slide your dick into her beautiful pussy," Dax continues, his nipples peaking and his cock growing in York's hand.

I shudder involuntarily, and my skin scatters with goose-bumps, a combination from the cooler air and the excitement I feel.

"Fuck, man," York mutters, as Dax presses the flat of his thumb against the slit of York's cock, then rubs it over the head in a circular motion. "You're good at this."

Dax grins darkly, his gaze still fixed on me. "I have a cock. I know how to use it," he responds.

"Good to fucking know," York mutters back, watching me.

Climbing out the jacuzzi, Zayn stands behind me, he draws my hair back away from over my shoulder and starts to kiss and lick my neck. "Fuck, Pen. Do you know how much you turn me on?"

"Xeno, condom," Dax says, still focusing on me as I moan at Zayn's words and his touch.

Xeno nods, climbing out of the jacuzzi. A moment later he's back and handing Zayn a condom. "I'm going to watch you fuck our girl," he says to Zayn, then walks around the opposite side of the jacuzzi, sliding beneath the water a little over from Dax. Now all three of their gazes are fixed on me.

Behind me, Zayn kisses a hot trail down my spine, then pulls my hips backwards so that I'm arched over the side of the jacuzzi. For a moment he licks and kisses the very base of my spine where my tailbone meets the crease of my arse. When his tongue dips lower, licking the rim of my arsehole, I let out a whimper, enjoying the unusual but not unpleasant sensation.

"Fuck her, Zayn. Now!" It's York this time, and I can see how his stomach muscles tense and his cock jerk in Dax's hand. I'm guessing he wasn't joking when he said Dax was good at handjobs.

Zayn laughs darkly, and stands behind me. I hear the rustle of the foil being opened, and a moment later his heavy cock is resting on my lower back. "Spread your legs, Pen," he says, gently stroking his fingers over my hips and arse.

With my fingers curling over the rim of the jacuzzi and my lower stomach pressing against the ledge, I spread my legs. Heat blazes over my skin, sending goosebumps scattering as Zayn lines his cock up with my entrance. I know I'm wet, and it isn't a result of sitting in the jacuzzi. I'm wet and achy and desperate to be fucked because these men, *my* men, are fulfilling every fantasy I've ever had right here, right now, for me. I feel like the luckiest woman on Earth.

"Please, I'm already so close," I beg, pressing my arse back against Zayn. He doesn't need to be told twice. With one firm thrust he's entered me and I'm clenching around his cock, screaming out his name, my pleasure twining with the rest of theirs.

His hips piston as he thrusts into me, his fingers holding my hips in a bruising grip as we all groan and grunt, moan and pant. My fingers curl over the ledge as I fixate on Dax and York, and how their fists pump each other's cocks faster, matching the tempo of Zayn fucking me from behind. Sweat beads on my forehead from the heat of the jacuzzi and the heat building deep inside.

"Tiny, I could watch you get fucked all day, every day, for the rest of my life and never, ever tire of it," Xeno says hoarsely, the muscles in his arm tensing and flexing as he jerks himself off.

"I'm going to come," I say, panting as Zayn reaches around and slides his fingers over my clit.

"Then come, my love," York urges, his icy-blue eyes flaring with heat before his eyelids drop and he lets out a long groan, his hips jerking and his stomach muscles clenching as he comes. I watch with greedy eyes as Dax slows his hand movement down, ringing out York's orgasm, white, thready cum releases from his cock in spurts.

"Fuck! York exclaims, breathing heavily.

For a beat, he lets his orgasm wash over him, his fingers loosening around Dax's cock for a moment. Then, like a true gent, he makes sure to finish off Dax, who's currently eye-fucking me. The muscles in his neck are tight, his veins popping beneath his skin as he reaches climax. When he comes, he grips the side of the jacuzzi and pushes up into York's hold, cum spurting into the water. Xeno follows shortly afterwards, calling out my name just as Zayn's cock grows impossibly large inside of me.

My internal walls clamp hold of Zayn's cock as I feel my own impending orgasm rush up from my curled toes, along the backs of my legs, up over my arse and back, reaching for the tip of my head. Then the feeling centres in my clit and pussy, a white-hot pleasure that makes my eyes roll in the back of my head until it explodes like a freight train out of a tunnel. I let out a strangled cry, everything going black for a moment as I milk Zayn's cock and he empties himself inside of me.

When the fog clears, Zayn is gently pulling out of me, and the guys are climbing out of the jacuzzi, grabbing towels from a small cabinet in the corner of the room. I watch as York wraps his arm around Dax's shoulder, slapping his hand against his chest, Xeno looking on and grinning.

"I've got one final request," Xeno says, with a sly smile.

"And what's that?" Dax asks him.

"I'll pay ten grand into Lena's university fund so I don't have to clean that motherfucking jacuzzi."

"Fuck you, I'll double it," Dax retorts.

"Come on, York jizzed all over your hand. I figure you'd be cool doing the job."

"I tell you what, I'll pay thirty grand into Lena's fund to watch you *both* clean it," York says.

In that moment, as the three of them fall about laughing and Zayn hugs me back against his chest, I know that this kind of love we all share is one in a million, and come what may, I will protect it with my life.

17

Pen

"PEN! Fuck! It's so good to see you!" Clancy says the second she sees me standing on her doorstep the following Monday.

Before I can even respond, she throws herself into my arms, almost knocking me over from the force. Fortunately for the both of us, York is standing directly behind me and places a steadying hand on my lower back.

"I've been worried sick. I've missed you so much!"

"I've missed you too, Clancy," I whisper, my throat thickening with tears as I hug her back.

The guys have been really supportive, wonderful even, but I've missed her friendship, advice, and her special brand of quirkiness that always manages to put a smile on my face.

"When I heard what happened, I wanted to come see you

straight away. If you asked I would've been there for you in a heartbeat," she says, pulling back and searching my face.

"I know you would've, but I needed time to wrap my head around everything, and I had to be there for Lena."

"Of course you did. That's what incredible big sisters like you are for. How is she doing?" Clancy asks, then pulls a face. "Sorry, stupid fucking question."

"She's... sad," is all I can say in response.

"And you?"

"I guess I'm doing better than Lena," I lie, and when it comes to the grief side of things, I am. "You know how it was between me and mum, we didn't exactly have the best relationship in the world." I shrug, but that feeling of guilt for not feeling more, still burns my gut.

"No need to explain. I understand." She gives me a warm smile then flicks her gaze to York standing behind me, as if only just noticing him. "Hey, York."

"Alright, Clancy? For a minute there I thought I was invisible," he responds with a wry grin. "Miss me, too?"

"Not nearly as much as Pen. River's been amazing and all, but he can't replace my bestie... I've been lonely without my Pen."

"Thanks a bunch, Clancy," River says, stepping out of his flat on the opposite side of the hallway. Clancy giggles and blows him a kiss and I know he's forgiven her in an instant. Besides, we all know that they adore each other.

"Hey, River," I say as York moves to the side and he gives me a warm, friendly, hug.

"Hey, Pen. I'm sorry about your mum."

I nod tightly, gritting my teeth on the response I want to say: *I'm not.* "How have you been?" I ask him.

"Aren't I meant to ask that?" He smiles at York who nods his head back in greeting.

"Yeah, that's why I asked you first. Saves me from the pity."

He gives me a wry smile. "I've been good. Spending time with Clancy, trying to avoid the evil stepsister."

"What's she been doing now?" I ask.

"Ugh, she's been *extra* since you've been away. Jesus, that girl has it bad for you."

"Yeah?" I sigh, needing her shit like a hole in the head.

"Just swerve her as much as possible. She'll get over her infatuation eventually," he suggests, then looks at his wristwatch and pulls a face. "I'm so fucking sorry. I gotta run. I'm late already for my class."

"That's okay. We'll talk later, yeah?"

"Definitely." River gives me another quick hug before turning to Clancy and grasping her cheeks, kisses her thoroughly. She makes these little whimpering noises, then grins when he pulls back and slaps her on the arse. "Catch you later, Little Tapper."

"Catch you later, sexy," Clancy responds, and with that he's gone. She turns back to face me, pulling a smiley wide-eyed face. "Seriously though, that man packs all the goods and knows how to pleasure a woman. Last night he did this thing with his cock that blew my mind—"

York bursts out laughing. "You girls really do dissect everything together, don't you?"

Clancy wrinkles her pretty, button nose. "Too much information?"

"It's totally fine," I reply with a grin. "And in answer to your question, York, girls really do dissect everything. So you better make sure it's good because Clancy here won't be impressed if it isn't."

"That's right, *lover boy*," Clancy responds, leaning against the door frame. "I need to know you're a ten out of ten every time otherwise I'll be disappointed."

"Well, I can assure you, I've most definitely got that covered."

We all burst out laughing and I feel my heart lift. Being around Clancy is like a breath of fresh air. It's only been a minute that I've been in her company and I already feel as though I'm a normal twenty-year-old woman just chatting with her bestie about life stuff, and not a girl fucking terrified of her evil older brother no matter how much she tells herself that she isn't.

"Have you settled in with the guys okay? When I saw Dax and Zayn emptying your flat they told me you were moving in with them and wouldn't be at the Academy for a while. I wasn't expecting to see you so soon, honestly," she blurts out, her words coming out in a concerned rush. "But I'm so glad you're here."

"We should take this conversation inside," York suggests when Sophie and Tiffany step out of Tiffany's flat at the end of the corridor. They both give me a blank stare, no empathy or kindness, not even any of the usual disdain. Just... nothing. It's kind of creepy and fucked up. Then again, what did I expect? Why should they care if I've lost my mum? We're not friends. Never will be.

"Fuck, of course! Look at me keeping you talking on the doorstep. Where are my manners? Come in. We can have a cup of tea before lessons start." Clancy waves us into the flat, heading off to the kitchen. York shuts the door and gives me a sympathetic smile. He knows I want some alone time with Clancy, but also won't leave my side.

"You don't need to be here, York," I say, whispering under my breath. "Clancy isn't a snake. She's my friend and she'd never hurt me."

York grabs my hand. "I know she isn't, but the guys would cut my bollocks off if they knew I left you alone even for a second, and honestly I'd do the same to them. We're not taking any chances when it comes to you, so you'd better get used to it. Besides, our tap class starts in twenty minutes anyway, so I thought I'd stick around and catch up with Clancy too." he says, squeezing my hand.

"I get it," I say, because I really, really do. I think I've called and texted Lena every five minutes since we left the flat this morning. The rational part of my brain knows that she's safe with Gray and the ghosts protecting her, but I can't help but worry.

"She's gonna be okay, Titch. Lena has the best men watching her," York says, instantly understanding what's on my mind.

"This is even harder than I thought it would be." Sighing, I step into his arms as he hugs me close, pressing a kiss to the top of my head.

Behind us Clancy coughs, breaking up our brief, intimate moment. "You two really are so fucking cute together. Seriously, it's sickening." We all laugh, and it's like a warm balm to my aching heart.

"I really have missed you," I say, giving her another hug the second I'm close enough. She squeezes me back then grins, handing us both a mug of tea. Glancing around the room, I notice a pretty dance costume of gold and black, hanging over her armchair.

"That's from last weekend's show at Tales," Clancy explains. "Grim's a pretty amazing woman. She lets us keep the costumes, and her pay is really generous."

"She really is," I agree. "I haven't had a chance to thank you for covering me at Tales. You've been incredible, and I know for a fact that Grim's been really impressed with you."

"It's no problem at all! I love dancing there. It's such a rush! You never quite know what's going to happen. Last weekend Beast had to knock out this guy who was catcalling me and the girls during a show. He was drunk as hell and forgot who's club he was sitting in. I don't even think Beast punched him all that hard, but he went down like a sack of potatoes. It was *brilliant!*" she says, enthusiastically. "I'm going to miss working there."

Her face drops, but she hides her disappointment with a smile, and I decide then and there to have a conversation with Grim when I meet up with her later this week as planned. We've been meaning to have a conversation about me coming back to work at Tales, and even though we haven't outright discussed it, I know the guys aren't keen. Truth be known, I'm not sure how I feel about it myself. Despite my promises to the guys and to myself, I still feel anxious about dancing in any capacity right now. I know I need to sort my head out, but it's easier said than done. Today is basically a test to see how I cope, and honestly I'm ninety-five percent certain I'm going to fuck it all up. Regardless, I need to just push through all these warring emotions and get back to some kind of normalcy. Like Grim and the guys have told me countless times, I can't let David get into my head.

"Titch?" York questions, his voice pulling me back to the present and away from my thoughts. "You okay?"

"Sorry, for a moment my head was elsewhere."

"Thinking about how nice it would be to have some alone time, yeah?" Clancy asks with a wink.

"Actually, no. I was thinking about the fact that I'm heading to Tales later this week to speak with Grim about getting back to work, and wondering if you wanted to come with me? Maybe between us we can persuade her to take you on permanently too."

"Really?" Clancy's eyes widen in surprise. "You'd do that for me?"

"Of course I would. She'd be mad not to offer you a job. You're an incredible dancer, Clancy. Plus, it would be good to divide up the weekend shifts. I don't want to be working both weekend nights. It wouldn't be fair to Lena."

Squealing, Clancy places her mug on the side and does a little happy dance. "Oh man, I hope Grim agrees! How cool would that be to get to dance with my bestie all day at the Academy and then work with you at Tales! It's a dream come true."

I laugh at her exuberance, but York just frowns. "You didn't mention anything to us about this."

"I only decided last night. Grim needs me back at work, and I need the money to pay you all back for everything."

"Titch, you don't owe us a thing—" he begins, giving me the same look he did at the funeral when I said that I would pay them back. I know they hate me even bringing up the subject but it's something I just need to do.

"I want to," I reply, cutting him off.

"We'll talk about this later..." York says, clearly not wanting to get into a heated discussion with Clancy looking on. I know this isn't just about the fact I want to pay them back. He's concerned for my safety too, but the security at Tales is tight now so he doesn't need to feel concerned about that side of things anymore.

"Anywaaaaay," Clancy says, pulling a face. "I am so looking forward to getting back in the studio with you guys. It hasn't been much fun rehearsing for the show with bitch-face one and two for company."

"Let me guess, Tiffany and Sophie have been giving you and River a hard time too?"

"Yep, they've been their usual catty selves, of course. River was gonna knock Tiff out last night after she mouthed off about you guys."

"What did she say exactly?" York asks, his voice darkening.

"Oh, just the usual shit. She was bitching about you all having time off. That kind of thing," Clancy says, waving her hand in the air, but I can tell she's holding back. Knowing Tiffany, she would have had a lot more to say about the situation than that.

York takes a seat on Clancy's bed. "I bet she did."

I perch on the mattress next to him whilst Clancy leans against the counter of her little studio kitchen. "I really don't get what her issue is with me."

"I do. You're talented, beautiful and dating the four hottest guys in the Academy," York says with a smirk.

Clancy leans her head to the side, as though thinking about it. "Hmm, three of the hottest," she says with a wink. "I'm not sure about one of them..."

"You best be talking about Dax being the ugly one because we all know *I'm* fucking stunning!"

Clancy rolls her eyes, and I laugh. "So River didn't punch Tiffany then?"

"No. D-Neath stepped in and broke the two of them up."

"*D-Neath* has been at the rehearsals?" I ask, surprised. I figured he's been busy with Hudson, Grim and the guys. I cast a look at York who nods to confirm it, and I wonder why he hasn't been at the meetings with the rest of them, or why they haven't mentioned that.

"Yeah, but he's been distracted. I'm pretty sure D-Neath and Madame Tuillard are on the rocks."

Frowning, I turn my attention back to Clancy. "What makes you say that?"

"Well..." Clancy says, her eyes lighting with mischief. "The other day I passed her office, and they were having one heck of an argument. Like, they weren't screaming at each other or anything, but it was that reigned in kind of argument when they know that someone might hear and they're whisper-shouting."

"Oh yeah? Did you hear what they were arguing about?" York asks nonchalantly, placing his mug of tea on the side table. He's acting like he's not really interested when I can tell that he very much is.

"Bits and pieces. She was going on about him being all secretive and shit. She mentioned that it felt like the first time, or something, and that she deserves to be treated better. I'm pretty sure he's having an affair. It would explain her anger and the fact he's always on his phone. In rehearsals the other night he barely looked up from his bloody phone. It was really annoying actually."

York shrugs. "It's not really any of our business what he gets up to. Tuillard knew what she was getting into when she got together with him. He's hardly got a glowing resumé when it comes to relationships and shit."

"Oooh, Yorky, sounds like you know way more than you're letting on right now. Want to spill?" Clancy grins, pulling the most ridiculous face.

"No more than anyone else," he fires back. "D-Neath has got a reputation. He's a player. Always has been, always will be."

Clancy huffs. "Urgh. Is this some kind of bro-code or something? You do realise that D-Neath, though totally hot and dangerous and all that, is a complete dicknugget of the highest proportions, right? No need to protect him."

York laughs. "I'm not protecting him. I just don't know anything."

"Whatever," Clancy retorts in a faux American accent, dragging out the r before heading towards the bathroom. "I need to pee and sort out my hair before class. Give me five minutes."

As soon as she's locked the door, I turn to York. "Spill!" I demand.

"What?"

"You know what? Is he having an affair?"

"How the fuck would I know? We're not that close."

"Then why have him and Tuillard been arguing?"

"I suspect it's to do with what's going on," York surmises, lowering his voice and flicking his eyes towards the bathroom.

"But, honestly, I really don't care what's up with their relationship, so long as it doesn't fuck anything up for us."

"But he's your friend."

"No, he's an *acquaintance*. We've all been thrown together for the soul purpose of taking down Santiago," York whispers. Not that he needed to bother as Clancy has just started singing *Sexy Back* by Justin Timberlake at the top of her voice and is doing a good job of crucifying the song. It's all I can do not to laugh out loud. I've really, *really* missed her.

"So why has he been overseeing the rehearsals and not meeting with you guys then? Do you suspect D-Neath?"

York shakes his head. "He might be a prick at times, but he's not a complete fool. That would be suicide. Beast would carve him up into little pieces before we ever got close to him."

"Then why?"

"Xeno asked D-Neath to cover the rehearsals. He didn't want things to get behind whilst we were away, and despite the fact that Clancy is right and he's a douche when it comes to matters of the heart..."

"Matters of the dick, you mean?"

"...We trust him," York continues, ignoring my snarky comment. "Besides, Hudson feeds back all the relevant details so he's kept in the loop. That's probably why he's been so distracted on the phone, not because he's having an affair. Though I wouldn't put it past him to be honest. He *is* a player."

"Then maybe you should've thought of someone else to oversee the rehearsals, because according to Clancy he's been doing a terrible job."

"Yeah, you're right. Probably wasn't the wisest decision.

Xeno's not going to be happy when he finds out D-Neath hasn't been pulling his weight."

"Why?"

"What do you mean, why?"

"I mean I get that it's frustrating for everyone, particularly for Clancy and River who are getting pulled into all this bullshit without even knowing it. This performance we've all been working towards is to showcase their talents as much as mine. I can even understand Tiffany and Sophie feeling pissed off, even if I don't like them. But for Xeno...? He's got bigger things to worry about right now than the end of year show at an Academy that he never wanted to be at in the first place. You run your own businesses alongside everything else, this is just another distraction you don't need."

"Believe it or not, this end of year show is important to him, to all of us."

"Because of me?"

York shakes his head. "Yes, of course because of you. This is your chance to shine, Pen. The show will be broadcast across the entire UK. It's going to launch your career. I know it."

"You have a lot of faith in me."

"Of course I do." York sighs, taking my hands in his. "Listen, we came back into your life and fucking steamrolled all over your dreams. We've brought trouble right to your door and we owe it to you to make sure that nothing gets in the way of that."

"David has always been trouble. You didn't bring anything that I didn't already have," I point out.

"We both know that you wouldn't have been back under the spotlight of his attention if we hadn't shown up here. His jealousy has always ruled him when it comes to you and us."

I shake my head. "That's bullshit. He would've turned up and ruined my life eventually."

"No, it's a fact. Why do you think we were all so determined for you to return to the Academy? It wasn't just because of our needs—because honestly we could dance with you anywhere—it's because training and learning the craft here at the Academy was always your dream, Titch. We owe it to you to make sure that you see it through."

He hugs me then, pulling me into his arms, I press my nose against the crook of his neck, breathing him in. "I just hope we haven't made another huge mistake returning to the Academy, and rubbing his nose in it. David's unpredictable. There's no telling what he'll do next."

York is prevented from responding when Clancy steps out of the bathroom mid chorus. She stops singing and places her hands on her hips. "You two really are fucking beautiful to look at. Are you certain you don't need an extra member in your harem?" she asks, a huge grin lighting up her face.

York grabs a pillow from the bed and throws it at her. "You really don't give up, do you?" he asks with a shake of his head and a smile on his lips.

"I'll take that as a no then, shall I?"

"Yes, Clancy. That's a no," he confirms as we head out of the flat.

"You don't sound that certain. A girl could get mixed messages here," she jokes. I throw my arm around her shoulder, laughing at her antics, and try my best not to let the low level anxiety in my stomach bring me down. Stepping back into the studio is going to be as hard as I thought.

18

Pen

"HOW DID THAT FEEL?" York asks as we head out of Studio 5 an hour later.

"Better than I'd hoped," I lie, plastering on a fake smile. Truth be known, for my first real attempt at dancing since everything has happened, it sucked.

York frowns, reaching for my hand, but I fold my arms across my chest, not wanting him to feel how badly being back in a dance studio is affecting me right now. I'm covered in a sheen of sweat, not just from the physicality of dancing but because of my warring emotions, and my hands are shaking uncontrollably. Right now there's this huge expectation to be able to dance like I had before my brother came back into my life like a wrecking ball. The Breakers want me to embrace dance for them, for me, and I want to, so badly, but that other side of me, the newer, more violent part, won't allow me to fully embrace it, not until David's dead.

It's fucked up.

"You aced it, Pen," Clancy says, giving me a warm hug and a huge grin, hiding the fact that it was, in fact, a train wreck.

"You don't need to do that. I know I wasn't at my best. I still got shit to work through," I admit, giving her a weak smile and internally cursing myself. I've never had a problem keeping up with choreo, but in that lesson I couldn't follow the steps. I kept fucking up, too distracted thinking about Lena, about my mum, about my bastard brother and what he's going to do next, about the Breakers' need for me to be that girl they love and failing so fucking spectacularly.

"You'll get there. We all have bad days," she says kindly, squeezing my arm.

"I need to go to the toilet. I'll only be a second," I blurt out, suddenly feeling like I can't fucking breathe. Pushing the door open into the ladies room, I stride into one of the free cubicles, locking the door behind me. Resting my head back against the door, I force myself to suck in oxygen to fight off the black dots spotting my vision. I really, really don't need to pass out right now.

"Hey, Pen, you okay?" Clancy asks, moments later. "York's about to come busting in here."

"I'm good. I just needed to pee!" I say breezily, even though my hands are shaking, and I want to throw up.

"Okay, cool. I'll wait here for you then."

"No, just go to class. I'll catch you later, yeah?"

"You sure?"

"Clancy. I want to pee, and I don't want you hearing me. Go!"

"It's not as if I haven't heard you pee before. So long as you don't need a number two, I'm good," she says, chuckling.

"Clancy!"

"Fine, fine. I get it. You and York are going to have a make out session and you need to get rid of the third wheel," she replies, laughter in her voice. "But you might want to wait until the other person in here finishes up before you get down to it, yeah?"

I groan and roll my eyes even though she can't see through the door. "Tell York to go to class too. I'm good."

"Is that code for, *come on in and take me now, lover boy?*"

"No, Clancy. If I wanted to fuck York I would've just pulled him in here with me."

She bursts out laughing. "Yeah, true. See you later, Pen. I really am so fucking glad you're back."

"Me too," I whisper. "Me too."

When she pushes open the door, I hear York asking her if I'm okay and Clancy telling him not to be so clingy and get off to class. I'm not sure what his response is because the door slams shut, and I'm left with just my thoughts once again. Trouble is, being inside my own head isn't doing me any favours so I pull out my phone from my gym bag and fire off a quick text to Lena asking how she's doing for the hundredth time this morning. Chatting with Lena is the distraction I need, and I'm so relieved when she replies almost instantly.

Lena: Gray is about as entertaining as a pig in mud.

Me: I thought they were your favourite farm

animal?

Lena: Ha ha. I swear he barely talks, let alone smiles. What's his problem?

Me: He's just doing his job. Next week the tutor will be starting. You won't be bored then.

Lena: Oh, fuck... Actually, Gray doesn't seem that bad after all.

Me: I thought you might say that.

Lena: Are you certain I can't go back to school?

Me: Not until this is over.

Lena: I hate this.

Swallowing down the guilt I feel at keeping my sister away from her friends, I heave out a sigh. *Me too, Lena. Me too.*

Me: It's not going to be for long. I promise.

Lena: But you're at school...

Me: With chaperones 24/7. Gray can't follow you into school.

Lena: Neither can David.

Me: I'm sorry, this is just the way it has to be right now. I love you.

For a moment Lena doesn't respond, but just when I'm about to slide my phone back into my gym bag she messages again.

Lena: I know it is. Sorry. I love you too.

Standing, I slide my phone back into my bag, take a pee then unlock the door only to come face to face with Tiffany.

"Well, if it isn't Penelope Scott, and here I was hoping we'd seen the last of your skank arse. I guess we can't always get what we want, now can we?"

"Fuck off, Tiffany. I'm in no mood for you today," I reply, turning on the tap and washing my hands.

Tiffany bites out a laugh, resting her perky arse against the wash basin next to mine. "I heard mummy dearest died."

"Really. You're gonna go there?"

"What were you expecting, *sympathy*? Well, you won't get it from me. Clancy might want to get into your knickers. She might've been crying to River about how your mum took one too many happy pills and how sorry she feels for you, but I really don't give a shit. Boo-fucking-hoo."

"I don't expect a thing from you except this bullshit. You really are messed up, aren't you? Find someone else to bother, because it's getting boring," I say evenly.

Not to be deterred, she continues. "Was your mum that disappointed by her pathetic crotch goblin that she had to get high to forget about you and managed to off herself in the process?"

It's a low blow even for Tiffany. Then again I shouldn't be surprised, she's a cold, calculating bitch that will do whatever she can to hurt me. But if she thinks talking smack about my mum is going to do that, she's barking up the wrong tree. I've built up very thick skin when it comes to my mum. I haven't even cried for her, for fuck's sake. Does she honestly believe a few spiteful, nasty words will get me to break? Now it's my turn to laugh as I level my gaze at her.

"*Crotch goblin*? What are you, five? You're losing your touch, Tiffany. I thought I told you the first day we met that words don't hurt me. Now get out of my way, because I happen to have one of my very delicious, *sexy-as-fuck* boyfriends waiting for me on the other side of that door." Tiffany's fingers wrap around the wash basin, her long red nails scraping across the ceramic as her mouth pinches into a hard line, but still she refuses to move. No bother, I'll just step around her. Swinging my gym bag over my shoulder, I do just that.

"We're not done!" she snarls, her long, slim fingers wrapping around my upper arm.

I roll my eyes at her. Despite her ugly words, and tight grip on my arm, I'm surprisingly calm. Dangerously calm, actually.

"Did you not hear me? Do I need to repeat myself?" I ask, tapping my forefinger hard against her temple. She flinches, but she doesn't let go. I see how it is. If she really is gagging for a fight, then I'll give her one. I'm in no mood to deal with jealous bitches today.

I. Am. Over. It.

"You know what you are, Pen. You're nothing but a *whore* who opens up her legs to get what she wants. We all know Tuillard chose you as the dancer for the marketing gig because you've been *fucking* Xeno. Looks like being a teacher's pet gets you to the top after all, huh?"

"Yeah, yeah. That's right I fucked Xeno to get the gig. This petty jealousy bullshit is really getting boring. Do you seriously not have anything better to do than *try* and upset me?" I ask, making sure to look at her from head to toe and back again with a bored expression.

"You fucking bitch!" she exclaims, her face reddening. She hates the fact that she's not able to get to me and it just makes me smile harder.

"Yeah, yeah, I've heard it all before. It's all just water off a duck's back..." I say, wiping off imaginary lint from my shoulder. "The truth of the matter is, I've got bigger fish to fry than spend any more energy on some jealous bitch who can't stand the fact that I'm a better dancer, better *person*, who has not one but *four* hot as hell boyfriends who love *me*. It's no wonder you're bitter. You're so fucking *ugly* that no one wants to have anything to do with you except for Sophie who has the personality of a gnat."

Tiffany releases me with a shove, spinning away from me to hide her expression. "What's the matter, Tiffany? You can dish it out but can't take it?"

"Fuck you, Pen." Her voice is quiet, and I swear I hear it crack like she's about to cry. I don't know if it's that or the fact her shoulders start to shake that makes me pause.

"Look..." I begin, heaving out a sigh, all of my anger draining out of me at her sudden show of weakness. "We'll never be friends, but I am done with this shit between us. I don't know what the fuck I did to make you hate me, and honestly, I don't care, but I'm willing to let all this go if we just remain civil. We have a routine to perform together with the rest of the troupe for the end of year show and we need to be tight. We don't have to like each other, but we do have to work together. Let's just call it quits, yeah?" It's an olive branch, one she doesn't fucking deserve, but I offer it to her regardless.

Her shoulders start to shake even more, and her head drops as she leans over the sink. I reach for her automatically, that part of me who gives a shit about people feeling sorry that she's so upset. "Don't cry," I say, but she turns around to face me.

She isn't crying, she's *laughing*.

When her eyes fix on me, I see something all too familiar. It's the same look my mum and David used to give me. It makes my skin turn cold. Tiffany doesn't just hate me, she *despises* me. She steps closer as I back off, and her silent laugh gets louder and louder until she's cackling like some fucked up evil witch about to slide a poisonous knife into my heart.

"You really haven't got a fucking clue, have you?" she asks, clutching her stomach and wheezing with black laughter.

"A clue about what?"

"He'll get tired of you eventually."

"Who Xeno? Dax? Zayn? Or wait, is it York that you want? Because you've been all over every one of them like a fucking bitch in heat since the moment we started here. It doesn't matter though, none of them want you, Tiffany. They're *mine*."

That just makes her laugh harder. I know I should walk out and leave her to it, but for some reason my feet are stuck to the floor and I can't move. Behind me the door to the bathroom swings open and York steps in.

"What the fuck is going on in here?" he asks, looking between us both. It doesn't take long for him to figure out that Tiffany is being her usual nasty self. "Tiffany, what the fuck is wrong with you? Move the fuck on, will you. This bullshit lady-boner you've got for Titch is getting tedious."

"Honestly, York, just leave it. She's finally lost it," I say, pushing against York's chest at the same time as I open the door. I can see he wants to say and do a lot more, but I don't need him jumping to my defence and getting into shit for it.

"Lost it?" Tiffany hisses. "The only person who's going to lose everything is you, Pen. *I'm* the best dancer in this Academy and *I'm* going to be the one to win the solo dance. You'll just be some distant memory once *I'm* on centre stage."

"You're fucking delusional," York snaps.

"And you're fucking ruled by your *dick*!" Tiffany screams back, the veins in her neck standing rigid against her skin. She's got barely enough fat covering her to hide them. In fact, she looks painfully thin. Sick almost. My momentary sympathy, however, is lost when she starts spouting more shit. "You think you're so special don't you, huh? Prancing around the Academy like you own the place. Sucking up to every single teacher to get what you want. Even Sebastian, our *gay-boy* ballet teacher has a fucking hard-on for you."

"You sad little bitch," York says, shaking his head, because she really is just that. The girl's got issues.

"You can't talk," she snaps, glaring at York. "She's got you wrapped around her little finger. Talk about pussy-whipped."

York throws his head back and laughs. "If you're calling this pussy-whipped then I'm gonna bend over and take every last, arse-stinging lash and fucking *love* it."

"You pig!" Tiffany hisses "You'd do anything for her, wouldn't you? You disgust me."

"What can I say? I'm talented like that. It takes a real woman to know how to please her men," I say with a grin that just infuriates her further.

"Talented at twisting people up inside so all they can do is think about you, you mean!"

"Talking from experience, are we?" York asks, scoffing.

"I don't get it," she sneers. "You're nothing but a worthless, dirty, little, street-rat whore. You were never meant for the stage. No one wants to watch *you* dance..."

She drones on and on, her barbs and spiteful words familiar. I've heard them all before from my mum and David over the years. They hit home, but not in the way she wants them to. They don't hurt me. In fact, they do the complete opposite. It's like a switch has been flicked back on and I'm vibrating not with anger, but with the realisation that I *can* do this, that I can still fight back *and* dance, I step into Tiffany's personal space and reach up to cup her cheeks in my palms. She stills, her eyes blazing with righteous anger and surprise.

"Thank you," I say, stroking her cheekbones with the pad of my thumbs.

"What?" she whispers out, disbelief paling her skin.

"Thank you. I needed to be reminded how that feels."

"How *what* feels?"

"To feel hated as much as you hate me."

"That makes no sense," she mutters as I lean in closer, my lips brushing against hers in a gentle kiss. She gasps, and I grin as I pull back.

"I keep telling you that words don't hurt me, all they do is fuel my fire, my passion to prove to myself that I AM WORTHY. All you've done with your little jealous outburst, Tiffany, is show me that I *am* worthy of these men. I am worthy of my place here at the Academy, and I'm sure as fuck worthy of that spot centre stage. So keep on spitting out your bile if it makes you feel better, but know this, it only makes me *more* determined, not less."

"I will ruin you!" she spits, but it's half-hearted and lacks the fire from before.

"Bring. It. The. Fuck. On!" I respond with a grin, and thanks to Tiffany I leave the bathroom with a new resolve burning in my chest. I came here to prove that I'm a good dancer, but I'm going to leave here the best dancer this Academy has ever seen, and not my brother, not the memories of my mum's hate, or that bitch Tiffany are going to stop me.

19

Dax

PEN SWIPES the sweat dripping from her brow and scowls. She looks so fucking sexy all sweaty and wound up, determined to get me on my back.

"Come at me again," she demands, a fierce concentration on her face as she stands on the training mat in the corner of the gym that's situated on the lower ground floor of the Academy. It's barely used, most of the students are fit enough already from the gruelling lessons each day and don't bother coming down here, which has been great for us. Plenty of privacy to run through some basic self-defence over the past few days since we've been back.

I shake my head. "That's enough for one day. We've been training for the past hour and Madame Tuillard wants us to do a run-through of the final dance at six. You need to conserve a bit of energy. Now that we're back she wants to see how much we've caught up."

"That's comical, what with Tiffany acting like a complete spoiled brat and Sophie following her lead every rehearsal, the group dance is whack. I really don't know how we're going to pull it off. Those two hate me so much they're willing to ruin it for everyone, including themselves. It's bullshit."

"Precisely why Tuillard wants to see a run-through. If Tiffany wants to continue to throw a hissy fit she might just find herself thrown out of the troupe for good."

"Really?"

"Yeah, really. Xeno messaged me earlier today after he met with Tuillard and D-Neath this morning. Tuillard's pissed off. This is her arse on the line and if we can't be tight for the show, then it's going to make her, and the Academy look bad."

"Then tell her to sort out Tiffany. Fuck knows I hate the bitch, but at least I'm willing to put that aside for the sake of the show."

"Which is precisely why you're the better dancer," I say, stepping towards her and reaching down to cup her beautiful arse, but she whacks my arm away with one hand before attempting to hit my chin with an elbow strike, just like we've been practising.

"It's like that is it?" I laugh because unfortunately for Pen, she's not tall enough to reach my face without leaping up in the air to get a good hit in, allowing me to jerk back from her attempt. She lets out a frustrated cry as I grasp her around the waist and flip her around so that her back is pressed against my chest. When I have her firmly held in place, I lean over and press my lips to her ear, "You're turning me on. If we don't leave now, I might just fuck you right here in the gym."

She chuckles. "Then let me go."

"No can do," I reply, tightening my hold around her waist and pressing a kiss against her bare shoulder. I'm fully aware I'm taking advantage, but our training session is over, and I want to pleasure my girl before our torturous fucking rehearsal later.

"Then I'll just have to make you," she mutters, shifting her hips to one side and slamming the palm of her hand against my groin. She catches my rapidly hardening dick, and even though she has the tiniest hands, it feels as though she's just hit me with a sledgehammer.

"Fuck!" I groan, my arms loosening around her waist as I double over from the pain. She uses the opportunity to twist beneath my arm then slam her knee into my stomach, winding me momentarily. The combination of my balls shrinking back into my body, and her perfect hit on my diaphragm has the desired effect. I drop to my knees like a motherfucking sack of potatoes.

"Shit! Fuck! Are you okay?" Kid asks me as she crouches down. I can hear the laughter in her voice, and whilst my own pride takes a battering, I'm also fucking proud of her. She's a quick learner.

"I've just been taken out by a 5ft 3inch pocket-rocket. My cock isn't the only thing feeling bruised right now."

"Oh, Dax, I'm sorry. Can you stand? Should I get you ice or something?"

"I'm not sure. I might need help getting up."

She reaches for me, her hands resting on my shoulders. The moment her guard is down, I pitch forward, knocking her off balance. As soon as she's on her back, I'm straddling her waist and pinning her arms above her head, grinning mercilessly. "First rule of self-defence. Once your attacker is down, you run. Understand?"

"But you're not my attacker, you're my boyfriend and I hurt your cock. I happen to like that cock. It does special things to me." She bites on her lip provocatively and my cock jumps to life like the good soldier it is. It doesn't give a fuck if it's feeling a little bruised, when it thinks it's getting lucky, it stands to motherfucking attention.

A slow grin spreads across my face as I lower myself over her. "Is that so?" I ask, keeping her arms in place with one hand whilst I shift my weight between her parted legs and lower my mouth to hers. Pressing a gentle kiss against her lips, I slide my tongue along the seam. She groans into my mouth, her hips bucking as I kiss her deeply.

"I really do love your cock. I'm sorry I hurt it, and your ego," she says, smiling against my lips.

"And my cock loves your sweet, tight pussy," I reply, branding her neck with kisses and wishing we had more than one measly hour until the rehearsal.

Ever since that night back at the flat, I've been permanently turned on. Pen had been so damn sexy and brave sharing her secret desires with us all. It was fucking insane what York and I did, but in some ways inevitable. We've toed the line between friendly banter and out and out flirtation for years now. I love the jerk, like I love Zayn and Xeno, and even though I would never dream of entertaining anything sexual between just the two of us, when Kid had dared us to kiss and jerk each other off, I knew that I wouldn't turn her down. If I can beat someone to death with my bare hands, then I can make my best friend come for the girl I love more than anything in the world.

Letting her wrists go, I slide my hand under the waistband of her legging and knickers and slip my fingers between the plump folds of her slit. "Fuck, you're so wet."

"Oh God," she groans as I find her clit and gently circle the nub. Her hips buck, seeking out the pleasure, whilst my mouth latches onto her neck and I suck, marking her with my mouth.

"You keep making those noises and I'm not going to last long enough to slide inside of you," I say, my voice hoarse. I'm not even remotely joking either, I can feel the telltale sign of my balls tingling. There's no way I'm coming in my boxers, my poor ego and dick would never live it down.

"Then what are you waiting for?" she asks breathily, her hand sliding between us as she rubs my cock through my trousers. I groan, grinding against her hand and wishing I wasn't still wearing clothes.

"I need us both to be naked, right the fuck now."

"What if someone walks in?" she asks, her chest heaving from excitement and probably a dash of fear.

"I locked the door. No one's coming in," I reassure her as I cup her breast and slide the material of her vest top and sports bra lower to reveal the tight pink bud of her nipple.

"You did...? Someone might think you planned this..." She pants, gasping when my lips wrap around her nipple and I suck it into the wet warmth of my mouth. She wriggles beneath me, her hand finding its way beneath my joggers and boxer shorts. When her warm fingers slide over the head of my cock and her thumb smears precum over the tip, I swear to fuck I almost jizz then and there. That tingling sensation gathering in my balls and lower spine intensifies.

"Kid, I need to be inside of you."

"Yes, please," she replies, smiling up at me whilst removing her hand from my dick so that she can wiggle out of her leggings and knickers. I rear upwards on unsteady feet, and jog over to my gym bag, snatching a condom from the side zip, before shucking off my trainers, joggers and boxer shorts. My cock bobs between my legs, long and thick and fucking proud as I stride back towards her.

"Kid, I'm gonna ask you not to judge me on this occasion, because I'm so fucking turned on I might just come in 2.5 seconds flat," I say, ripping the foil with my teeth and sliding the condom over my cock in one smooth move. Pen giggles as she lies bare before me, her sweet pussy on display.

"I really hope that's a euphemism for *quick, dirty sex that's going to blow my mind*."

"That's exactly what this is going to be," I reply, her gorgeous brown eyes drinking me in as I rip off my t-shirt and get fully naked. "Though I'm not selfish enough to fulfil my own needs until you've come long and hard first, screaming my motherfucking name."

Kid's cheeks flush a deep rouge, matching the inner lips of her pussy that I want to feast on, right the fuck now. She presses her thighs together, her pupils blown wide as she stares up at me. Having her look at me like this, like I'm the centre of her universe and so fucking loved makes me want to get down on my knees and beg her to be my wife. The only thing stopping me is three other men who love her as wholly and deeply as I do. Once this shit is over, we're gonna need to figure out how we move forward with this relationship between the five of us, make a commitment to each other. I don't even know how that will work, but I want it to.

"I really hope that there are no cameras in here," she says, oblivious to my roaming thoughts as her cheeks blush furiously.

"There aren't. I checked that too."

"You really have come prepared."

"I'm always hopeful," I mutter, kneeling between her parted legs, and grinning wryly as my hands smooth over her thighs.

"I'll never get tired of looking at your body. All that artwork. It's beautiful," she says as I lean over her, my hands either side of her head. She reaches up and runs her fingers over the fallen angel tattooed on my chest. Her touch makes the fire inside me burn bright, it's a flame that has never gone out. Even when we weren't together it was still there deep in my chest, a flicker that I tried hard to ignore. I've always had this need to protect her and that hasn't changed. It cuts me up inside, what he's been doing to her. Fuck! If David so much as touches a hair on her head...

"Dax?" she whispers, stroking my face, drawing me back to her. She both calms me and turns me on, it's a combination that has my heart thrumming and my cock weeping. Shaking my head, I rid myself of thoughts of her cunt brother and concentrate on her instead, allowing my gaze to slide from her face and over her body to where my cock is resting against her mound. "Where did you go?"

"I was just thinking about how much I fucking love you," I say, sliding my dick through her folds. I can't help but watch the angry red head of my cock as it slides between her plump pussy lips. She looks too, her mouth parting as she drinks me in.

"That really is a weapon of mass destruction," she says, lovingly trailing her fingers over the head of my cock. It weeps for her, bobbing at her touch.

I chuckle, trying my best to concentrate on her funny sense of humour and not her fingers teasing my cock. "Whatever it is, my dick is all yours. I'm all yours. *Forever*," I rasp as she reaches between us and plays with my balls. "Fuck, Kid. Don't do that. I'm going to lose it." She pulls her fingers away, her cheeks flushing with lust and a little bit of pride. I love that my reaction to her makes her feel good about herself.

"I have so many dirty thoughts when it comes to you all," she says, her warm, gentle fingers trailing up the v-muscle I work so damn hard on maintaining. "Sometimes I think that I'm a bit of a pervert," she admits, biting on her lower lip in that way that drives me fucking crazy.

"There's nothing dirty about fancying your men. I'd be worried if you didn't have dirty thoughts about us or fantasies you wanted to fulfil," I say, grasping the base of my dick. I lock eyes with her and smile as I run the head of my cock gently over her clit. She makes a sweet sound that goes straight to my dick. "The amount of times I've imagined you tied up and at my mercy..."

"You want to tie me up?" she pants, her face open, not judgemental.

"Ever heard of Shibari?" I ask, torturing us both slowly as I rub up and down her slit.

"No?"

"It's the ultimate act of trust. I tie you up with rope..." I say, pressing a kiss against her collarbone, "...Until you can't move. Then I make you come, over and over again."

"Oh God," she moans, grinding her pussy against my dick.

My cock aches at the spiralling tension. She gets wetter with every stroke of my dick, coating my cock in her juices as her skin flushes with heat. I can't hold back any longer.

"Please, Dax," she begs, lifting her hips and telling me with her body what she can't seem to manage fully with words right now.

"Fuck, I love you so damn much," I confess, not able to deny her a thing, especially this. Sliding into her slowly, I relish the feel of her tight warmth, only giving as much as she can take.

"Dax..." Her mouth pops open as her eyelids flutter shut. "I love you too. Sometimes it scares me just how much."

"You never, ever need to be afraid of loving me, Kid," I say before kissing her deeply.

Our tongues dance, a slow, sensual exploration of each other's mouth. With every second that passes, her body relaxes, accommodating my length, allowing me to ease inside of her, inch by excruciating inch, until I'm fully seated. Settling there, I cup Kid's cheeks, my teeth gently biting on her bottom lip before I release it.

Staring up at me, Kid smiles. "What?" she whispers.

"When I'm with you, joined like this, I feel like I'm finally whole. Do you know what I mean?"

"I do," she pants, her hips gyrating gently beneath me, her legs wrapped around my back.

For two people so very different in size, we fit like we were made for each other. It's fucking beautiful how perfect she is, how perfect we are, *all* of us together.

"Dax, please, fuck me," she says breathlessly.

Pressing another kiss against her mouth, I start to move,

edging slowly out, then sliding back in. With every stroke of my cock, her pussy fists me tight, her walls clamping down as we kiss with building passion, the previous sensuality we shared replaced with hunger. Her fingers grasp my arse as she pushes up to meet me stroke for stroke. Our teeth clash, our tongues duel as I fuck her with even, steady thrusts.

"Yes, like that," she whimpers, her tongue sliding across my collarbone, her teeth biting down. the sharp pain mixing with the growing pleasure.

Cupping the back of her head, I hold her against me then slam into her, giving into my basic need to fuck, wildly and freely. With every thrust she cries out, clutching, clawing at me, begging me to make her come. So I do just that. I drive into her sweet, tight pussy and I fuck her with all the love I feel inside until we're both screaming each other's name.

20

Pen

"ENOUGH! What's going on? That was a mess!" Tuillard shouts, slamming her hands on her hips as she glares at us all.

She's not wrong. This whole routine *is* a mess, and it isn't for lack of trying, at least not on our part. Tiffany just doesn't want to make it work, at least not for the benefit of the rest of us. Rather than dancing as part of a troupe, she's intent on getting all the attention and fucking up the synchronicity to do it. Even Sophie, her sidekick, seems to have had enough. All through rehearsal she's been throwing glares Tiffany's way when she thinks she isn't looking. Of course, Sophie would never call her out on her bullshit directly. That's the problem siding with a bitch like Tiffany, you turn your back on someone like that and you're their next victim. It's a shame, because despite the fact Sophie is clearly a sheep that lacks a spine, she *is* a good dancer.

Madame Tuillard shakes her head and points at Tiffany, her eyes blazing with fury. "I want a word with you."

Tiffany rolls her eyes and strolls to the front of the class, placing her hands on her hips as she stares Tuillard down. I've seen Tiffany act this way towards me and anyone else she hates, but I've never seen her look at Madame Tuillard in the same way. She's most definitely losing her mind.

"Is there a problem, Madame Tuillard?" she asks, her voice dripping with sarcasm. She manages to sneak in a glare at me and I just shake my head. For someone who badly wants to get the solo dance, she's going about it the wrong way.

"A problem? Of course there's a problem. You've spent the entire routine trying everything in your power to mess it up. You need to put your overinflated ego aside and shape up, young lady, or you will very quickly find yourself out of the show altogether."

I catch Clancy's eye and she pulls a face, surreptitiously crossing her fingers behind her back whilst she mouths the words we're all thinking. "Fucking, *please*."

"My overinflated ego?" Tiffany replies, her skin blanching.

"Yes. If you hadn't noticed, this is a *group* dance. There is no single dancer here who owns the spotlight. This dance will only come together as Xeno and Zayn have envisioned if everyone, *including* you, work as a troupe."

Tiffany huffs, folding her skinny arms across her chest. "What about her?" she asks, pointing her finger at me.

"What about Pen?" Madame Tuillard counters.

"Well *she* seems to get away with being centre fucking stage in every goddamn routine so far. So why the fuck can't I?"

Madame Tuillard shakes her head, disappointment written

across her face. She sighs heavily. "Am I really having to deal with jealousy here, is that it, Tiffany?"

"I am not fucking jealous!" she screams, stamping her foot like a five year old.

"Fuck me, what *is* she doing?" River mutters under his breath as the rest of us watch this car crash unfold. "She's a crazy bitch, but she's never lost it like this before."

"I've seen jealousy tear careers apart. Don't be that person," Madame Tuillard says calmly. "You're an exceptional dancer in your own right, but that doesn't mean to say I will allow you to sabotage this routine just to spite someone you dislike. You must maintain professionalism at all times regardless of how you feel inside."

"Really? If that's the case why is Mr Tyson, a *teacher* at this Academy, fucking one of his students then, huh? Why have you turned a blind eye to that?" Tiffany counters.

"It's not as if you haven't tried to get into his pants often enough, sweetheart," Dax interrupts with a scathing look. "Just because he turned you down multiple times and hurt your feelings, doesn't mean to say you get to throw shade at Kid like that. So why don't you do us all a favour, stop the tantrum bullshit, suck it the fuck up and dance!"

Tiffany snorts, scowling as she levels her stare at Dax. If looks could kill, he'd be ten feet under by now, and even though I know Tiffany is no match for him or any of my Breakers, I know a woman scorned when I see one, and that makes her unpredictable, dangerous even.

"Of course you'd stick up for her! Clearly the four of you don't mind sharing skank-arse pussy!"

"Shut up, Tiffany!" Clancy says, shaking her head in disgust.

"Don't you dare," Tiffany retorts, her face all twisted up and bitter. The prominent bones of her ribcage slide beneath her too loose skin as she glares at Clancy. "You're no better, following her around like some lovesick puppy. She's a fucking tease. Pen will never fuck you!"

"Who's got the popcorn?" York jokes, winking at me.

"You should calm down, Tiffany," Xeno says with barely restrained anger. A muscle leaps in his jaw as he bites back the words he really wants to say. I think I know him well enough to know that *bitch*, and *get the fuck out of here* are just a moment away.

"Don't tell me to calm down, *Mr Tyson*," she spits, her chest heaving.

"This clearly isn't getting us anywhere today, Tiffany. I think you should—" Madame Tuillard pauses as D-Neath enters the studio.

"What did I miss?" he asks, something flickering in his gaze as he looks between the two.

Tiffany tips her head back and laughs. "What have you missed...? *Fucking everything.*"

"Okay, well then..." he pulls a face, amusement and a dash of something else shading his features. He gives Madame Tuillard a smile, his gold tooth glinting in the overhead lights. She doesn't smile back.

"Duncan, what can I do for you?" Madame Tuillard asks, pinching the bridge of her nose in exasperation.

"Nothing. I'm just checking in."

"Don't you have *more important* things you need to be getting on with?" she counters.

"Not tonight, no."

"Okay, fine, back to the point in hand," Madame Tuillard says, focussing back on Tiffany. "You will remember that at the beginning of term I said that any issues there might be between dancers is kept off the stage. Either you work with us or you don't at all. It's your choice."

"You're giving me an ultimatum?" Tiffany scoffs, pressing a bony finger into her chest.

"You aren't giving me a choice. The only problem we appear to have right now, is you. Either you pull yourself together or we'll replace you in the show. It's as simple as that. What's it to be?"

For a moment Tiffany is too shocked to retaliate, which is laughable given everything she's done to sabotage this dance and her own career. Then she breathes in deeply, her nostrils flaring before turning her attention to me. Her expression is livid, her hate for me seeping out of every pore. "I will not dance with that bitch one fucking moment longer."

"Then I guess you've made your choice because Pen is staying in the troupe. Gather your stuff and leave the studio. The rest of us have work to do," Madame Tuillard says, folding her arms across her chest.

"Gladly!" Tiffany spits, striding over to the other side of the studio. She grabs her gym bag and motions to Sophie. "Come on. Let's go."

Sophie looks at her with wide eyes. "Tiffany..."

"Now!"

Sophie shakes her head. "No. I'm staying." Her voice is quiet but firm.

Tiffany's fingers curl tightly around the strap of her gym bag. We all watch as she leans over and whispers something into Sophie's ear. The girl's face pales, all the blood rushing from her skin. Whatever Tiffany's *threatened,* it's clearly spooked her.

"Hey, leave Sophie out of this. She doesn't need to suffer because of you," I say, stepping in. I don't owe Sophie shit, but I won't stand about and watch the bitch torment someone else because she refuses to step in line.

"I don't need you to stick up for me," Sophie says, suddenly growing a backbone. She looks back at Tiffany and says, "I'm done Tiff. This is my career, my future, and I won't throw it away because of you."

"You think they'll accept you now?" Tiffany laughs, jerking backwards.

"I'm not here to make friends. I'm here to dance. That's what I should've been doing all along," Sophie mutters back, but Tiffany is no longer interested in what she has to say.

"And you!" she snaps, rounding on me.

"Yes?" Zayn moves to stand in front of me as she approaches, but I step out from behind him and rest my hand against his arm. "Let her say what she needs to say."

"That's it, move aside like a good little boy. She's got you all trained so fucking well, hasn't she?" Tiffany snarls before leaning in and whispering in my ear. "This isn't over."

I just laugh, stepping back. "Yes, it *is*. Get out of here, Tiffany."

Shoving past me, Tiffany strides across the room stopping in front of Madame Tuillard. "I was offered a spot at the Royal Academy of Dance yesterday. I was going to stay here and help this shithole of an Academy get the good press it so desperately needs, but do you know what? I really don't give a fuck anymore. You can shove your scholarship up your old, *frigid* arse."

If Madame Tuillard is upset by her words, she doesn't show it, instead she's resolute. "Goodbye Tiffany. I wish you well."

River's mouth drops open in shock. "Did you know?" he asks Clancy.

"About the Royal Academy? No clue. We're not exactly close. Fuck, I hate being related to that bitch."

"Imagine *choosing* her as a friend, probably not the wisest move of the century," Zayn comments, sliding his gaze to Sophie who's currently staring off into the distance looking like she's about to throw up.

Madame Tuillard huffs out a breath, then plasters on a smile. "Right then, shall we start from the top?" Her gaze falls on me and she gives me a nod. It's a simple gesture, one of solidarity. I dip my head, silently thanking her because, unlike Tiffany, I won't turn my back on the woman who gave me an opportunity to fulfil my dreams.

"Actually, I think we should pick this up again in our next rehearsal session. Start fresh then," Xeno suggests.

"Yes, fine," Madame Tuillard concedes without argument. "We need to find another dancer to replace Tiffany anyway. I'll have a think about who would be most suitable, and let you know tomorrow."

"It's not your fault," D-Neath says. "You couldn't have dealt with that situation any better *mi cielo*. Don't beat yourself up. Tiffany was a fucking pain in the arse. Much better this way."

He reaches for her, but she steps away from his touch, folding her arms across her chest in a defensive gesture.

"That's not helpful, Duncan," Madame Tuillard snaps, her professional mask slipping momentarily. "I've just lost a very talented student. It's a blow to the Academy. You may not seem to appreciate that, but I do. This show, the *Academy*, is important to me as you well know."

"Oh, come on, she might've been talented but let's get real, no one liked her. She was a stuck-up bitch. It's a fucking relief to be rid of her, am I right?" D-Neath asks, turning his attention back to the rest of us, and even though he *is* right, not one of us agrees with him. Instead, we all gather our things and leave.

21

Pen

"ANOTHER DRINK?" Grim asks me as I sit, propping up the bar in Tales a week later.

"No. I'm good, thanks," I say, taking a sip of the drink she poured for me twenty minutes ago.

It's seven in the evening and the club won't open for another couple of hours yet, but I don't feel like getting drunk.

"How's Lena doing? She seems in good form today..." Grim says, smiling as she watches Lena talk a mile a minute at Gray who is doing his best to focus on her and not the dancers practising their routine. Clancy is currently taking them through the choreo we came up with together after Grim agreed to hire her. His eyes keep slipping back to the dancers and I hear Lena's sharp voice snapping his name.

"Gray! Would you listen? Jeez, show a man some tits and

arse and he turns into a mindless hard-on," Lena says in that snarky way of hers that she's perfected.

Grim laughs, walking out from behind the bar and sitting on the stool next to me. "She's just like you, Pen. Full of fucking spunk."

"I bloody hope not," I reply with a laugh. "That would be a concern."

Grim's face pales. "I meant as in feisty, not as in cum."

"I know you did. I'm just joking." Taking another sip of my drink I watch Lena's exuberance and allow myself a small smile. "She's taking it upon herself to be the one to crack Gray's professional facade. Focusing on pushing his buttons is helping her to forget the shitty situation she's in. So far she's not doing a very good job at it. He's a tough nut to crack."

"Oh, I don't know. Gray's not the type of guy to put up with teenage tantrums. I think he likes her."

"He tolerates her for sure. He's very good at his job. Thank you for choosing him."

"Hey, only the best for my friend and her little sister. Seriously though, how is she really doing?"

"Not good, despite how she seems on the surface," I reply, watching her laugh at some cold remark from Gray. I don't think I've ever seen him smile or say more than a few words to her. But like me she's stubborn and won't rest until he reacts either positively or negatively to her efforts. She'll keep on poking until he has no choice but to respond. "Nightmares. Every night without fail."

Grim nods. "And living with you and the Breakers? Is that not helping?"

"It's not home, at least not her home, not yet anyway. I'm

hoping that will change as time goes on." I chew on the inside of my cheek, tasting blood. "The guys are great with her though, and she wants for nothing... Except her mum of course."

"Your mum too. She wasn't the only person to lose someone," Grim says, watching me closely. "In my experience, no matter how much you love *or* loathe a person, you feel their absence regardless. That's especially true of a parent."

"Not for me."

Reaching for my hand, she wraps her cool fingers around mine. "By the time Beast brought me my father's heart, I hated my father passionately."

"But you shot Beast because of what he did."

Grim pulls a face. "He went against my explicit request, and at the time we were having this power play tug-of-war... Anyway," she says, waving her hand in the air. "My point is, my father wasn't the man I thought he was and every notion I had about him was shattered by his betrayal. Didn't stop me from missing him though. Love is fucked up like that."

Sighing heavily, I wince. "She was never a mum to me. I never loved her."

"Sometimes love and hate are so tightly wrapped up in each other that it's impossible to tell the difference. But you do know that it *is* okay to feel love for someone who was cruel, who hurt you, especially when they're your parent. It doesn't make you weak, Pen, it makes you human."

Grim's words are kind but they pack a punch that winds me, and for a moment I find I can't breathe all that well. Her thumb rubs my knuckles as she waits for me to absorb her words, to let them truly sink in, and a memory that I've buried for years suddenly filters to the surface of my consciousness. I take a deep breath and blow it out slowly.

"When I was around five, before mum got pregnant with Lena, we went to the local park. It was summer and I remember I was wearing this white dress with red strawberries printed all over it. It was the only item of clothing I had that wasn't second hand. I loved it. The day before it had rained heavily after weeks of blistering heat, and mum took us both out to enjoy the cooler weather."

Grim cocks her head to the side. "Sounds like a happy memory, was it?"

"Yes and no," I admit. "It's been a long, long time since I've thought about that day." Grim nods, but doesn't say anything. Instead she waits for me to continue. "David was being his usual mean self and when I walked past this huge muddy puddle, he decided to push me into it. I fell face forward into the mud. The dress was ruined. I remember David taunting me, laughing."

"What happened then?"

"Mum was furious and when she strode over to us both her fingers were curled into fists with anger. I remember clutching the material of my mud-soaked skirt in my hands and dropping my head, waiting for the slap to come. It never did. Instead, mum told off David then hauled me up into her arms, not caring that she got covered in mud too. She *hugged* me. She let me cry and she held me like a mother should. It was the first and last time she ever gave me affection. I clung onto her for as long as she would let me."

"Pen..." Grim begins, her voice trailing off as I shake my head.

"At that moment, I had loved her. I had loved the mum she

was in those five minutes. Even when I buried that memory deep down inside, I held onto the hope that one day she would return. It's the only fond memory I have of her..."

"There's more, right?" Grim gives me a sad look.

"Isn't there always?"

"With parents like ours? Yes, yes there is," she agrees.

"That day there had been a good looking man with fair hair and light eyes watching us at the park. I remember her flirting with him for hours and all that time she was the best mum I'd ever known. Nine months after that, Lena was born." I fix my gaze on Grim, and heave out a sigh. "That five minutes of kindness she'd shown me wasn't because she loved me, or even cared that I was upset. It was for that man's benefit, not mine. The sad thing is, I would've done anything to have that woman as my mum, even if it was only a pretence. I loved *that* woman, the lie, but I've hated the real version my whole life."

"I'm sorry, Pen."

"Don't be, because that experience made me understand what true love is. What I feel for Lena, for the guys, *that* is love and right now I'm focussing on that. When I see Lena sad I just want to take away the pain so she can be happy. I want to be that woman who picked up a little girl in her mud-splattered dress and make her *real*."

"You're already so much more than that," Grim says.

"Thank you, I appreciate you saying that..." My voice trails off as I move my gaze from Grim to Clancy who's currently running through the second half of the routine we're going to perform this weekend. She's been an amazing friend and taken up some of the slack whilst I've juggled being a parent to Lena and dealing with her emotional needs.

"Clancy's good at what she does. I'm glad you persuaded me to hire her," Grim remarks, watching Clancy as she high fives the dancers. "Her personality is infectious."

"It is. Thank you for hiring her. I'm sorry I can't do more right now."

"You've no need to thank me or apologise. Clancy is an asset and you're my friend. This works for all of us. Are you certain you're good to perform this weekend? You know I won't push you to come back until you're ready. *If ever...*" She adds that last part as a friend who understands that I have four boyfriends who are struggling right now with my decision to return to work.

"Yeah. I am. I need to get back out there, for me as much as anyone else. Besides, this place is locked up tight with all the security now. I feel safe here with you all, despite the slightly nefarious characters who walk through the doors to this club every night."

"Slightly?" Grim laughs. "Seriously, Pen, I wouldn't be offended if you wanted to drop this gig altogether. It'd hurt my purse, but not my heart," she says, taking a sip of her tea as we watch Clancy and the girls rehearse.

"Good to know, but despite everything, I *like* dancing here." We fall silent, and just watch Clancy and the girls run through one of the best routines we've put together so far. It's going to be amazing, and yet I can't fully enjoy that fact because no matter how much I try to push thoughts of my brother aside, he's always there in the back of my head, taunting me.

"You know, I keep expecting David to jump out of every dark corner," I say after a while. "I hate the fact he's out there somewhere just waiting to make his next move."

"That's understandable, but you have to know that we'd never let anything happen to you or Lena, right?"

"I do know that. The guys are on high alert twenty-four seven. They're trying to hide it, but I know how stressed they all are. It feels like we can never catch a break. Ever since we've known each other, we've gone from one crisis to another. I don't see an end in sight."

"They love you, Pen. They're not going to rest until your brother is dead and Santiago is behind bars. I don't think any of us will..." Her voice trails off as she taps her finger on the bar counter, a thoughtful look crossing her face.

"Then why does it feel like we're just sitting ducks? He has the upper hand, Grim."

"Hudson has *every* avenue he can think of covered. Between us, we've hired more ghosts to protect the clubs we own just in case David or Santiago send another crew in an attempt to take us down. Interpol have upped their surveillance. Not to mention your boys have stepped up and gone into protective mode."

"I'm not being funny, but Interpol doesn't seem to be doing much at all, other than taking ages to find out anything."

"It's an issue. Doing everything correctly according to the law takes time. There's a lot of red tape to cut and bullshit legal documents to get in place before they can even take a shit, let alone start pulling hundreds of hours of CCTV footage from across various areas of London."

"But they hid what Zayn did. So really, what's the big deal?"

"Your Breakers made a very tight deal with Interpol that meant they couldn't be arrested for any unlawful activity whilst working on this case, including killing someone in self-defence, which is why Zayn literally got away with murder. Believe it or not, covering up a crime is a lot easier than dealing with various police forces and council departments over differing London boroughs to gather CCTV footage. It's likely that David travelled quite a distance that night he murdered your mum, and that means several different warrants need to be raised for each local authority before they can even access the CCTV footage."

"I didn't realise it was so complicated."

"If it isn't handled correctly then the whole operation could be put at risk. There are too many people who can blow the whistle. Plus, hours of manpower is needed to trawl through the tapes, and that's only the ones the local authority have jurisdiction over. It doesn't include the hundreds of privately owned CCTV systems dotted around London."

"I wish there was an easier way."

"Right? I'm all for using the unlawful way to get what we want, so believe me it's just as frustrating for me as it is for you that we can't. I'm not concerned though; between all of us, we have enough ears to the ground and eyes on the street that it won't be long before David fucks up, and when he does, we'll be ready for him. He can't hide forever."

"This is all a sick, twisted game to him. It's part of the fun. Those notes he left for me; I keep expecting another to turn up..." I swallow down the bile I feel rising in my throat, forcing it back down and closing a door on the memory of my mum's wide, staring eyes.

"*Eenie, meenie, miney, mo...*" Grim whispers, repeating the words that haunt my dreams. I flinch. She meets my gaze, and I see the sympathy she has for me harden into hate for my brother. "He might enjoy playing games, Pen, but he's fucking with the wrong people. We've got this covered."

"And Santiago?" I ask.

"You, sweetheart, *don't* need to be worrying about that fuck. You've got more than enough to worry about," Beast says, appearing behind me like a ghost. I jump, and he grins.

"Don't do that!" I admonish, slapping the back of my hand against his broad chest and regretting it instantly when pain ricochets up my arm. He's basically made of rock. I've really no idea how anyone can beat him in the cage.

Beast chuckles, nudging me with his arm, the force of which would've had me falling backwards off the barstool if I hadn't been ready for it. I'm used to his quirks by now. He doesn't care that I'm 'a girl', he treats me exactly the same as he would the guys. Well, maybe he dials it down a notch, but still, I like that about him. He doesn't treat me with kid gloves.

"What's up, Pen, you feeling delicate today?" Beast asks, poking me with a finger on my upper arm.

"Leave Pen alone, you brute," Grim admonishes with a glare, though there's a smile in her voice that she only seems to reserve for Beast. Angering Grim is a risk for the general population. Beast, however, can wind her up to the max and she'll let him. Well, she might break his nose or shoot him if steps over the line, but he loves her enough to take the punishment. We all know they're mad about each other.

"Hey, babe, no need to go all *mama bear* on me," he says, his already deep voice dropping an octave or two. If I weren't so in love with my Breakers I'd be squirming in my own seat right about now at the sexy look he's giving her. No one can doubt how much he adores her, and when he leans down to give her a kiss, I have to look away. By the time he pulls back, Grim's cheeks are flushed, and her pupils are blown.

"How did the sparring with Dax go?" she asks him.

"Good, babe. He got his arse whooped though," Beast chuckles, wrapping his arm around her shoulder before giving me a look, screwing up his face.

"What? Please don't tell me I need to get Dax seen by Joey? I don't trust that old quack," I say.

"Nah, nothing like that," Beast says. "Dax did tell me that he's teaching you how to fight. How's that going?"

"Good, actually. Why?"

"No reason."

Grim laughs, rolling her eyes. "Beast was offended that you didn't ask him for help. He thinks he's the better man for the job."

"I don't think, I *know* I'm the better man for the job."

I smile. "Don't let the guys hear you say that..."

"Too late, just fucking heard it, " Dax says, striding over to us. He's changed out of his workout gear and into his clothes, and smells nice and clean. No doubt using the showers here at the club.

"What? You know it's true. I'm almost ten years older than you, and I've barely broken a sweat. You on the other hand have just pissed out a litre of water from your pores sparring with me. I'm the don of bare-knuckle fighting. You know it. I know it. Everyone knows it. Pen should be taught by the best. Am I right?"

"Maybe I should be calling the Deana-dhe then? After all, I'm pretty sure you said *they* were your betters," I comment, my lips quivering with a smile.

"Fuck, no! I don't want you within ten miles of those dangerous fucks," Dax warns, wrapping his arms around me and hugging me close. I lean into his hold, breathing in his clean scent.

"I'd have to agree with you, mate. As much as I respect them—"

"*Fear* them," Grim points out.

"Babe, I don't fear anyone. Well, except perhaps you..." Beast counters with a laugh before continuing with his point. "As much as I *respect* them, those lads aren't people I would feel comfortable leaving my woman alone with."

"Speaking of which, have you heard from them lately?" A look passes between the two that has me frowning and wondering about The Masks. Aside from that time when Beast and I met with the Deana-dhe in Tom O'Brien's pub, no one's mentioned Malik Brov or his crazy sons for weeks but that doesn't mean to say the threat has gone away, just that they're hiding the problem from me.

"No, I haven't. But if I do, you'll be the *last* to know about it," Beast retorts with a smirk. Grim scowls. "Babe, I'm kidding. Tom's going to let me know when they're back in London or if he hears from them."

"Good." Grim presses a kiss against Beast's cheek. "Drink anyone?" she asks, giving him a sweet smile.

"I guess that's your cue to start serving," Dax says, smirking.

"Well of course it's his cue. I'm a pregnant woman and need to get off my feet every once in a while."

"Wait a minute... Whenever I suggest you get off your feet and rest, all I get is an ear bashing and sent to the spare room for being a chauvinistic pig. That shit ain't fucking fair," Beast retorts, grumbling under his breath.

Dax blurts out a laugh, and I elbow him in the ribs when Grim glares at him. He immediately slams his mouth shut knowing better than to piss off Grim. Beast, on the other hand, either has a death wish or gets off on the fact that he's always a few seconds away from losing his dick.

"Babe, you know it's true," he counters.

Grim grins sweetly, but her eyes are glaring daggers. "That's my prerogative, and frankly, you'd better get used to it, because if you continue to piss me off, I'm going to be doing more than sending you to the spare room. I'll be chopping your cock off and stuffing it down your throat."

Beside me Dax is desperately trying to hold in a laugh, and I'm biting my lip to stop myself from doing the same. Poor Beast, he really is trying his best, but Grim isn't making it easy for him with her hormonal mood swings that flip on a dime. Perhaps the Freed brothers were onto something with their little wager after all.

"What's going on? Why does everyone look like they're straining to go for a crap?" Lena asks as she approaches with Gray. It's all we need to set us off, and everyone, including Grim, roar with laughter.

22

Pen

"GOOD TO SEE YOU ALL," Hudson says a couple of days later as we gather together at *The Noble Arms*, the Irish pub I visited once before with Beast.

"What are we doing here?" Xeno asks, cutting a look at the same group of men who were here that night Beast and I spoke with the Deana-dhe. Tom O'Brien's bodyguards are playing a game of cards, but every now and then they look over at our group. There's no hostility coming from them, more curiosity than anything else.

"Beast called. He wanted to meet us here," Hudson explains. "Apparently one of his contacts has some news that might be of interest to us."

"Finally," D-Neath says, grinning. He slides an e-cigarette between his lips and starts puffing on it. The smoke that pours out of his mouth is thick and smells like liquorice. In other words, it's disgusting. I wave my hand in front of my face and try not to choke. Opposite, Zayn, Xeno and York talk quietly with Hudson, whilst Dax collects our drinks from Tom at the bar. The rogue catches my eye and winks. "How are ye *álainn*?"

"Good, thank you, Tom," I reply evenly.

Across the table, York scowls. He might not understand Irish Gaelic, but he certainly understands flirting and he's none too pleased about Tom's friendliness, even if it is harmless.

"So, I bet you're glad to be rid of Tiffany, eh? She really didn't like you very much did she?" D-Neath says, leaning his forearms on the table as he looks at me. His wrists are adorned with thick gold chains to match his gold tooth, and I briefly wonder how much all that jewellery is worth.

"We weren't friends, no," I reply instead.

"Funny how she took a real dislike to you. Why do you think that might be?"

I shrug. "Your guess is as good as mine."

Sucking in another lungful of simulated smoke, he nods, watching me carefully. "You're a great dancer. Not everyone can appreciate that without feeling jealous."

"Thanks," I reply, not feeling comfortable with the compliment in the slightest.

"You've got that fire in your belly. I see it. Only kids who've grown up in shitty environments like us carry it inside of them. Pretty sure everyone sitting around this table has the same spark," he remarks.

"And Tiffany didn't?"

"Nope. She comes from privilege. That girl ain't struggled

for anything in her life. The spoilt little rich bitch has lived a life of luxury."

"Maybe once upon a time, not anymore."

"Regardless, she ain't experienced trouble like we have. She doesn't understand what it means to really fight for what you want."

"I don't know, she seemed pretty troubled to me. Just because she came from money once doesn't mean she didn't have problems. Money just makes it easier to hide them."

D-Neath nods his head. "Maybe that's true in some cases, but believe me, Tiff ain't had to work hard for anything in her life."

"You seem to know an awful lot about her, D-Neath, any reason for that?"

He laughs. "Not particularly. Just reading between the lines, that's all."

Opposite, Xeno shifts in his seat as the bell over the door to the pub rings. Grim and Beast walk in, followed by Arden, Carrick and Lorcan. Everyone turns their attention towards the three men and my skin pricks with goosebumps. I really, really don't like those guys.

"You've got to be fucking kidding me. This is who we're here to meet?" Xeno mutters whilst Hudson flashes him a curious look.

"Do I need to be concerned?" Hudson asks.

"Watch your back with these three. They have a reputation for being merciless bastards," Zayn explains quietly.

"Yeah, these guys aren't to be fucked with. I don't know what Beast is thinking, but you don't want to exchange a debt for information from these guys," Xeno warns, eying Hudson. "Seriously, watch your back."

"Noted."

"They don't look all that scary to me," D-Neath remarks, raising a curious brow.

Zayn cuts D-Neath a look. "Then you're a fool. Those guys are possibly *the* most dangerous men you'll ever come across."

D-Neath raises his brow, unconvinced. Nevertheless we all quieten, watching the group with wary eyes. A feeling of disquiet creeps up my spine as my internal warning bells start ringing loud and clear. My gut is screaming at me to get the hell out of here and as far away from the Deana-dhe as possible. It's not often I ignore my gut, but given everyone else is rooted to the spot, I keep my arse seated too.

"Good to see you, mate," Beast says, striding over to the bar so he can shake Tom's hand. He slaps Dax on the back next, introducing him to the Deana-dhe, and even though Dax is acting relaxed, I can see the tension in his jaw. Grim, on the other hand, just waves at Tom then walks over to our table and takes a seat next to me, giving me a quick one-armed squeeze before she throws a look at D-Neath.

"Don't smoke that shit around me," she snaps, motioning to his e-cigarette and the plume of dense smoke. D-Neath opens his mouth, presumably to protest, but she cuts him a look that would make any man piss themselves. He wisely places the offending item on the table.

"Evening, Beast, do you want to introduce us to your friends?" Hudson asks, assessing the Deana-dhe with one quick sweep of his gaze as Dax, Beast, and the scary threesome join us.

"Evening," Arden says, taking a seat. Lorcan and Carrick

remain standing behind him, looking nothing less than intimidating. At least to me, anyway.

"Arden, this is Hudson, the man I was telling you about," Beast explains. Arden cuts Hudson a look, acknowledging him without saying a word in greeting. "And these are the Breakers. Dax you've just met," Beast continues, nodding to Dax, who is currently handing out a round of drinks. "This is Xeno, York and Zayn."

"I know who they are," Arden replies ominously, raising guarded looks from the guys.

"And you've already met Pen."

"Pen," Arden says, his strange amber eyes lingering on me a little longer than is comfortable. I wilt beneath his stare, swallowing heavily. Beneath the table, Grim grips my hand, sensing my fear. I can't even look at any of the guys. If they knew the depths of just how uncomfortable I felt right now they might start a fight, and honestly, I'm not sure it's one they'd win.

"Who's this?" Arden asks, jerking his chin towards D-Neath. Though by the look in his eyes, something tells me he already knows exactly who D-Neath is.

"Duncan Neath. Owns The Pink Albatross on Fenchurch Street. He's working with us," Beast explains.

"Is that so," Arden raises a brow, and D-Neath shifts uncomfortably in his seat. I get the distinct impression that Arden has taken an immediate dislike to him. Then again, he looked at my guys in exactly the same way, so perhaps he just dislikes everyone he meets.

"Beast says that you have some information that might be useful to us?" Hudson asks, cutting to the chase.

"That I do. I heard you have history with Santiago Garcia, is that correct?" Arden fires back, his Irish accent lyrical and deceptively alluring. I find myself relaxing to the sound of it, even when everything else is telling me to run.

"I do, yes."

"And you're seeking vengeance?"

"*Justice*," Hudson corrects him.

"I see." Arden takes a sip of his Guinness, and a seam of white froth lines his top lip. He stares at Hudson, licking his top lip clean. "Why?"

"Why what?"

"Why do you want justice?"

"It's not something I wish to discuss."

Arden raises a brow, turning his attention to me. "Do *you* know?"

"You don't need to speak with her," Xeno butts in, his voice thick with menace.

"Are you her keeper?" Arden questions, his long, thick fingers tapping on the table top.

"No, I'm her fucking *soulmate*," Xeno snaps, and it strikes me as odd that's the term he uses to describe our relationship. I mean, it's true, but still... odd.

"It looks like Pen has more than one of those," Lorcan says, his strange grey eyes looking between my guys before resting his gaze on me.

"I do," I respond firmly, somehow feeling that it's important that I acknowledge that fact. "They're *mine*. I belong to them and they to me."

"Is that so," Carrick says, cutting me a look. His black eyes glittering with sudden interest. I try not to shiver.

"What the fuck *is* this?" D-Neath mutters, clearly not

getting the weird power play on display here. I'm not sure I understand it either. Regardless, no one answers him.

Arden strokes his neck as he contemplates us all, and I find myself fixated on the butterfly tattoo that covers the long column of his throat. Taking another sip of his drink, his Adam's apple bobs below the skin, making it come to life suddenly. I could've sworn it was way more colourful the last time I saw it. Now the butterfly has grey wings edged in black and red, a skull sitting in the bottom half of each wing. Something about that makes my pulse beat erratically, and my stomach suddenly flutters with deadly butterflies just like the one I'm staring at now.

"If you need compensation for coming here today and speaking with us, I'm more than willing to oblige. It's very important Santiago is brought to justice for what he's done," Hudson says.

"Very important to whom?" This time it's Carrick who asks the question. He pins Hudson with his hawk-like eyes. "To the Breakers? To D-Neath here? To Penelope Scott? What about Beast or Grim?"

"To me. It's very important to *me*," Hudson clarifies.

"Then the debt is yours to pay when the time is right," Arden says.

Hudson frowns, cutting a look at Grim who grits her teeth. "I don't wish to be in debt to you. I wish to pay you for the information you have. Providing it's worth it, of course."

"Whether you believe it to be worth it, is irrelevant. Agree to owe a debt that we will claim at a time of our choosing, and we will give you the information we have. Don't agree and we walk, and you'll be none the wiser."

"What's the debt?" Xeno asks, leaning forward and pressing his elbows on the sticky surface of the table.

Lorcan shifts his gaze to Xeno. "That is none of your concern."

"Hudson's my friend. That makes it my concern."

"*Our* concern," Dax, York and Zayn chime in. Hudson dips his head at the four, acknowledging their loyalty and friendship.

But Arden doesn't seem to give a shit. "No. It *isn't*," he insists, smiling with what can only be interpreted as malice. He doesn't even bother to hide it.

Beast coughs into his fist, looking between the two groups of men. He's definitely nervous and that's something I've never seen before. "Listen, we're all friends here. No need to take this down a road none of us wish to visit. Yeah?"

"Oh, I don't know, some roads lead to interesting destinations," Arden says, turning his attention back to me. "Wouldn't you agree, Pen?"

"The only journey I've ever wanted to be on is with the Breakers. We travel together, no matter how difficult the path. That's the way it's always been, and *always* will be," I answer quickly.

All three of the Deana-dhe stare at me, and I feel like they're stripping me back layer by layer, trying to reach right into the very essence of me. I've no idea why, but I feel it's important that I don't look away. They can strip me bare, but the truth of my words won't change.

Eventually Arden nods, looking away, and I find I can breathe again. "Understood," he says, and I swear to fuck the whole pub takes a breath, let alone the people sitting around this table. *Who are these men?*

"Is this guy for real?" Xeno growls, about two seconds away from starting a war. York rests his hand on Xeno's arm, shaking his head.

"Let's get back to the point at hand," Hudson says. "Fifty thousand for whatever information you have."

Arden cocks his head. "We don't take money as payment. We have enough of that already," he says with a slow, easy smile.

"Property then?" Hudson counters. "I have property all over the world. I can show you my portfolio, you can take your pick."

"You want Santiago that bad, huh?"

"I need to put this to bed. Once and for all."

"Ah! So this is about revenge. He hurt someone you love and now it's time to pay?"

Hudson leans back in his seat and crosses his arms. "Something like that."

"Love is man's one true weakness," Arden remarks, taking another sip of his drink. Behind him Carrick yawns, clearly bored. Lorcan, however, looks like he's itching for a fight. He smirks at Xeno before trailing his hot gaze over to me. Smiling, he licks his lips provocatively. My cheeks flush with heat, not because I'm attracted to him but because he makes me feel so uncomfortable.

"Take your eyes off Pen. Now!" This time it's Dax who's had enough, he pushes up from the table, but Zayn grasps his shoulder and forces him back down in his seat.

"Enough!" Grim snaps. "Pen is off limits."

Arden grins. "We had to be sure."

"What the fuck is that supposed to mean?" Zayn asks.

"That she's definitely yours."

"Fuuuuckkk... Is shit getting weird or what?" D-Neath mumbles under his breath. For the first time ever, I'd have to agree with him. There's more to the Deana-dhe than meets the eye, that's for sure.

Lorcan crouches down and whispers something in Arden's ear. He nods, returning his attention back to Hudson. "We don't want money. We don't want property. We deal in *debts*. Information for a debt of our choosing. That's how we work. Take it or leave it."

"I'm a businessman, I don't make deals when I have no idea what the debt is. Whatever you know isn't worth compromising myself like that."

Arden nods, a flicker of respect crossing his features before he shuts it down and stands. "Then we shall be on our way."

"*I* will take on the debt," Grim suddenly cuts in.

"The hell you will!" Beast shouts, standing. His chair scrapes across the floorboards and in seconds he's standing behind Grim, his hand on her shoulder. "Arden, no!"

Arden slides his gaze to her and nods. A look passes between them, and despite Grim's relaxed demeanour, her hand tightens around mine beneath the table. "Done," he agrees, arching a brow at Beast who's the palest I've ever seen him.

"No, we are not done. There's no deal. Grim owes you nothing, thank you for your time, gentleman," Hudson says quickly, understanding that Grim has promised something that goes beyond money or property, something far too personal.

"What the fuck have you done, Grim!?" Beast shouts.

Arden smiles slowly. "That's between Grim and the three of us now. You know better than to question it."

Beast's mouth slams shut, but his grip on Grim's shoulder tightens. She winces, but doesn't make a sound. Behind the bar, Tom looks up. He shakes his head, takes a bottle of brandy from the shelf and pours two generous glasses.

"Beast, there's a drink here with your name on it," Tom says, jerking his chin.

Grim untangles her hand from mine and squeezes Beast's. "Go have a drink with Tom. We'll talk about this later."

"Don't you fucking dare dismiss me," Beast counters. It's the first time I've seen him speak in anger towards Grim, and it's the first time I've seen Grim look cowed. What the fuck?

"I've got this in hand, Beast," she says quietly.

"The fuck you have," Beast snaps, turning his attention to Arden. "Regardless of what debt you come up with, there are things I won't accept. She is *mine*, and I will protect what is mine to the death. You know this about me. I fought hard for Grim. There's isn't a damn thing in the world that I wouldn't do for this woman. You hear me Arden Dálaigh?"

Arden nods his head. "This we know, and because you are a friend of the O'Brien's who are friends of ours, when it comes to settling the debt I won't take what Grim isn't willing to give. You have my word."

Beast visibly relaxes, but the rest of us watch the exchange with confusion and apprehension. "I have your word. All or yours?" Beast insists, looking at Lorcan and Carrick too.

"Yes," the three agree simultaneously.

Drawing a breath through his nostrils, Beast nods once then strides over to the bar and sits down heavily on the barstool opposite Tom. He knocks back the drinks in quick succession. Tom grips his shoulder, squeezing tight.

"The information, Arden," Grim insists, squaring her shoulders as she stares him down.

Arden shifts in his seat, leaning forward, his palm's flat against the table top, his fingers spreading out before him as he speaks.

"Santiago Garcia's pride is his weakness, but you know that already, don't you?"

"Yes," Hudson agrees. "We're counting on it."

Arden nods. He raises the pint glass to his lips and slowly drinks the rest of the Guinness. "But what you don't know is that there is someone close to home who isn't who she seems. When you find her, you find Santiago."

"What? *Who?*" D-Neath pulls a face.

"That's all I know," Arden shrugs, schooling his features into a hard, unreadable mask.

"What the fuck good is that?"

Before anyone can even blink, Arden has pulled out a knife from the waistband of his jeans and has slammed it down onto the table between D-Neath's pointer and middle-finger of his left hand that's currently resting on the table top. I watch in morbid fascination as blood starts to spill from a cut to his middle finger. The edge of the blade slicing through his skin like a warm knife through melted butter.

"What the *fuck?*" D-Neath exclaims, pulling his hand back and inspecting the wound as blood trickles down his finger, dropping onto the table. "You just fucking *cut* me."

Arden pulls his knife from the table and tucks it back into the waistband of his jeans. "Next time I'll be sure to take the finger off, I didn't out of respect for Grim and Beast, but you ever talk to me like that again and I don't care who your friends are, I will chop off each finger and shove them down your motherfucking throat until your choke to death," he says, his pretty Irish accent wrapping the threat in honeyed vowels.

"Go wash up. There's a toilet out back," Grim says to D-Neath, jerking her chin towards the back of the pub, effectively dismissing him.

Once D-Neath is gone, cursing under his breath with every step, Arden returns his attention to Grim. "Santiago left his estate in Manzanillo three weeks ago with a man I believe you're also very familiar with," Arden says, looking directly at me.

"My brother?"

Arden nods. "You will have one opportunity to bring them down, and you will succeed, but not without sacrifice. Someone sitting at this table is going to have to pay a high price."

A chill runs down my spine at his words. "Who?" I whisper, my heart squeezing in my chest.

Arden's amber eyes burn into my skin as he contemplates his response. "We look forward to seeing you dance at Tales this weekend, Pen. If you're willing to dance for us privately, then perhaps I'll tell you." With one final nod of his head, Arden gets to his feet and walks out of the pub, Carrick and Lorcan following behind.

"Can someone tell me what the *fuck* just happened?" Yorks asks, breaking the heavy blanket of silence. "Who the fuck are those men really, and what is their story?"

Grim sighs. "Truthfully. No one really knows. There are many rumours, none of which they've denied. Some people say they're only partly human, others that they're from a world within our world."

"You're *shitting* me?" Zayn comments. "People actually believe that horse shit?"

"People are willing to believe anything if the ones telling the story are persuasive enough, but I would have to agree with you, Zayn. The Deana-dhe might want everyone to believe that they're gods dressed in human skin, but they're just very clever, very perceptible young men who've built their reputation on stories and *make believe*," Grim explains.

"Clever," Hudson states.

"Indeed," Grim agrees. "They exchange information for debts, and they obtain that information by living up to their very fierce reputation."

"So they're bullshitters who happen to be good fighters, is that what you're saying?" Dax asks.

"No, they don't bullshit. They follow through on *all* of their threats. They're undefeated fighters in the world-wide under-ground fighting circuit, and they're also merciless killers. Rumour has it they've killed a thousand people each."

"Fuck," York exclaims.

"You shouldn't have stepped in Grim," Hudson says. "I had it under control. Now you owe them a debt, and that's on me."

"No, that's on *me*. I know how to handle the Deana-dhe," she replies, her body language shutting down any talk on the matter. They exchange looks and something tells me that Hudson isn't going to let this lie, but for now at least he lets it go

"And the information they gave us...? Can we trust it?" Hudson asks.

Grim nods. "Yes. Without a doubt. They're not liars. Part of the reason why they're so respected is that they never give incorrect information. Ever."

"Except when they're making shit up about themselves," Xeno points out.

"They've never made up a single story about who they are, they've just never stopped anyone else from doing the same. They're smart. That is how legends are born. One man can tell everyone he's a god, but that will only become true if enough people *believe* it."

"Fucking devious bastards, " Zayn mutters.

"And Arden's prediction about us being able to take down Santiago and David? He said we would succeed but only if someone at this table pays a high price. What about that? Is he a psychic or something?" I ask, goosebumps rising across my skin at the thought.

York laughs, shaking his head. "Just a lucky guess, Pen. We always knew we were gonna finish this, and it ain't too much of a stretch to think one of us might get a little hurt in the process."

"He said someone would pay a *high price*. That doesn't usually mean a punch to the jaw, York," I retort, casting a look at Grim. "Should I dance for them?"

As soon as the question comes out of my mouth, all four of my guys are expressing their thoughts with a series of colourful curses that turn the air blue. I block out their reactions, waiting on Grim's response.

"I guess that all depends on whether you believe the rumours are true."

23

Pen

THE AIR THRUMS WITH HEAT, with anticipation, as we enter the cage slowly one by one. Clancy is first to step onto the canvas, her red, knee length dress floating around her bare legs as she moves seductively. Behind her six dancers follow, all wearing the same red dresses, made edgy with black leather straps that criss-cross around their breasts. Like me, their eyes are shadowed with black liner, their lips red slashes, hair hanging loose. With every step, we bang our black canes onto the floor, the pounding of our bare feet adding to the sound and drawing the attention of the audience who begin to quieten in anticipation of the show. My fingers curl over the handle of the cane, a silver gun, chosen purposefully for the aesthetic of this performance.

Lola, the dancer that Clancy has been seeing on and off over the last few weeks, looks back at me, her long, tight curls falling over her shoulders. She's a beautiful woman, sexy, sensual. I can see why my best friend is so attracted to her. River too, according to Clancy. They've already been on a few dates together as a trio and shared a bed.

"Ready?" she whispers.

"Ready," I reply softly, feeling the familiar tingling beneath my skin that I always get just before a performance. Tonight I draw on that feeling, immersing myself in the moment, and forgetting everything else.

Around us the chattering dies down as the warehouse falls into darkness, the flickering candles on each table the only discernible light as we take up our positions in the cage. Somewhere in the audience, Grim and Beast sit with York and Xeno, the pair opting to accompany me this evening. Zayn and Dax are back home with Lena, keeping her company whilst Gray has his first night off in weeks. I'm also eerily aware of the Deana-dhe who are also here tonight, somehow feeling their eyes on me even though the whole place is steeped in darkness. Their attendance hasn't gone unnoticed, and throughout the evening there has been talk of the mysterious, dangerous men deigning us with their presence.

"Let's do this, girl," Lola says, reminding me that the show must go on.

A smoke machine starts pumping out dense vapour that creeps across the canvas, grey tendrils tumbling and whirling as we stride across the floor. Clancy stands to my left, and Lola to my right. The rest of the girls crouch down behind us, their palms pressed against the canvas, and their canes lying on the floor by their sides.

Start a War by Klergy begins to play, and the cage is suddenly illuminated with an eerie blood-red light, turning the grey smoke into a sea of blood. If the title of the song wasn't a dead giveaway, then our costumes and stage design is. This is a dance about fighting our enemies and winning. I may not be able to see into the future like Arden appears to be able to do, but I am certain of one thing, David might've started this war, but *I* intend on finishing it.

Whilst the three of us stamp our feet, marching on the spot in time to the music, the rest of the dancers rise up slowly from the floor. They twist their bodies, making shapes with their arms, like immortal creatures returning from the dead. Once they're standing, chins tipped up, canes held out in front of them, the silver gun handles pointing at the audience, they start marching on the spot too, synchronising their steps with ours.

When the next beat drops, and the pounding of the drums becomes more frantic, we transition seamlessly into the next portion of the dance. This is all about timing, control. Every step, every move I make is mirrored by the others. We dance as a unit, like an army, and it's fucking powerful. I feel the surge of energy rising up from my feet, right to the tips of my fingers. Bending forward at the waist, I lift my head and pump my arms as though running into battle, my cane clutched in my right hand.

With every step that follows, every jerk of my torso, slide of my leg and twist of my head, I feel a rush of adrenaline, of power spreading through my veins. My hair whips around my face, and as I slam the cane onto the canvas, it's my brother's face I imagine pummelling. I take out all my frustration, fear, anger, and anxiety on the cage floor, using my feet and my cane to beat down the image of my brother in my mind's eye.

But with every war there are the innocent bystanders drawn into a fight that doesn't belong to them. Casualties of war. My mum wasn't an innocent bystander in this war between me and my brother, but she was still a casualty. Her death is on my hands as much as it is David's. I had the power to protect her like I did Lena, but because of my feelings towards her, it didn't even cross my mind. That's on me.

As the rising tide of the song hits its crescendo, I imitate being shot, flinging my arms to the side, my cane still clutched tightly in my hands. That fantasy bullet rips through my chest and I stumble back, pressing my hand over the centre of my chest as though stemming the flow of blood. But I'm not knocked down. None of us are. We keep marching. Another shot is fired, and I fall to one knee, only to rise up again. Using the cane as support, I fold my hands over the handle and push upwards, twisting my hips and throwing my leg out to the side, following through the movement.

Then we really sink into the dance. We're nine women in perfect synchronicity. Powerful, sexy, *compelling*.

We twist and turn, fighting an imaginary enemy. Legs kick, fists curl and punch, the canes we're holding onto become both our shields and our weapons. Around us, our blood-red skirts flare with every turn and pirouette, whipping up the smoke and making it tumble over the edges of the canvas and out into the warehouse where it disperses. Our dance speaks of violent things, it deals in murderous thoughts, savagery the only currency running through our veins.

Then the lighting changes subtly from a deep red to a bright crimson and it's our cue to transition into the next portion of the dance. Bringing the cane around in front of me, I straighten up, kicking the base and flicking it up. I catch it with my other hand so that it's held horizontal against my body, then lift it above my head. Like Clancy and Lola, I tip my head back between my shoulders, shift the position of my hands so that the cane is held vertically above me now. Behind me, one of the dancers takes the cane from my hands so that I can slide my arms through a loop of red silk that has been lowered from the ceiling. With the silk nestled safely around my back and beneath my armpits, I tighten my hands around the material and nod. Either side of me, Clancy and Lola do the same. As we're hauled upwards, about ten feet off the ground, a rush of air lifts the skirt of our dresses giving the impression of blood blooming from a wound. Adrenaline pumps through my body, and although I know I'm safe, there's still an element of fear that I could fall, and that makes this all the more exciting. Even from this height, it's impossible to see anything other than dark, shadowy figures of the audience. Knowing that Xeno and York are watching gives me a boost of confidence. Tonight, I'm proving to myself, to them, that I can both dance and still hold onto the violence that I need in order to kill my brother.

I funnel it now, that violence, that hate and anger, and I use those emotions in this dance. It doesn't make me weaker like I thought it might. It makes me stronger. Strong enough to fight my demons, not the internal ones like my Breakers battle with daily, but the very real ones that are intent on hurting me and the ones I love. Xeno was right, I can still dance and face my brother. I knew that deep down, but like always, I allowed David to get into my head.

Not tonight.

Below us, the girls dance with fury and passion, summoning up their own strength from whatever experience that might have brought them to their knees in the past. They use that to dance better than they've ever danced before, and a rush of pride fills me up. These women are incredible dancers. These shows are as popular and as successful as they are, not because I'm dancing in them, but because, *together*, we put on a spectacular show.

As we dance, the remaining tendrils of smoke disperse revealing warriors who've battled and won. My skin covers in a sheen of sweat as I use my upper arm strength and strong core muscles to keep dancing suspended in the air. Tipping my head back, I smile knowingly and wait the fraction of a moment it takes before fine water droplets fall from the rain machine rigged up above us. Red dye has been added to the water and as the rain pours in bloody droplets over the three of us, tingles rush up and down my spine. This was Clancy's idea, and it is incredibly provocative. Grim was right to hire her permanently, she has a brilliantly creative mind. I can put together an amazing routine, but Clancy? She can put on an incredible show.

With one final push, the dancers below kick up the water with their dance steps, and we're lowered back down to the stage so that we can join them. Releasing my arms from the loop of silk, I put every last ounce of energy I have into the final portion of the routine, and dance with a focus that I've never felt so acutely before now. My wet hair whips around my head, lashing my skin as I move, and the skirt of my dress sticks to my bare legs. Despite my damp, cold skin, I feel a rush of heat rise up my body as awareness flickers in my belly, followed by fore-boding blooming in my heart.

As the final, haunting verse plays out over the speakers and I stand with a heaving chest, droplets of bloody water cascading over my body, my attention is drawn to York and Xeno as the lights in the warehouse brighten. I find them instinctively, bound in some inexplicable way since we were kids. They're both staring at me with a look of wonder, awe and love on their faces. I dip my head in acknowledgement, a rush of love and fierce protectiveness rampaging through my veins.

They're mine. The Breakers are mine to love, to dance with, to fight for, to protect. Always.

With that thought in mind, I seek out the Deana-dhe, imme-diately sensing their penetrating gazes as they sit at a table in the centre of the warehouse. All three are watching me closely. I look from Carrick to Lorcan, finally settling my gaze on Arden. Nodding my head once, I tell him without words that I will dance for them, because I know, without a shadow of a doubt, that one of my Breakers is the person Arden was talking about, and I'm determined to find out who.

With trepidation creeping through my bloodstream, I turn on my heel and follow the dancers out of the cage to the sound of cheers and whistles, the club erupting with appreciation. All the while my body is shaking, not from the rush of adrenaline after a good show, but from *fear*.

Dancing in front of an audience with the girls by my side is one thing, but dancing for the Deana-dhe privately is something different altogether.

I know it, and so do they.

24

Pen

I'VE CHANGED into my after show outfit that I picked out for tonight, and instead of my usual jeans and hoodie combination, I'm wearing a mid-thigh, black halter neck dress paired with flat pumps. Clancy looks up from her spot at the dressing table and smiles.

"Are you off to somewhere nice with Xeno and York?" she asks me, pulling on a pair of tight, leather hot pants and shrugging on a cropped, faux fur coat over her tank top.

"We're hanging out here for a little while before heading home," I reply, brushing through my still damp hair. I don't tell her I'm about to dance for three of the scariest guys I've ever had the displeasure of meeting. Knowing Clancy, she'd want to meet them not realising that she'd just be another sheep walking into a lion's den.

"That's great. You all deserve a little R&R."

"Where are you off to tonight?"

"Foxtrot, in Bermondsey. Lola and I are meeting River there. We've got an uber coming in five to collect us."

"Foxtrot? I've heard good things about that club."

"Yeah, us too. It's got three floors apparently, and each floor has a different theme. Tonight it's seventies disco, club classics and hip-hop. We're probably going to spend most of the night on the club classics floor."

Lola laughs. "Not all night, love. I reckon River wouldn't mind hanging with me on the seventies disco floor. You know how much he loves John Travolta aka Tony Manero from Saturday Night Fever." She rolls her eyes and Clancy bursts out laughing.

"Yeah, true! God, if I didn't love him so much I'd seriously worry about his taste in men."

"Oh, I don't know, Travolta circa 1994 in Pulp Fiction is pretty fucking hot," Lola retorts with a smirk.

Clancy rolls her eyes. "Which is why you both get on so well. The two of you have the same taste."

"Well of course we do, we happen to adore the same beautiful redhead," Lola counters, holding her hand out for Clancy to take. She stands, and side-by-side the contrast of their appearance is stunning to look at. Clancy is a redhead with freckles and pale skin and the perfect opposite to Lola, who has ebony colouring, deep brown eyes and tight curly hair. Lola is tall, athletic, with curves in all the right places, and Clancy is petite with a toned figure. They make up a beautiful couple, add in River's quirky, good looks, and the trio is fucking gorgeous.

"Anyway, we gotta run," Clancy says, giving me a quick hug. "Tonight was epic!"

"Have fun," I reply, stepping aside as the pair leave. I hear them chatting briefly to someone in the corridor and when I poke my head around the door, I see Grim striding towards me. She smiles, but it doesn't reach her eyes.

"The Deana-dhe are waiting for you in the gym. Arden says you agreed to dance for them?"

"I did."

Grim sighs. "You can back out. This isn't a debt. You don't owe them anything."

"I need to know who Arden was talking about."

"I thought you might."

"You believe him then? You think he can see into the future somehow?"

"I believe there are some things that can't be explained. I believe that there are some people who are more sensitive than others. I also believe there are fakers and crooks out there who prey on people's weaknesses and exploit them." She crosses her arms beneath her breasts and leans against the doorframe.

"Do you think the Deana-dhe are fakes and crooks."

"Like I said before, I think they're clever and manipulative. I also believe that Arden was telling the truth, which is why I don't think you should go through with this."

"Why?"

Grim bites on her lip, watching me carefully. "Would knowing the answer make a difference to the outcome? There are some things you can't change, fate is one of them."

"You sound like you're talking from experience, Grim. Don't tell me you're some kind of witch as well as a badass gangster." We both laugh at the direction this conversation has headed. I haven't even had a drink tonight, let alone any form of drug that might explain why we're even entertaining this notion. Maybe that's the power of the Deana-dhe right there.

"I'm pretty sure there are quite a few people who've called me a witch in the past and meant it," she grins. "But seriously, I trust my gut and intuition, but I'm not gifted, if you can call it that. For some, seeing things is a curse. I suspect it's like that for Arden despite how things appear to the contrary."

"Who?" I ask, intrigued now. I never thought Grim would buy into this kind of thing, but here we are talking about psychic shit like it's as real as we are. I guess I must believe a little in it too given I'm about to dance for three men who'd kill first and not bother to ask questions later.

"Christy..." Grim's voice trails off when she meets my gaze.

"You're half-sister?"

"Yeah. She's been known to predict things. Scares the life out of Beast, and as you know, he's not scared of anyone, but he *is* wary of Christy, just like he's wary of the Deana-dhe." Grim smiles then, a genuine, warm smile that lights up her face. "Christy is formidable. A beautiful ballet dancer with this inner strength that is remarkable given her history. She's a lot stronger than she seems on the surface."

"She sounds incredible."

"She is. She's been through a lot emotionally, physically too. Her past has scarred her in more ways than one."

"I'm sorry to hear that."

"People often misjudge her, much like people have misjudged you. I think you'd like her."

"I'd love to meet her one day," I say, meaning it.

"You will. One day." Grim flicks her gaze down, worry creasing her brow.

"What is it?" I ask, resting my fingers gently on her arm.

"Just something Christy said to me on the phone the other day. Nothing that should concern you." Grim plasters on a smile, but before I can push further, her attention is caught by footsteps striding along the corridor. "It's Xeno and York, neither look particularly happy," she says.

"Better leave them to me then."

Grim squeezes my arm, then walks towards her office at the other end of the corridor and gently closes the door behind her.

"I've just had a very interesting conversation with Arden," Xeno says the moment I step out into the corridor. His eyes rove over my outfit, his teeth clenching tight.

"Is that right?"

"Yeah, he said you'd agreed to dance for them," York continues. "Want to tell us what the fuck is going on?"

"I need to know who he was talking about," I reply. "I don't expect you to understand. I know how you feel about them, but I *have* to know." Stepping around them, I walk towards the gym area where Beast and Dax trained the other day. It's separate from the main warehouse floor and sits on the far side of the building.

"It's bullshit. You know that right?" Xeno asks, his hand clamping around my upper arm as he prevents me from going any further.

"You can't trust a word they say, Titch," York adds. "And I sure as fuck don't trust their intentions. They were interested in you, that much was clear from our meeting."

"They're not going to abduct me, if that's what you're worried about," I counter.

"Of course that's what we're worried about. The Deana-dhe never take an interest in anyone, but all of a sudden they're willing to give you information for a dance? Fuck that!" Xeno exclaims. "You're not doing it."

"I think that's Pen's choice, don't you?" Arden says, appearing in the corridor like a fucking ghost.

"Where the fuck did you just spring from? Don't tell me you've got mystical powers to add to your *all-seeing eye*?" York says with an arch of his brow.

Arden barks out a laugh, completely dismissing York's sarcastic remark and looking directly at me. "I can see why Malik Brov wanted you," he says. "There's something so alluring about a woman who has multiple men willing to die for her. Not to mention your ability to dance. He would've had you locked up in his castle and doing unspeakable things to you if Beast hadn't ended his life."

"You fucking cunt!" Xeno exclaims, rushing forward just as Beast steps into the hallway from the warehouse.

"Woah! What the fuck is happening here?" he exclaims, reading the situation in an instant, and holding his hand out to prevent Xeno from getting any closer to Arden.

"Pen here has agreed to dance for us, and her men aren't happy about it."

"No shit... Pen?" Beast frowns, questioning me with his eyes.

"I'm not doing this because I want to. I'm doing it because I *have* to. I can't lose any of them. I can't."

"You *won't*. How many times do we have to tell you this?" York says, frustrated.

"Lose them? What the fuck did I miss?"

"That night we met up with Hudson at Tom's. Arden here filled Pen's head with his fucking sorcery bullshit."

"Where the fuck was I when this was going down?"

"You were at the bar nursing a couple of shots after Arden agreed to take a debt from Grim."

"Fuck, man." Beast grits his jaw.

"Psycho here said that we will defeat David and Santiago but that one of us sitting at the table would pay a high price," Xeno explains.

Beast's face pales. "Who was sitting at the table?"

"That's irrelevant when it's horse shit! "Please don't tell me that you buy into this crap too," York counters, trying to edge around Beast.

Beast throws his arms out, preventing York from moving. "Who was sitting at the table?" he repeats, firmer this time.

"Me, Xeno, Dax, Zayn, Pen, Hudson, and Grim. D-Neath was in the toilet and you were at the bar," York says.

Beast looks at me, swallowing hard. "And to find out who it is, you have to dance for them?"

"*Privately,*" York stresses.

"It's just a dance, that's it," I say, casting a look at Arden.

"Right," he agrees, but there's something about his expression that gives me pause.

"Arden, these people are my friends... Is this really necessary?"

"It is if she wants to know," Lorcan says, striding down the hallway with Carrick close behind him. The three of them all give off the same menacing vibe despite their relaxed demeanour. They're so certain of themselves, so sure that they're untouchable and it irks me. I wonder what it would take to bring them to their knees. Not me at any rate.

"*She* has a name, have a little respect and fucking use it," York counters.

Lorcan laughs, but it's dark and filled with menace. "Make me."

"That's enough!" Behind us, Grim approaches. "This is my club, and I won't have any fighting here. Understand?"

"We're not interested in fighting tonight. Just having a friendly discussion," Carrick says looking bored, especially when he focuses on me. "I'm not all that bothered about seeing her dance, anyway. On the other hand, that fiery little redhead sure looked interesting."

"Leave Clancy out of it!" I snap.

"So she does have teeth," Carrick says, chuckling. "Maybe you're not so boring after all."

"Shut. Your. Mouth!" Xeno snaps, Beast's fingers curl into his top, shooting him a warning stare as he shoves Xeno back none too gently.

"Look," I say, breathing deep and refusing to rise to the bait. "I'm not doing anything other than dancing. I just did the same out there in front of dozens of men and women. This is no different."

"Nothing is cut and dry when it comes to the Deana-dhe. You get that, right?" York says, turning to me. He reaches for my face, cupping my cheek in his hand. "Let's say that Arden can somehow see into the future, what makes you think knowing who's gonna get hurt will change anything?"

"That's exactly what I said," Grim mutters, shaking her head.

"I'm doing this with or without your backing," I say stubbornly, refusing to answer his question and stepping around him before he can stop me. I duck under Beast's arm and walk towards Arden.

"Wait! I have a proposition," Xeno says, stopping me in my tracks.

Arden grins, and in that instant I know that this is what he wanted all along.

"Xeno, no."

"Cold feet?" Arden asks.

"Maybe we'll let fate decide what happens after all. Like everyone keeps telling me, we can't change fate, right?" I ask, swallowing heavily as Xeno steps up beside me and entwines his fingers with mine.

"Are you sure you want to take that chance?" Carrick asks, his black eyes boring into me.

Xeno's nostrils flare. "If she dances for you, then so do York and me. She does this with us or she doesn't at all."

York flanks my left side. "Take it or fucking leave it."

"Well, shit just got interesting," Lorcan says, and I try not to tremble at the way his grey eyes cut like a steel blade right through my chest.

Arden pushes off the wall, locking eyes with Xeno. "I'm not an unreasonable man. I'm willing to bend my own rules just a fraction. I will tell Pen what she wants to know if you dance as a trio... On *one* condition."

"Oh, here we fucking go," York mumbles.

"And what's that?"

"No holding back."

"What the fuck is that supposed to mean?" Beast mutters.

"Done!" Xeno agrees, taking my hand and striding past the trio. Behind us, York follows.

25

Pen

CARRICK AND LORCAN sit down on a sofa that has seen better days whilst Arden waits for us on the large gym mat in the centre of the room. Carrick pulls a joint from the pocket of his shirt, lighting it. His black eyes settle on me as he takes a hit before passing it to Lorcan who takes a deep drag, a slow smile pulling up his lips as he regards us.

Without even turning around to see who's holding the joint, Arden says, "Bring it here, Lorcan."

Getting up, Lorcan strides over, passes the joint to Arden who sucks in a lungful. He purposely blows the blue-tinged smoke in our faces and when I draw in a breath, I'm surprised to find that it doesn't smell like the marijuana we used to smoke as kids. It has a sweet scent, almost floral.

"What's in that?" I ask.

Xeno grips my fingers tightly.

"Nothing good," he grinds out.

"All natural ingredients, no synthetic bullshit in this," Arden counters.

York scoffs. "Opium is a natural ingredient. It's still fucking dangerous."

"Then let me rephrase that. This drug isn't addictive, nor is it dangerous to your health. It is, however, mind-altering."

"Mind-altering? Fuck, that's never a good experience," York comments.

Arden shrugs. "That all depends on what frame of mind you're in. Pretty sure that dancing with your girl should make it a good one."

"With three fucking psychos looking on. Yeah, it's bound to be," Xeno snarls, jerking his chin and daring Arden to bite.

Arden grins and offers the joint to York who shakes his head. "I can't dance high. It fucks with my coordination."

"You won't have that problem with this," Arden says. "It *heightens* your perceptions, not dull your senses."

York shakes his head, refusing. "Still, no... *thanks*," he adds as an afterthought.

"It will open you up in ways you can't even imagine," Lorcan adds, his black eyes impossibly dark now that his pupils have blown wide from the high.

"Yeah, and fuck with our ability to fight you off when you *try* and take Pen from us," Xeno grinds out.

"If we wanted to do that, we would've done it already," Carrick points out from his spot on the sofa. "Besides, we don't take what's already owned by another, no matter how tempting. She's your soulmate, and there's no fucking with that. Believe me, we've tried before and failed."

"Carrick, *enough!*" Arden snaps, anger flaring before he shuts it down with a smile that is as fake as the faux leather sofa Carrick's sitting on. I briefly wonder if he ever feels joy, and something tells me that isn't an emotion that often blesses him. If ever.

"She was *never* ours," Lorcan mutters, before turning on his heel and sitting back down next to Carrick. I can tell by the furious look on Arden's face that the '*she*' Lorcan's talking about isn't me, but some mysterious woman in their past, or perhaps, even their present.

My mouth drops open and Xeno is suitably stunned, but it's York who latches onto that piece of information and grins. "Ah, so there's a chink in the Deana-dhe's armour. Looks like you're not as infallible as you want everyone to believe. Is that why you're all so fucking obsessed with soulmates because you haven't found yours?"

"Take a drag," Arden responds, shutting down completely.

Xeno looks over his shoulder at the door. I follow his gaze and see Beast looking through the small square window. He nods at Xeno, telling him without words that he has our back. "Do it," Xeno says.

"If you say so, brother. In for a penny, in for a pound, right?" York says, winking at me as he takes the joint, places it between his lips and draws in a lungful. He smiles around the smoke, blowing it out over Arden whose expression darkens.

"Careful, York."

"Fuck me!" he responds, completely uncaring.

"You okay?"

He nods. "This shit is... *wow*! What the fuck is in it?"

Arden smirks. "If I told you that, I'd have to kill you, and I'm not in the mood tonight."

York laughs, and I'm not sure if it's the drugs he's just inhaled or the fact he thinks Arden is kidding. Either way, he isn't remotely bothered by the implied threat.

Xeno's fingers tighten over mine before fixing his eyes on Arden. "Enjoy the show," he says, before placing the joint between his lips and dragging in a deep breath, the bright tip of the joint sizzling. He passes the joint back to Arden, then keeping the smoke in his lungs, he cups my face in his palms. I smile, understanding his intentions as he lowers his mouth over mine. With his bottle-green eyes fixed on mine and his thumbs stroking my cheeks, Xeno blows the smoke into my parted lips. I draw it deep into my lungs. The hit is immediate and powerful.

My eyes drift shut momentarily, as tingles rush out over my skin and a burst of bright, white light explodes behind my eyes. I'm momentarily blinded, but when that brightness recedes I find myself feeling weirdly energised, like currents of electricity are thrumming through my veins.

"Tiny?" Xeno questions, his hands still cupping my cheek.

"I'm good. I'm... *better* than good," I reply, my eyelids fluttering open as a slow warmth blooms out from my middle. When I focus on Xeno, my lips part on an exhale of breath, words lost beneath my surprise and awe as I drink him in.

"Do you see it too?" he asks.

"Yes," I whisper. Xeno is surrounded in a halo of white light. I've never seen anything more beautiful in my life. In my peripheral vision, York steps close, and I see the same white light surrounding him too.

"You look like the brightest star, Titch," York whispers, and I feel the heat of his body wrap around me like a warm blanket at his nearness. When his fingers graze over the bare skin of my back and he presses a kiss against my shoulder, the tip of his nose trailing up my neck as he inhales, I shudder, my blood flooding with pleasure hormones.

"Oh God," I exclaim, reaching for Xeno, my hands pressing against his chest to steady myself. "You feel like silk. You smell like fucking sunshine," York continues, his hips pressing against my back. He's hard. Turned on. I realise I am too, but it's a subtle feeling. When we're together usually there's no denying that we want to rip each other's clothes off. What I feel now... it's different, pleasurable but not overpowering. Soothing but also invigorating, a strange concoction.

"I feel..."

"...Fucking amazing," Xeno fills in, his pupil's blowing wide at my touch.

"The effect of the drug heightens your senses as well as your perception. It will only remain that way for a short while. I'd enjoy it while you can. Follow your instincts. *Dance*," Arden demands, pulling our attention back to him.

"Oh my God," I whisper, stepping away from Arden the moment I lay my eyes on him. He isn't lit up with light like Xeno or York. No, he's bathed in shadow, his features indistinguishable. The only thing that has any life, any definition, is the butterfly at his neck. It flaps its wings slowly, droplets of blood sliding down the delicate edge, dripping from the tip.

"*Dance*," he repeats, his shadowy figure striding towards Carrick and Lorcan, both of whom are bathed in shadow just like he is.

"This drug is fucking intense," York mutters, but what I'm feeling and seeing now is nothing compared to the auditory overload when music begins to play in the room.

Like a flood of water seeping out of the speakers, *Waves* by Dean Lewis begins to play and the three of us are immediately swept up in the current of the notes as they float around us. Like Xeno and York, the need to move swells inside of me, and I kick off my shoes wanting to feel the floor against my bare feet. Under the influence of this powerful drug, it feels as though I'm wading through warm water, sand moving and shifting beneath my feet. I undulate my body, my arms stretching out in front of me, my hands weaving and twirling like seaweed moved by the current of the ocean. I close my eyes briefly and can almost feel the salty water embracing me, making me light, weightless, as though I'm standing at the bottom of the ocean. It feels so *real*.

Turning in a pirouette, I allow myself the freedom to embrace what I'm feeling and just go with it. For a moment I'm alone dancing beneath the waves, being pulled by a current. I spin and leap, twist and twirl. My arms flare, I make shapes with my limbs. Sharp angles, followed by smooth, fluid motion. I'm aware of Xeno and York dancing around me. We don't touch, we simply dance.

There's a simplicity to the way we move, a rise and fall, just like that of a gentle ocean. Every now and then we touch, hands feathering over skin, like waves lapping against the shore. Soothing, calming.

When the music begins to swell, so do my movements. Every step becomes more defined, sharper, purposeful, and the lightness I feel becomes heavier with every step, the weight of the water suddenly suffocating. I fall to my knees, and roll onto my back, my back arching, my arms spread wide, as I fight off the feeling of heaviness. Darkness moves close by. I feel the ripples of it, and I don't know if it's something within me or something on the outside. The sudden freedom I felt, turns in on itself, twisting into something I fear. In that moment I understand that this is what I've buried within me. All the fears I've been battling drift to the surface of my consciousness. My brother's face appears laughing, twisted up into the monster of my nightmares. He disappears only to be replaced with my mum's dead eyes that suddenly come alive, her harsh words and hate flow into me, shifting again into my sister screaming. Lena's cries are replaced with mine as I stare at my Breakers, the men I love, *dead*. All those fears tumble over one another drowning me. My face suddenly awash with tears, a whole ocean erupting from within.

"Come back to us," a voice says, pulling me back from that dark abyss where dangerous creatures lurk, where darkness lives, where my fears reside. "Titch, I'm here. Come back, my love."

Warm fingertips glide gently over my face, running down my neck, the centre of my chest and over my stomach. I arch my body, chasing the warmth, the crackling electricity drawing me back from the brink. I open my eyes to find York staring down at me. He smiles, and it's a brilliant smile that gives me my breath back, instead of taking it away.

My fears disperse, just like that.

In my periphery, a sudden movement catches my eye, we both look, drawn to the energy barrelling towards us both. It's Xeno, and for the briefest of moments I think he's going to push York over to take his place above me. Instead, he twists his body to the side and leaps into the air, rolling over York's back only to tumble away, caught up in his own momentum as he continues to dance around us. I feel his energy as he dances, as though he's battling his own demons and winning.

"Take my hand," York urges.

Sitting up, I reach for him, and as our fingers meet, a zap of electricity surges down my arm all the way to my toes. He pulls and I push up from my feet, leaping into his arms in one smooth motion, wrapping my arms and legs around his body as he spins away, taking me with him.

We turn together, like a shoal of fish glittering in a crystal clear ocean. My loose hair whips around as we spin, and I find myself letting go of my arms. I trust York to keep me safe, and I lean back, flinging my hands above my head. Laughter bubbles up from my throat, bursting free. I feel weightless. Happy. *Free.*

As York slows down, something moves closer, twisting and turning, tumbling and leaping just like the current of the ocean. It teems with life and beauty, but with darkness too. Not the same kind of pitch black of the abyss in the distance. No, this darkness is more like the night sky dotted with stars. It's beautiful.

"Xeno," I whisper.

Dropping to my feet, I cup York's face and kiss him gently, turning in his arms so my back is pressed against his chest, then hold my hand out to Xeno. He takes it, stepping into my body, cushioning me, Xeno at my front, York at my back.

They fold around me, keeping me safe between them.

For just a moment we breathe each other in. Three best friends, soulmates buoyed by our love for each other. I feel a deep sense of belonging in their arms and an unbreakable bond that binds us together. Dax and Zayn might not be with us physically right now, but are carried with us always. We belong to each other, the five of us.

We always have.

As the music cascades around us, Xeno steps backwards and York and I step forwards, our bodies grazing over each other. We move as though we're one entity, and when York steps out to the side, Xeno and I follow, our movements mirrored, in-sync in a way that shouldn't be possible, but is.

Together we dance, the ebb and flow of our bond moving our feet, synchronising our steps all whilst we're joined in some way. A touch of a hand, a brush of lips, arms folding around each other, fingers sliding over bare skin as we lift each other, guide each other, move in sequence, in harmony. The words of the song filter through my consciousness, feeding our movements. It's like nothing I've ever experienced before. I'm carried away by the motion, the wonder of our movements. I feel their hands everywhere, on my hips, curling around my wrists, running over my thighs, my arms, cupping the back of my head as we dance. York and Xeno are joined too, they touch each other, support each other as we dance free from outside pressures, worries or pain. We dance with love, friendship, passion and hope. We dance with the kind of magic all dancers hope to find through movement. It whips up the air around us, an indescribable feeling of something unexplainable, *powerful*.

Xeno grasps my hips and lifts me up in the air, and I feel as though I am drifting on a current as my legs spread out into the splits. I land on light feet only to be passed into York's arms as he dips me backwards, his fingers trailing over my chest, a wave of pleasure zinging beneath my skin at his touch. When he draws me back up, Xeno steps close behind me, the heat of his body flooding mine. His hands splay over the flat of my stomach, sliding upwards, stilling beneath the curve of my breast. York's mouth trails over my jaw, sliding over my lips.

Our chest heaves, our breaths coming thick and heavy, full of unspoken words, full of need and love. So much love. I breathe York in, my hand clasping his cheek.

We kiss.

Xeno groans, his mouth dropping to my neck, sucking, kissing the delicate, sensitive flesh.

Light and heat sweeps over my body. It fires through my veins, igniting me from the inside out.

I want them badly enough that I don't care who watches.

I don't care that the Deana-dhe are in this room with us now.

And neither do York and Xeno. Their erections grind against my stomach and back, their hands, mouth and teeth tease. I turn into liquid heat, warmth pooling between my legs, seeping into the thin material of my knickers.

Let those dark, shadowy men see what it means to truly be loved. Let them see.

With the effect of the drug still flooding my veins I grind my hips against the rigid length of York's cock, needing the friction, wanting more, *needing* more. I think I might burst if I don't get it. Behind me Xeno groans, his fingers playing with my nipples over the material of my dress. His breath is heavy as his teeth and tongue slide over the bare skin of my shoulder.

"Tiny..." he laments, and I understand in that plea what he wants because I want it too.

"I don't care. I don't care. Fuck me. Please just *love* me."

"Always. We'll always love you, until the end of fucking time," Xeno replies, his voice thick with emotion, brimming with love.

"My love, come here," York says, his hands sliding over my arse. He lifts me up and I straddle his waist, understanding how this is going to play out and not caring about anything other than seeking the ultimate high with these two men, two portions of my soul.

With one hand, York holds me firmly against his chest, with the other he unzips his trousers and frees his cock. Behind me, Xeno slides his hand beneath my dress and pushes the thin material of my knickers to the side.

I'm so wet that his fingers slide through my folds with ease. Circling my clit, Xeno draws out my pleasure, his fingers replaced by the head of York's cock.

"Oh God," I cry as York and Xeno bring me to the edge just by their gentle, teasing touches. I'm on the verge already, the heat of their bodies causes mine to flush, a sheen of sweat covering my skin. They're so close that I don't know where I end and they begin, the drug rushing through our veins heightening every feeling. It's indescribable.

Held between them, I'm hidden from view, the only thing on show are my legs and arms cinched against York's back and neck. My head falls back against Xeno's shoulder as I release a low, throaty moan.

"Tiny, I need to be inside you," Xeno murmurs, cupping my chin with one hand as he angles my head and slides his lips over mine. We kiss and we kiss, and we kiss, our tongues twirling, our lips fusing as York continues to slide the thick head of his cock through my folds, making me wetter, hotter, desperate.

It's too much. It's not enough. I feel like I'm both within my skin and out of it. I'm fuelled by lust, by love, by this feeling of magic and wonder, just like the song suggests.

"You are ours," Xeno says, his fingers sliding around my arse, one finger dipping in, followed by another, stretching me. I grind into his hand, against York's teasing cock, seeking more, chasing the pleasure.

"Please," I beg against Xeno's lips.

York squeezes me harder against his chest and guides his cock to my entrance, pushing inside of me with one smooth thrust. Stars burst behind my closed eyelids as I take him in, fisting him deep inside. Xeno draws back, allowing me to kiss York who fucks me in slow, smooth thrusts, holding me steady in his arms. Our tongues twine, dancing, twirling seeking warmth, stirring up the light that surrounds the three of us. Then slowly, gently, Xeno removes his fingers in my arse and replaces them with his cock. He slides into me, inch by delicious inch. York stills, a low groan releasing from his lips as he tips his head back, eyes rolling, feeling the slide of Xeno's cock as much as I do.

When Xeno is fully seated, they move in unison, their cocks separated by a thin wall of muscle. Heat builds, the light that surrounds us expands, reaching out to the corners of the room. Nothing but the feel of them moving within me and our love surrounding us enters my thoughts. Held between them like this, with their lips and tongues sliding over my skin, fingers gently twisting my nipples, cocks sliding, fucking, a finger pressed against my clit drawing out my pleasure, I come undone. We come together, crying out in unison. The white light around us flaring, blinding us, *binding* us together. Slowly as I come down from the most incredible orgasm I've ever experienced, the waves of pleasure ebb away along with the effects of the drug.

"That was..." I begin, words failing me.

"Incredible," Xeno and York answer in unison.

We laugh in wonder, still very much in our own bubble. It isn't until Xeno and York pull out of me gently that I tense, reality settling back in as I realise what we've just done. "The Deana-dhe," I whisper.

"Are gone..." Xeno says, pulling my skirt down over my hips and arse as York lowers me to the floor and tucks himself away.

"When? I didn't notice them leaving."

"Me either," York says, removing his t-shirt and dropping to his knees. He swipes the soft cotton between my legs and when he's done, balls up his t-shirt and stands. "I'm sorry. I didn't use..."

"A condom. Fuck!" Xeno whispers.

"Don't. Don't apologise. We couldn't help ourselves," I say softly, cupping his cheek. I'm not panicking about it, far from it. I just feel warm, loved.

"You're not mad?"

"No. I'm not mad."

"But what if..."

"Then we deal with it."

He nods, unspoken words crossing his features, then flicks his gaze to Xeno, his expression darkening. "Those motherfuckers. They got their kicks for the night, then fucked off without telling Pen what she wanted to know."

"Are you surprised?" Xeno asks, blowing out a steady breath, his fingers flexing and curling into his palm.

"Wait," I say, noticing a sheet of paper on the sofa, a discarded pencil left lying next to it. My throat tightens and my stomach flips over as I step closer. When my eyes land on the perfectly drawn image, I can't help but gasp. "No."

"Tiny?" Xeno asks.

With shaking hands I pick up the piece of paper, drawn on it is an exact copy of a tattoo that I know only too well. The detail is perfect, right down to the shading. In the corner of the piece of paper is Arden's signature, a message written above it: *there's no tricking fate.*

"Titch, what is it?"

I turn around slowly to face them both just as Beast steps into the room. "I made sure that they left before you all started fuck—" he begins, his words cut off by the expression on my face.

"The person Arden was talking about..." I swallow hard, tears pricking my eyes, "It's Dax," I whisper, turning the piece of paper around and showing them a perfect replica of his dark angel tattoo.

26

Pen

"THE QUICKEST WAY TO kill a man is a bullet to the head at close range," Xeno explains, pressing his mouth to my ear as he stands behind me. The shooting range Xeno has brought me to on this quiet Sunday afternoon is empty, which is just as well. I don't much feel like having an audience.

"Yeah, I know," I reply, forcing away the memory of Jeb blowing the brains out of his security guard that night at Rocks. It doesn't matter how much time has passed since that night, I still see the image of blood and brains exploding out of that poor man's skull. There was so much blood.

"There is very little room for error, and death is swift. Messy, but swift."

"Is that how you killed people, at close range?" I ask.

The thought of Xeno doing the same to his enemies turns

my blood cold. Then again, I've been perpetually cold ever since I laid eyes on the image Arden drew of Dax's tattoo last weekend. They've all tried to persuade me that the Deana-dhe were just fucking with us, but I know, deep down, they're scared too. They just won't admit it. Dax is the most blasé of them all, even though I see the fear in his eyes anytime the subject is brought up.

"Most of the time, yes," he replies, and the hairs on the back of my neck lift at the empty hollowness of his voice.

"Most of the time?" I whisper, my fingers skirting over the cool metal of the guns laid out on the bench before me.

"On a couple of occasions when I wasn't able to get close enough to the target, I would use a sniper rifle. Though it wasn't my preference, too impersonal," he says, picking up one of the smaller handguns. "This is a Glock G43x. A perfect fit for your hand size. How does it feel to hold?"

"It feels fine," I reply, my voice as taut as my body. I want to ask him how many people he's killed over the years, but I don't. It's probably better that I never know the number. At least if I kill David it will be one less life he has to take.

"It's important that you hold the gun correctly. You should hold onto it firmly, but not in a death grip," Xeno explains, placing the gun in my hand and adjusting my fingers until he's satisfied they're in the correct position. "Now support your hold with your other hand, like this." Again he arranges my fingers then slides his hands beneath my forearms and raises my arms so that they're extended out in front of me. "Align the sights with the target, then when you're ready, pull back on the trigger in one smooth, continuous motion."

"Okay," I respond, shivering a little when he presses a kiss against my cheek before placing a pair of noise cancelling head-phones over my ears and adjusts my protective glasses.

When he steps away I force myself to concentrate on the target, and not on the fact that someday soon something terrible is going to happen to Dax. Taking one last steadying breath, I pull the trigger just like Xeno taught me to do. The first shot rings out, muffled by my headphones, and the kickback is more powerful than I'd anticipated. I miss the target.

"Fuck," I mutter, and determined not to miss again, I hold the gun firmer. By the time I empty the magazine, I'm no longer shaking, and I've at least hit the target.

"You did good," Xeno remarks once I place the gun back on the table and take off the headphones and glasses. "The more you handle the guns and practice shooting them, the more confident you'll become."

"Thanks."

Xeno nods then picks up the handgun I'd just used, reloads it with more ammunition, then flicks the safety on and hands it to me. "This is yours."

"Mine?"

"You need a gun. This is your gun. I'd suggest you carry it on you at all times given the circumstances. I'm not sure Madame Tuillard would appreciate you taking it into dance lessons at the Academy, but I don't really give a fuck," he says with a wry smile.

"No, I guess not. But what she doesn't know won't hurt her, right? I'll just keep it in my gym bag."

Xeno grins. "Come on, let's get out of here."

Five minutes later, with my gun tucked safely into my hand-bag, we're in the car and on our way home. It's just past six o'clock, and the sky is already dark. Outside, the streets of Hackney are filled with people leaving work, or grabbing last minute items from the shops before they close for the evening. As we drive through our hometown, I find my thoughts returning to Dax and what Arden had written on the corner of the page he'd drawn the dark angel tattoo upon: *There's no tricking fate.*

"Xeno, can I ask you something?"

"Sure, of course."

"Do you believe in fate, that there are things that are beyond our control?"

"Tiny, we've talked about this..."

"I know. You think the Deana-dhe are bullshitters. That specifically, Arden is a bullshitter. That's not what I'm asking. I'm asking if you believe in fate."

"I believe in the here and now. I believe in us."

"So you don't then...?"

"No, I don't."

"I do..." I whisper, hating that it's the truth, because if it is that means I believe in Arden's prediction. "I believe I was meant to be dancing in the park that day when Zayn and I first met. I believe York was supposed to find me standing under the oak tree that night when I ran away. I believe Dax was always supposed to be my first kiss and that you and I were destined to dance together. I believe fate had a hand at bringing us together, and I'm terrified she's going to tear us apart."

"Screw that. Nothing is set in stone. I don't buy into something that takes away my power to protect the people I love. Fate can go screw herself, and the Deana-dhe can fuck off with their bullshit too. This is what they do. They get into people's heads and they manipulate them."

"I hope you're right. I really, really do."

"I am right. Believe in that if you want to believe in anything."

I nod, and for a while we sit in silence, slaves to our thoughts until I can't bear it anymore. "What did you mean when you said that using a sniper is less personal?" I blurt out, forcing myself to think about something else.

"Sorry?" Xeno glances my way, frowning.

"At the shooting range, you said it was too impersonal using a sniper. What did you mean by that?" I ask, watching him closely.

When we come to a standstill due to some traffic, he eases out a breath, then looks at me. "It's easy to pretend you're not guilty of taking a life when there's some physical distance between you and the target. Using a sniper meant I could walk away without seeing what I'd done. I chose to kill at close range when I could so that I would *never* forget the look in the eyes of the men I killed. I had to fucking see it, Tiny. I had to see what I'd done."

"Why would you do that to yourself?"

"I told you that killing numbed me, didn't I?"

"Yes, you did."

"It stopped me from feeling altogether and I knew, deep down, that wasn't necessarily a good thing."

"I hate that. I hate that you needed something so violent in order to stop you from feeling anything at all," I admit.

Xeno swipes a hand through his hair, his jaw gritting. "I think I knew on some level that if I didn't look those men in the eyes before I killed them, then what little humanity I had left inside would be gone for good."

I nod with understanding. "But you're not that man. Not anymore."

"I'm still that man, Tiny," he replies with a sigh, "But I'm also the man you love and the boy you grew up with. I'm all of those things."

"And I accept all of you. Every part. All of the ugliness and all of the beauty..."

"You're too good, Tiny."

I laugh at that, but it isn't a happy sound. "Too good for you, is that what you're saying?"

"Yes... *No*. Fuck, I don't know. Most days I don't feel worthy of you, if I'm honest." He lets out a harsh laugh at that. "Admitting that to you is difficult, but it's true."

My heart lurches inside my chest and I hate that he thinks that way after everything we've gone through together. "Xeno, I'm going to tell you something, and you're going to listen, okay?"

"And what's that?" he asks me.

"You've done bad things, I *know* that, but I also happen to know that you've done them for good reasons. Does it make it right? Maybe not, but who the hell am I to judge? I wasn't in your shoes, but I understand how it feels to want to protect the people you love. You're a *good* man, Xeno. Believe me, I know what a bad man looks like. Men like my brother don't feel the things you feel or love the way you do. You've struggled your whole life with your emotions because you feel *everything*. David feels nothing but a twisted kind of ownership. When I look at you, when I look into your eyes I don't feel fear, Xeno. I don't feel afraid for my safety like I always did in David's presence. I only feel loved. So fucking loved," I say, my voice trailing off as Xeno's fingers curl around the steering wheel in a tight grip as he battles internally with his own feelings about himself.

"The men I killed might have been criminals, they might have been bad men like your brother, Tiny, but killing them didn't make me a good man either. You need to understand that. I'm flawed. *Dangerous*. You've no idea just how much. I keep it contained for you."

"I know who you are, Xeno. *I know who you are*," I repeat fiercely.

Xeno reaches for my hand and squeezes it tightly. "Well, I'm glad one of us does," he laughs a little, but it's forced, broken. "Truthfully, Tiny, the only time I ever feel like the real me is when I dance with you, with the guys. That's the honest, fucking truth. Aside from the fact dancing is who we are deep inside, it's why we *have* to keep dancing. Why you *need* to keep dancing with us all. It's crucial to our survival, to yours. You understand that now, right?"

"I do. I understand completely, and that's why I'm back at the Academy. That's why I've kept my job at Tales. That's why I will always dance with you whenever you need me to."

"You've kept your job at Tales because you still feel like you have to repay us. You don't. Being our girlfriend, loving us all, it's enough. It's more than enough. We can take care of you. We want to do that."

"And I appreciate the sentiment, you know I do, and whilst I do want to pay you back, I'm not just working at Tales because of that fact. I need to earn my *own* money. It's important to me."

"Then it's important to us too." Xeno responds. When we

stop at the next set of traffic lights, he turns to me. "Are you hungry?"

"I could eat," I reply.

"Good. I need to pop into Jewels and check on the new security set up and make sure the updated fire alarm system is working as it should. I'll get the chef to throw together something whilst we're there. He starts around this time to get set up for the evening."

"What about the guys and Lena? They'll be expecting us home. We only said we'd be gone a couple of hours."

"The guys can just suck it up," he says with a smirk that has me laughing out loud, "But maybe give Lena a call so she doesn't start worrying."

TURNS out the chef at Jewels is more than happy to *throw together* a three course meal that is so well thought out that I can't help but wonder whether Xeno had this planned all along.

"That was delicious," I say, licking the last of the chocolate mousse from my spoon and letting out a small moan of appreciation. Trent, the chef, has skills for days. If I wasn't already deliriously in love with four men, I'd totally have the hots for him.

Xeno leans back in his seat, his eyes zeroing in on my mouth as I wrap my lips around the spoon. "Very," he agrees, taking a sip of his brandy as he regards me.

"I feel kind of guilty that the others didn't get to enjoy it."

Xeno places his drink on the table, then stands, holding his hand out to me. "I don't. You're my girl as much as theirs, and if

I want to take you on a date, I will. They just need to up their game."

"So you *did* plan this then?"

"Yep," he says, popping the *p*. I laugh at his honest response then place my hand in his. "Besides, I may have had an ulterior motive."

"Oh, yeah?" I reply, following him onto the dance floor knowing exactly what he wants, what he needs, and I'm more than willing to give it to him because I never, *ever* want to see him hold a knife to his own chest again. Never.

Xeno turns to face me, giving me a small smile before flicking his gaze to someone over my shoulder. He nods his head and music starts playing over the sound system.

"The Chainsmokers?" I ask, recognising the tune as *Don't Let Me Down* starts to play.

"Bachata version," he corrects me, the underlying bachata beat, familiar and welcome.

"I like it. Good choice."

"What can I say, I'm full of surprises," he retorts with a slow smile as he lifts my arms into a classic bachata hold. "Dance with me?"

"Always," I reply, feeling more and more confident in my ability to both embrace dance and the still very violent need to kill my brother. They live side-by-side now, neither one cancelling out the other. I feel stronger for it, not weaker.

"I'm so fucking proud of you, Tiny. Today you fired a gun. You're taking control. If David walked in here right now you'd have the ability to kill him. Dancing doesn't change that fact," he says, swaying his hips in time to the beat.

"You're right, it doesn't."

"Follow my lead, okay?"

"Okay," I reply as he leans in and brushes his lips across my cheek, leaving a trail of wild heat across my skin.

"I fucking adore you, Tiny. Everything about you turns me the fuck on. For the next hour you're mine," he says with a possessive growl.

"I've always been yours," I remind him, cocking my hip and feeling immediately comfortable in his hold as we dance together. He's so sure of himself as he guides me with a touch to my hip or the slide of his leg between mine. We've never danced to this song together before in any style, let alone bachata, but that doesn't matter, because Xeno is an excellent partner and I know him well enough to be able to follow his cues.

As the beat gets more intense, so do our movements. This isn't a slow bachata, this is punchy, sexy, *invigorating*. When Xeno grasps my shoulders, slides his thigh between my legs and rotates his hips, I'm forced to follow the movement, my crotch grinding against his thigh as he presses his forehead against mine and locks gazes with me. It's a dominant move, and highlights his ability to take control, just like he does in everyday life.

"Do you feel that?" he asks me.

"Feel what?"

"*Free.*"

"Yes."

"We don't need a drug to make us feel that way, it was in us all along..." he says thoughtfully.

I nod in agreement, my body humming with energy as Xeno slides his hands down my ribcage and over my hips, the palms of his hands pushing against my hip bones, showing me how he wants me to move.

My soul practically weeps with relief as he spins me around so that my back is pressed to his front and we rock together. I can feel his cock thickening, his love and lust for me growing as we dance. In response, my heart thrums with blood, a rush of endorphins overwhelms me as the heat of his body seeps into mine as he lowers his lips to my neck, kissing me gently.

"I think I've found a better addiction," Xeno mutters, turning me in his arms and cupping my cheeks as we really sink into the mood of the song and the growing, undeniable attraction between us.

"Addictions aren't healthy," I counter, sliding my hands up his arms and gripping his wrists.

"That all depends on what the addiction is. I think you'll agree that dancing with you is an addiction that's good for my mental wellbeing." He grins and I can't help but laugh.

When he lets go of my face and steps between my legs, I tighten my fingers around his wrists, recognising the move instantly. My thighs clench his leg and I tighten my core as he lowers me backwards.

"You remembered?" he asks, his eyes flashing with hunger as my lips part and my cheeks flush at the memory.

"How could I forget? You picked Tiffany to showcase this move. I was sick with jealousy... and *lust*. I wanted so badly to be her."

"I was such a prick."

"Yeah, you were, but we're past that now. I forgive you."

Xeno pulls me back up and I let his wrists go, taking his proffered hand. "Let me make it up to you," he says, lifting our joined fingers over the back of my head before encouraging me to turn beneath his arm.

"How do you plan on doing that?" I ask, laughing as he yanks me back against his chest, his hands trailing down to my arse and squeezing tightly.

"Do you feel *that*?" he repeats, a mischievous glint in his eyes as he grinds his hips against me, his erection pressing against my abdomen.

"Yeah. I feel that. So, what are you going to do about it?" I ask, biting on my lip.

Xeno's eyes flash with the challenge. "Oh, Tiny, never mind the fucking stars, I'm gonna make you see the whole damn galaxy."

Siding his hands over my arse, Xeno lifts me up and I straddle his waist, my arms wrapping around his neck as he kisses me deeply. Blinded by his kiss, I'm only aware that we've moved when he lays me down on one of the other tables that surround the dance floor.

"I've never fucked on a table before," I say, smiling up at him as he stares down at me.

"Well, this is a first that I'm going to enjoy taking," Xeno responds, his eyes glazing with need.

Someone coughs, interrupting us. "You might want to bench that thought for now..."

27

Pen

DAX STEPS onto the dance floor, his arms folded across his chest as he regards us both.

"You've got to be fucking kidding me," Xeno grumbles, pulling back and drawing me upright as we both turn to face him.

"What is it? What happened?" Panic rears its head as my thoughts turn immediately to Lena.

"Lena's good. She's with Gray. The ghosts are guarding the flat."

"Why, where are the others?" Xeno asks, as we gather our things from the table.

"Gone straight to Hudson's office. We should head there now. He has some news."

"They've found David?" I ask, both filled with hope that we

can finally end this nightmare once and for all, and fear that nothing is ever as simple as that.

"Not exactly. But Max and Bryce have managed to uncover some information. Come on, we should go."

Less than half an hour later we're stepping out of the escalator and into the penthouse of the Freed brothers' office building. The place is swanky as hell, with floor to ceiling windows that provide an incredible view over central London, minimalist decor that screams money, and all the technical equipment any self-respecting multi-million dollar businessman should have at their fingertips.

"Good, you're here. Come on in," Hudson says, waving us over to the huge conference table situated in the centre of the room. Already sitting at the table are York and Zayn and two more men I've never met before but recognise from the photos I saw dotted around their huge mansion when we stayed there. I give York and Zayn a tremulous smile and they smile back, if a little guardedly. It's obvious they're as anxious as the rest of us to find out what Hudson knows.

"I'm Pen," I say.

"Nice to meet you, Pen. Sorry about my brother, he can be a complete dick sometimes," the dark-haired of the two says with a grin that instantly transforms his face. He's tall, built, and has an impressive, groomed beard.

"Apologies," Hudson says, pointing at his two brothers in turn. "This is Max and Bryce."

"It's good to finally meet you at last. Louisa had nothing but kind words to say about you," Max, the smiliest of the three, says to me. He's got a flop of hay-blonde hair, tan skin, and is dressed down in a loose hoodie and black jeans unlike his brothers who are both wearing suits.

"Right, now that we've got the introductions over and done with, let me show you this. Please, take a seat," Hudson urges.

Xeno squeezes my hand and guides me towards the table, pulling out the chair opposite York, who winks at me when I bite on my lip worriedly. "You good?" he asks quietly.

"I'm okay," I reply, nodding.

York frowns but doesn't press further, we both know I'm not okay, but there's really not much either of us can do about it right now. I just need to put on my big girls pants and just deal with whatever this turns out to be.

"We're just waiting on Grim and Beast to arrive. They're coming up in the lift as we speak," Hudson explains, looking briefly at a second laptop opened up on the table. I can see from where I'm sitting that the laptop must be connected to a camera in the lift, because Beast is currently pressing Grim up against the wall and kissing her passionately. He has her chin gripped in his tattooed hand and is thoroughly fucking her mouth with his tongue.

Max notices and chuckles. "I've never understood what she sees in that arsehole, but right now both of them seem to be enjoying the rush of hormones pregnancy brings. I miss those days with Louisa," he says, glancing at me and winking.

Behind us the lift doors open and Beast and Grim step out. Her cheeks are flushed, and Beast is grinning like the cat that has just got the finest cream. "Alright everyone?" Beast asks, one arm slung around Grim's shoulder, the other carrying her coat in front of him. It doesn't take a genius to work out what he's trying to hide.

Max shakes his head. "Good to see you, mate. You too, Grim. Enjoy the *ride* up? We certainly did," he says, amusement dancing in his eyes.

Grim narrows her eyes at Max, then shoves her hand against Beast's chest, clearly blaming him for their little indiscretion being caught on camera. Rather than responding to Max's very obvious ribbing, she approaches me and gives me a peck on the cheek. "You doing alright?"

"Yeah."

"Good." Squeezing me on the shoulder, she rounds the table and sits down on the empty seat between Bryce and York, focussing her attention on Hudson. "Let's see what you've got, Hud."

"Coming right up," he replies, typing some kind of command into the laptop. A moment later a grainy image appears on the screen, but it's all pixelated and I can't quite make out what it is.

"Pregnancy suits you, Grim," Bryce whispers under his breath, whilst Hudson types some more, his finger clicking on the mouse as he tries to make the image clearer.

"Thank you, Bryce. I like the beard," she reaches up, giving it a playful tug.

"All I did was kiss my woman. Nothing wrong with that. How was I supposed to know these fuckers have cameras every-fucking-where?" Beast grumbles, plopping down in the only empty chair left, which happens to be the furthest point from Grim. She smiles over at him sweetly, but I can tell he's in deep shit. Clearly public displays of affection aren't really her thing, even though it totally wasn't his fault.

"Hudson, as much as we all enjoy watching Beast squirm,

do you want to fill us in on why we're here?" Xeno says, squeezing my thigh beneath the table.

"Interpol has managed to pull up footage of a man fitting the description of your brother entering a shopping centre in Waltham Forest about thirty minutes after Jefferson saw him leaving the flat the night your mum was murdered."

"About fucking time!" Zayn says.

"Face recognition technology has confirmed a ninety-five percent match based on photographs of your brother from three years ago before he left for Mexico," Hudson explains. "Once I've been sent the footage, I will forward it onto you so you can officially identify him."

"Okay," I reply with a curt nod.

Dax shifts in his seat beside me, his hand closing over mine. "So where did he go after that?"

"He entered the underground station situated beneath the shopping centre and got on the Central Line towards Epping," Hudson says. "They managed to trace him all the way to Debden, but then lost him. The cameras at Debden station were vandalised the night before he took the journey."

"How fucking convenient," Beast says. "I'll give him props. He's a conniving son of a bitch."

"Fuck!" Xeno exclaims, banging his fist against the table top.

"My thoughts exactly. Anyway, there's more," Hudson says. "Give me a minute, the footage sent over isn't the best and I need to just sharpen it up a little. He twists the laptop screen around so that it's not in my direct line of sight.

"I didn't know you were a techy," Beast remarks, looking mildly impressed.

Hudson shrugs, his attention focused on the screen in front

of him. "I guess you could call it a hobby... Here we go." Grabbing the remote control that's sitting on the table beside the laptop, he presses a button and the wooden panelling making up one wall in the office starts to slide open, revealing a huge TV screen. "About an hour ago Max got a call from a friend of ours, a man called Maguire Fitzpatrick. He sent this footage over to us after his security team found it when searching through their CCTV."

Xeno leans forward. "Wait, who's Maguire Fitzpatrick?"

"He's the owner of a number of shipping ports in the West Country," Hudson explains. "We've been waiting on him to get back to us."

Bryce shifts in his seat and rests his forearms on the table, interlocking his fingers. "After Max and I met with him and explained what we needed, he got his security teams to search through the CCTV footage at each port he owns for any unusual activity over the last few weeks."

"And?" Grim prompts.

"And this is what they just sent me," Hudson says, clicking the enter button on his laptop. "What you're looking at is footage of a fishing boat that docked at Newlyn Port just over three weeks ago."

On the TV screen a grainy image appears of a fishing trawler pulling into the dock. We all watch as several fishermen walk down the gangplank. I've never seen a fishing boat in real life before, but as far as I can tell nothing looks out of place. Beast must think the same because he leans forward in his seat and says, "Fucking brilliant, the guys have hauled a pretty big catch... And?"

"Just wait," Hudson urges.

Maybe half a minute or so passes then two men step out of the cabin that sits on the deck of the trawler. One is an older man wearing a fisherman's cap and overalls and the other is wearing a hooded jacket and jeans, and even though he's facing away from the camera, I know who it is.

"Is that the little psycho causing all this shit...?" Beast scoffs, looking between the screen and me. "What a twunt!"

"Twunt?" Max snorts, then straightens his face when Beast glares at him.

"I wanted Pen to confirm his identity," Hudson says, before turning his attention back to the laptop screen. He pauses the footage just at the precise moment when David turns around. It's a clear shot of his face and there's no denying who it is.

"Yeah, that's him."

York catches my eye and gives me a reassuring smile. It's enough to make me swallow down the bile I feel rising up my throat and ignore my sudden need to bolt. I hate that that's my reaction. Instinctively, I reach for my handbag, comforted by the firm shape of the gun resting inside.

"Okay, so we have absolute proof that David's here and we're not dealing with some copycat fucker or rival gang member doing his dirty work, but we knew that already, right? So, my question to you, Hudson, is this: what's the real reason you brought us here tonight?" Xeno asks, squeezing my jittery leg beneath the table.

"Xeno has a point," Grim agrees.

"I didn't want to tell you this news over the phone. I figured you should hear it in person."

"Don't tell me you're pregnant too?" Beast asks, folding his arms across his chest and smirking.

"Funny," Hudson reports, pressing play once again. "David wasn't the only passenger on that fishing trawler that day."

Grim sits forward in her seat, her elbows resting on the table as she looks between Hudson and the screen and back again. "You're kidding," she asks.

Hudson shakes his head. "I wouldn't kid about something like that. Watch."

For the next minute or so David stands and chats with the captain of the fishing boat. Then there's movement in the cabin and another man steps out. He appears to be a lot older than David, definitely in his sixties given the lines on his face when the camera zooms in. He's wearing a floor length black coat and a matching black fedora hat that screams old school gangster.

"Oh, look, it's Al Capone," Beast comments, a smile in his voice.

"Not Al Capone, Beast, but Cuba's very own homegrown version of him. That, my friend, is Santiago Romero Garcia."

"Well fuck me with a side of fries," Beast remarks, darkly. "Let the motherfucking games begin."

Grim locks eyes with Hudson, her expression serious. "Louisa and the kids?"

"On their way to the airport with my father-in-law and security team as we speak. Our jet is waiting to go. They'll be staying in our chalet in Alpes d'Huez until this is over. Max and Bryce are heading to the airport to join them as soon as we're finished up here."

"You know I'm happy to stay behind. We don't need to both go. You're going to need back up," Bryce says.

"The fuck you are. I need you and Max watching over Louisa and the kids," Hudson replies firmly.

Bryce tugs on his beard in frustration. "They're going to have an army of ex-marines guarding them, and as much as I hate the thought of being separated from them, I know they'll be safe with Max and the team."

"I don't give a fuck. You're going," Hudson replies, and it's clear to everyone sitting around the table who the leader of this trio is. I might've respected that if I didn't feel like punching Hudson's face in right now as a sudden rush of anger rises up my chest.

"Wait! Just hold on a minute," I say, glaring at Hudson. "You're sending your family away because Santiago's *that* dangerous and yet you're happy for my family, for Grim and Beast, to be in the line of fire all to get your revenge? It must be nice to have the means to protect the people you love like that. What about the rest of us?"

"Sweetheart, Grim and I are here because we want to be, and the same applies to your men. None of us are afraid of some twunt psychopath and a two-bit drug baron who dresses like he's stepped out of a mobster movie set in the 1950's. This is all in a day's work," Beast says, giving me a wink that doesn't reassure me in the slightest.

Hudson closes the lid of the laptop and looks me directly in the eye. "I should've sent them away sooner. Admittedly, there was a part of me that wasn't even sure Santiago would come and I selfishly kept them close because like you, Pen, it's difficult to part with the ones you love. I'm not immune to making bad decisions, but I am good at rectifying them. With that in mind, Lena has a ticket with her name on it. Gray is welcome to accompany her if that makes you feel better about her leaving.

She can go and be safe with my family, and all the guards I've got protecting them will protect her too."

"We'll look after her," Max adds. "We'll treat her as family. Louisa wouldn't have it any other way, and neither would we."

"You want me to send my sister away with a bunch of strangers?" I ask quietly. "She doesn't know you. She doesn't know any of you well enough to go and live with you all, even if it's only for a little while."

"As soon as this is dealt with, they'll be home," Hudson says, trying to reassure me.

"Lena's just lost her mum. Her world has been upended..." I counter, feeling sick at the thought of her going away and sick of the thought of her staying.

"I swear we're good people," Max insists. "I might have a weird sense of humour, and Bryce might have a small animal growing on his face right now, but Lena will be safe with us."

"I don't know... This is all happening too fast." I chew on my lip, trying to decide what to do for the best.

"Yes, you do, Kid. You've been protecting Lena your whole life. You know what the right choice is," Dax says, reaching for my hand and squeezing it.

"You should go too, Pen. No one here would think any less of you if you did," Hudson says.

"No!" I retort, shaking my head. "I'm not going anywhere. Do you honestly think I'd let the men I love stay behind and deal with this after everything that's happened?"

"No, I figured you'd want to stay, but the offer is there, regardless."

"No. Absolutely not. I'm staying. Besides, I *know* David,

he'll only come after me. We end this together, right here and now."

"And Lena?" Grim asks me, her voice gentle. "Is she staying put or is she going?"

Swallowing hard, I lock eyes with Hudson. "Can you guarantee her safety?"

"Yes. My family is my top priority. I wouldn't send them away without me if I didn't think the people guarding them weren't up to the job."

"Then she goes with them. I want her safe whilst we finish this."

"Alright then," Zayn says then stands up. "We should get going so Pen can say her goodbyes to Lena and help her pack."

"Actually, there's one more thing I need to say before we all head off..." Hudson begins.

"Does it happen to have anything to do with a certain Duncan Neath?" Beast asks, steepling his fingers beneath his chin and grinning a little too maniacally for my liking.

"The fuck?" York exclaims, clearly making the same assumptions as the rest of us. "You're not suggesting—"

"What do you know?" Hudson asks Beast, ignoring York for the moment.

"Well, I know he ain't here sitting with us right now, which tells me one of two things. Either he's dead, or you think he's the snake and you're cutting him off."

"Well, he isn't dead—" Hudson points out.

"—yet," Grim finishes, her eyes flashing dangerously. She looks as surprised as the rest of us, but recovers quickly. "He isn't dead *yet*. By the time Beast finishes with him he's going to wish he was. I knew there was a reason that I never liked the creep."

"Fuck!" Xeno mutters.

"You honestly think he's the snake?" York asks, frowning. "He can be a bit of a twat, but really, fucking all of us *and* Interpol over, that's suicide."

"I think it's the only possibility," Hudson says.

"But why him? He's set to lose a hell of a lot if that's the case," Zayn points out.

"Yeah, starting with a bollock," Beast interjects without so much as a hint of a smile.

"He's the only one who knows the full extent of what's going on. He's fully aware of our connection with Grim and Beast and their role in this. It's the only logical explanation... Unless it's one of you four," Hudson says, looking between my men. Immediately my hackles rise. How dare he even suggest that?

"Of course it fucking isn't!" Xeno snaps before I can. He glares at Hudson menacingly, and for the briefest of moments I see the man he's trying so hard to protect me from. Taking a steadying breath he reigns himself in. "We want this to be over so we can the move the fuck on and have a life like you have with your family. Do you honestly think we'd put the woman we love in danger? Do you think we'd risk our lives and our free-dom, just to be under the thumb of Santiago fucking Garcia?"

"Actually, no I don't, which is precisely why it has to be D-Neath," Hudson counters calmly. "Don't tell me you hadn't considered it?"

Xeno grits his jaw, refusing to answer that question. "I

trusted him. I shouldn't have," he says turning to face me. "I'm sorry, Pen."

"It's not your fault."

Hudson squeezes Xeno on the shoulder. "We all trusted him, which makes this so much harder to swallow, but the fact of the matter is, Duncan could gain a lot more than he could lose out of this situation."

"Like what exactly? Because the way I see it, he's set to lose every damn thing, including his bollocks," York points out, glancing at Beast who has a sudden look of bloodlust in his eyes.

"Believe me, Santiago can be very persuasive. If Duncan has bought into whatever Santiago is promising then I imagine, for him, being a turncoat is worth it."

"For him?" I ask.

"Duncan has always hungered for power and notoriety," Hudson explains. "The Pink Albatross wasn't his club originally. He got it through nefarious means."

"Well that's a shock," Grim remarks with more than a little sarcasm.

"The club was originally owned by someone called Nicholas Allen, a millionaire playboy in his day. Before Duncan went down for drug racketeering he won the club in a game of cards. Nicholas Allen lost everything, including his wife who left him."

"To be fair, if this Nicholas dude was stupid enough to gamble his business in a game of cards then he deserves all he gets, if you ask me," Zayn says. "Doesn't mean he's guilty of being a snake."

"That's a fair point," Hudson agrees. "But there's more. My team has been doing some digging on the side."

"On the side, as in without Interpol's approval?" Grim asks.

"Precisely."

"Well, look at you bending the rules and shit," Beast says with a grin.

"Not only did I find out about how he came to own The Pink Albatross," Hudson says, choosing to ignore Beast's remark. "I also found out that Duncan has recently looked up flights to various holiday destinations."

"Okay, so he's an opportunist and he wants to go on a holiday. That doesn't make him a traitor. He's with Tuillard. Perhaps it's just a romantic getaway, and after this shit is over he wants to treat her. I know I wouldn't mind getting away with our girl," Dax points out, playing devil's advocate.

Grim scoffs. "Duncan, romantic? Yeah, and I like flowers and candy."

"No babe, we all know you love *hearts*," Beast quips, drawing an exasperated smile from Grim's lips. "What? It's true..."

"I thought it could be as innocent as that, but given everything that's going on I had to be certain. When my team delved a little deeper, some pretty interesting results came up on Duncan's internet search history. Namely extended stays in Cuba, specifically at the resort our very own Santiago Garcia happens to own."

"FUCK!" Xeno exclaims, banging his fist on the table. "I'm gonna murder that bastard."

Now it's my turn to rest my hand on Xeno's leg, trying to calm him a little. "Have you informed Interpol? Surely this is enough evidence to send him back to jail?"

"Fuck Interpol," Beast says with a growl. "Let me have a

word with him. He'll be singing like a canary after five fucking minutes."

Hudson grits his jaw, then nods. "I was hoping you would say that."

$$\text{\textsubscript{}}$$

"I DON'T WANT to go, Pen. Don't make me do this!" Lena cries, clinging onto me as we stand on the Freed's private air strip just outside of London.

On any other day, my mind would've been blown by the fact the Freed brothers own an airplane let alone an airport. Today isn't that day. My heart is way too heavy to be impressed by material things. "You have to. I've told you what's going on. I've been completely honest with you. David isn't the only person who would hurt you given the chance. You need to go. You need to be safe."

Lena casts a brief look over her shoulder at the jet sitting on the tarmac behind us. Her eyes are wide with fear. "I don't like flying."

"You've never been on an airplane before, Lena. How do you know you won't like it?" I point out with a small smile.

"What if it crashes?"

"It won't."

"I don't know anyone..." she argues..

"That's not true. You know Gray and you've met Louisa before. She's really nice, Lena."

"What if that's all a front and she's really some wicked witch who wants to torture me?"

I raise a brow. "You don't really believe that, do you?"

"No. Of course not. Bar you, she's probably the nicest person I've ever met," she says quietly.

"You know that I wouldn't send you away with them if I didn't think they were good people. Think of this as an adventure. That's all you need to do. Forget everything else."

"But, Pen—"

"No more buts. It's time to go," I say, firmer this time. We both know the longer we draw this out, the harder it's going to be. We've already held them up ten minutes longer than necessary. Louisa, Max, Bryce and their two kids have already climbed aboard, as well as the ten ex-marines who Hudson has hired as their security team. Everyone's just waiting for Lena to peel herself off of me and get onboard with Gray, who's currently standing at the bottom of the stairs leading up to the open door of the jet. He's watching us both with professional detachment, and when I meet his gaze he lifts three fingers telling me that our time is running out.

"But what about you? Don't *you* need to be safe?"

"I *need* to finish this."

"No you don't. You can leave it to everyone else. Let the Breakers finish it. Let them, Pen!" Lena's fingers curl into my arms, pinching my skin despite the fact I'm wearing a coat.

Shaking my head, I cup her face in my hands, brushing away the tears that won't stop cascading from her eyes. "If I go with you, David will follow. He wants me most of all, Lena. You staying here will only put you in more danger, me going with you will only put you in danger. We can't be together right now. You *have* to go with them. I will come and get you when this is all over."

"No!"

"Yes."

"Pen, I'm sorry we need to go," Gray says, stepping forward and interrupting our conversation, he rests his hand on Lena's shoulder, but she shakes it off.

"No!" Lena protests.

"I'll make sure she's safe. I swear on my life, Pen."

Blinking back the tears threatening to fall, I nod. "I know you will, Gray. Thank you."

"Pen, *please*," Lena whispers as the wind picks up her hair, whipping it across her face. Above us, standing in the open doorway of the airplane, is Louisa. She gives me a warm smile and I know, no matter how hard this is right now, that it's the right decision. Lena will have Louisa to watch over her for me. I've only been in her company a couple of days, but I already know she's a good woman. Far better than our mum ever was.

"You're going to France, Lena. They'll be snow, skiing, and building snowmen with those beautiful kids. The place sounds amazing, and as soon as this is over I'll be there with you all. I promise."

"I'm scared."

"I know, but you have to be brave."

"I'll try."

"Gray here is gonna watch over you for me. I trust him to look after you."

I realise as I say those words that I really do trust him, that I'm not just saying it to comfort Lena. There's something about Gray that screams *good guy* despite his standoffish attitude. My gut tells me he will look after Lena with his life, and my gut is never wrong.

"I appreciate you saying that," he says.

She looks up at him then and a tumultuous smile pulls up her lips. "For an old guy, he *is* kind of cool..."

"Old?" he laughs briefly, before shutting it down and maintaining that professional mask.

"Don't mind Lena, she thinks anyone above twenty is old," I say, pulling her in for one more fierce hug before letting her go. "Call me the second you get there, okay?"

"I will. Speak soon, Pen?" she frames her response as a question, as though there's a possibility that we'll never speak again, let alone see each other.

"I love you. Everything is going to work out. Now go!"

She nods, and with Gray gently urging her forward, she climbs onto the plane and straight into Louisa's welcoming hug.

28

Pen

"Madame Tuillard, can I have a word?" I ask, knocking on her office door and stepping inside without waiting for a response.

She looks up from behind her desk and smiles warmly. "Pen, shouldn't you be in class?"

"I snuck out a little early. I needed to speak with you."

"Sounds ominous. Please don't tell me that you're leaving the Academy too?"

"No, it's nothing like that."

"Okay..."

Biting on my lip, I wonder for the thousandth time this morning whether I'm making the right decision coming here and speaking with her. Then I think about what Beast is going to do to D-Neath today, and I get this sinking feeling in my stomach that somehow they've got it all wrong. I don't particularly like D-Neath, not in the slightest, but something's been bugging me all night and I need to figure out whether my hunch is right or if I'm barking up the wrong tree. Either way, the outcome for D-Neath won't be good.

"There's something I wanted to ask you."

Noticing the seriousness of my expression, she places her pen on the table before her, and nods. "I guess you'd better come in then."

Closing the door behind me, I take a seat. I'm due to meet the guys for lunch in ten minutes and if I don't turn up, they'll come looking for me. This isn't a conversation I want Madame Tuillard to endure in front of an audience, so I need to make it quick. "When we spoke before, you said that you trusted D-Neath? Do you... still trust him, I mean?"

"Why are you asking me this?" Something close to concern flitters across her face, but she shuts it down.

"It's important."

"It's *private*."

"You said that he hurt you before, but that you trust him now," I push on. "Is that still true?"

"Yes," she blurts out, but despite the certainty of her answer, her body language is telling a different story.

"You don't seem certain. Has he done something to break your trust recently?" I press.

For long moments she just stares at me, but then eventually she nods. "I don't know..."

"You don't know?"

She heaves out a sigh, clearly debating whether she wants to talk to me about this very personal matter. "I *want* to believe he's changed. I think he wants to be a better man. I love him, but lately I've begun to worry that I've made the wrong decision putting my trust in him."

"Why?"

"Over the past few weeks he's been different, *distant*. I put it down to what's going on and the stress he must be under, but my gut is telling me it's more than that..." She clasps her trembling hands together on the table and meets my gaze. "Are you saying that I've made the wrong decision trusting him? Is there something going on that I should know about?"

I chew on my lip, wondering how much I should be telling her. She knows about Santiago and the drugs, but has no idea about my brother or the fact that he murdered my mum. She doesn't know that there's a traitor and that everyone thinks it's D-Neath. Honestly, I'm not even sure why I'm here trying to find a reason why he's *not* the snake. I don't even like him all that much.

"Pen. Tell me."

"When you said before that D-Neath hurt you emotionally, what did you mean exactly?"

"That isn't something you need to know, Pen."

"Like I said, I wouldn't ask if it wasn't important."

She crosses her arms over her chest in an almost self-comforting way then meets my gaze. "Do you remember when I said that the attraction between Duncan and I was immediate and explosive...?

"Yes."

"Well, it happened to be the same for several other girls, not just me."

"So he did cheat on you?"

"You make it sound like you knew that all along..."

"People talk. I'm sorry."

"Well those people were right. Duncan and I were together for several years before he went to prison, and in that time I lost count of the amount of times he slept with other women."

"And you stayed with him?" I ask, shaking my head in disbelief. For me, cheating is the ultimate sin. How could someone so successful, so put together, be such a walkover? It makes no sense.

"I did. Back then I believed it when he told me those women meant nothing, that he loved me. After all, he came back to me every time."

"But he *screwed* other women."

"I was young. Foolishly in love. In some ways, Duncan going to prison saved our relationship. You can't cheat when you're stuck behind bars with a load of men. Granted, he likes sex, I would even suggest that he has an addiction to it, but he's very much into girls." She laughs at that, but the sound is hollow.

"And now...?"

"And now what?"

"Do you have any reason to believe he's gone back to his old ways?" I ask, remembering how he'd looked at me that day the filming crew had been at the Academy. Back then I'd thought he was a creep, that he was probably cheating on Madame Tuillard. Now that seems even more likely especially after what Clancy mentioned when she'd overheard them arguing. In which case, D-Neath's not necessarily the snake, but maybe whoever he's been sleeping with *is*, and I have a hunch who that might be.

"I guess the question really should be, do *you* have a reason to believe Duncan is cheating on me?" Madame Tuillard counters.

"For his sake I hope he is..." I mutter.

"What did you just say?" Madame Tuillard asks, her voice laced with hurt.

"I know how much you love him, and that's partly why I'm here. You deserve to know what's going on."

"What *is* going on, Pen?"

I don't answer her question, instead I ask one of my own. "Do you believe that D-Neath is having an affair?

Her eyes fill with tears and when one tips over her lashes and slides down her cheek, I don't need to hear her answer to know that he is. Eventually she nods. "Yes. I think he is. In fact, I'm almost positive." Her voice cracks and she looks away, opening up a drawer in her desk. Pulling out a piece of paper, she lays it on the table. On it is a mobile phone number. "Like I said, he's been acting *off* for a little while now. Initially I put it down to the fact that he was involved with the whole Santiago, drugs thing. But he's become more and more withdrawn... *Intimately*. That's when I knew. I recognised the signs. So, when he was in the shower last week, I looked at his phone. He's been making calls to this number regularly for the past few weeks. The calls are mainly made after I've gone to sleep."

"Any text messages?"

"No. Just phone calls. I've not been brave enough yet to call the number. I'm not sure I want to confirm that he's having an affair even though not knowing for certain is killing me."

"I can understand that..." Pausing I chew on my lip.

"What?"

"There's something else."

"Could that something be why you're so keen on finding out if D-Neath is having an affair?"

"Yes... *Shit,* I don't know how to say this."

"I'm a big girl, Pen. Spit it out."

"D-Neath is currently being questioned," I say, not wanting to actually tell her that he's most likely being tortured by Beast as we speak.

"What do you mean questioned?"

"The guys believe D-Neath has been feeding information to my brother."

"Your brother? I didn't know you had a brother..." She gives me a confused look. "But why would Duncan be giving information to your brother? Who is he exactly?"

"My brother works for Santiago Garcia. They think D-Neath has betrayed them."

"What kind of information?"

"The dangerous kind." I don't tell her about my mum, about the truth surrounding her death. It wouldn't change anything if I did.

"But that makes no sense. Duncan doesn't want to go back to jail, that much I do know," she replies.

"They believe that Santiago has offered D-Neath something he can't refuse, and I believed that too until..."

"Until?"

"Until I was reminded of something Tiffany said to me the other day."

"*Tiffany?*" Madame Tuillard stiffens, her gaze darkening. "What did she have to say exactly?"

"She confronted me the day I returned to the Academy. Amongst spouting off about the fact she thinks I'm a shit dancer and not deserving of my place here at the Academy, she also said a couple of things that I didn't question at the time."

"Like what?"

"She said that I was clueless, but more specifically she said that '*he'll tire of me eventually.*'"

"Clueless about what? Who will tire of you eventually?"

"I thought she was just being a bitch and trying to insinuate she was sleeping with one of my men, that she meant Xeno or Dax would tire of me, maybe even York or Zayn, but that isn't who she meant..." Swallowing the bile I feel rising up my throat, I lock eyes with Madame Tuillard.

"You think she was talking about D-Neath, that he has a thing for you?"

"No," I shake my head. "I think she was talking about my brother, David."

"I don't understand."

"I believe she's been sleeping with D-Neath, using him to gather information to pass onto my brother in the hope to gain *his* affections. I think *Tiffany is* the snake. It makes sense. She hates me, she hates the men I love, and my brother is *very* manipulative. He can turn on the charm when he wants to."

Madame Tuillard's mouth pops open as she allows that information to settle. It can't be easy to hear that the man she loves has been fucking a student, an *ex-student*, let alone that he's been careless enough to let information slip about what's been going on, but here we are.

"I'm sorry, it's a lot to take in. This can't be easy to hear, but I needed to be certain."

"There's really only one way to be certain that your suspicions about Tiffany are true," she says, pointing at the piece of paper with the mobile number written across it. "Though, I'm not sure she'll answer the line if she sees the call has been made from my office at the Academy."

"Good point. But she'll answer the phone if D-Neath calls, right?"

"If what you're saying is true, then yes. I imagine she would," Madame Tuillard agrees with a tight nod of her head.

"I should go," I say, picking up the slip of paper and pocketing it. "I need to tell the guys what I've discovered. I really am sorry to be the bearer of bad news."

"Don't be. You've only confirmed what my heart has known for some time," she sighs, forcing herself to smile. "I will ask one favour though."

"What's that?"

"When you see D-Neath, can you pass on a message?"

"Sure I can..."

"Will you tell him that he has 24 hours to remove his stuff from my home and that he no longer has a job at my Academy."

"Of course," I say, reaching for the door handle.

"Oh, and could you also tell him to go fuck himself."

I meet Madame Tuillard's gaze and smile. "That I'd happily do."

29

York

"SO YOU'RE TELLING me that *Tiffany* has been feeding information to your brother?" I ask Titch just to be certain I've heard her right, because fuck if I'm not a little gobsmacked by the news. Given the looks on Xeno, Dax and Zayn's faces they're struggling to wrap their heads around the idea too. We all know Tiffany's a crazy bitch, but getting mixed up with David and Santiago? That's batshit crazy. Then again, she's the type of woman who'll do anything it takes to get what she wants. So maybe it ain't too much of a stretch.

"Yes. I've just explained this," Titch says, looking at us all in exasperation as Beast places a round of drinks on the table in front of us.

We're all back at Tales once again, but this time D-Neath isn't joining in on our little tête-à-tête, because he's currently tied to a chair beneath our feet in the basement, being guarded by one of the ghosts and most likely shitting his pants. Everyone knows that if you enter Beast's basement you don't come out of it again. Sucks to be him.

"It makes perfect sense," she continues. "Tiffany has tried to get into bed with all four of you at some point, but you turned her down because of me—"

"Conniving little bitch," Grim says, rolling her eyes. "Doesn't she understand girl-code?"

"Nah, she only knows bitch-mode," I say, winking at Titch.

"Anyway, when she couldn't get into your beds, the next logical person to try was D-Neath. It wouldn't have taken much for my brother to persuade her to sleep with D-Neath if he had something good enough to barter with. Don't you think it's a little suspicious that she's suddenly got a spot at the Royal Academy of Ballet? That's *the* most exclusive ballet school in the world. It's all a little too convenient."

"And you really think your brother has pulled some strings to get her the spot there in exchange for sleeping with D-Neath?" Xeno asks, knocking back a shot of brandy.

"Yes, I do," she replies.

"But David's a *criminal* who specialises in drug racketeering and selling women in the sex trade. He hasn't lived in the UK for three years. How is he suddenly able to secure her a place at the Royal Academy between murdering your mum, setting Rocks alight and sending sick messages? He's only been back in the country a few weeks," Zayn adds.

Beast shakes his head. "Come on now, don't be so thick in the head. There are *plenty* of posh nobs with skeletons in their closets and secrets in their beds. I'm willing to bet Tales on the fact that whoever gave Tiffany that spot has some pretty nasty shit they need to hide."

"Beast is right, they're exactly the type of people who have the money and the means to buy anything they want. From drugs to human slaves, sexual or otherwise. This makes a lot of sense," Grim agrees, reaching for her phone that's resting on the bar. "I'm going to call Hud, fill him in. He's been held up with something at work, but whilst he's there I want him to do a little background check on this Tiffany girl. You don't happen to know her surname?"

"I don't, but Clancy will. Let me drop her a text," Titch replies, pulling out her phone.

"No, don't do that. She'll only ask why you want to know, and we don't need to get her involved in this if we can help it. Let me call Tuillard instead," Xeno suggests.

"Yeah, you're probably right." Titch tucks her phone away and we all wait whilst he strides over to the cage and makes the call.

Less than a minute later, he's back. "You'll never believe this."

"What?" Dax asks, leaning forward and placing his fore-arms on the table. I swear the guy has got bigger overnight. He's like the motherfucking Hulk, except he ain't green, doesn't rip out of his clothes when he gets angry and can be a gentle fuck when he wants to be. I'm pretty sure he's been working out extra hard as a way to block out this stupid fucking prediction hanging over his head. He won't admit that it's got him all paranoid.

"Tiffany's surname is *Allen*."

"And? Pretty fucking standard surname if you ask me. What's the big deal?" Beast asks.

"Hold on. Allen, as in *Nicholas Allen?*" I ask, remembering what Hudson had told us about The Pink Albatross nightclub D-Neath owns and how he won it from a dude with the same name in a game of cards.

"Fuck!" Zayn exclaims.

Dax whistles and Titch's mouth drops open. "Do you think she could be...?"

"Nicholas Allen's daughter? Given everything we now know, I'm betting on it," Xeno says. He exchanges looks with Grim who grabs her phone, calling Hudson.

"Well, fuck, ain't this all coming together in a nice little bow," Beast says, slurping on his pint of Guinness.

Titch frowns. "You don't sound so certain."

"In my experience, when something is too good to be true, it normally is. I'm going to reserve judgement about this whole theory until we've had a little chat with our buddy, D-Neath."

ℓ

"YOU HEARD HER, answer the damn question. Have you been fucking around on Madame Tuillard?" Beast snarls, gripping D-Neath's jaw roughly, before letting it go. "Be careful how you answer. This might be a life or death situation right about now."

"Come on, man. Pussy ain't got shit all to do with this. I ain't no snake. Let me go," he replies, struggling against the restraints. His wrists are red, raw from the tightness of the rope wrapped around them and his persistent struggle to get away. He should know by now that the only way he's getting out of here alive is if Grim or Beast allow it. D-Neath looks at Xeno, jerking his chin. "You know I ain't about to sell you out, *right*?"

Xeno folds his arms over his chest, his expression a well-trained mask. "I don't know D-Neath, this is all looking pretty fucking suss to me."

"This is bullshit," he mutters, futilely yanking at his restraints.

"You need a piss break, squirming around like that?" Beast comments, laughing when D-Neath looks at him hopefully. "Yeah, not gonna happen. You need to take a piss, go right ahead."

"Fucking gross," I mutter. Like any of us need him pissing his pants and adding more noxious fumes to the disgusting stench of this blood and piss encrusted concrete room situated in the basement of Tales.

"We're waiting. Have you been fucking around on Madame Tuillard?" Beast insists, folding his arms over his chest.

"Why the fuck does it matter *who* I'm banging?"

"It matters, *dipshit*, when the person you're fucking is passing on information to David and Santiago!" Beast counters angrily as we all watch on. There isn't one person in this room who doesn't want to knock D-Neath's lights out. Grim is staring at him stone-faced. Xeno, Dax, and Zayn all look like they want to murder him, and Titch is glaring at him with a mixture of disgust and pity. Her heart's way too good for this place. Frankly, the fact that she's even down here doesn't sit right with me, but she insisted and so here we all are.

"What the fuck?!" he exclaims, shaking his head. "No, man,

that can't be right. I ain't said jackshit to anyone. I swear on my life."

"Cheaters lie, right? So what makes you think we'd believe anything you'd say?" Beast replies, slapping D-Neath's face before bringing his fist back and following it up with a punch. He hits him so hard that D-Neath's head snaps to the side and he topples to the floor with the chair still strapped to his body, out cold.

Titch gasps, her hand flying to her mouth. "Beast, what are you doing?"

"I told you, Pen, just because you've gone all *detective* on us, doesn't mean that what you believe to be true *is* actually true."

"This makes the most sense," she counters. "You said so yourself."

"Look, whether you like it or not we gotta be sure he's just a cunt who thinks with his dick and not a dick who is selling us out to some bastard cunt," Beast counters, flexing his fingers. "Because believe me, there are two very different outcomes depending on what is *actually* going on."

"So you're going to beat him until he confesses?"

"Pretty much."

"Does that usually work when someone is *actually* telling the truth?"

"Every single person who ends up in my basement is a liar. The truth always comes out, one way or another, and I'm an expert at getting the fuckers to spill it."

"Tiny, I think you should go upstairs with York. You don't need to witness this," Xeno says, jerking his chin towards the door whilst keeping his gaze pinned on me. I expect he wants me to take her, and whilst I agree that she shouldn't be down here, I shake my head. There's no way Titch is going to leave and I'm not going to be the one to force her either. Her sense of right and wrong is the most evenly balanced out of all of us. Maybe we need her here to temper the rest of us hotheads. I don't really give a shit about whether D-Neath lives or dies, but on the other hand we don't really need another murder on our rap sheet, it's already a mile long.

"I'm staying. If only to make sure Beast doesn't kill him," she retorts firmly.

"Seriously, Kid, you should go," Dax says, backing Xeno. Like me, he knows this isn't going to end well.

"No." She cuts him a look then glares at Zayn who is about to say the same thing. "I'm staying."

"Suit yourself," Beast says as he yanks D-Neath upright. "Wakey, wakey, rise and shine!"

Duncan's head lolls to the side and it takes another minute or so for him to gain full consciousness, even with Beast slapping his face and shaking him. Eventually, when his eyes focus and he's back in the room with us, he swallows hard staring at Beast who's currently right up in his face.

"I swear on my life, Beast. I didn't say anything to anyone," he says.

"You didn't need to. Turns out that pretty piece of pussy you've been fucking around with has been extracting information about our plan right from under your nose, most likely when you've passed out from an orgasm coma. Did no one ever tell you to password protect your shit?"

D-Neath's face pales. "The fuck?!"

"Yeah, fuck indeed. Clearly you keep your brains in your cock," Beast says, grabbing his split lip and squeezing hard. D-

Neath groans. "Because that girl *you've* been fucking has been feeding information back to David, and David has been sharing that information with Santiago. Which means, *fuckface*, that your cheating arse has blown this whole thing wide open all for a bit of pussy. Now we're on a back foot because of you."

D-Neath bares his teeth, blood staining them red as he tries to speak. Beast lets his lip go and waits. "Look, I get you're upset, but I made a mistake. How was I to know who that bitch was working for?"

"That's your apology?" Grim makes a scoffing noise then strides across to the back of the room where an array of weapons are spread out on an aluminium tray. She takes her time strolling up and down in front of them before picking up a serrated-edged blade. In her leather trousers and black shirt combo, paired with high heels and dash of red lipstick, she looks the perfect part of villainess. If my heart and soul didn't already belong to Titch, I'd have a hard-on for this woman.

"You know what I hate more than liars, Beast?"

"No, what's that, babe?" he asks, as she steps up beside him, waving the knife in front of D-Neath's face.

"It's a liar *and* a cheat." Handing the knife to Beast, she says, "Chop his dick off and pickle it. Madame Tuillard can keep it as a souvenir."

"What the fuck! No! Jesus fucking Christ! I'm sorry, okay? I'm sorry."

"Grim, Jesus!" Titch exclaims, the blood draining from her face. "He might be a cheating bastard, but he didn't knowingly do this."

Grim folds her arms across her chest and sighs, reverting her attention back to D-Neath. "Sorry really doesn't cut it. But luckily for you, Pen is here today, and she requested that we don't chop off any appendages. *This* time."

"Thank you. Thank you, Pen," D-Neath says, and I can't help but cringe a little at the way his teeth chatter from the rush of fear chased up with a shot of adrenaline. If he pisses himself I might just have to bleach my eyes out. He's gone from someone we all respected, if not liked, to someone we wouldn't piss on if he were on fire.

"Don't thank me," Titch replies. "We're not friends. I just don't want anyone I care about getting sent to prison because they murdered your sorry, *cheating* arse."

"It's an addiction..." he mumbles, trying to gain our sympathy.

"Fuck off, Duncan," Zayn says, curling his lip in disgust. "You've got a beautiful woman willing to put up with your bullshit and you go fuck around on her with some little conniving whore. What the fuck's up with that?"

"I'll make it up to her. I swear it. I know what I've got. I love her..."

Titch laughs. "Got? Don't you mean *had*?" Titch steps closer to D-Neath, narrowing her eyes at him. "Madame Tuillard wanted me to pass on a message."

"Yeah?" he asks.

"You've got 24 hours to get your shit out of her flat."

D-Neath's shoulders drop and for a moment he looks genuinely sorry. "Thought that might be the case."

"Oh, and one more thing..." Titch adds, glaring at him. "She also asked me to tell you to *go fuck yourself.*"

Grim throws her head back and laughs. "I like this Madame Tuillard. She's my kind of woman."

"Look," D-Neath begins. "I know I fucked up. I'll do anything to put it right. I swear to fuck I didn't know what she was doing. We can still see this through. Let me make this right. I'll do anything."

Grim raises her brow. "Actually, there *is* something you can do. I need you to dial this number," she says, holding up the piece of paper Titch gave her earlier.

"Sure, whatever you want," he agrees.

"I need you to take your bitch on the side for a nice swanky meal for two tonight at Chez Rouge on Grafton Street."

"Why?"

"Well it ain't because we want you to get your leg over, dipshit," Beast says. "Fuck, I really did hit you hard, didn't I?"

"We want you to wine and dine her, get her nice and tipsy, then steal her phone. We'll put one of the ghosts on her tail too, see if we can't get her to lead us right back to David and Santiago."

"No problem. I'll do it."

Grim smiles, but it's not the same smile that she gives to Beast or one of her friends. No, this is a smile she reserves only for her enemies. If D-Neath wasn't in her good graces before, then he sure as fuck is on her shitlist now. She nods to Beast and he cuts the rope from one wrist so that D-Neath can take back his mobile and dial the number.

"Put it on loudspeaker," she orders, "And you'd better hope to fuck that your bitch on the side answers because if she doesn't and it's David or Santiago, then you'll be leaving this room in a bodybag. Got it."

"It won't be them. I swear to you."

"Then what are you waiting for?" Beast asks. "Dial the fucking number."

D-Neath nods, tapping in the digits.

"Hello? D-Neath?" a familiar voice answers after the third ring.

"The fuck?" I whisper.

Beside me, Titch wobbles on her feet and I'm forced to slam my palm over her mouth to stop her from saying something to give us away, because it ain't Tiffany on the other end of the line, but Clancy.

30

Pen

"D-NEATH IS THAT YOU?" Clancy asks, her voice sounds odd, quivering, like she's been crying.

My throat tightens. My stomach flips over. I want to throw up, but I can't do that given York's hand is pressed over my mouth. Hauling me back against his chest, he wraps his arm around my waist like he's afraid I'm going to snatch up the phone and give us all away. He's right, because that's exactly what I feel like doing. I can't believe it's her. I was so certain it was Tiffany that D-Neath has been fucking.

But *Clancy*?

She's my friend. Our friend. She wouldn't betray us.

She wouldn't.

I flick my gaze to the rest of the guys. Xeno is shaking his head in disbelief. Zayn is scowling and Dax has his attention focused on me, a look of sympathy in his gaze.

"D-Neath?" she questions again, and it spurs Grim into action.

Stepping towards D-Neath, she cuts me a look. I can see the questions in her gaze, and the anger. Grim is all about loyalty and right now she's as confused and as hurt as I am, though she hides it better than I do. She jerks her chin at D-Neath who is looking between us all. He's as stunned as the rest of us, and something about that makes my thrashing pulse calm a little.

"Is this *Clancy*?" he asks, a question in his voice as he stresses her name.

That question changes everything. York lets me go and I bend over sucking in lungfuls of air. I feel him rub my back as I try to regain control of myself as quietly as possible.

"Y—yes," she stutters out.

Straightening up, I step forward, wanting to snatch the phone up and find out why Clancy is answering Tiffany's phone, and why she sounds so upset. This time Dax catches my hand and pulls me back, shaking his head. He raises his finger and rests it against his lips. Something's wrong, that much we all know. Grim looks at D-Neath tightly and nods. She wants him to continue with the conversation.

"Where's Tiff, Clancy? I'm surprised you answered her phone... This is, erm, awkward," he says, playing the part well.

"She's...Oh, God!"

Dax's releases my hand and throws his arm around my shoulders pulling me tight against his chest. He knows this is bad. We all do. Under normal circumstances Clancy would've questioned why he was calling Tiffany, and given her own suspicions about D-Neath having an affair, would've given him a piece of her mind. She likes and respects Madame Tuillard just as much as I do. So for her not to say anything is a huge sign that something is terribly, terribly wrong.

"She's what, Clancy?" D-Neath asks, his voice surprisingly gentle.

"She's in the hospital. My step-mum and Dad are talking with the doctors now. Everyone thinks she took an overdose of a street drug called *Dancing Shoes*."

"Fuck!" D-Neath exclaims, taking the word right out of our mouths.

"Wait, hold on," Clancy says, her hand folding over the mouthpiece. We all wait as the muffled sound of people talking comes through the loudspeaker. There's more static and then Clancy speaks, "Sorry, the doctor and my dad returned. I've left the ward so I can talk to you in private." Her voice wobbles, but she holds herself together. "I didn't even like her all that much, but she didn't..."

"But she didn't, what?" D-Neath asks as Beast quietly unties his other wrist.

"But she didn't deserve this. I wouldn't wish this on my worst enemy."

"Is she conscious?"

"No. They don't think she's going to make it. All her organs are shutting down. It's happening so fast. She's dying. There's nothing they can do." Her voice cracks as she tries to get a hold of herself.

"Which hospital is she at?" D-Neath asks, standing. He takes a towel from Beast and presses it against his split lip, wiping away the blood. For a man who talked about Tiffany like she was nothing more than a good fuck, he sure seems concerned about her. Maybe he isn't a complete arsehole after all.

"Chelsea & Westminster."

"I'll be there within the hour," he says, and I'm not sure if he's saying that because he genuinely cares about Tiffany or if he thinks it'll somehow get him out of this mess.

"No! You can't come here."

"Why?"

"Because the police are looking for you."

"Looking for me? Why would they be looking for me?"

"She left a suicide note. She said that you were her lover but that you didn't want her anymore after you found out her dad was the man you stole The Pink Albatross from."

"What? Her dad was Nicholas Allen?" D-Neath slams back down onto the chair in shock. Clearly he had no clue. He looks at us with wide eyes, disbelief casting his features in shadow.

"So you did steal the club?" Clancy asks in a hushed tone.

"It wasn't like that. I *won* it..." he slams his mouth shut when Grim shakes her head, scowling at him. This isn't the time for confessions.

"She also said in her note that you got her addicted to *Dancing Shoes*, that you've been pushing the drugs to the dancers at the Academy, that you're basically responsible for what she did to herself."

"I'm not. I didn't give her those drugs, Clancy. I fucking swear it."

"I believe you," she says, her voice no more than a whisper.

"You do?"

"Yes."

"But why?" he asks.

"I'm scared..."

Clancy pauses and I can tell that she's trying her best not to fall apart. I believe that she's genuinely upset for Tiffany, but this is more than that. She's *afraid*. Grim senses it too and encourages D-Neath to keep her talking. I know what she's thinking, because I'm thinking it too. This was David, this was my brother's doing.

"What's going on, Clancy?" D-Neath presses, swiping a hand over his head. "You can tell me. I promise it'll be okay."

"I don't know what to think. Who to trust..."

I look at Grim, pointing at the phone and then my chest. She nods. "Clancy, it's me, Pen," I say.

"Pen? What...? Why are you with D-Neath?"

"There isn't much time to explain everything now, but it's really, *really* important you tell us what's going on. Why are you so scared?"

"Us?"

"I'm at Tales with the guys, Grim and Beast are listening in too. Please, Clancy, we want to help you."

"There are too many people around, I'm going into the stairwell. Hold on."

Whilst she heads to somewhere more private, I take the chance to look about the room. Aside from Xeno who appears to be firing off urgent messages, presumably to Hudson, everyone else has their attention focused on the phone gripped in D-Neath's hand.

"Clancy," I prompt.

"There was a man..."

"A man? What do you mean?" I say slowly, my stomach flipping over.

"I had some free time today, so I decided to go home to see my dad. It'd been a while since I'd been back. Anyway, when I got in no one was home. I totally forgot that Dad and my step-mum had an event to attend for my Dad's work today, an extended lunch with the partners at his law firm with their wives and husbands. Rather than head straight back to the Academy, I decided to grab some things from my room whilst I was there..." She pauses, swallowing hard.

"Clancy, what happened?"

"Tiffany turned up. I didn't want to speak with her after what happened at the Academy that day she left, so I stayed in my room. I was going to sneak out once she'd gone to her own room, only I heard a male voice... *Fuck!*" Clancy chokes back a sob and takes a few deep breaths.

"It's okay, Clancy. Take your time."

"It wasn't long after that I heard her making weird noises. I thought, at first, they were having kinky sex or something, but when I heard her choking, I knew something was up. I should've called the police then and there, I didn't." She swallows hard, takes another breath then continues. "I watched them through a gap in her bedroom door, Pen. The guy she was with had a gun to her head."

"What the fuck?" D-Neath exclaims.

"What happened then?"

"In front of her was a bag full of these pills. He made her swallow handfuls of them down with water. She was crying and choking, trying to swallow them, all the while begging for her life."

Beast scowls, his arms folding over his chest. He's furious, just like we all are. "Then he forced her to write a note."

"The suicide note you mentioned?"

"Yes."

"What did you do then?" I ask her.

"I left her with him." She's sobbing now. It takes her a full minute to stop crying enough to continue, and in all that time my heart is in my throat and my legs are like jelly. "He had a gun, and I was scared. I knew if I tried to help, he'd kill us both. So I crept back to my room and called the emergency operator. I was only just giving them our address when the man entered my room. I hadn't even told them what was happening yet. He had the gun pointing at my head..."

"Jesus fucking Christ," York cuts in.

"He shook his head at me, and I knew if I said another word, he was going to kill me..."

"What did you do?"

"I dropped the phone. It was still connected to the operator. I hoped that he would say something, and they would know that there was someone dangerous in the house, but he didn't say a word. Instead, he made me leave the room and sit on Tiffany's bed. She was slumped over her desk, her eyes glazed, tears pouring down her face. Her lips were turning blue. I wanted to help her, but when I moved towards her, he just jerked his gun at me. I had to watch him gathering up his coat and bag whilst Tiffany was losing consciousness. In the distance, I could hear a police siren and I thought for sure he'd kill me, but he just smiled."

"He smiled?"

"Yes," Clancy whispers, shock evident in her voice. "He

smiled at me and said that if I so much as breathed a word of what really happened to the police, that he would kill my dad and step-mum whilst I watched... T—that he would kill me too. He said that I should tell the police that I'd found her like that."

"Did you recognise him at all?"

"No. I've never seen him before in my life."

"What did he look like?"

"Around twenty-five I think, mid-brown hair. About 5'11. London accent, but with tanned skin, like he'd been on holiday... Shit, I probably shouldn't be telling you this. What if he comes after my family? Pen, what am I going to do? I lied to the police!" Clancy screeches, her teeth chattering. I can just picture her now, blotchy from crying, her freckles pronounced against her pale skin, her hair as wild as her fear. God, I wish I could hug her, but my own feelings of guilt rush through me, making me feel sick to my stomach.

"Clancy I'm so sorry," I say, hating myself for not warning her. It was stupid. So fucking stupid. If David has been using Tiffany to gather information then of course she would have mentioned my friendship with Clancy, and that only gives him more ammunition to hurt me by hurting her. He could've killed her. He could still kill her. That thought has me swaying on my feet once again.

"Just before he left, he said something else to me too," she continues, not understanding that my apology isn't because I feel pity but because I feel guilt.

"What was it? What did he say?" I ask, forcing myself to remain upright.

"It doesn't make any sense..."

"What was the message, Clancy?"

For a moment the line goes eerily quiet. Then she swallows hard. "Eenie, meenie, miney, mo...."

The breath leaves my body in a rush and black spots dance in front of my eyes. Dax rushes to my side, holding me up whilst stars spot my vision. Hearing those four words are like a sucker punch to the gut, even though deep down I was just waiting for her to say them. Forcing air into my lungs, I grip hold of Dax and lock my knees. I can't pass out now. This was my brother's doing, the least I can do is stand here and listen to every word she has to say.

"Did he hurt you?"

"No. He left right before the police and ambulance turned up... Pen, I lied to them. I did exactly what he said... Oh God, I think I'm going to be sick," she says, echoing my own struggle right now. "What do I do? Should I tell the police?"

"I don't—" I begin, but Grim clears her throat.

"Clancy this is Grim."

"Grim?"

"Yes, it's me," she says, taking the phone from D-Neath and holding it tightly in the palm of her hand. "I want you to listen to me very carefully, okay? We know who hurt Tiffany. He's a dangerous man, Clancy, and it's imperative you're not alone. I want you to go back into the ward with the others. All of you need to stay there. Do it right now."

"Why? What's going on?"

"Clancy, move your arse!" Grim orders.

"I'm heading back there now."

"Where exactly are you in the hospital?"

"The third floor. Stairwell of the West Wing."

Grim cuts a look at Beast who nods. "On it," he says, tapping out a message on his phone.

"Are the police with you at the hospital?" Grim asks.

"No. They left about half an hour ago. I think they went to the Academy to look for D-Neath."

"Then get your arse back to the ward. We're making some calls. Once you're back with your family I want you to stay in the ward. Don't go *anywhere* until the police return, okay?"

"Why?"

"Just do it!"

"Okay." We hear what sounds like a door swinging open and for a moment I assume Clancy is heading back into the ward to her family and my shoulders relax a little, but then a familiar laugh echoes around the room. I freeze.

"So we meet again... How is Tiffany?"

David.

"No!" Clancy shouts her fear forcing me into action. "Pen!"

"Leave her the fuck alone!" I scream, pushing out of Dax's arms and stumbling towards the phone. My head fills with white noise as I snatch the phone out of Grim's hands. "I swear to fuck, David! I will kill you if you hurt her!"

There's a struggle on the end of the line, like Clancy is trying to fight him off, then nothing. "Clancy?! Clancy?! Answer me!"

She doesn't respond and I stare at the phone, my attention fixed on the screen, afraid that if I look at anyone else in the room our connection will be severed. There's a lot of muffled noise, the sound of doors opening and closing, footsteps, people talking, background noise, a plane flying overhead, a car horn honking. He must have some kind of weapon because there's no way she'd go anywhere with him without a fight.

"What's going on?" I ask, "Talk to me, Clancy," I say, my own voice no more than a whisper. Part of me wants to scream and shout down the phone so someone comes to her aid, but another part of me is terrified that without a second thought he'd use whatever weapon he has pressed against her in an instant. Given where they are, it's probably a knife, something he can hide between them, keep her terrified and him in control. Something he could easily slip into her body in some quiet corner of the hospital and walk away whilst she bleeds out.

"Pen, *help—*" she whispers.

"Shut the fuck up. Or you'll find yourself with a severed spinal cord," my brother replies, his voice whisper-tight, confirming all my fears. Silence fills the room momentarily, not one of us breathes as we listen to this all play out. Then Clancy's voice is replaced with David's.

"Get in the car. Now!" he seethes.

I know that voice only too well. I can picture him now, with his teeth gritted and a smile plastered on his face. Always that fake smile, fooling anyone who might be looking that he's a man you can trust and not a certifiable psychopath. My heart shrivels up as I hear the muffled sound of Clancy quietly pleading with him and a car door slamming.

"Now, listen up, *Penelope*," David says a few moments later, his voice loud and clear now that he's in a vehicle and can speak more freely, "This is what's going to happen—"

"You hurt her and I swear to fucking God, David...!" I blurt out, panic, anger and rage making my mouth run away from me.

"What, do you swear to do, Penelope? Because right now

you can't do jackshit. One more fucking word from you and I will slit your little friend's throat. I don't give a shit."

"Now, let's not talk stupid," Beast interjects, his voice hair-raising, threatening in a way I've never heard before. "If you were going to do that, you would've by now. You need her alive, am I right?"

"Who's this?" David asks, whilst another male voice mumbles something in the background. He has help. Santiago maybe? I dismiss the idea, from what I've heard, a man like Santiago wouldn't lower himself to kidnapping, he'd just get some other sick fuck to do it. Namely my brother. I imagine whoever the other man is, he's driving the getaway vehicle because there's no way you can drive a car and hold a knife to someone at the same time.

"If you don't know then I guess that poor bitch you preyed upon didn't quite do her job properly," Beast responds.

"Well, you ain't D-Neath and you sure as fuck ain't one of those traitorous Breakers my sister has been fucking like the skank-arse whore she is... Speaking of which, I'm betting they're with you too, Penelope. Am I right?" David asks.

I cut a look at Dax who's gritting his teeth so tightly, I'm worried he might break a few. I don't answer. I refuse.

"Well, well, well, given you've clammed up, Penelope, I'm betting they're listening in too. Still protecting them I see," he continues. "Hello, boys, what's up?"

"Is there a point to this, you little cunt?" Beast prompts, losing his patience.

"Ah, I know who you are! The inimitable Beast. Are you really as fucked up as they say?"

"You little chump, you're gonna find out soon enough," he replies. "We're coming for you."

David just laughs. "Yeah, you and whose army?"

"*My* army," Grim interjects, her voice cool, calm. "You've fucked up, David."

"I don't think so, *Grim*. I think I've got you running around like a tit in a trance. *You* fucked with the wrong people, *sugar tits*."

Beast snarls and Grim smiles, long and slow. David might not be able to see her face, or feel the air of confidence she gives off so effortlessly, but I can. *I can,* and that gives me strength. She turns to me then and nods, and without even saying a word I know she's reminding me of the promise she made. She'll make sure that I'm the one who gets to kill my brother. I've heard all the rumours about Grim, but I've only really seen the nicer side to her personality. She's known to be a formidable opponent and in that one look, I can see that she will never, ever, let my brother best her or me.

Clancy *will* be okay, and my brother *will* die.

"Let's cut to the fucking chase," Dax interjects, taking the phone from me. He's vibrating with anger, and I see that same violence I feel inside, reflected in his eyes.

"Ah, there they are! Which prick are you? You'll have to forgive me. It's been three years..."

"What do you want?" Dax insists, not rising to his bait.

"What have I always wanted? Penelope of course."

"You can't fucking have her!" he retorts.

"Then Clancy dies." And with that finale statement, David ends the call.

31

Pen

"THE POLICE ARE at the hospital with Tiffany and her family right now. They'll be under Interpol's protection from this moment onwards until we get Clancy back safely and Santiago and David are dealt with," Hudson explains, sitting down with us. Xeno had texted him whilst we were on the phone with Clancy, and he came straight over to Tales. It's been thirty minutes since the phone call and every second of it has passed by agonisingly slowly.

"How are her dad and step-mum?" I ask, guilt churning in my gut.

"They're scared, upset, panicked," he replies, pulling out his laptop from his bag and laying it on the table in front of him. There's barely any room, given the table is covered in various handguns and scary looking knives. A war is imminent, if that wasn't already clear by all the weapons littering the table, then it sure as fuck is from the tension that fills the air.

"And Tiffany?" I ask, dragging my eyes away from the table and back to Hudson.

"Not going to make it," he says heavily. "It's just a matter of time."

I swallow hard, forcing myself not to fucking lose it. I may not have liked Tiffany, but like Clancy, I wouldn't have wish this on anyone. She had her own demons and chose to trust in the wrong people. Making David pay isn't just for me and Lena anymore, it's for Tiffany, Clancy and her family too. I won't rest until Clancy is safe and my bastard brother is dead.

"And now that there's been a kidnapping *and* another murder, are the police going to pull their fucking fingers out of their arses?" Xeno asks, as frustrated as the rest of us.

"As we speak, the team at Interpol is checking all the license plates that were recorded exiting the hospital carpark at the time you were on the phone to David."

"That won't turn up anything. David is probably using a stolen car or a stolen number plate," Beast points out.

"You're right. Regardless, we should have details within the next hour or so. Once they have a registration plate, they'll be able to obtain a registered address and that line of investigation can be ruled out."

"The next hour? Clancy could be dead by then!" I shriek, my whole body trembling.

"He won't kill her, Pen," Zayn says, wrapping his arm around me. My fingers curl into the material of his top, knuckles bone white as he tries and fails to soothe me. "He needs some kind of leverage."

"If we don't do as he asks. He *will* kill her, then he'll find someone else to use as bait. It won't end until he has what he wants!" I shout, letting go of Zayn's top and slamming my fist against the table top.

"We are *not* turning you over to him, Titch. That isn't going to happen," York says calmly, though I see how that calm is just a front, that he's just as fucked up over this as I am. Of the four, he was closest to Clancy. I know he cares about her.

"Then Clancy *will* die. Just like he said."

"It's non-negotiable, Kid. We'll find another way to get her back." Dax is stoic. Unmoving on the matter.

"There is another way," Hudson says, opening up his laptop on the table. He punches in the password and waits for the screen to load up.

"We're all ears," Beast says, folding his arms across his chest. "Spit it out. Coz the clock is ticking."

Hudson taps on the keyboard some more, frowning in concentration before looking up at Beast. "Over the past couple days I've been thinking a lot about what Arden said. From what I understand of the Deana-dhe, whilst manipulative, they do barter in truths."

"Not being funny but they could've just given us Tiffany's name. It would've made shit a lot simpler and it might've saved her life," D-Neath remarks, swallowing a gulp of neat vodka. He winces, his lip swollen and still weeping blood.

"But he wasn't talking about Tiffany. He was talking about someone else. Tiffany is a piece to this puzzle for sure, but she's not the person Arden was referring too."

"Is anyone else fucking lost?" Zayn asks, looking between us all. His fingers linger on the handle of his knife that's currently resting on the table. I know it comforts him, despite the fact this knife has ended many lives, and every single one of them haunt him.

"Just give me a moment and I'll explain," Hudson continues. We all watch him tap away at the keyboard, pulling up information on the laptop screen. "Based on what Arden had insinuated, my men did some digging. Believe me, it wasn't easy. The trail was covered well, but not well enough. Just as Xeno texted me this afternoon, we finally got a breakthrough."

"Well, who the fuck was Arden talking about if it wasn't Tiffany?" Beast asks, getting impatient. "Because I'm not being funny, Clancy's life is on the motherfucking line right now, and I'm not down with one of our girl's lives being threatened. She's a good kid. So hurry the fuck up."

"This is Mila Garcia," Hudson says, twisting the laptop around to face us. He clicks a button, and a pixelated image of a face starts to slowly take form. "She was awarded a scholarship at the Academy under the name of *Sophie* Miller. I don't know her, but I believe you all do."

"*Sophie* is Santiago's daughter! The fuck?" Zayn exclaims, his mouth popping open in surprise.

"Yes. From the information I've been able to uncover, Sophie and her mum appeared to arrive in the UK when she was just six years old, and given the lengths she's gone to hide her daughter's true identity, we can assume that she doesn't want her to be found. Santiago has been married to his wife Maria for thirty-five years, his other children are hers. I suspect Sophie's mum was someone he had an affair with."

"Well, if I had the misfortune of falling pregnant by

Santiago I wouldn't want him to have anything to do with my child either," Grim comments.

"Indeed," Hudson agrees. "She entered the UK, changed her name and effectively went into hiding. But Sophie's mum passed away six years ago. Since then Sophie has been looked after by her step-dad and his new wife. Clearly, neither of whom new about Sophie's heritage."

"So she ends up coming to the Academy, making friends with Tiffany and wham, Santiago finds his long lost daughter," York says, a frown creasing his forehead.

"In a nutshell, yes."

"Okay, so Sophie's his daughter. Fucking great. Then let's go get her. We can end this shit now," Beast exclaims, getting to his feet. "We'll do an exchange, Sophie for Clancy."

"What, so we drag Sophie into this, just like that? We might not be friends, but I'm not cool with that," I say.

"Do you want to get Clancy back or not?" Beast asks.

"Of course I do, but Sophie's mum kept her hidden for a reason and now we're just going to offer her up like a nice slab of meat to a starving lion?"

"We'll use her as bait. If Santiago wants his daughter badly enough, he'll come get her," Beast says with a shrug. "How that man chooses to let things play out is up to him. If he gives a shit about his daughter, then he won't do anything to hurt her."

"What makes you think Santiago hasn't already gotten to Sophie?" York points out, folding his arms across his chest. "In fact, what makes you think that she's an innocent bystander in all of this?"

"York has a point," Dax agrees, looking at me. "Kid, Sophie has disliked you from the very start. She's been Tiffany's side-bitch from the get-go. Maybe she's been more involved in all of this than any of us realised."

"Ah fuck," D-Neath interjects.

"What?" Grim snaps her head around to look at D-Neath, her eyes narrowing.

"Tiffany and Sophie are thick as thieves. Always hanging out together. Tiffany would often meet me at The Pink Albatross to... you know," he falters, looking guilty as fuck.

"Yeah, we know," Beast grunts, jerking his chin. "Keep talking, arsewipe."

"On a couple of occasions she brought along Sophie. At first I thought maybe they wanted..."

"A threesome?" Beast growls and D-Neath nods once. "You fucking prick."

D-Neath has the decency to look ashamed, but pushes on regardless. "It wasn't the case. I let Sophie sit in my office whilst Tiffany and I would make ourselves comfortable in one of the booths..."

"For fuck's sake man! You really are a piece of fucking work, aren't you?" York grinds out.

"I had no reason to believe either of them were fucking with me," he counters.

"Because you were too busy fucking one of them, that's why!" Grim snaps. "How could you be so stupid?"

He doesn't respond because there really isn't anything he can say to that. Ruled by his dick, D-Neath has fucked up royally.

"So you think Sophie's been in on this too?" I ask for clarity's sake.

"It's a real possibility. If she was brought over to the UK by her mother at six years old then she would've known her father in those first few years, missed him perhaps. If Santiago reached out to her..." Hudson hesitates.

"What?" Xeno asks.

"Fuck!" Hudson swipes a hand over his face. "Why didn't I see that before?"

"See what?" Dax asks, shifting in his seat.

"They've known all along! Damn it."

Zayn frowns "Who've known? What, Hudson?"

"Interpol. This whole thing has been a ruse to get Santiago's attention on the Academy. They knew he wouldn't come to the UK just because someone fucked with his drugs. They needed to shine a light on his daughter because she's the only thing he'd step back into the UK for. This whole elaborate plan that I bought into—"

"That *we* bought into," Xeno corrects with a scowl.

"—was designed purely so that Santiago would look in the direction they needed him to."

"Fuckers could've given us a heads up!" York points out.

"What does it matter? Their plan worked," Beast points out. "He's here. That's what you all wanted, right? Plus his psycho sidekick is too. Let's end this shit right now."

"It matters, Beast, because people have been hurt," I point out. "Mum's dead and Tiffany's dying. Clancy is in danger right as we speak. If we'd known about Sophie then maybe things could've been done differently, maybe that could've been prevented."

"Let's face it, Pen. All of that's on your brother. Knowing about Sophie earlier wouldn't have changed that. He's fucked in the head and would've killed your mum anyway," Beast points out.

"I agree with you to a certain extent, Beast. But Pen's right, David has played this all to his advantage. If Interpol had filled us in, we could've handled this all very differently. I don't much like being played a fool." Hudson sighs, scraping a hand over his face. "But none of that matters now. What matters is Clancy. What matters is ending this, once and for all."

"Then lets fucking do this shit!" Beast grins, bloodlust in his eyes. "We'll go grab Sophie and do a little bartering of our own, yeah?"

"Hold up. I've got an incoming call," Dax says, pulling out his phone. He glances at the screen, his eyebrows shooting up in surprise. "It's Jefferson Sloane."

Zayn frowns. "Mad Dick?"

"Yeah, the one and only." Dax presses the loudspeaker button. "Jefferson, I've got you on loudspeaker. What's up?"

"You asked me to call you if I ever saw that guy again. Well, I'm looking at him right now."

Dax stands, his chair sliding out behind him. "Where is he?"

"He just walked into a dive bar on East Street, Tower Hamlets. There's a girl with him."

"Describe the girl to me."

"Short, redhead. She doesn't look too great. I think she might be drunk or something. The younger guy's practically hauling her across the pavement."

"Clancy," I whisper, my stomach flipping over.

Zayn grips my hand tightly in his. "This is good news. She's still alive. Focus on that," he mutters under his breath.

"Are they on their own?"

"No, there's a guy too. He's an older man, smoking a cigar and wearing a floor length coat."

Beast pumps his fits, grinning. I know what he's thinking. That we've got them. That this will be over soon, but I'm not so certain.

"What's the name of the bar, Jefferson?"

"*Duffers*. It's known for illegal shit. The police around here swerve the place. Pretty sure Rourke has the local PD in their pockets."

"I know it," Grim says. "Owned by Rourke Dempsey, great grandson of the late Billy Dempsey, a very well known, well connected East End gangster back in the forties and fifties. He runs a protection racket." I've no idea who Grim's talking about, but by the look on her face the Dempsey family aren't the kind of criminals you want to mess with.

"Is that Grim?" Jefferson asks.

"The one and only, mate," Beast replies, winking at Grim.

"Alright, Beast?"

"Funnily enough, much better now that you've called with this information. You did good. Next time we fight in the cage I'll let you get some good hits in before I knock you flat out."

Jefferson laughs before Dax cuts in once again. "Is there any way you can get into the bar? We need eyes on the pair at all times."

"Not a chance, Fuck Boy has—"

"Fuck Boy?" Grim pulls a face.

"I mean *Danny*. The stupid fuck burned our bridges with Rourke when he fucked his daughter, Emilia, then her cousin, and her cousin's best friend. Emilia's a woman scorned, and Rourke wants his head. So, no, we can't go in."

"Okay. So why the fuck are you there tonight?" Dax asks.

"Danny's got a hard-on for Emilia's sister, Juliet. He only slept with her sister and the other two to make her jealous. It didn't work. So he's being a fucking creepy arse stalker and hoping to catch a glimpse of her tonight. We're just here for the ride. Anyway, the point is, we can't go in, but we can hang out where we are for as long as you need."

"Where are you exactly?" Dax asks.

"Chilling in a friend's flat in the building opposite. It overlooks the entrance to *Duffers*. I was just smoking a joint on the balcony, and saw them."

"Are there any other entrances or exits to the club?" Beast asks.

"Not as far as I remember. One way in, one way out."

"Good. Stay right where you are. You need to take a piss you get one of the others to cover you. I want to know the second they leave the building. Got it?" Dax orders.

"Yeah, I got it... So, we're still good with that deal we made, yeah?" Jefferson asks. I throw Dax a look and he winks, reassuring me he hasn't promised something that he can't follow through on.

"I'm a man of my word. When you need to cash in that favour, you know where to find me."

"I do."

"Good. Now keep an eye out." Dax hangs up the call and looks between us. "So we know where they are. What's the plan?"

"I'm going to call Tuillard. We've got one opportunity to get this right and we need to make sure Sophie doesn't leave the Academy," Xeno says. "Whoever he's sent to collect her, you bet your arse it won't be an Uber driver."

"My thoughts exactly," Grim agrees, tapping her manicured nails against the table top. "Best go prepared."

"I agree," Hudson says, grabbing the Beaumont-Adams revolver nearest to him. The fact I can even identify the majority of the guns on this table is a testament to how well Xeno has trained me. He's a good teacher, both at the shooting range and at the Academy. Maybe in another life that's something he could've become if he hadn't got drawn into the Skins.

Xeno makes the call, putting it on loudspeaker. Madame Tuillard answers after a couple of rings. "Good afternoon, Xeno, got what you needed from Duncan?" she asks, without even bothering with the usual pleasantries. Her voice is tight, hurt, but there's an inner strength that I hear within it. That D-Neath hears. I see the shame in his eyes.

"Pretty much," he replies. "I need to speak with Sophie."

"You're the second person to ask me that today."

"The second person? Who else have you spoken too?"

"Her father. He called five minutes ago, wanted me to pass on a message to her."

"And what was that?" Xeno cuts a look at Hudson who swears under his breath.

"What's going on, Xeno?" she counters. "Should I be concerned?"

"No time to explain. What did he say?"

"There's been an emergency of some sort. He wants her home for a few days. I think she's packing up a weekend bag as we speak. He's sending a car to pick her up. It'll be here shortly."

"Can I ask you to do something for me?" Xeno asks.

"I guess that depends on what that something is."

"I need you to keep Sophie at the Academy until we get there. It's *really* important that she doesn't leave."

"Xeno, what's happening?"

"I'll explain everything to you as soon as we arrive. Just tell Sophie that you want to see her solo dance before she goes home. Take her to the theatre. We'll be there in twenty minutes tops. Whatever you do, don't let her leave."

"Fine. I'll do it," Madame Tuillard agrees before hanging-up.

Xeno grabs his car keys off the table. "We need to move," he says, motioning to Hudson. "I'll drive."

"What about Clancy?" I ask as we all get to our feet.

"The only way Clancy is going to survive is if we have something to barter with. Right now, we know Clancy's alive, and we know where she is," Xeno says, a grim look on his face. "We need to get to Sophie before Santiago does. That has to happen first."

"David won't care about Sophie," I protest. "He won't trade her. He'd sooner kill her."

"David might be a fucking psycho, but he's not a fool. This is Santiago's daughter, someone he left Cuba for. We get a hold of Sophie, and we have a chance of getting Clancy out of this alive. I know it doesn't sit right with you handing Sophie over, but I have no intention of allowing that man to leave this country with his daughter. This ends tonight," Hudson says, giving me a tight smile. I swallow hard and nod curtly, a deep sense of foreboding swimming in my stomach.

"York, Zayn, you're with me. Dax, I want you here with Pen," Xeno says.

"Fuck that. I ain't sitting here doing jackshit," Dax grinds out, glaring at Xeno.

"You're not doing jackshit. You're watching over our girl. That's what you do best, Dax. I know you won't let any harm come to her," Xeno replies, stepping around him.

Dax slams his palm against Xeno's chest. "If you're keeping me here because you've bought into that bullshit prediction—"

"I don't buy into that shit and you know it. Stay the fuck here and protect our girl. Got it?"

"Not being funny, but I'm pretty sure that me and ten ghosts have got shit covered this end," Beast says. "You go get Sophie with the others and bring her here, and I'll protect your girl, yeah?" He winks, waggling his eyebrows. Dax's nostrils flare.

"Fine, I'll stay." He cuts Xeno a look then turns on his heel, heading towards the far side of the warehouse.

"Where are you going in a huff?" Beast teases, always making light in the tensest moments.

"I'm gonna go check on the ghosts. Catch them up," Dax snaps back.

The moment he walks away a look passes between York and Xeno, one that makes my blood run cold. Whether they want to admit it out loud or not, they're worried and that only fuels my own fear. Gritting my teeth, I focus on the moment and don't allow my thoughts to linger on something that may never happen.

"I'm coming too. Despite what you all think, I do actually give a fuck," D-Neath says. "This is on me. I wanna fix it. Besides, the woman I love is there."

Grim scoffs at that. "*Love?* You've got a funny way of showing it."

"Regardless, I'm coming too."

Xeno nods, levelling his gaze at D-Neath. "Fine, but you get in our way or cause any shit, I'll kill you. Understand?"

"Understood."

"Then let's move," Hudson says, turning on his feet and striding across the warehouse.

Zayn nods, then presses a chaste kiss against my lips before grabbing his knife. I watch as he slides it back into the holder at his hip, then picks up a gun from the table and pulls on his jacket.

"Are you planning on using those?" I ask.

"I'm not taking any chances," he replies, giving me a tight smile. "We don't know what we might be walking into. There's no telling how this is going to play out." He gives me a tight smile then catches up with Hudson.

York doesn't say a word. Instead, he grabs a black revolver from the table, tucks it into his back pocket then pulls me in for a hug. Pressing a kiss against the top of my head, he squeezes me tighter then lets me go. Xeno is already halfway across the ware-house when I call out to them. "Please be careful." My voice cracks, but I force the worry deep inside. This day was always going to come, I can't fall apart now. I refuse.

Xeno hesitates, then jogs back to me. He reaches up behind his neck and a second later has unclasped a familiar necklace. It's the one the Breakers gave to me when we were kids. "This is our promise to you, Tiny. We're getting that happy ever after," he says, before placing the necklace around my neck and securing it in place.

"Come back to me," I whisper.

"Oh, we will," Xeno assures me, then cups my jaw in his hands and slams his lips against my mouth. He kisses me roughly, deeply, and then he's gone.

32

Xeno

IT'S JUST past seven in the evening when we enter the carpark at the back of the Academy. Madame Tuillard's car is still parked there, otherwise the place is empty. All of the students would've left by now, which is just as well because I have no doubt that tonight is going to get bloody. York knows it, so does Zayn, and given the way Hudson keeps touching the gun tucked in the back of his jeans, he does too. Apart from D-Neath, who I don't trust with a weapon right now, we're tooled up and ready for a fight. Santiago and David might be out of the way at *Duffers*, but that doesn't mean jack when there's a BMW X5 SUV with blacked out, reinforced windows parked in front of the Academy. That sure as shit ain't no Uber.

"Did you see that car?" Zayn asks as we enter the building.

"Yeah, I did," I reply curtly. "We need to make this quick,

because whoever Santiago sent to pick up Sophie isn't going to wait for too much longer."

"Agreed. Which way are we headed?" Hudson asks, flicking his gaze along the corridor.

Jerking my chin, I indicate left. "There are two entrances to the theatre. One further along this corridor," I say pointing down the hallway, "And another on the other side of the theatre, in a corridor that runs parallel to this one."

"Got it," Hudson says.

"York, Zayn, I want you to head around to the other side so you can cover that entrance just in case Sophie bolts or we get an unwanted visitor or two from our *friends* in the BMW."

"On it," Zayn says, and with his hand resting on the knife at his hip, he strides down the corridor and hits a left, disappearing from view.

"See you in a few," York dips his head, winking at me, before he jogs off, pulling his gun out as he moves. He doesn't need me to tell them that I want a sweep of the floor, and heads off in the opposite direction to Zayn in order to do just that.

"If shit's about to go down, then I'm gonna need a weapon," D-Neath says, flicking his gaze between me and Hudson. One eye is steadily swelling shut, and a deep purple bruise is beginning to form around it. Beast punched him hard, and it wouldn't surprise me if he's got a fractured eye socket. Not my problem.

"Do you honestly think I'm going to put a weapon in your hands after the bullshit you pulled?"

"I *fucked* the wrong girl. I didn't snake you out. I don't want to go back to prison and I sure as fuck don't want to see *mi cielo* get hurt. Let me help."

"Fine, but you don't get a gun." I pull out a four inch flick knife from my back pocket and hand it to him. "Knock yourself out."

"What am I supposed to do with this if someone's firing fucking bullet at me, use it as a shield?" he asks, flicking the knife open and pulling a face.

"It's all I got. Take it or fucking leave it," I retort, striding off down the corridor.

"Fuck's sake," he mutters as we head towards the back entrance of the theatre.

"You should wait here," I say to them both. "I'll head inside. If Sophie bolts and I can't get to her first, you'll be here to grab her. It's the nearest exit to the stage."

Hudson cuts me a look and nods. "Got it."

D-Neath jerks his chin. "Let's get this done."

Pushing open the door, I step into the backstage area. It's dark in this portion of the theatre, there are stage props dotted around, and hanging rails full of costumes from past performances. Dim lighting penetrates the gloom and allows me to traverse through the semi-darkness without banging into something. Heading towards the side of the stage, I peer around the black curtain that wraps around the stage in a semicircle. From my position, I have a good view of Sophie, but not of the stalls where Madame Tuillard is sitting. It's difficult to look out into the audience area without the possibility of being seen, and I'm wise enough not to walk out onto the stage without knowing who else might be in the audience. Right now my gut is telling me that I need to be cautious, I never ignore my gut.

For a moment I stand and watch Sophie dance to *Paradise* sung by Dermot Kennedy. She's caught up in the music, her skin is covered in a sheen of sweat as her plaited hair flies around her head like a whip as she moves. She's a natural hip-hop dancer, full of fire and precision, but right now she's dancing street mixed with contemporary. It's a well thought-out choreographed routine and a more appropriate style of dance for the song. Standing here watching her, I can see why Madame Tuillard picked her to dance in the troupe for the final show. Perhaps her light hasn't shone as brightly under the blinding star that is Pen, but she's still talented. The dancer within me appreciates her passion as she moves, but the man I am doesn't give a fuck if I'm about to destroy her dreams. It's her for Clancy, because it sure as fuck isn't going to be Tiny that we're trading to that cunt.

Crouching low to the floor, I wrap my fingers around the curtain and take a peek into the audience. I see Madame Tuillard first, her gaze fixed on Sophie dancing on stage, but my attention is quickly pulled to the man sitting directly behind her with a gun pressed to the back of her head.

"Fuck!" I exclaim under my breath. From this angle there's no way I can get a clear shot of him. He's whispering something into her ear, and she nods imperceptibly at whatever he's saying. I have to give her props, despite the fear in her eyes, she's not falling apart like someone else might do in the same situation. She's got balls, I'll give her that.

Rising slowly, I step back into the shadows trying to figure out how I'm going to play this. With my gun cocked and ready to fire, I look around me, trying to see if there is anything I can use to stand on so that I can get a better shot at the fucking prick threatening Madame Tuillard's life. To my left are more stage props and discarded dance shoes from whatever rehearsal has taken place here recently. The song is coming to an end, and if I don't act soon then I'm going to lose the element of surprise.

"Fuck. Think, Xeno," I tell myself. Then I remember that there's a ladder backstage that leads up to a walkway that hangs above the stage. It's used to access the lighting and will give me the perfect platform to get a good shot. Stepping back into the shadows, I move as quickly as I can and climb up the ladder as quietly as possible. Once I'm safely in position, I hunker down, flick off the safety on my gun and line up the sights. Drawing in a deep breath, I wait for him to move positions. When he does, I blow the air out of my lungs evenly, blocking out all other thoughts before pulling the trigger slow and steady, just like I taught Tiny to do.

The guy never stood a chance.

The bullet hits him right between the eyes and blows his brains out of the back of his head, the force throwing his whole body backwards alongside fragments of skull, half his brain and a shit ton of blood. Madame Tuillard screams, flinging herself forward and dropping down in the space between the row of seats.

"Stay the fuck down!" I roar, as the door to the theatre bursts open and both York and Zayn come running in. Below me on the stage Sophie falls to her knees, her hands covering her head.

"Xeno!" Zayn shouts, as he races down the central aisle towards the stage.

"I'm up here. Grab Sophie!" I shout, running along the walkway and climbing down the ladder just as Hudson and D-Neath enter backstage.

"You good?" Hudson asks me, giving me a quick once-over.

"I'm good, but we need to split."

"Where's *mi cielo*?" D-Neath asks, panic rampaging across his face.

"She's here," York replies as he steps around the curtain with Madame Tuillard. She's pale, leaning into York's side. Shock rendering her speechless.

"What the fuck happened?" D-Neath asks, traversing around us both. He takes Madame Tuillard from York's arms, sliding his arm around her waist. She allows him to help her, too in shock to do much else.

"One of Santiago's men had a gun pressed against Tuillard's head. We need to get out of here, right the fuck now, before anyone else turns up," I say.

"Let me go!" Sophie shouts, struggling in Zayn's hold. She elbows him in the stomach, but the fucker's got a six pack that's hard as a rock. He barely flinches.

"Keep still," he demands, pulling her back against his chest, his thick, tattooed arm holding her firm. "Don't make this difficult for yourself, Sophie!"

"Fuck you, arsewipe! When he gets his hands on you, you'll be fucking sorry! He'll kill you like he kills everyone who fucks him off," she screams, confirming what we already believed to be true. Sophie isn't an innocent bystander. Zayn's arm tightens around her, his jaw gritting.

"What's going on? What's happening?" Madame Tuillard blurts out, Sophie's outburst forcing her into action. "Let Sophie go, she hasn't done anything wrong." She's visibly shaking now, the cool calm she managed to maintain with a gun pressed to her head, gone. "That man just came into the theatre and threatened my life. He said that *I'd* fucked with the wrong family and watching Sophie dance would be the last thing I'd ever see."

"*Mi cielo*, be calm. We need to leave," D-Neath murmurs against her ear, but that only seems to spur her into action and she forcefully shoves him away.

"This is on you, Duncan! Bringing trouble to my door. I should never have trusted you, any of you!" she shouts, glaring at us each in turn. "How dare you do this to me! What the hell has Sophie got to do with any of this?"

"We haven't got time for this shit! Get to the motherfucking —" My order is cut short when my phone vibrates incessantly in my back pocket with an incoming call. I snatch it up, answering the second I see who's calling. "Dax, what's up?"

"Jefferson just called. They're on the move, left about five minutes ago. Santiago and Clancy are in one vehicle. David in the other."

"Why would Santiago take Clancy and not David?" I ask.

"Your guess is as good as mine. Either way, you need to haul arse."

I look at the guys and jerk my head. They know me well enough to know that things are hotting up. Zayn shifts Sophie in his hold and walks her towards the exit, rest of us follow. "We've secured Sophie. We're leaving now," I reply as we all head down the corridor and towards the door that leads out into the carpark.

"Any trouble?" Dax asks, his voice tight. Stressed.

"Santiago sent one of his men to collect Sophie. He's dead."

"Anyone else?"

"No, and we're not sticking around to find out if there are any more on the way."

"Good..." Dax hesitates.

"What is it?"

"*Fuck!*"

"Dax?" Holding my hand up, I indicate for the group to stop walking. I'm straining to hear what's happening over Sophie's incessant muffled screaming. I glare at Zayn and he lifts the gun to her temple.

"Quiet," he snaps. She instantly shuts up.

Madame Tuillard's face pales further. I see the questions in her eyes and the disgust. So be it. This isn't about who's morally right or wrong, and I switch off that part of me that allows the emotions in. Sophie is Santiago's daughter, and therefore the enemy. That's all I need to know in the moment.

"Dax, talk to me. Right the fuck now!" I put him on loud-speaker so the others can hear.

"We're under attack. There must be at least thirty men surrounding Tales." He's running, that much I can tell from the heavy breathing coming down the line.

"We're coming. Keep her safe!" I yell. The line goes dead and in that fraction of a second I snap out of the fear that's suddenly clawing at my heart, I become the cold-blooded gang-ster I need to be in order to get through this.

"He won't fucking take her, Xeno, and *no one* is dying tonight," York says, reading my mind. His ice-blue eyes strip through the rapidly growing armour I'm erecting around myself with that one look. I grit my teeth, refusing to acknowledge how he's managed to uncover my fears.

Instead I turn my attention to Hudson.

"Call the cavalry. They're needed at Tales."

"On it," Hudson replies, pulling out his phone and barking

out orders as we step outside into the carpark. I've never trusted the cops, and given how they fucked us over not telling us about Sophie, I trust them even less now, but I'm also a realist. They can't fight off thirty men on their own and we might not get there in time. We need the police.

I turn to D-Neath and Madame Tuillard. "Lay low until this is over. You've done enough already," I say to D-Neath, and I don't mean it as a compliment. He knows it, and so do I. Frankly I'd rather he was out of the fucking way. Besides Madame Tuillard looks like she's about to collapse. D-Neath wanted to take care of her, well now he could. Gritting his jaw, D-Neath nods, then guiding a still shell-shocked Madame Tuillard out of the carpark, flags down a passing Taxi and gets in.

"Where are you taking me?" Sophie grinds out, her dark eyes flashing with anger.

"To your father."

"He'll kill you *all* for this. No one threatens me. No. Fucking. One," she snarls, revealing the true nature of the beast right here in the backseat of my car. "That bitch, Tiffany, trying to force *me* into doing what *she* wanted? Fuck her. Fuck that. You'll all die too."

"Wow. You really are your father's daughter, aren't you?" Zayn remarks, keeping the gun pressed into her side.

"You know *nothing* about me or my *father*."

"We know enough," Hudson says, casting a look over his shoulder at her before looking at me. "They're on their way."

I nod. "Good, because this ends tonight."

"He's untouchable and he'll kill you all," Sophie spits, her face twisted up with rage and spite as she shifts forward in her seat, totally ignoring the fact she has a gun pressed to her side.

York throws his arm across her waist preventing her from launching herself at me.

"We'll see about that," I reply, flicking my gaze to Zayn in the rearview mirror and nodding sharply. He lifts the butt of the gun and gives her a sharp tap to the base of her skull, knocking her out cold.

Putting the car in drive, I press down on the accelerator, my wheels spinning as I shoot out of the carpark. On the radio *Arise* by The Siege is playing. It couldn't be more apt. Turning up the volume I drive like a bat out of Hell, breaking every fucking rule and law in the book as I traverse the streets of the town I grew up in.

Tonight we're going to fight for our lives, and we *will* survive.

All of us.

33

Pen

THE MUFFLED sound of gunshots ring out in the air around us, and every single one is like a bullet to my heart. Grim grabs a gun from the table, loads up the magazine, and then hands it to me.

"Shoot first, ask questions later. Got it?" she says, grabbing her own gun and picking up a knife, sheathing it at her waist.

"Got it," I reply with a terse nod of my head. My eyes scan the table and I reach for a flick knife, tucking it into the back pocket of my jeans, remembering what York had told me. Gun first, then knife, failing that I should use my fists. More shots ring out just as Dax enters the main portion of the warehouse and sprints towards us.

"Move your arse now!" he yells, Beast and four of the ghosts close behind him. "Get behind the bar!"

He sprints across the warehouse just as the door we use to enter Tales by is riddled with a round of bullets. They splinter the wood and send shards flying into the open space. Throwing his arm over my shoulder, Dax shields me with his body as the door flies open and more shots ring out. I see one of the ghosts hit the ground, blood and brain matter splattering out from the gaping hole in his head as Dax shoves me in front of him.

"Fucking cunts!" Beast shouts, grabbing Grim's hand and pulling her forcefully behind the bar. Dax and I follow them whilst the remaining ghosts run for cover.

"They came out of fucking nowhere," Dax exclaims, his chest heaving as he peers around the side of the bar. "There's too many."

"Santiago and David?" Grim asks, gunfire ringing out around us. Whilst I'm fucking shaking at every shot, she's eerily calm.

"Without a doubt. They're bringing the battle to us."

"Good, let them," Grim says tersely.

"We should've fucking known they'd pull a stunt like this. Motherfuckers!" Beast seethes.

"Are David and Santiago here too or have they sent these cunts in to die first?" Grim grits out. She releases the magazine of her gun, double checking the number of bullets she has then slides it back into the grip.

"Jefferson only just called. It will take them at least ten minutes to get here from Tower Hamlets. That's if they're both coming here. David got in one vehicle. Santiago and Clancy in the other."

"What? Oh God," I say.

"Then we should have time to bring in reinforcements,"

Grim states, she rests her fingers on my arm, squeezing briefly. "Focus on what's happening now. You can't afford to be distracted in a situation like this."

I grit my teeth and nod.

"I called Xeno already. They're on their way back," Dax says, peering around the bar.

"Good. These motherfuckers have messed with the wrong woman. I'm not about to see any of the people I care about hurt. They want a fight, they're gonna fucking get one," she says, and right in that moment, I see the warrior within her. This is a woman who isn't afraid of anything, and her fierce resolve gives me strength. Forcing myself to breathe, I try to take a page out of her book.

"What about the rest of the ghosts?" I ask. "They're trained killers. Surely one of them is worth at least five of these bastards trying to kill us."

"Four are on the roof, taking some of the cunts down who are still on the outside. One is dead. Two now," Beast corrects himself, remembering the ghost who got his brains blown out no more than a minute or so ago.

Grim nods tightly. "How many are we looking at?"

"From what I could tell, at least thirty," Dax says.

"We need to get to my office. It has a fortified door. We can call more reinforcements when we get there."

"Let's move," Beast says, placing his hand on Grim's back. She nods once and a look passes between them, one I recognise only too well. It's fierce protectiveness and a soul-deep love. These two were made for each other.

"I'll grab the door, keep low to the floor. On three, okay?"

Beast clips out, one hand on Grim's lower back, the other clutching his gun tightly. "One, two, three!"

He races for the door, hauling it open as Dax fires shots into the warehouse giving us the opportunity to make a dash for it. Grim moves fast, head down, gun held out in front of her. I follow, liquor bottles exploding as stray bullets smash into the shelves above our heads, raining shards of glass and alcohol over us.

"Fuck!" I shout, a sliver of glass embedding itself into my cheek. I reach up brushing at my face, feeling blood, something sharp, but no pain. Later, I'll deal with that later.

"Move!" Dax hollers, his hands on my back as he shoves me through the door, slamming it behind him. It's a thick, three-inch fire door, and there's no doubt in my mind that it saves Dax's life from several bullets that embed themselves into the wood and not his back. I send a silent prayer to whatever God is out there for keeping him safe from harm.

Beast takes off in front of us and I'm forced into action. Pushing all thoughts of Arden's prediction away, I haul arse racing after Grim who has no trouble keeping up the pace, she's meters ahead of me, Dax at my back. We get to the T-junction at the end of the corridor, and come to an abrupt stop. My heart feels like it's going to explode out of my chest from the stress and exertion. Forcing myself to take in lungfuls of oxygen, I battle against my fight or flight instinct. Everything is telling me to keep running, yet doing so now would be foolish. We've no idea what might be waiting for us around the corner.

Beast peers to the right, holding his arm up to prevent us from moving any further. Dax steps up close behind me, I can feel his back against mine as he takes up the rear, covering our backs just in case the ghosts left behind in the warehouse are unable to keep our enemies at bay. Which is highly likely given we're outnumbered.

"We don't have much time!" Dax grinds out. I press my body against the wall and peer around him as one of the ghosts I recognise pushes out of the door we just exited from. He's limping, obviously wounded. Pressing his back against the door, he uses the brief reprieve to tie a tourniquet around his upper thigh. He nods his head in acknowledgment at Dax, then holds up his arm, his fingers fisted before he opens his palm and flashes us five fingers. He does that twice more.

"Fifteen men left in the warehouse," Dax relays, keeping his back to me. "They've taken out over half already!"

"Four men to the right!" Beast shouts back.

Grim grabs my hand squeezing it tightly. "Remember what I said. Shoot first, ask questions later. You can do this."

I nod tightly. "Don't worry about me. I'm ready."

Letting my hand go, she holds her gun like a pro and if I wasn't so damn terrified, I'd appreciate the whole *badass bitch* look she's got going on right about now. Beast casts a quick look over his shoulder at us both, blows out two breaths in quick succession then leans around the corner and fires out several shots. I hear the distinct cry of pain and returning gunfire, and grit my teeth. Taking a shot at a target in the safety of a shooting range is one thing, firing a bullet into a living, breathing human, something else altogether.

"Two men down!" Beast grunts. "I'm out."

Grim takes his gun, and passes him hers just as more bullets spray past his head and embed themselves into the wall opposite, sending up a spray of plaster into the air from the impact.

He fires off more shots down the corridor and the return fire abruptly stops.

"They're dead." Beast steps into the corridor and motions for us to follow. "GO!" he roars.

Grabbing my hand, Grim yanks me behind her, letting me go only when she knows I'm following, but after a few more steps I realise Dax isn't behind me and I stop running. Grim and Beast continue, passing another door on the right-hand side that leads into the main warehouse. Just as they barrel past and run towards her office, three men step out into the corridor between us. With my feet stuck to the floor, time seems to slow down, a countdown of horrors unveiling before my eyes.

Five bullet holes in the wall to my left.

Four dead men, rivers of blood pooling beneath them.

Three enemies intent on killing the ones I love.

Two friends out of ammo.

My dark angel, roaring at me to run.

Zero fucking time left.

"PEN!" Grim shouts as time speeds back up, her eyes popping wide as she screams out my name. One of the men drops to his knee and fires a shot that misses Grim but hits Beast square in the shoulder as he shoves her out of the way. He grunts, blood spraying from the wound, but he doesn't appear to register any pain. He just lifts her off her feet and within a few strides has pushed open the door to her office and slammed the door shut behind him.

"KID, MOVE!"

I hear the panic in Dax's voice, and I turn on my heel sprinting back towards him, firing off shots wildly behind me. I reach him in record time and he practically lifts me off my feet, wrapping an arm around my shoulder as we run. I'm vaguely aware of the ghost who'd been shot in the leg covering us as we head for cover. Barrelling through the next door on the left we stumble into the gym, slamming the door behind us. Dax frantically looks around the room, trying to find something to push against the door.

"Here, help me with this," he orders, sweat dripping down the side of his face as he runs across the other side of the room and grabs hold of the beat-up sofa. Before I even reach him, he starts dragging it across the floor. Dropping my gun to the floor, I push the sofa as he pulls. Beyond the door more gunshots ring out as we half carry, half drag the sofa across the room. With one last inhuman effort, Dax shoves the sofa vertically up against the door, covering the small glass window and giving us a moment's reprieve.

"What about the guy?" I ask, breathing heavily as I press my back against the base of the sofa and look at him with wide eyes. Boxing me in, Dax rests his sweat covered forehead against mine, then cups my face, and gently pulls out the tiny shard of glass embedded in my skin. I feel a trickle of blood slide down my cheek, which he swipes at with the pad of his thumb.

"You're the most important person to me. What counts is that *you're* safe. He can take care of himself," Dax reassures me, even though we both know that he's already wounded and no match for a warehouse full of men with guns.

"What are we going to do?" I ask, my whole body violently trembling. "This won't keep them out."

"We just need to hold out for a little bit longer. The guys will be here in no time and I've no doubt Hud has called for back up from the police. They fucking owe us. It'll be over soon."

"Beast was shot," I blurt out, the image of his blood splattering against the wall mingles with that of the dead men on the floor in the corridor.

"Beast is a tough son-of-a-bitch, do you honestly think one little bullet wound is going to put him down?"

"Maybe not..."

"Kid, concentrate on the here and now. Worrying about them isn't going to help you get through this."

"Fuck!" My hands tremble so much that I have trouble cupping his face. Adrenaline right now isn't my friend.

"Just breathe."

Time passes and Dax just holds me whilst the battle continues outside. We've no way of knowing how many more ghosts might have been injured or killed, but when it suddenly becomes eerily quiet, I don't feel any safer. If anything, I'm *more* terrified.

"Where's your gun?" Dax suddenly asks, as though he too is coming out of the fog of shock.

I point to the other side of the room where I left it discarded on the floor. Stupid. I should've kept it on me. Dax runs across the room and picks it up, releasing the magazine so he can check how many bullets are left.

"Two," he says, returning just as someone pushes against the other side of the door. I plant my feet on the floor and push back. Dax joins me in my efforts.

"That's not enough."

"Only one person can come through this door at a time, Kid."

"I'm scared, what if—"

"Knock, knock, who's there!" a familiar voice sing-songs.

David. He's here.

My whole body goes rigid at David's laughter and the nausea I've been holding onto threatens to spill out of my mouth. Dax grips my hand and shakes his head. "I'm here. I got you," he mouths.

"Everyone's dead. Beast and Grim are hiding out like the chickenshit's they are, and we've got the place surrounded. If you stop putting up a fight, I might allow Dax to live. It is him in there with you, am I right? My men tell me you ran scared with the infamous *Teardrop Dax!*" He laughs again and I grit my teeth, pushing back against the sofa as they try to force their way in.

"Come on, Penelope, let us in," he wheedles out, his voice like nails scraping down a chalkboard. "If you don't, Dax is dead."

"Get fucked!" I scream, that fear encasing my heart making way for rage. It boils beneath my skin, erupting like lava through my pores. How dare he do this! How fucking dare he! "I'll fucking kill you!"

Dax reaches for me, yanking me to the side so that we're facing each other. "Now you listen to me," he whispers urgently. "You do not stick your neck out for me. None of this saving my arse bullshit. If it comes down to it and you get an opportunity to run, you take it regardless of what's happening to me. Understand."

"No!" I retort, shaking my head. "We get out of this together, or not at all."

Dax grasps my face in his hands. On the other side of the

door my brother and whoever he's with are pushing against it. The sofa shakes, but we hold firm. "Don't you fucking dare disobey me. I made a promise to myself a long time ago that I'd protect you. I failed you once before. I won't fucking do it again. You run. I can't fight them off if I've got one eye on you."

"You can't fight a *bullet*, Dax! Let me be your shield. He won't shoot me to get to you."

"Have you seen our size difference, you can't shield anything, Kid," he replies, a broken laugh breaking free from his lips. "Fuck, if only there was another way out of this fucking room!" The despair in his voice nearly undoes me. He knows we're on borrowed time as much as I do. He looks around frantically, then his gaze stops on the slim window situated above a running machine over the far side of the gym. I know what he's thinking, and I shake my head.

"I won't leave you. We can hold them out—"

"Do it."

"NO!" I shout, loud enough to capture the attention of my psychotic brother on the other side of the door.

"I'm getting a little impatient Penelope. Open the mother-fucking door now, bitch!" Shots are fired and I hear the muffled thuds of the bullets spraying into the door behind us. It's not a thick fire door and some bullets manage to pass through, embedding themselves into the sofa instead. We both look at each other wide eyed as we feel the thump, thump of two bullets hitting the stuffing just behind our backs.

"You go, now!" Dax shouts, pushing me away from him.

"Please, Dax."

"No. Go!"

"*Please,*" I beg.

"MOVE IT NOW!" he roars, and the sheer panic on his face forces me to act. I sprint across the room, hauling myself up on the running machine. Grasping the ledge and standing on my tiptoes, I manage to lift the latch on the window, shoving it open. The window is wide enough for me to fit through, but because I'm so short, I can't get enough lift with my hands in order to push through the gap. I press my feet against the wall trying to find purchase, but I keep sliding back down.

Behind me, Dax is struggling to hold them off as he turns around and pushes against the sofa with his hands. The door shakes, the sofa moves, and his feet slip and slide against the floor as he tries desperately to force them back.

"Kid, fucking move!" he shouts over his shoulder as more gunshots ring out. I see one penetrate through the sofa, missing his head but taking off part of his ear. Blood splatters from the wound and a scream rips out of my mouth. I forget about trying to escape. Instead, I make a split second decision and jump off the running machine, hitting the floor awkwardly and crying out in pain as I twist my ankle. But the pain is nothing to how I feel seeing blood flooding down the side of Dax's face, most of his ear missing. I run towards him as he runs towards me, eyes wide, roaring my name.

Behind him the sofa crashes to the floor and Dax twists as he runs, firing a shot at the intruder. It misses, slamming into the plasterwork instead. He lets off another shot, his last one, just as he reaches me, his body slamming into mine. As we both fall to the floor I notice our intruder crumple into a heap as blood spurts from his mouth and pours out of the bullet hole in his neck.

It takes less than the time for two more men to enter the

room for him to die. I forcefully shove Dax to the ground. Stepping in front of him.

"Don't. Don't kill him, *please*," I beg.

My brother follows those two men into the room, at least half a dozen more behind him. They fan out across the gym in a line beside my brother, and for a moment I'm struck by his sheer cowardice. One-on-one Dax would kill my brother, even wounded and bleeding as he is right now. He's a fucking pussy, and knowing that gives me hope because if there's something my brother hates more than being a pussy, it's being called one in front of his people.

Narrowing my eyes at him, I laugh. "Is this what you need to take down a handful of men, a fucking army? You're pathetic," I spit, making sure to look him up and down from head to toe.

"No, actually, scratch that. What you are is *weak*. You haven't changed one bit, David. When are you gonna grow up and be a man and not a pussy, huh? Hiding behind Santiago and *his* men. You're not worthy to stand in the same room as Dax, let alone the same fucking country."

"I'm not hiding behind anyone, *whore*. Santiago ain't even here." He tips his head back and laughs and all I can do is watch. My fingers curl into fists, and my body shakes not in fear, but in anger. Rage.

"What do you mean?" I bite out.

"Oh, you thought that the man I arrived with was Santiago? That man is my *valet*, José. My fucking *driver* and Santiago's half-brother."

"What?" I bite out.

"He's slow in the head. All he's good for is driving my cars. I kept him when my men and I *killed* Santiago and his most loyal followers nine months ago."

"That's bullshit," Dax comments, attempting to get to his feet, but I push him back down, trying to cover his body with mine as much as possible. He was right, I am too small, and he is too big, but for now no one's shooting at him and that has to be my priority. If I can keep David talking, I can buy us time.

"Like Dax said, you're full of shit," I comment, sneering at him.

"You don't think I'm capable?"

"No. I don't. You pick on the weak because it makes you feel like a man. You're not a man. You're nothing! You're insignificant. You couldn't organise a piss-up in a brewery let alone take down someone like Santiago."

"Shut your fucking mouth, bitch!" He snaps, and the soldier to his left cocks his gun, just waiting on his order to shoot.

"Why, it's the truth?"

He steps towards me, smiling slowly. "When Santiago returned to Cuba after fucking up the deal *we* made with the King a year ago, I decided it was time that someone younger, and far cleverer took the mantle. That someone was *me*. My men and I razed his motherfucking complex to the ground, all in the dead of night. It took us just eight hours to take him and his most loyal men out. I've rebuilt and reformed his businesses with these two hands," he says, holding them up to me and staring at them like they're plated in gold. "You've all been chasing a fucking ghost!"

"I don't believe it," I reply, refusing to accept that everything the Breakers have done, everything we've been through together has all been for nothing. They've been trying to lure out a man who's dead, and instead got my brother.

"I don't give a shit if you don't believe me. It's been easy to fool the international police given José has an uncanny resemblance to Santiago despite having different mothers. Whilst they've been concentrating on José—who does whatever the fuck I tell him to do—I've been running the biggest, most profitable sex trafficking business right beneath their noses. What was Santiago's is now mine, including his home, his widow, all his children, and that pretty little cunt, Sophie. Fucking a mother and a daughter is just the cherry on the cake. But you, Penelope, you were always the cake that I could never take a bite out of. That's gonna change tonight when I kill everyone you love and take you back home to Cuba, alongside that feisty redhead. I'm going to enjoy breaking her in."

"If you've hurt her...!" I grind out, my teeth scraping together.

"Oh, believe me, I've been *very* tempted to take a bite out of her, but thought I'd savour the moment when I've got you both alone. I'll fuck her first and then when I've used her up. I'll fuck you."

"The fuck you will. I'll rip your fucking throat out with my teeth before I allow you to take her," Dax exclaims, getting to his feet. I hold my arm out, and widen my shoulders, trying to somehow make myself bigger.

"Dax, don't!"

"She's feisty, and you know I *like* them feisty," David says, more intent on hurting me than Dax right at this moment.

My stomach flips over, bile burning my throat, but I refuse

to give him the satisfaction of watching me throw up. "Where is she?"

"Right now her and José are being driven to a small fishing port in Penzance. Just as soon as I have you, we'll be following them."

"And you expect us to believe you?" Dax asks, his voice eerily steady, calm. "That you'd give up all this information, just like that."

"Like I said, I don't care if you believe me. You're gonna die soon, so it makes no difference to me if I tell you the truth now."

"You honestly think you'll get away with this?" Dax asks, changing tactics. "Even if you did manage to kill us, in a few minutes this place is going to be surrounded by police. You ain't going nowhere. You were a fool to ever step foot on British soil."

David shakes his head. "You're not the only one who's got immunity from the law. I know people in very, *very* high places. You wouldn't believe the list of people I supply women and drugs too. They call me the secret keeper. Knowledge is power, and I'm fucking untouchable."

"Jesus Christ," Dax mutters.

My heart plummets to my feet, because in that moment, as he looks me dead in the eye, I know he's telling the truth. All of this is so much bigger than any of us had anticipated. The only way we're getting out of this is if David dies, and with an army backing him, that isn't going to happen. If I can't convince him to fight Dax one-on-one then there's no hope for either of us. I have to do something. I have to convince him to fight.

"You think I'm impressed by that, David? I don't give a fuck about who you know, or what you did to get to where you are. You're still that twisted, sick fuck with a superiority complex and a miniature dick. A real man wouldn't hide behind other men. I dare you to fight Dax without weapons and see who fucking wins then!"

David sneers at me, false bravado painting a mask on his face, but I know I've got to him. I can see it in his eyes as he glares at me. "I don't need these men to take you from Dax. Look at how he cowers behind you. The only pussy in this room is him."

"Fuck you, *cunt*. You wouldn't last a minute with me. This battle between us has been a long time coming. Question is, are you fucking *man* enough?" Dax taunts, following my lead and poking the lion.

More soldiers aim their guns at Dax, but David holds his hand up. "No! He's *mine*. Let's fucking do this," he says, handing his gun to one of his men and smiling broadly. "I should've beat your arse years ago, just like your daddy did over and over and *over* again."

It's at that moment, I know we've got him. He might've been able to beat upon a helpless child and murder a recovering addict, but one-on-one he's no match for my dark angel. Dax will kill him with his bare hands. I'm as certain of that as I am of my love for him.

Reaching for me, Dax rests his hand on my shoulder. Squeezing gently, he lowers his lips to my ear and whispers under his breath. "I'm going to finish this once and for all," he promises before stepping out from beside me and moving towards David.

"Let's fucking do this," David says, his lips pulling back over his lips in a feral scowl.

Dax rolls his head on his shoulders. Blood flicks from his

torn off ear and coats his face and shoulder, but he doesn't seem to notice. I watch him with trepidation in my heart and a fierce love in my soul.

"Get ready to die, motherfucker, because you're not gonna win."

For a split second I believe Dax. For the briefest fragment of time I allow hope to enter my heart and I convince myself that Arden was wrong. That tonight the only person who's going to pay the highest price is David and these men that stand before us now.

I was wrong.

Because like Arden said, *there's no tricking fate.*

As Dax runs towards my brother, David reaches behind his back, pulls out a shotgun, aims it at Dax and fires.

34

Dax

I DON'T FEEL any pain.

I don't feel much of anything as I fall to the floor, blood and bone exploding in the air, and a strange whooshing noise rushing in my ears.

A *dead* weight.

That's my passing thought as black spots blur my vision, and the light begins to dim.

The Deana-dhe were right after all...

Here I am paying the highest price and I didn't even get to save her.

I *promised* her.

I made a vow far more sacred than that of marriage.

I vowed to protect her.

My heart.

Our lucky penny.

My soulmate.

Kid.

Screaming.

She's screaming.

Gunshots.

More of them.

Outside.

Bang. Bang. BANG.

Shouting.

Voices mingle, sound shatters my thoughts.

Someone is dragging me across the floor. Crying and tugging and dragging and I can't help.

I can't help.

My eyelids are so heavy. So, so heavy.

Light flickers above me.

A face bathed in sunlight.

It's so bright. So pure. My heart. It's *her*.

"Kid?"

"Dax, stay with me!" she begs, leaning over me.

Panic is the only emotion she wears now.

Blind panic.

Her fingers run over my face. Her lips press against mine.

"Stay with me, stay with me, stay with me," she chants over and over and over again.

"Run!" I shout, but it comes out as a whimper.

It's a boy's voice. A child. I'm that child again. A boy, helpless. Unable to stop the pain. Unable to move, to fight back. Useless.

Something tugs at my arm. Something tight wraps around my bicep. Pulling. Tighter. So tight that I *feel* it.

Throbbing. Blinding pain.

I try to flex my fingers.

Nothing but pain.

Pain. So much pain.

I want to be sick.

But even that seems like a monumental effort.

Her fingers grip my jaw as she forces me to look at her.

"Open your eyes goddamn it! Hold on. They're here! Hold on!"

Bang. Bang BANG!

A voice shouts.

Someone familiar.

Someone I love.

Xeno?

"Hold on!" she screams, tears and breath and love and fear falling like rain over my face. "They're here. Hold on!"

I blink back the fog. I focus on her. My light. My love. Our lucky penny. *Kid.*

I will not die tonight.

I refuse.

More pain rushes in, almost knocking me out. I will myself awake.

Sleep is too easy, and I've never, not once, taken the easy route.

For her. For them. My brothers.

There's no dying tonight.

"Stay the fuck away from us!" she shouts, her head snapping up as she stands, stepping over me.

My girl. So strong. So *brave*.

I turn my head to the side.

He's standing there.

Him.

Her fucking monster.

I was supposed to slay him.

That was my job and I failed.

He grabs her, and she fights, the world behind her a blur of noise and violence, and blood.

Rivers of it.

He can't have her. He can't.

I feel a burning inside my chest. My heart fucking sets alight right behind my dark angel tattoo that I had inked into my chest for her.

It rages, my heart. It refuses to let him take her.

I flip onto my stomach pushing up on my hands.

Hand...

Where's my other fucking hand?

I see a bloody, tattered stump where my forearm should be. A white, jagged bone, sharp like a knife, pokes out of the sinews of tendons and muscles hanging in strands. A leather belt is pulled tight around my bicep. Blood drips but not pours.

Fuck.

Bile rises, I swallow it down.

Black spots float in my periphery. I ignore them.

No.

She needs me.

Kid screams, but it's not a scream of fear. It's a mother-fucking war cry. She's done. Enough is enough. I hear her intent over every other noise in this room.

She'll kill David, or die trying.

Kid!

My head lifts up as I see him drag her across the room, but she fights.

My God, she fights.

Everything I taught her, she uses.

She's a warrior.

Claws, teeth, fists, elbows, feet, knees. She uses her body, and she motherfucking fights.

That's what I have to do.

Fight.

Around her, men battle. Inside the room. Outside of it. I see a flash of white-blonde hair.

York.

He's coming to help.

That's when I hear it. *Audacity* by Stormzy. It plays in my head, and I don't know if I'm having an auditory hallucination, or it really is playing out whilst the battle rages.

Either way, I don't care. I embrace the anger and the rage in the song. Absorb it. Use it.

The fucking audacity of David.

Pushing up on my good arm, I brace myself. Willing myself to push harder, using every ounce of strength I have left. I can't let her down. I won't.

He grips her by the hair and tugs, she flies back onto her arse, legs flailing, fingernails scratching at his forearms. Nausea rises, my head drops between my shoulders as I sway on my hand and knees.

Kid screams. Ear-shattering, heart-breaking.

I breathe in deeply through my nose.

Motherfucking cunt.

I'm going to kill the bastard. I'll wrap my hand around his throat and squeeze. I'll do it with a smile on my face and peace in my heart. I'll watch with glee as the blood vessels pop in his eyes, as they bulge out of his motherfucking head. I'll absorb his oxygen like some soul-sucking monster and enjoy every last fucking breath.

He dares to come after my brothers?

He dares to threaten the girl I love?

He dares to taunt her with messages that have twisted her up inside?

He doesn't get to fuck with her, with us.

He *will* die.

Snapping my head up, my fingers curl into my palm. My muscles tense with adrenalin. My heart fucking kickstarts into a higher gear as I will myself to get to my feet.

Xeno was right when he said that violence was brewing inside of me.

I feel it now. It's an inferno, burning me up from the inside out. I've felt it smouldering inside my chest ever since Frederico had a knife pressed against Kid's throat. Wait, who am I trying to fucking kid? It was ignited ever since the moment I allowed the only girl I've ever loved back into my heart. It's grown in size since I held her in my arms and fucking loved her with every part of my tainted, broken soul. Loving us has put Kid in danger and that knowledge has fuelled the fire inside. My need to protect her spreads like liquid heat inside my veins with every passing day. I made a promise to her as a kid, and I will not break it. Not now, not ever.

We sealed that promise with a kiss, her first kiss, one that scorched away all kisses that came before that point until they were nothing but dust. I had known in that moment, when she'd looked up at me with flushed cheeks and love in her eyes, and asked me if I'd always protect her, that I would. That I would *die* to protect her. She was always my hope, my *home*, and I was always her dark angel.

So, you see, it doesn't matter that I'm bleeding out.

It doesn't matter that my skin is pale, and my heart is fighting to keep me alive.

It doesn't matter that Xeno is roaring at me to stay the fuck down, or York is beating a man to a pulp to get to me. It doesn't matter that Zayn is cutting through more men to do the same, his knife glinting in the light, blood dripping from the blade.

All that matters right now in this fucking moment is Kid. If it's the last thing I ever do, I will kill that cunt David. I will set her free of the cage he's inflicted on her soul.

That's my final vow as I push myself up off the floor and stagger towards him.

"No fucking more!" I roar.

I stumble towards her. Focused.

She sees me. She screams for me to stop.

I don't.

This is it.

This is my last gift.

I'm going to save her from that bastard before I leave this world for good.

Forcing myself to move. Forcing my heavy limbs to hold me steady. Forcing my heart to keep beating through sheer fucking will. I move towards her.

Tears pour down her face as David yanks her up against his chest.

And right before my eyes, my girl, my fucking beautiful Kid shifts her hips to the side, elbowing him in the diaphragm just like I taught her.

He's winded.

I take another step on heavy, heavy legs.

She doesn't stop there.

She ducks out of his loosened arms, pulls out a flick knife from her back pocket, snaps her wrist, releases the blade then ducks under his arm and slams it into his armpit. The scream that rips out of her mouth is one of fury and hate, rage and violence as she yanks it free.

I drop to my knees a few feet away, a weak cry escaping my lips.

David stumbles, but she doesn't stop. Instead, she shoves him to the side and crouches low, slicing the back of his knee.

He screams.

My breath is heavy as I pant. I'm fading fast.

I blink away the darkness. I need to see it. I need to see her safe.

With absolute fury, Kid kicks David to his knees then lifts the blade and rams it into the base of his skull, and in that moment as death comes to claim me, Kid slays her motherfucking monster.

35

Pen - One week later.

"I LOVE YOU, PEN," Clancy says, gripping my hand tightly in hers. Her red hair is splayed across the crisp, white cotton of her pillow, reminding me of all that blood splattered across the walls and floors in Tales...

So much blood.

I push the thought away. I can't think about that. Not now. Clancy might be laid up in hospital, but she's alive. She's alive and for that I'm so, so grateful.

"I love you too. I'm so sorry about it all," I reply, my throat tight, thick with unshed tears. I've cried so much over the past few days. I'm surprised that I have any tears left honestly.

"It's not your fault. None of it is. David was evil."

"He murdered Tiffany, my mum. So many are dead... He

shot Dax..." I gulp, not able to say the words. "I should've protected them. I should've protected *you*."

"We've been through this Pen. You can't save the world from the evil within it. His actions don't reflect on you. You hear me?"

I nod my head, forcing myself not to cry. "Sophie has been charged with the premeditated murder of Tiffany. I found out earlier."

Clancy sighs. "I can't believe she was involved with your brother. That she would do such a thing."

"Me either. We all knew she was a mean girl, but a murderer? Not that. Never that."

"It's difficult to wrap your head around it," Clancy mutters.

"It really is... How's your step-mum? Your dad?"

"Devastated. Heartbroken. Tiffany might not have been my friend. She was cruel and heartless, but I had hoped that one day, maybe we could've been..." Clancy sighs, then gives me a tremulous smile.

"I'm so sorry. If there's anything I can do... *Anything*."

"You did everything you could, Pen. You fought him and you *won*." Shifting her position, she winces as her hand presses against her side, reminding us that she has several broken ribs.

"He hurt you," I counter, my fingers gently brushing over the yellowing bruises on her arm. There are so many more hidden beneath her hospital gown. He beat her, like he used to beat me because she fought back.

"And now he's gone. He can't hurt anyone anymore," she says, firmly. "It's over. I don't blame you. My family doesn't blame you. I swear it."

My head drops as I place my forehead against her hand. She

reaches for me, her fingers stroking my hair. "It's going to be okay, Pen," she murmurs, and I hear the tears in her voice too.

"How can it be? How can it ever be okay again?" I ask, lifting my head and blinking back the tears.

"It will be. You have to believe that. There's one less monster in the world."

"Too many people have died. Too many people have been hurt because of him."

"And you heard what Hudson said yesterday, many, many more women are safe now because of you all. Your brother is dead, and the women he was trafficking are free."

"Are you still having nightmares?" I whisper, knowing that she's not the only one who will suffer from bad dreams because of my brother. He might be dead, but his evil somehow lives on. And the worst thing, he was just the tip of the iceberg. Every layer that Interpol has uncovered since his death is as shocking as the one before it. So many sick men and women who've used their privilege and money to buy what they want, to fulfil their fantasies. Hudson may not have got the personal vengeance he sought, but he has helped to take down one of the biggest sex trafficking rings in recent history.

She bites her lip, nodding. "I won't lie to you. Those were the worst twelve hours of my life, but I'm alive and right now *that's* what counts. He can't hurt me in a dream, Pen. I'll be okay."

Swallowing hard, I nod. Across the room, the door opens, and River and Lola enter. The smile on Clancy's face and love in her eyes are enough to warm my heart.

"Ah, here they are," she grins.

"Hey babe, how're you feeling?" Lola asks.

"Good. Much better," Clancy replies, accepting a kiss and a gentle hug from her girlfriend. I feel a warm hand on my shoulder and look up to find River staring down at me.

"Hey, Pen," he says.

"Hey, River."

Squeezing my shoulder gently, he nudges Lola aside and leans over Clancy, planting a tender kiss on her lips. "Time to go home," he says.

"I can be discharged today?"

"That's right, babe," Lola says with a wide grin. "The doctor has given you the all clear. Let's take you home. River and I are going to take care of you at my place."

"I'm not sure Dad will agree with that."

"He already has."

"He has?" she asks in surprise.

"Your dad *loves* us. We're both pretty persuasive..." Lola says, flinging her arm around River's shoulder and pressing a kiss against his cheek.

"And bloody charming."

They laugh and whilst I can smile at their happiness, my own heart's too heavy to join in with the laughter.

"Go on, make yourself useful and pack up my stuff," Clancy orders, pulling back the cover and swinging her legs over the side of the bed.

River salutes her. "On it, boss," he says, and the pair start gathering her things.

"Help me with this?" Clancy asks motioning to her top. "I want to change out of my pyjamas."

"Sure," I reply, and just as she removes her top, there's a knock at the door. Whoever's on the other side doesn't bother to wait for an answer and barges right in. Lucky Clancy's wearing a bra.

"York, did no one ever tell you it's rude to barge into a room like that?" River says, folding his arms across his chest.

York pulls a face. "Sorry, mate. I'll look the other way whilst your missus gets dressed." Only he doesn't look away, he stares right at Clancy and grins. "You're looking better."

It's the first smile I've seen in over a week. My heart lifts, a bubble of hope expanding in my chest. Something good must've happened.

"Is that finally an offer, York? You know River, Lola and I are willing to combine harems..." she jokes, winking at me.

"We are?" Lola and River say simultaneously.

"Yours isn't strictly a harem, more of a *menage*... Besides, I'm more than happy with Pen and my guys."

"Fair enough. How's he doing?" Clancy asks.

"*Awake*. Dax is awake."

I stand abruptly, the chair scraping over the floor. "He's awake, awake?"

"Yep, for about an hour now." York's smile widens. It's a beautiful, glorious, sunshine-through-clouds kind of smile that makes happiness burst inside my chest. "He's grumpy as fuck, but can at least string a sentence together that isn't drug-induced nonsense."

"And you're only telling me this now! Why didn't you come get me sooner?" I screech.

"He demanded to know what happened and then wanted to make himself presentable for you."

"How did he take the news?" I ask, referring to the fact he's now an amputee. The doctors here were incredible, managing to save his elbow joint so that sometime in the future after he's healed and has had some rehabilitation, he'll be able to wear a prosthetic arm if he wishes.

"Like a fucking champ. We've just finished helping him shower, shit, and shave. I swear, the things we do for the people we love, eh?"

"You know he can't shower. He'll get his dressings wet!"

"By shower, I meant a bed bath," York says, wrinkling his nose. "At least he doesn't smell like a pile of dirty laundry now."

"Oh my God!" I laugh, just imagining the three of them giving him a bed bath. I turn to Clancy and she grins, shooing me out of the room.

"Go! I'll see you later."

Kissing Clancy, then River and Lola on the cheek, I sprint down the hallway to Dax's private room in The Wellington Hospital located in St John's Wood, in record time. My heart fit to burst with every step. This past week has been hell. I've lived at this hospital refusing to leave Dax's side. When he's been asleep, which has practically been the whole time, I've kept Clancy company. They've had the best possible care money can buy, all paid for by the Freed brothers. I'm convinced it's been the specialised, very expensive treatment Dax has received this past week that has kept him alive after such a traumatic, life-threatening injury. Now, after a week of him being in and out of consciousness due to the heavy pain medication and fourteen hour operation he's had to endure, he's finally awake enough to have a proper conversation.

I burst into his room, the door slamming open in my haste. "Dax!" I yell, running over to his bed and throwing myself against his chest, forgetting myself. He groans and I instantly pull back.

"You might want to take it easy on the poor fuck," Zayn says, laughter in his voice. "He's still feeling delicate."

"I am *not* feeling fucking delicate," he counters, laughter rumbling up his chest as he cups my face with his good hand. "Well, you're a sight for sore eyes."

"I've been here every day. You don't remember?"

"The guys said I've been pretty out of it the past week. I don't remember much of it." His gaze falls to his stump, and he shakes his head. "Look at the state of that."

"Does it hurt?"

"Like a bitch. I'm looking at my non-existent hand right now and I swear I can feel my fingernails digging into my palm. It's fucking weird."

"That's the phantom pain. The doctor said that can go on for quite some time," I explain, leaning into his hold. "I'll help you through it. We all will."

"Fucking hell, don't tell him that, he'll be milking this for all it's worth," York comments, rolling his eyes.

"You're damn right I will. It's not every day you get your hand blown off," Dax retorts, grinning. Reaching up, I gently stroke over the bandage wrapped around his head, that covers what's left of his ear. My eyes well with tears that are both happy that he's alive and sad that he's lost so much.

"How are you *feeling*?" I ask, cupping his cheek gently.

"Better now that you're here," he mutters, drawing me in for a kiss. It's gentle and soft and filled with so much love. It's just as well I'm sitting down because my knees go weak.

"I'm sorry I wasn't here when you woke up," I say, pressing another kiss against his lips, unable to help myself.

"It's just as well that you weren't, Titch. Big boy here got a bit of a shock when he woke up. Not being able to grab hold of his boner with his wanking hand can do that to you," York says, laughter in his voice.

A beat passes, my eyes widening at York's crass joke. Dax blinks, then he grins, and that grin turns into a full blown smile that releases a deep, joyous laugh. We all join in and the sound is music to my ears

"You fucker," Dax says, shaking his head in disbelief. "I'm never gonna *ear* the end of this, am I?"

"You didn't just..." Another laugh bursts out of my mouth as I shake my head. "That was terrible, Dax!"

Zayn smirks. "Pen, you haven't heard the worst of them. York's been thinking up all sorts of one-armed, one-ear'd jokes. Are you ready to endure the next sixty years of York winding up Dax?"

I flick my gaze to Zayn, grinning. I'm willing to spend every single minute of the next sixty years doing just that. "That bad, huh?"

"They really are terrible," Xeno agrees, stepping up behind York and grasping his shoulders. He looks as exhausted as the rest of us. Dark circles under his eyes and his chin and cheeks are covered in a week-old stubble. I itch to touch it, him. All of them. I just want to hold them for the rest of my life and never, ever let them go.

"You know, I warned York to take it easy on Dax," Xeno says. "But he wouldn't have it. So I had to remind York that Dax could still beat his arse, *single-handedly*."

"What the fuck was that?" York exclaims, screwing up his face as we all chuckle at Xeno's poor attempt at a joke.

"Alright, alright," Xeno says, holding his hands up in surrender. "I'm fucking tired. You'll have to allow it."

"You're losing your touch, mate. I, on the other hand, am not afraid of Dax here," York continues, not to be deterred. "We all know he's 'armless.'"

"Oh for fuck's sake. It had to be me that lost a motherfucking limb. It couldn't be one of you arsehats, could it?" Dax groans, shifting position. He winces and my gaze is drawn back to the bandaged stump, and the tube that's draining off excess fluids, sticking out of it.

"Do you need more pain medication?" I ask, worry creasing my brow.

"No, I'm good. I've been hopped up on morphine and fuck knows what else for too long. It feels good to have a clear head."

I chew on my lip, my gaze roving over his stump and up his arms to his broad chest. Instinctively, my fingers press against his dark angel tattoo and I sigh. I'm so, so happy he's alive. That's the most important thing, but I can't help feeling how cruel this injury is. He'll never be able to dance like he did before. There are just some moves he won't be able to perform, and that kills me. Arden was right, Dax did pay a *high price*.

Dax covers my hand with his and draws my fingers to his lips. "Don't do that, Kid. Don't pity me. It's not good for my ego."

"I don't pity you, Dax. I love you. I'm sad for what you've lost."

"I've lost nothing. Just an arm. I've got another one," he says nonchalantly, but I know this has affected him. He's just putting on a brave face for me.

"But..."

"No buts. I'm going to heal, and we'll dance again. Whatever it takes. I'll make sure of it."

"Okay," I agree. "Whatever it takes."

York coughs, breaking up our serious moment with a roll of his eyes. "I'm not being funny, Dax, but it could've been worse..." York's gaze drops to Dax's crotch. "Would've been a crying shame if your monsterdick was blown off. Thank fuck David was such a crap shot."

I choke down a laugh, my hand covering my mouth.

Dax snorts. "You lot are on fire today."

"Yeah and now that the playing field has levelled, we can all get a crack at the whip when it comes to Tiny's attention. You're about as handsome as we are now," Xeno adds.

"Ha! Whatever, mate. I might've had my wings clipped, but I'm still Kid's dark angel and don't you ever fucking forget it." Dax grins as he rests his hands on my thigh and squeezes. When I catch his gaze I see the love and lust firing within them.

"Woah! Steady, *big boy*. You might want to bench that thought. You've got a lot of recovery time ahead of you," York says, serious for a moment. "Don't get carried away. You need every drop of blood in your whole body, not just your gigantic cock."

"I'm beginning to think you're obsessed with my dick."

York shrugs. "No more than my own."

"York's right, you need to concentrate on getting better. We'll be happy to take up the slack. Won't we, boys?" Xeno adds, with a shrug and a wink.

"Oh, my God. Stop it! Leave the poor man alone." I admonish.

"Yeah, you heard Kid. Leave me alone. In fact, why don't you all fuck off for a moment so I can remind our girl just how much better I *really* am."

"Not a chance in Hell. None of that for you, my friend," Beast winks as he steps into the room, Grim and Hudson following behind. "You might've defied the odds and survived the worst fucking injury in history, but Pen here is a badass bitch and she'll fucking kill you if you so much as pass out before you give her the big O!"

Grim slaps his chest. "Sorry about Beast. You would think he was shot in the head and not in the shoulder with the amount of shit he's been coming up with lately."

"Lately? Are you kidding? Beast has been spewing crap ever since he lost his head over you," Hudson counters with a laugh.

"Yeah, and you've been a pain in my arse the whole fucking time. Anyway, haven't you got a family to go home to?"

"I do," Hudson agrees. "In fact, I came here to let Pen know that Gray will be dropping Lena back home in a few hours. The plane lands at four o'clock."

"Thank you Hudson. For *everything*," I say, grateful that his family looked after Lena for me this past week or so whilst we dealt with David and looked after Dax.

"No. Thank *you*, Pen. I'm indebted to all of you, and I'm also fully aware of the monumental fuck up on my part."

"Don't be. You didn't know that David took out Santiago and used José as a doppelgänger. He fooled the police too," Dax says.

"I should've dug deeper. Looked closer. That's on me. I

dragged you into something that was all smoke and mirrors. I'm sorry."

"Well, fuck. The great Hudson Freed apologising... As I live and breathe," Beast remarks, chuckling.

"It happens on occasion, but don't get used to it."

"Look, man," Zayn says, swiping a hand through his hair. "We can all go around in circles about who's to blame, but we got what we wanted out of this. David is dead, and our girl *never* has to be afraid of that piece of shit hurting her again."

"Regardless, I will forever be in your debt. If there's anything any of you need, any time. You know where I am."

"Don't tell the Deana-dhe that," York jokes, and this time none of us laugh, no matter how ironic the joke might be. We all remember the deal Grim made and not one of us is happy about it. "Sorry, verbal diarrhoea."

Grim waves her hand in the air, batting away everyone's concern. "Like I said before, I know how to handle the Deana-dhe."

"Well, that makes one of us then," Beast mutters, scowling.

Grim flashes him a look, not wanting to have another row. This past week I've witnessed plenty, but despite their fiery relationship I see the enduring love they have for one another. Their love story has been full of ups and downs. I'm aware of some of the downs already, but I'm hoping someday soon Grim will have the chance to share their full fairytale with me, bloody hearts and all.

"Oh, before I forget, I have something for you," Hudson interjects, returning his attention back to Dax.

"Yeah, what's that?" he asks.

Hudson reaches into the pocket of his jacket, pulling something out. "Catch," he says, before chucking a small, clear plastic container to him. Dax catches it with his good hand. There's something small, metal and twisted inside.

"What the fuck's this?" he asks, holding up the pot between his finger and thumb, peering into it.

"It's the bullet that Doctor Morris dug out of your wound. He just gave it to me. I thought you might want it." Hudson says.

"Actually that's a slug not a bullet," I point out, glancing over to Xeno who nods.

"Knowledgeable and beautiful, that's my girl," he says.

Dax shakes his head in wonder as he stares at the slug. "You wouldn't think something so small could cause so much damage."

"No shit," Beast says. "You totally trumped me on the sympathy vote, that's for sure."

"You should have it made into a necklace or something, a reminder that what doesn't kill you makes you stronger," York remarks, serious for once. He takes the container from Dax, unscrewing the lid and drops it into his palm. "Twisted bullet..."

"Slug," Xeno corrects him.

"No, I mean, that's a pretty fucking cool name for a club. *Twisted Bullet*," York clarifies.

"Are you thinking of changing the name of one of your clubs?" I ask, frowning as I glance between York and the guys. They all look like they've been caught with their fingers in the cookie jar. I narrow my eyes at them. "What?"

"Nothing, my love. Just thinking out loud, that's all." York grins and curls his fingers around the slug, pocketing it.

"Yeah, let's concentrate on the sick and wounded. How are

you *really* feeling, mate?" Beast asks, and I can't help but think that they're all up to something. For now, I let it go.

"How am I?" Dax muses, rubbing a hand over his smoothly shaven chin. "That's an easy question to answer."

Hudson smiles. "It is?"

"It is." Dax's gaze flicks between each of us in turn. "I'm fucking grateful to have you all as friends. You three included," he says to Grim, Beast and Hudson.

"Likewise, mate," Beast replies for the three of them.

"I'm also fucking grateful to be alive. I know it was touch and go for a while..."

"Why do I sense a but coming?" I prompt.

He reaches for me, taking my hand in his. "But most of all I'm wondering how long it will take me to heal so that I can dance with our girl again."

36

Pen

FIVE MONTHS *later*

MY BARE FEET press against the wooden boards of the stage as a cool breeze lifts the strands of my hair and the soft, thin material of my white dress. This is my third costume change for the evening, and the last dance.

Our finale.

The air is thick with anticipation as the audience waits patiently, blanketed within the darkness of the auditorium. The only noticeable light is the red spot of a camera recording our performances live to the entire British public. All night, here in the theatre of the Academy of Stardom, our nearest and dearest have enjoyed performances by the remaining dancers in the troupe. Clancy and York duetted their tap piece. River, Zayn and I danced the trio. And our group dance to Survivor by 2WEI, featured everyone beside Dax who hasn't quite recovered enough to take part in such a strenuous routine.

But this dance we're about to perform. This dance wasn't part of the original line-up. This is something personal, *special*. Clancy and I have been working on this routine with the dancers of Tales, River and the guys for the past couple of weeks.

Now it's ready.

In return for allowing us to perform this routine, Madame Tuillard requested that the Breakers and I teach a dance class every week to disenchanted kids from the local community. Of course we agreed. How could we not? Perhaps if we'd had a similar opportunity as kids, things would've turned out differently for us all. The five children I teach had never stepped into a dance studio before they started my class. They're inexperienced, but that matters little to me because no matter your age, your sex, your level of ability, so long as you can move your body, you can dance.

Dance allows imperfection. It embraces difference, challenges perception. It shines a light on all of the beauty, and all of the ugliness inside a person. It's freeing. Uplifting. Cathartic. Joyous. Dance gives hope to the hopeless. It brings people together. It brought *us* together, and I don't just mean the Breakers. I mean Clancy and River, Grim, Beast, Madame Tuillard, the dancers from Tales, and the Freed family. Every single one I count as friends, and alongside Lena, they're my family now. Those who aren't dancing on stage are sitting in the audience, supporting us with their presence.

All of those thoughts run through my head as *Move Me* by Ruthanne begins to play. The piano chords and her haunting voice fills the vast expanse of the theatre, a perfect song for the most beautiful, heartfelt routine I've ever had the pleasure of performing.

"Ready?" Xeno whispers to me in the darkness, his fingers whispering over my skin as they trail down my bare arms.

"Yes."

A spotlight turns on, a circle of white light illuminating Dax's hunched over figure a few feet away from us. He's bare chested, his tattoos and injury on display. A pair of thin, white cotton shorts the only item of clothing he wears. He wanted people to see. He wanted people like him, who've suffered such terrible, irreversible injuries to know that nothing need stop them from doing what they love.

He's worked hard to recover over the past few months. He's dealt with phantom pain and his own emotional reaction to losing a limb, and here he is now, astounding us all.

My heart blooms with love, with pride and joy. With happiness. We all agreed, unanimously, that Dax should take the solo spot.

He's earned it.

With his hand pressed against the boards, Dax slowly rises out of the tumbling, twirling dry-ice pumping from the smoke machines at the edge of the stage. My throat tightens as he raises his arm in the air and kicks his leg out into a pirouette. A perfect turn despite the fact he dances without complete balance. Because of the loss of his lower arm, he's had to learn to dance again, to find a slightly different centre of gravity. It was hard, but he overcame, just like we knew he would.

Silent tears pour down my face as we watch him.

Every single step is a miracle.

I could've lost him. We could've lost him.

But here he is dancing with such poise, with indescribable power and a muted kind of passion that is controlled, composed, but also free. He dances with joy, happiness and love. Dance has always healed us, and it has helped to heal Dax these past few months too. He's alive. My dark angel is alive, and I will never, ever, take him or any of my Breakers for granted. Life is so precious, so very, very fleeting. I've learnt many things recently, but above all else, that realisation has had the most defining impact. Not one of us knows what's around the corner.

As the music builds, and Dax continues to dance with a beautiful fluidity, another spotlight switches on above me and Xeno this time. Grasping my waist, Xeno lifts me up and I leap into the movement as he helps me glide through the air, the skirt of my dress fluttering over my legs. The audience gasps and I drop back to the floor, turning in his arms. Clasping my hand above my head, Xeno spins me beneath his raised arm as we dance in a circle around Dax. For a moment we're two separate entities, me and Xeno orbiting Dax in the centre, then our spotlights become one. In that moment, Xeno lets me go so that I can step into Dax's arm.

He captures me, dipping me low. "Hey, beautiful," he murmurs.

"Hey, Dax," I reply, before he captures my mouth in a brief whisper of a kiss that is completely unrehearsed, before lifting me back up. Xeno reaches for me again, and supports us both as we dance together as a trio. He becomes Dax's missing arm, and between them I'm lifted into the air supported with both Xeno and Dax's hand on my waist.

We dance like that, *together*. Every step is choreographed so that we are never parted, always touching, caressing each other with our movements. For a portion of the song I dance with two of the four pieces of my soul, always conscious of the missing pieces close by.

As we get to the end of our choreographed trio, the spotlight turns off, dropping us into darkness briefly before a row of light-bulbs are switched on behind us in an arc. Each lightbulb sits upon a stand and is controlled by one of the dancers from Tales. Then from the left of the stage River and Clancy enter together, and from the right, Zayn and York. They dance in their duets, whilst we move aside a little, still dancing but in a muted way so the audience's focus is on the two couples.

Turning and twisting, tumbling and rolling around each other, they dance with the same passion as we did. The way they move in their duets is compelling, effortless, touching and poignant. When they dance it becomes more than movement, it surpasses a routine or a series of steps. It has meaning, it bares the truth of who they are as people.

It is compelling.

As the dancers from Tales flick the light bulbs on and off, casting shadow and light across the stage, Zayn and York dance towards our trio whilst Clancy and River continue to dance to the left of the stage. I've watched Zayn and York perform their duet together dozens of times before tonight, but the way they dance now? My God, I don't have any words for just how stunning they move. Two powerful men, dancing with grace and a gentleness that belies the cold, hard, callous men I know they can be, that I've witnessed them to be. They dance as a couple, as best friends, as brothers. Supporting each other, lifting each other up. It's powerful to witness a love so pure.

Dance truly unveils the truth of who we are beneath the walls we've built over the years. Dance peels back the layers, and with every step those layers fall away one by one, like leaves from a tree in autumn. As we dance, the stage becomes littered with all our past mistakes. It's both a completely personal experience and a shared one.

Right here and now, we shed any last remaining feelings of resentment, of disappointment, of pain, revealing what's important to us as people, as couples, as lovers and friends. Clancy and River embrace the dance as wholly as the rest of us, unveiling more about their relationship in these few minutes than perhaps they have ever before. They dance with us, and I love them for the friendships they've given me and look forward to years of friendship in the future.

Right now, for all of us, this dance is our finale.

It's the culmination of a year filled with so many ups and downs, with friendship and laughter, love and heartbreak, rage and fear. This dance is our goodbye to that period of time in all of our lives, but also, for me and the Breakers, it's a goodbye to a past riddled with pain. It's the start of new beginnings. It's the first step into a future we've all been longing for since we met each other as broken, fucked-up kids, our bond sealed in the basement of number 15 Jackson Street.

Zayn spins away from York and strides over to me, reaching out a hand of friendship, just like he did as a kid. I take his tattooed covered fingers in mine and spin in his arms, the spotlight highlighting us as we move. For the briefest of moments, we just breathe each other in, swaying in each other's arms as the undeniable connection we share wraps around us both. Then with a gentle smile, Zayn lifts me up above his head, my hands resting on his shoulders as he turns. He grins up at me with his beautiful chipped-tooth smile and I nod imperceptibly, telling him that I'm ready. Zayn bends his legs then throws me up into the air, and just like we've practised, York catches me in his arms.

I laugh, I can't help it.

York grins, my heart soars. Then he lowers me to my feet and kisses me, rough and hard. This isn't part of the routine, and the audience seem to understand that as they clap, cheering and whistling.

"Only you," Dax chuckles over the music, reaching for me and pulling me against his chest. Not to be outdone, he kisses me long and hard. The crowd roars in appreciation as he lifts me up one armed and drops me into Xeno's arms. We too kiss and there's more cheering, more clapping before I find myself in Zayn's arms once again, his plump lips dusting over mine.

Right then and there my heart knows that everything we've been through, both together and apart, has all led to this one pivotal moment. Like the song suggests, this is beauty, right here on the stage. This is what we were always meant to be, before life and our choices took us on separate paths. None of that matters now as the five of us dance together as a crew, as lovers, as friends. As soulmates.

Together, we perform with love in our hearts, with trust and compassion. We dance fluidly, like the first rays of sun passing through a darkened room. We're the tiny motes of dust, and the particles of light. We're the peaceful silence of happiness and joy, and the step in each other's dance. We're the warmth in each other's hearts, and the love in each other's souls.

And whilst this might be our final performance at the Academy of Stardom, I know that it's just the beginning of a lifetime filled with love, friendship, laughter, joy and most of all, *dance.*

EPILOGUE

Grim - Two months later

STEPPING INTO THE TWISTED BULLET, I rub a hand over my very pregnant belly. My little girl kicks in anger at the loud music that wakes her up from her peaceful, muffled slumber. I already know she's going to be feisty just like me, and a talented fighter just like her daddy. Any day now she'll be here causing chaos, and I can't wait.

"Would you like a mocktail, babe?" Beast asks me as we head towards Pen's office that's situated behind the dance floor at the back of the club.

"A mocktail? Sure, why not. I'll have a Pina Colada minus the rum." Our daughter kicks me again and I smile, envisaging her as a teenager keeping court with a bunch of unruly men at her feet. She's going to be remarkable. I know it.

"Coming right up," Beast replies, pecking me on the cheek and patting me on the arse as I stride past him.

When I knock on the door, there's laughter and the sound of people rushing around for clothes. I don't step into the room, knowing full well that Pen and one of her guys are up to no good. I made that mistake once before, and whilst I appreciate the view of a man's firm arse, I'm not sure Pen appreciated the intrusion. When York pulls open the door, flushed cheek and his hair dishevelled, I grin.

"Alright, York?" I ask, my gaze flicking to his jeans and his zipper that's still undone. "You might want to zip up."

He barks out a laugh and shrugs. "You know how it is, I've got to get in there when I can now that Pen's busy running the club and putting on the best motherfucking dance shows this town has ever seen. No offence."

"None taken. I know she's the best at what she does and I'm not in competition with her. Besides, Clancy is a pretty fucking amazing dancer too, and we have a totally different client base."

"Yeah, you can keep the criminals. I think Pen's had enough of them to last a motherfucking lifetime."

"I hope not," I say with a wink.

"Excluding you guys, of course."

"Anyway, I gotta dash. Xeno will kick my arse if he finds out I've been skiving off." York leans in and gives me a peck on the cheek, then crouches before me and whispers to my bump. "You be sure to keep your parents on their toes for Uncle Yorky, okay little one?" he says, before rising up and winking at me. I shake my head and smile, watching him as he swaggers down the hallway back into the main portion of the club, disappearing from view.

"Hey Grim, how are you?" Pen asks as I step into the room and take off my jacket, throwing it over the back of the chair before sitting down. Her cheeks are flushed, and she gives me a wry smile.

"Feeling like a bloated whale, you?" I ask with a raised brow.

She laughs. "I'm feeling great, thank you very much, and you look beautiful, as always. Can I get you a drink?"

"Beast is bringing me one. He's at the bar as we speak."

"I love how dedicated he is to keeping you happy. I didn't know he had it in him."

"There are a lot of things you don't know about Beast. He hides a lot."

"Don't tell me he gives you foot massages and head rubs too?"

I grin. "Shh, don't tell anyone."

"Well, I'm glad he's looking after you so well. It's really good to see you, though I was a little surprised you wanted to come here tonight. I know you're crazy busy with Tales. Clancy tells me that her shows are a hit."

"They are. She's working those girls hard, but they love it. I couldn't want for a better bunch of dancers." I grin. "How are things here? I know you were looking for some more dancers to add to the troupe. Found any yet?"

"Not yet. I'm starting auditions next week."

"How's it been, dancing in the shows and running the place?"

Pen laughs. "Bloody hard work, but also amazing. I just feel so... *lucky*, I guess is the right word. Not everyone gets to live their dream. Most days I have to pinch myself."

"It's not luck, Pen. You deserve all of this and more..." My voice trails off and I sigh, hating to burst her bubble.

Pen cocks her head, looking at me thoughtfully. "Come on, Grim. Spill. Why are you here? You've given me all the advice I could ever want or need over the past month since we've opened up, so I know you're not here on business. Is everything okay with you and Beast?"

"Of course. We're good. Really good."

"Okay then, so what is it?" she asks gently, moving around the table and dropping into the seat next to me.

"I'm worried about Christy," I blurt out. Coming here was a difficult decision, but ultimately I trust Pen and her guys just as much as I trust Beast and Hudson. I couldn't go to Hudson because he's already busy with his family and businesses, so Pen was the obvious choice.

"Why?"

"Remember I told you once that she's... *sensitive* to things?"

"Like the Deana-dhe, you mean? Or at least Arden, I don't know about the other two." She shivers involuntarily, but hides her instinctive fear behind a smile. She's right to be scared of them. They may just be men, but they're far darker than many I've met in my life, just in a different, more unexplainable way.

"Yeah, like them."

"So what's going on with Christy?"

"She's been having these dreams... visions I suppose. They've become more and more regular lately, and a lot clearer."

"You're worried about her... mental health?" she asks, trying to understand. I know it's not easy to wrap your head around stuff like this. It took me a long while to accept what Christy was telling me to be true, but she's never been wrong. Not about anything.

"Not her mental health because she isn't sick, Pen... I'm worried about what she's seeing in her visions." Blowing out a long breath, I place my hand over my belly. I've never felt more strong or as weak in my entire life carrying this baby. It's been a sobering experience, that's for sure. "The past couple of nights she's dreamt of men shadowed in darkness. They come for her in the dead of night."

"Shadowed in darkness?" Pen asks. Her face pales, and I know what she's thinking.

"This isn't the Deana-dhe, Pen. I know what you saw that time you danced for them at Tales, but this isn't them."

"How can you be sure? What if that's the debt, Grim? What if Christy is payment?"

I shake my head. "No. They said they wouldn't ask for something I wasn't willing to give. My family and friends are something I will protect until my last breath. They know that."

"So who then...?" Her voice trails off when she sees the look in my eyes. "You don't think..."

I nod. She's correct in her assumption. "Last night Christy dreamt that she was lying in a room with iron bars at the window, in a place far away from here. She described three men standing in the shadows, each of them wearing a mask..."

"Oh God, Grim. What can I do?"

"If Christy's right and they come, whenever that may be, I'll need someone to look after our baby."

"You want me to..." Her face pales as her eyes drop to my stomach.

"Yes. Christy is gifted, Pen. She sees things that no one else does. If she says this is going to happen, then there is nothing I can do to stop it, but that doesn't mean to say that I won't do everything in my power to get her back. So will you help me? Will you and the Breakers look after our little girl when the time comes?"

"Yes. You know I will," she replies immediately.

"Thank you," I whisper. "There is one other thing..."

"What's that?" she asks.

"Just in case something happens to us, I want our little girl to know where she came from," I say. Reaching into my handbag, I pull out a diary and hand it to Pen. "This is Beast's and my love story. It might not be the fairytale she'd expect, but it is our fairytale and she's a part of that too."

Pen takes the diary from me and clutches it against her chest. "I'll take care of this, and I'll do what you ask if anything bad happens. I *promise.*"

And I know, without a doubt, that she will.

The End

WANT SOMETHING TO READ NEXT?

Their Obsession duet featuring Grim's half-sister Christy and The Masks is out now. Start with ***The Dancer and The Masks.***

Read on for the prologue

THE DANCER AND THE MASKS

EXCERPT

PROLOGUE

Jakub

My brother and I watch as Konrad shackles our newest acquisition to the stone wall with chains. Manacles secure her wrists and ankles, spreading her feet and arms wide apart and showing off her perfectly proportioned figure. She's naked and cast in an orange glow from the flaming torches attached to the wall. Yet, despite her ample breasts, small waist, bare pussy, curvaceous hips and long, dark hair, I feel nothing but apathy.

Even her screams bore me.

"Your efforts are a waste of energy, *Twelve*, no one will hear your screams," Konrad reminds her, his middle finger swiping at the tears that cascade from her dark brown eyes and slide over her smooth olive skin. He places the jewelled teardrop in his mouth, tasting her fear.

"Fuck you, *hijo de puta*! My name is Carmen. Car-men! I

am not a number!" she screams, yanking at the chains and darkening the bruises around her wrists and ankles further.

"Hush now. Don't make this any harder for yourself," he whispers, his voice a warm caress as he slides his fingers over her collarbone and down the centre of her chest all the way to her bellybutton which he circles lazily with his finger. "Allow yourself to feel the pleasure."

"Touch me again and I'll...!" she warns, hissing between gritted teeth.

"And you'll do what, *Twelve*?" he taunts, baring his teeth in a slow smile and showing a glimpse of the man he could be if pushed too far. He wears his mask with pride, just like Leon and I do. It covers the majority of his face, leaving his mouth, chin, and left eye free. We wear these masks not because we wish to hide our identity at this point, but because they instill a level of fear in our acquisitions. No one leaves the castle once inside of it, no one, but nevertheless the masks we wear remain on our faces. The only time we remove them is in the sanctity of our private rooms.

"Please," she whispers, her instincts kicking in. Her anger subsides, replaced instead with fear and the innate need to please the one man who she believes has the power to free her. Whilst that might be true, and Konrad could very well let her go, he won't, because the man with the ultimate power is *The Collector*, our father, and he wields that over the three of us like an iron fist.

"Giving up so soon?" Konrad taunts.

"You don't have to do this..." Twelve continues, her fire tempered.

She glances at me hoping that I'll step in and stop what's

happening. Instead, I watch with detachment. She's just like all the rest, breakable, malleable, and ultimately submissive, though not in a way that gives her power, but in a way that relinquishes it. Eventually all of our acquisitions come to accept their life here, and are comfortable, even. Once they accept their fate, we treat them well. No harm will come to our Numbers from any of the clients we entertain. The last person who tried to fulfil his fantasy on Eight without her permission is now a rotting corpse in the catacombs beneath our home. Leon's wrath that night was exquisite to behold. We protect what belongs to us. Always have. Always will.

"Keep any marks to the bare minimum," I warn Konrad.

Leon smirks. "Let him have his fun. Besides, this one likes it."

Of the three of us, Leon is by far the most dangerous. I've seen what happens when he lets go, and it's not pretty. He may be beautiful, with thick black hair and deep set, pale green eyes but there's nothing *pretty* about him. Like Konrad and me, Leon thrives in the darkness. The masks we wear are more our true faces than the ones we were born with.

"I know the rules, Brother..." Konrad's voice trails off as he strokes the flat of his hand over Twelve's stomach and hips, caressing her gently. She flinches away from his touch, the shackles rattling. "She's exquisite, no?"

"Yes. She'll draw the attention of many of our clients," I agree, adjusting my mask.

"Such a fine specimen," Konrad growls, the low rumble of his voice intoxicating to many.

Yet her appearance, however beautiful, isn't why our father acquired her. No. This woman—who from now on will only be referred to as Twelve—is a soprano. Her voice is enchanting, beautiful, and the real reason why she's here now. Ten women, and one man have come before her. Aside from their beauty, they have one thing in common, they're all artists and they will live the rest of their days in this castle to serve one purpose: to entertain our clients.

"I am *not* a whore!" Twelve screams, visibly shaking as Konrad cups her pussy, telling her without words, that we own her. *All* of her.

She'll be a whore if we ask her to, and she *will* enjoy it.

Eventually.

Her screams die down to whimpers as he coaxes her with his talented hands. Leon and I watch with mild interest as he gently fingers her. For someone with so much brutality inside of him, he certainly knows how to keep it under control when required.

"You're wet," Konrad muses, his thumb slowly circling her clit as he runs the tip of his tongue against her jaw.

"And you're *sick!*"

"Your body doesn't seem to think so," he chuckles, bringing his glistening fingers to his mouth and sucking on them. Twelve's nostrils flare and her cheeks flush as he reaches back between her legs and rubs her clit once again. She hates him, there's no doubt about that. Regardless, her body reacts to the pleasure he brings her, twisting her up inside, fucking with her head, just like he intended. That's the idea, break them down until they crack, then build them back up with a mixture of fear and pleasure. We train them to respond to both. They've all learnt to heel, craving the attention we give them. Good or bad.

So long as they behave, accept their lives here, we give them what they want, what they really, *truly* want.

For Twelve, that's passion, the high of an orgasm, being owned and taken without her permission, punished with a whip or a paddle. She may not like to admit it, but it's the truth nevertheless. It's why Konrad is the perfect man for the job. He studied her for weeks before she arrived, watched her social media posts, delved into her private chats that our hacker, Charles, managed to get hold of. He knows her better than she knows herself. Ultimately, he's giving her what her soul craves. That's the key to what we do.

It's different for each of the Numbers, and the three of us are masters at delving into the deepest parts of their psyches to draw out what makes them tick. To give them their ultimate sin.

We do it with ease, whilst never truly indulging our own wants or desires.

"My father will *kill* you for this!" she hushes out, still fighting, though with less rage and more passion now. The kind she thrives on.

Next to me Leon chuckles darkly. "Should we tell her that it was her father who betrayed her?"

"No. Let Konrad have his fun first. We'll douse the rest of her rage later with that knowledge," I reply.

"She'll be screaming his name and coming before long," Leon remarks, focusing on her peaked nipples. Like pretty little buds, puckered and desperate to be licked.

"No doubt. It's why he's the best man for the job. He knows what she wants. Can sense it. All that emotion has to have an outlet, yes?" I reply, pushing off from the wall. "Come on, our guests will be here in a few hours and with Father away there is much to do."

"I hope she's worth all the trouble," Leon says, referring to the latest girl our father has become obsessed with. It's why he's still in London, instead of entertaining our clients this evening.

"She must be. I haven't seen him this excited since he brought home Six. He thinks this girl will draw in clients from across the world. He even named her."

"He did?" Leon asks, his voice giving away his surprise.

"Yes, he did. *Stopy Płomieniach*."

"Feet of Flames? Fuck, he has got it bad."

"Indeed..."

"What?" Leon asks, resting his hand on my arm and stopping me in my tracks. On the other side of the room Konrad is currently too preoccupied with Twelve to be concerned with our hushed conversation. "Are you worried because he's named her?"

"No," I reply, shaking my head. "She'll become a Number the moment she steps inside these walls, just like all the rest. That's not the issue."

"Then what?"

"Grim has already claimed her. She's not for sale."

"*Grim?* Doesn't she own that fight club, Tales, in London?"

"Yes, she does."

"That's problematic."

"It is. This girl, Penelope Scott, means something to her."

"We both know that won't stop Father from collecting what he wants."

"Precisely. If she's held in such high esteem by someone of Grim's calibre then he'll only want her more. That's part of the excitement for him, he always wants what he can't have. It makes the acquisition all the more sweet once he's able to secure it by whatever means possible."

Leon nods. "So we might have trouble coming our way?"

"Without a doubt."

"Then we'll prepare for the worst, just like we always do," he reassures me.

"Fuck sake!" Konrad growls. "I'm trying to do a job here. Either be quiet and enjoy the show, or fucking leave." He levels his gaze on us both, his hand lazily rubbing between Twelve's legs, his fingers pinching and twisting her nipple, darkening her skin with bruises.

"Konrad. You know the rules. Keep within them," I warn. Again.

Despite the lingering hate in Twelve's eyes, her body reacts to Konrad's skilled fingers. He knows how to play the most diffi-cult of instruments, and it's a skill that we use to our advantage. Sometimes, however, my brothers need to be reminded that the Numbers aren't ours. Never will be. There's only so far we can go with them. He knows it, as do Leon and I.

"What? She likes it," he retorts as her hips grind against his hand, the slickness of her pussy glistening in the firelight. "See?"

"Fuck you!" she bites out, but it has less venom now. More acceptance.

"Regardless. Remember why she's here. She isn't yours."

Konrad smirks, catching my eye before dropping to his knees in front of her glistening cunt. Her hips buck as presses a gentle kiss against her bare mound, then winks at me. "Stay, you might enjoy it."

I shake my head. "You know me better than that."

"I do. Maybe we could keep this one to ourselves," he suggests. "You could do what you want to her without fear of Father's wrath."

"No." The truth is, I don't *want* any of the Numbers. Perfection turns me off. Beauty lies. It hides ugliness beneath a pretty shell. The three of us are the perfect example of such a truth. We three are handsome beneath these masks, but have twisted, black hearts. I don't deny that fact. Never have.

"Leon, are you staying?"

He shakes his head. "Not today, Brother."

"Suit yourself." Konrad shrugs before replacing his fingers with his lips and tongue and eats Twelve out.

She jerks against his face, a cry of pleasure ripping from her mouth, followed by broken sobs that wrack her body. She hates herself for reacting the way she does. Society has conditioned her to believe what she truly wants, *needs*, is wrong. She believes that her body is betraying her spirit, her soul. It isn't. It's showing her the truth.

When she realises that, she'll understand, and she'll never try to leave here. Our castle may have brick walls, and iron bars. It may have an ancient forest surrounding the castle that's so dense, escape is impossible, but contrary to popular belief, it is not a prison. At least not a traditional one. The Numbers stay of their own free will. Well, perhaps with a little coercion in the beginning. A few more weeks of this and she'll be under our spell completely. I already see her fracturing apart. Every orgasm she gives up, another chink in her carefully constructed armor. Eventually it will crumble, and like an addict she will look to Konrad for her next fix. She will chase the high. He will make her believe that he is the only one who can give it to her, and *that* is why she'll stay.

Reaching for the heavy, iron door, I release the latch and pull it towards me. I have no intention of spending any more time in this cold, dark chamber, preferring the darkness to be found in the forest than these cool dungeons Konrad thrives in, or the cold underground lake Leon prefers. Stepping out into the hallway, Leon following close behind, I come face to face with Renard, our elderly butler.

"Sir..." His face is pale, not because of what's happening inside the dungeon behind us—he's immune to such things now —but because something else appears to be troubling him.

"Renard, why are you down here?" My voice is sharp, reacting instinctively to the tension he holds.

"I have some news," he begins, the wrinkles around his eyes deepening as he frowns.

"What is it?" I demand. His gaze flicks to the girl and Konrad before returning back to me. "Speak!"

He swallows hard then nods. "It's your father. He's dead."

AUTHOR NOTE

So there we have it. Pen and her Breakers story is complete. I really hope that I've given them a fitting ending and that you don't hate me too much for the injury to Dax!

I always knew, right from the beginning of this series, that not all of her guys would come out unscathed. Happy ever after's aren't always perfect, and given the circles the Breakers move in, it would've been unrealistic to expect them all to come out of this situation unharmed. However, I also knew that despite his injury, Dax would want to continue to dance, no matter what. Dancing is fundamental to his character and the heart of Pen and her Breakers. The last scene, when they all performed to *Move Me* by RuthAnne, had me in floods of tears both when writing the scene and when reading back through it. In fact, there were many times during writing this book that I couldn't help but be emotional. When I write I want to be moved, I hope that translates to you as the reader.

If you're a member of my Facebook group Queen Bea's Hive, you'll know that I love to dance (not well, I hasten to add) and have watched every dance movie ever made. I guess, then, it was inevitable that one day I would write a series of books featuring dancers. I'm so grateful for all the love this series has had, and that you were willing to pick up a book about a bunch of dancers / gangsters and fall in love with them as much as I did. Thank you so much!

It's possible that you may have questions about the epilogue. What I can confirm is that this *is* the end to the Breakers story. They have got their happy ever after, and whilst they *may* appear as cameos in future projects, they won't get another story to themselves.

If you've read my other contemporary books, you'll know that, so far, they're all set in the same 'world' and that many characters cross over into each series / trilogy. You also might have noticed that there are quite a few new characters that have been brought to life in this series. There is some speculation about what / who I might be writing about next. I can confirm that The Masks (Malik Brov's three sons) and Christy are getting there love story and Their Obsession Duet is available now to read.

Before I go, I just wanted to thank you all for your continued support.

Much love, Bea xoxo

ABOUT THE AUTHOR

Bea Paige lives a very secretive life in London... She likes red wine and Haribo sweets (preferably together) and occasionally swings around poles when the mood takes her.

Bea loves to write about love and all the different facets of such a powerful emotion. When she's not writing about love and passion, you'll find her reading about it and ugly crying.

Bea is always writing, and new ideas seem to appear at the most unlikely time, like in the shower or when driving her car.

She has lots more books planned, so be sure to subscribe to her newsletter:

beapaige.co.uk/newsletter-sign-up

ALSO BY BEA PAIGE

Grim & Beast's Duet

#1 Tales You Win

#2 Heads You Lose

Their Obsession Duet (dark reverse harem)

#1 The Dancer and The Masks

#2 The Masks and The Dancer

Academy of Stardom

(friends-to-enemies-lovers reverse harem)

#1 Freestyle

#2 Lyrical

#3 Breakers

#4 Finale

Academy of Misfits

(bully/academy reverse harem)

#1 Delinquent

#2 Reject

#3 Family

Finding Their Muse

(dark contemporary reverse harem)

#1 Steps

#2 Strokes

#3 Strings

#4 Symphony

#5 Finding Their Muse boxset

The Brothers Freed Series

(contemporary reverse harem)

#1 Avalanche of Desire

#2 Storm of Seduction

#3 Dawn of Love

#4 Brothers Freed Boxset

Contemporary Standalone's

Beyond the Horizon

For all up to date book releases please visit

www.beapaige.co.uk